David Alex Jones

WALLS

The Survivor Trilogy: Book One

Apparently
Normal
Publishing

LAND ACKNOWLEDGEMENT

This book was written in Southwestern Ontario, Canada, on land located within the Haldimand Tract, land that was granted to the Haudenosaunee of the Six Nations of the Grand River, and is within the shared traditional territory of the Neutral, Anishinaabe, and Haudenosaunee peoples

TABLE OF CONTENTS

PROLOGUE

"In the internal 'houses' of people who survived childhood trauma, there are often many thoughts, feelings, body sensations and emotions that are … kept secret from the self and from others, as if they are kept behind locked doors and thick walls."

— Sandra Paulsen, PhD
Looking Through the Eyes of Trauma and Dissociation

FROM BEHIND the walls she had erected in her mind, Francesca Capellini was struggling to comprehend last night's real-life nightmare.

As though she was on autopilot, her lean, naked, 41-year-old body had been swimming mechanically, back and forth, through the cool cleansing salt water of the swimming pool for the past forty-five minutes. As she swam, her mind battled within itself to try to understand, but also to forget, the terror of last night.

The sun was low in the eastern sky, just beginning its ascent over the California desert and the isolated estate, high in the hills over Palm Desert, where Francesca and her husband, Philippe, lived their reclusive, luxurious lives.

She struggled to stay in the moment, and to keep herself focused on the calming sensations of the water flowing over her skin.

Her efforts to keep her mind present were in vain. It drifted back to her youth in Manarola, Italy. In those days, she had learned to find escape from the loneliness of her home, and from the shame of the sexual advances and humiliation of her older sister's husband, Paolo. Rising at dawn, stripping off her clothing, and swimming in the Mediterranean off the rocks surrounding the village's small marina, it was the one place where she felt free and could cleanse herself of the shame that seemed to cling to her after he had humiliated her or used her young body.

The memories of those dark times from her past began overwhelming her brain. Walls came up in her mind to block them, but it was too late. Those haunting memories from her past connected with images and sounds from the surreal events of the last few hours. The sensory overload of those old memories, plus the nightmare of the past few hours, was working its way up and over her walls, creeping into her consciousness. She saw ghostly images of the young Columbian man shouting at Philippe and heard distant screams of anger from Philippe in reply. Then there was the anguish and fear she'd heard in the young woman's cries. It was as if she was living it all over again. The images, screams, and cries from last night flooded into her consciousness as she swam.

Francesca felt cold fear course through her body. Her muscles tensed, her heart pounded, and her strokes became more labored.

Then, there was only darkness.

In her mind, Francesca felt the cold desert air of the February night chilling her to the bone. Her muscles were trembling, but she couldn't tell whether it was from fear or the cold. She was vaguely aware of sitting in the passenger seat of a car in the darkness.

In the distance, she heard a seemingly endless cycle of sounds: a shovel sinking into the gravel, occasionally striking a stone, a human grunt, then a brief pause before debris could be heard hitting the ground nearby in the darkness. The rhythm repeated itself until she had no sense of time.

Suddenly, the shoveling stopped and the implement dropped to the ground.

A voice with a heavy French accent barked out of the darkness in frustration.

"Are you going to help, or must I do everything myself?"

Francesca forced herself out of the car and moved reluctantly around to the trunk, where Philippe waited impatiently.

"Lift his legs!" he commanded.

Philippe grabbed the man's upper body. As Francesca's arms circled a pair of rigid legs, she caught a glimpse of the victim's lifeless white face. She gasped, her lungs and her legs momentarily paralyzed as she stared at the ghost-like visage.

Philippe tugged on the body. Francesca's legs and lungs jumped back to life. She struggled with the lifeless weight, doing her best to look away at the ground as they staggered towards the shallow pit in the desert floor.

There was a dull thud as the man's body slid out of her frozen hands and dropped into the makeshift grave. It was all she could do to keep from vomiting as she forced herself to repeat the same repulsive process with the young woman's corpse.

Francesca's body continued swimming on autopilot. She felt filthy and nauseated, trying desperately to refocus her mind on her swimming, and to bring it back into the present. As she glided out of the shadows and into a sunlit area of the pool, the brilliant morning sun blinded her, bringing her body and mind out of the darkness simultaneously.

Where did Philippe say he was going?

One part of her identity vaguely remembered them showering to remove all traces of the grime, sweat, and evidence after returning from the desert just before sunrise. Philippe was agitated as he followed her out to the pool afterwards. He was incoherent, and rambled on about having to go to Tijuana to dispose of the South American couple's rental car.

Then he abruptly left her alone, and Francesca started swimming.

As she swam, her mind escaped to Manarola, to the memories of swimming along the coastline of northwestern Italy. In her mind, she was rolling over and floating on her back. She felt as if she was twelve years old. The buoyant Mediterranean waters kept her afloat as she gazed up at the azure sky and the vibrant yellow, green, and pink buildings of the town, perched on the rocky cliffs. Her gaze swept to the green terraced vineyards that carpeted the hillsides along the five-mile stretch of coastline between the five peaceful little villages that made up Cinque Terre.

Twelve-year-old Francesca rolled over onto her stomach again and continued to swim for a few more minutes in the direction of Corniglia, the next village. In her mind, she heard the laughter of dolphins playing in the distance. Suddenly, a pair of the sleek mammals breached beside her, heckling and laughing at her each time they surfaced, then swimming circles around her. She envied their freedom and their playfulness. Yet, while swimming, she felt as free as the dolphins.

Then, as quickly as they had appeared, the dolphins disappeared. In her mind, she turned around for the imaginary swim back to the rocks and the marina at Manarola. Her strokes quickened for the return swim. She was late and had to get herself dressed and ready for school.

Getting ready? For school?

Francesca's mind became confused as reality jumbled together with her childhood memories. She started to remember Philippe's ramblings, and it dawned on her that the part of her identity that was a forty-one-year-old adult had to get ready for work at the hotel today.

Philippe Morel's French accent was much thicker than usual. He was mixing French words into his English, a sign of the intense anxiety and agitation he was feeling.

"Francesca, *ma chère*. You must go to work as usual today. You have to be calm. You must not show any sign that anything is different. Do you understand?" he said.

"And … and tell Carmen that I have the flu. I cannot come in today. You and Carmen will manage the guests as usual," he said.

The hotel. The guests.

Francesca struggled to keep herself connected to reality. She became vaguely aware again of the rhythm of her strokes and the gentle flow of cool water caressing her skin. Both sensations were helping to calm her and bring her back gradually, bit by bit, into the present. She noticed that the yellow streaks of sunlight had spread and were bathing much of the far side of the patio in light. The air was getting warmer. She realized it was time to shower, dress, and to drive into Palm Springs to the hotel.

Francesca pushed the nightmare of the tragic murders into the dark recesses behind her walls. She coasted to the end of the pool nearest the house and pulled herself up onto the deck. Her body was covered in water droplets, causing her skin to cool rapidly. She shivered as the hairs on her arms stood upright and her nipples became firm and erect. She always felt sad to end her swims, but she also loved the feeling of the nerves in her skin coming alive. It made *her* feel alive.

She reached for a large bath towel and hurriedly dried her shivering body.

Pull yourself together Fran.

She was finally starting to access the businesslike part of her personality that always helped her to manage in times of stress. This was the part of her identity she liked the most. It was a part of her that her American friend and mentor, Susan, had taught her during her teen years in Cinque Terre. It was the part that helped her feel strong when the darker parts tried to take over. It was Susan who first called her Fran, and it was Fran who became the businesslike, responsible part of herself.

She started to plan what she would wear and thought about the things she needed to do when she arrived at the hotel. She was beginning to win the battle within her mind for now. As she had learned to do in her youth, she pushed those parts of herself that were feeling afraid, dirty, and ashamed back behind her walls.

Fran continued to reassure herself while she quickly showered, rinsing the salt from her skin.

Philippe is right. Just focus on your usual routine and do not worry about anything. Philippe will take care of this mess. Everything will be alright. You will see. He will take care of you. He always has.

Fran emerged from the shower, dried quickly, and hurried into the large closet to choose some cool and casual clothing. She preferred to wear more informal attire to the hotel, which she helped Philippe manage and also worked as a part time massage therapist.

She looked for something white. Something that would help her to feel clean. She settled on a simple white low-neck cotton tank top that tastefully framed her breasts and décollage. Along with the tank top, she chose a pair of white capris and a gold belt. She picked out a pair of white running shoes with gold trim that matched her belt. Once the large items were selected, she quickly grabbed some white bikini panties, a white camisole, and a sheer bra with white lace trim that went well with the low-cut tank top.

As Fran slipped into her clothes and looked at herself in the mirror, she nodded approvingly. She felt and looked crisp and clean. Professional, but still casual. Finally, she reached for a bikini and a cover-up in case is was warm enough to give massages outside on the patio.

A glance at the clock told her that she had to hurry with her hair and makeup. Fortunately, her dark Mediterranean complexion looked good without much makeup and her short black hair was easy to maintain. She hastily applied a touch of lipstick and eye shadow, then the slightest hint of her favorite Italian perfume, and she was ready to go.

Fran paused and took a single, deep breath to calm and center herself.

It worked. Her businesslike persona was ready to go. She chose a matching white purse, swiftly transferred her belongings into it, and headed for the garage.

Although Philippe insisted on addressing her as Francesca, and preferred that she dress with class and style in a way that befitted the wife of a wealthy art agent and dealer, she often longed to be less ostentatious and formal. In her choice of a personal vehicle, a silver-blue Prius, Philippe allowed her to have some input in the decision for once. But when they went out in public, Philippe would still insist that they be seen together in his luxury Mercedes or a chauffeured limo.

Fran opened the driver door and slid into the Prius, once again pausing to catch her breath. There were only a handful of places where she felt she could be herself: when she was swimming, on those rare occasions when Philippe allowed her to go out by herself with her camera, when she felt her clients losing themselves in relaxation from one of her massages, and when she was alone in her Prius, as she was now.

She turned on the vehicle and heard the soft whine of the electric motor as she silently backed out of the garage. She felt a slight vibration from the gasoline engine as she shifted it into gear and drove slowly towards the main gates of their estate.

On either side of the massive wrought iron gates, in both directions, stretched an imposing ten-foot high, stucco-covered wall topped with coiled razor wire. Philippe maintained that it was necessary to keep their estate secure from outside intruders. She knew that it could also keep people securely imprisoned inside.

Although she had some freedom to come and go, she knew that Philippe was always aware of where she went. He ensured she didn't have the resources to go far on her own. In return, Philippe had always kept her safe. Until last night.

Fran reached for the remote control to open the gates. As she did, she felt a wave of nausea growing in the pit of her stomach. Her muscles tensed, her heart raced, and her chest tightened. Once again, she struggled to control her breathing. As the Prius gradually accelerated through the opening and the gates closed behind her, she realized she was driving out into a world that was suddenly dangerous and starting to careen out of control.

9

PART ONE: EDEN

CHAPTER 1

MICHELLE WHITNEY'S eyes opened suddenly in the dark room.

Where the hell am I?

Her breathing was rapid and shallow. Her chest felt like somebody was sitting on it. Her heart was pounding like a locomotive, and she was dripping with perspiration. She searched the room with her eyes, gradually starting to process the information that was surging into her brain. She began to wrestle some control over her body and mind.

I'm in somebody's else's bedroom.

At least she was aware that she wasn't in her own bedroom back in Warren, Michigan. Michelle surveyed the scene around her. The sheets and blanket were strewn aside, a sign that her legs must have been thrashing. The rumpled pile of sheets and blankets led to the shadowy outline of a man's head lying next to her. She gasped instinctively. Her brain scrambled to make sense of this new information.

Oh ... It's just Dan! A sigh of relief escaped from her lungs. *But where are we?*

Dan Whitney, her husband, was breathing with strange little puffing sounds, blissfully unaware of the commotion beside him. Michelle began to recognize her surroundings. She noticed a family photograph in the dim glow of the clock radio on the headboard. Her breathing and heartbeat immediately slowed to a more normal pace.

Of course. The guest room at mom and dad's place. We're still in San Diego.

It was starting to make sense now. She and Dan were nearing the end of their weeklong visit to San Diego for her parent's fiftieth anniversary celebration. They had flown from Detroit last Friday and were leaving today.

As Michelle's brain became oriented to time and place, a fragment of her nightmare crept back into her awareness. The recurring nightmare had visited her again. Her mind drifted away from the present and she started to relive the dreadful images.

In her dream, Michelle is always fully clothed in a swimming pool, her clothes weighing her down and dragging her under. She is unable to breathe and her chest feels like it's going to explode before she can breathe. She looks up and sees the bright yellow sun in a clear blue sky, glaring like a searchlight through the azure water overhead. She begins to panic. In desperation, she begins clawing at her clothing and tearing it from her body, finally escaping only when she is totally naked.

She struggles upward and breaks the surface, her lungs gasping for breath. Only then does she realize that the pool is surrounded by a huge crowd of her family and friends. When they see that she's naked, they point at her and laugh hysterically. She feels like she'll die from embarrassment, but there is no place for her to hide without climbing out of the pool and walking through the mocking crowd. She feels completely vulnerable as she displays her naked self to everybody she knows.

Michelle hated the nightmare, or variations of it, that reoccurred every three or four months. What made it worse was having a psychologist for a husband. She regretted ever asking Dan to interpret the dream the first time it happened. The memory of that conversation was still etched in her mind.

"Well," Dan said, after mulling it over for a moment. "When people dream about being naked in public, it often suggests they might be trying to be somebody that they aren't in reality. Sometimes they feel like they're impostors. Even worse, their greatest underlying fear is that others will find out that they're insecure: not the strong, confident person they want others to see."

"Are you trying to say I'm phony and insecure?" she exclaimed. Her tone was half-joking, but she was getting upset. Michelle's voice became lower, colder, and more serious.

"If you ask any of my friends, they'd say I'm the most confident person they know!"

While she outwardly rejected Dan's interpretation, unconsciously she was afraid Dan could be right. The thought left her feeling just as vulnerable as she felt with her nakedness in the dream. *Damn it, why did I have to marry a psychologist anyway? What does he know about me?*

Michelle watched Dan's eyelids flutter and listened to him as the air puffed rhythmically from his lungs. He was still sleeping soundly, deep in REM sleep. She covered herself and tried to go back to sleep, but her brain was already wide-awake.

This isn't going to work. I need to get up and pee.

She looked up at the clock on the headboard: it was six o'clock. Daylight was just starting to penetrate the sheer window coverings.

Damn. Mom and dad will be up soon.

Sleeping late wasn't an option at her parent's place. Michelle knew they'd make enough noise to ensure that anybody else in the condo would have to get up to join them for breakfast. She surrendered to her aching bladder and paddled naked into the bathroom to relieve herself, shivering in the chilly morning air as she sat down on the frigid toilet seat.

DAN STIRRED as Michelle returned to bed. He rolled over and snuggled up behind her, bringing his arm around her to stroke one of her breasts.

"Yeeooooow, Chelly," he groaned. "Your ass is freezing. You can't expect me to get into the mood with a frozen penis, can you?"

The sudden cold made Dan realize he also needed to relieve himself. "Oh man, now I have to get up too!"

He flipped the covers away and bounded quickly across the cold floor to the bathroom. When he was finished, he hopped across the frigid floor, jumped back into bed and cuddled up to his wife. He started nuzzling and stroking her bare skin amorously.

"Not now!" she whispered sternly. "The walls in this place are paper-thin, and mom and dad are up. Do you want them to hear everything? Can we save it for tonight after we get to Palm Springs?"

Chelly gave him a cool kiss and pulled away.

Dan felt himself being pushed away again. It was happening more often lately. Yet she was the one who was always accusing him of not being romantic enough. *What do I have to do to be romantic enough for her?*

There was an awkward silence. Chelly quickly changed the subject to put a temporary end to the tension.

"We only have to put up with their criticism and preaching for a few more hours," she whispered. "Then we can relax and have time for ourselves for a few days. Do you think we can wait that long?"

"I guess I can if you can," Dan sighed. "But my tongue is getting awfully sore from biting it for a whole week!"

"Well, thanks for being here for moral support," Chelly said. "Let's be thankful that Leo had to work this week. At least we didn't have to put up with his condescension too".

"No kidding. Does your brother ever have anything positive to say about you?"

"He hasn't liked me from the moment I was born. What did I do to deserve such a dysfunctional family?" Chelly said, laughing half-heartedly.

"So what are you going to tell them about where we're staying in Palm Springs?" Dan asked. "I can't imagine the sermon we'd get if they find out we're going to a nude resort to relax for a week!"

"Please. Whatever you do, don't say that word to them!"

"Don't worry, I won't. How are you feeling about it? Having any second-thoughts?"

"Of course. Wouldn't anybody be anxious about going stark naked in front of strangers? Weren't you nervous the first time you tried it?"

"Yeah, I guess. I was just afraid I'd embarrass myself and get hard in front of everybody. I should have realized I'd be too nervous for that to happen," Dan said, chuckling.

"I know you're nervous, but I know you'll do fine," he continued. "You do great in any social situation. It's what you do best, Chelly!"

"I'm just glad you scouted the place out and met some of the people. I can't wait to meet them," Chelly said.

"I know you'll like them," Dan continued. "And remember, the resort is clothing optional. If you don't feel comfortable being nude, nobody is going to say anything if you decide to wear a swim suit or just go topless."

"I'll manage" Chelly replied. "If my best friend Jenny can do it, then I guess I can too. Besides, you're the one who's always afraid of doing something bad. I can't believe you grew up liking skinny-dipping. You're such a goody-goody. It just doesn't fit your personality."

"Are you calling me boring?" Dan asked.

"I wouldn't say that," Chelly said. "You're just not adventurous. You never take any risks. I'm the one who likes to break loose and have fun. If you can handle being naked in front of strangers, then I'm sure I can handle it just as well, if not better!"

Chelly's tone was becoming more defiant.

"If they ask, let's just tell them that we're going to a fancy European-style spa for a week of relaxation and pampering."

Dan knew that the last thing Chelly wanted was a confrontation with her parents.

"Okay, I'm good with that."

"It's not a lie," Chelly said. "I'm just not telling them everything. What they don't know won't hurt them. Come on, I smell coffee brewing. Time to get up before they start pounding on the door! I'm going to go for a short run."

Before Dan could say anything, or even give Chelly a good-morning kiss, she popped out of bed and was scrounging through her suitcase for some shorts and a top. She dressed hastily, grabbed her running shoes and socks, opened the guest room door, and was gone.

Dan was alone.

The feeling triggered memories of the pain he first felt as a young medical student in Vancouver. He'd just found out that Brenda Cybulski, the love of his life, had lied to him about going home for the weekend to visit her parents on Vancouver Island. Dan was taking his regular route past her apartment on his way home from campus, when he saw Brenda and a strange man exit from a car. They embraced before walking into her apartment, holding hands.

He walked the rest of the way to his apartment in shock. As soon as he was home, he forced his fingers to dial Brenda's number. She answered, and when Dan identified himself, she spilled it out. She no longer loved him and was moving on. She was sorry he had to find out this way. She intended to tell him after the weekend. She didn't mean to lie. But he always remembered the pain of hurt and betrayal from being unceremoniously dumped.

Dan was jolted back to reality by the sudden sound of Chelly's dad slamming the condo's front door. He caught his breath and realized tears had formed in his eyes. He slowed his breathing and oriented himself back to the present.

His thoughts returned to Chelly and her running. *That's what she does whenever things get too close for her*. Dan suddenly felt the urge to go for a long swim, which he hadn't done since they left Detroit a week ago. Swimming always helped him clear his mind.

It generated a stream of consciousness that left him feeling rejuvenated.

He heard more noise and activity in the condo's kitchen. It was time to get up. He swung his legs over the side of the bed and headed for the shower. He started the water and noticed the tension in his muscles as he adjusted the taps and waited for hot water.

I can't wait to get to Chateau Eden. I just want to swim and feel like myself again! And I can't wait for those massages I booked for this weekend.

Dan let the soothing stream of hot water do its work, gradually melting away some of the tension in his body. He tried not to think about the lack of intimacy in his marriage, but his mind just wasn't able to let it go.

CHELLY EXHALED a long sigh of relief once her parent's condo was out of sight.

"That was exhausting! I miss seeing them, but after I've been with them one day, I can't wait to leave."

"Yeah, I agree," Dan said. "But you're lucky you still have them. Someday when they're gone, you'll miss them like I miss my parents."

"I know," Chelly replied. "I just wish I could relax and not let them get to me."

Dan turned his attention to the rental car's GPS, which directed him to Interstate 15 for the drive to Highway 79 into Palm Springs. "If traffic isn't heavy, we should be there in about two and a half hours," he said.

"I can't get there soon enough," Chelly answered. "They sure didn't pull any punches during breakfast, did they?"

"God has planned for you to be a wife and a mother. He intended for you to stay home with your children," Chelly said, reciting her mother's words.

"I hope you heard me try to stand up for you," Dan said. "I tried to put things into a more modern perspective for them."

"I noticed, and I appreciate it. But it didn't do any good. And dad sure didn't show any mercy to you and your profession, did he?"

"That's okay, I can take it. I see where he's coming from. But you'd think your parents would have more compassion for people who've been abused or suffered other kinds of trauma, wouldn't you?"

"Nope. Not a chance," Chelly huffed. "If people would just get over it, move on, and put their faith in God, there wouldn't be any need for psychologists," Chelly said, this time imitating her father.

"Well, I tried to see their side of the arguments, but it didn't help much. It sure must have been hard for you to grow up with all of that," Dan said.

"Thanks. Was it that difficult being around your parents when they were alive?" Chelly asked.

"Yeah, sometimes," Dan answered. "My parents had me when they were older. I think I was a bit of a surprise for them, because my brothers were ten and twelve-years-old when I was born. I always felt like I didn't belong, since they'd been a family for a long time before I came along. But, in other ways my family was different from yours. Mom and dad were warm and loving. I could always talk to them, there were lots of hugs, and my brothers spent a lot of time with me. They were usually supportive of everything I wanted to do. And even though my parents were religious, they weren't as judgmental as yours. I guess they didn't have the strict German upbringing your parents had."

"Well, I hated growing up with that German tradition," Chelly said. "I wasn't allowed to do anything! Leo got to do whatever he wanted because he was a boy and was older. He couldn't do anything wrong. Everything I did was always compared to him."

"Michelle, why aren't you doing well in math? Leo won the math prize and the teachers are expecting great things from you!" Chelly mimicked. "The worst part was that I wasn't allowed to have my own opinion about anything! If I disagreed or argued with them, I was told not to disrespect my elders. I felt like a little trophy; meant to be seen, but not heard."

Chelly's eyes were watering; the fair skin around her eyes and nose turned puffy and red as she talked.

"I remember a few times when I got my face slapped for talking back. I just wanted to feel like I was being heard. It made me feel so unloved!" she sobbed.

Dan felt her pain. He reached over and took Chelly's hand in his.

"I'm so sorry for what you went through," Dan said.

"Thanks. It's okay," Chelly sniffled. "I think the experience just made me stronger in the long run."

Maybe not as strong as you think, Chelly, he thought to himself.

Silence filled the car as Dan continued to stroke Chelly's hand. Before long, he saw her head falling sideways against the window. She had cried herself to sleep.

AS THEY drove northward, Dan was alone with his thoughts about Chelly and the strains in their marriage.

He knew that growing up in such a negative home had affected her self-esteem and contributed to her perfectionistic tendencies, particularly at work. She once said that her previous boyfriend, Derek, had become more emotionally abusive as he progressed through his anesthesia residency. But Dan knew the abuse probably took an additional emotional toll.

Chelly's mother's comments about children had also upset Dan. It was another source of strain in their marriage. He felt they were running out of time to have children. They were both in their early forties, Chelly's clock was ticking, and he didn't think it was fair for children to have elderly parents.

But Chelly was happy with the status quo. She loved her work, her lifestyle, and their social circle, which was composed mostly of childless couples like themselves. Chelly always managed to put up roadblocks to becoming parents.

What worried Dan most was her difficulty with physical intimacy. On one hand, she was a hopeless romantic, faithfully watching TV shows like *The Bachelor* and truly believing in the notion of romantic love. She made frequent comments to Dan, questioning why he couldn't be more romantic like the bachelors on TV.

Yet, when it came to Dan trying to be more romantic, nothing appeared to satisfy Chelly. She always found ways to sabotage his attempts to be more intimate. As a psychologist, his intuition was telling him there was something in her past she hadn't told him. But she swore that nothing traumatic had ever happened to her.

I hope our nudist vacation will put some spark back into our marriage. But, it seems the harder I try to make things better, the more distant she gets.

He looked at Chelly as she slept.

"I love you!" he said silently.

Tears were forming in his eyes.

What can I do to get closer to you?

The silence was finally too much for Dan. He turned on the radio for some company. The familiar voice of Don Henley filled the car.

Dan found himself tapping the steering wheel in time to the slow, driving rhythm of *Hotel California,* while Joe Walsh's guitar wailed in the background. *I love this song, but I still don't get it. Where would you find a hotel where you can check out, but never leave?*

He played around with the lyrics in his mind for a while without finding a satisfactory answer. His mind drifted. Before he knew it, he was back to thinking about the upcoming week with Chelly at *Chateau Eden.* The Eagles were fading into silence, only to be replaced abruptly by the grating guitar riffs of Aerosmith.

Dan turned down the radio.

I wonder what caused her to change her mind about nudism so suddenly? She actually made the suggestion to me this time!

He remembered the first time he asked Chelly if she'd ever be interested in trying a clothing-optional warm weather vacation.

"Are you nuts?" she replied. "With a bunch of swingers and perverts? Not a chance. I have no interest in letting everybody see my cellulite and saggy boobs." Then, one day last summer, she came home from work and casually mentioned that her best friend, Jenny, visited a nudist resort in Michigan with her husband. A few days later, he recalled hearing the two women talking about it one night over a bottle of Chardonnay.

"It was so different than what I expected," Jenny told Chelly. "Everybody was so friendly and casual. They made us feel so comfortable that I didn't want to come home on Sunday."

"It sounds intriguing!" Chelly squealed.

Dan always liked hearing Chelly when she was hanging out with the girls. She was more animated, and her voice always raised an octave to that higher pitch women use when they're together. She was a totally different person when she was with the girls. Especially when she loosened up with a bit of wine. One of the qualities Dan most admired in his wife was her loyalty to her friends. She'd do anything for them, often putting them ahead of herself. Her loyalty was without question.

Yet, her absolute loyalty was also the thing that irked Dan the most. While she was often critical or negative about things he suggested, she would instantly acquiesce to the same suggestions from her friends. While her voice was usually low in tone and serious with Dan, it was animated and excited when she was with the girls.

Why can't she let herself be that way around me? He wondered. Dan's mind returned to the night Jenny was telling Chelly about visiting the nudist resort. Their voices had moved into the higher register, and they were talking excitedly.

"You and Dan have to come with us and try it some weekend," Jenny urged. "You'll love it."

"I don't think I could go naked in front of people I know," Chelly giggled. "But you make it sound so awesome."

Chelly's confidence was rising, along with the alcohol level in her blood.

"Tell you what," she tittered. "Next time you guys are planning on going naked, bring a bottle of wine over and ask me again. I'll probably say yes!"

"That's my girl," Jenny said. "You need to take some chances and enjoy life a little. What's the worst that could happen? Some strangers see you naked and you never see them again?"

"You're right," Chelly said. "I'm always telling Dan to stop being so afraid to try new things. I guess I need to take some of my own advice. Maybe Dan and I can try it some place where I don't know anybody. He heard about a place in Palm Springs that sounds interesting. Maybe we can go there and I can try it out."

That's it! Dan said to himself, smacking his hand onto his forehead. The missing piece of the puzzle had just fallen into place.

All it took was one of Chelly's friends to suggest nudism. The last thing she could do was to back down or lose face in front of one of her friends.

Dan shook his head slowly from side to side, feeling a jumble of emotions from the revelation. It hurt that Chelly couldn't be the same person with him that she was when she was with her friends. But, in this case, it finally made her more open to the idea of spending a week together in Palm Springs.

I guess I have to be thankful for that.

DAN FOLLOWED the Highway-79 exit northeast towards Palm Springs. The turn had roused Chelly from her shallow sleep, but she was still lost in thought. Silence hung in the air like a dark cloud. They'd driven for about ten minutes when Dan's head snapped to attention. A car was pulled off on the shoulder of the road in the distance. Somebody was standing behind the vehicle, frantically waving a red object back and forth.

Chelly perked up in her seat when she saw Dan jerk to attention. "What's that? Is somebody in trouble?" she said.

"Looks like it. But I can't tell if it's a man or a woman, can you?" Dan slowed their car and squinted to see more clearly. As they drew closer, he noticed that the vehicle was a classic late-seventies Oldsmobile; chocolate brown with a cream-colored vinyl roof that was tattered and torn.

A gaunt woman stood behind the car, flapping a bright red kerchief in the air. She pre-dated the Oldsmobile by at least forty years. Her leathery skin was brown and wrinkled. Her hair was bleached blonde and looked more like straw than hair. Her bones protruded through the skin of her anorexic body. "I'm going to pull over. Can you roll down your window and ask her what's wrong?" Dan said.

"Do you think we should? What if it's a setup? What if somebody jumps out and mugs us?" Chelly asked.

"Don't be so paranoid. She's probably just broken down," Dan answered.

"Then she can call Triple-A on her cell phone like anybody else. Why do we have to stop?" Chelly asked again.

"C' mon, Chelly. She's an old lady. She doesn't look like she's got much money, if that old beater is any indication." Dan pulled up beside the woman and pressed the switch to roll down the passenger window. The woman leaned down, first glaring at Chelly then leaning in further to scrutinize Dan.

"Can we help you, ma'am?" Dan asked. He waited while the woman decided whether he and Chelly were trustworthy.

"Tire's flat as the Mojave and twice as cooked, young fella," she said, finally breaking the silence. "Can you gimme a lift into Palm Springs?"

"You don't have a spare in the trunk?" Dan asked.

"Don't rightly know. Wouldn't know what to do with it anyway," she admitted.

"Mind if I have a look? Maybe we can get lucky and get you back on the road," Dan said. Chelly threw Dan a disconcerted look while the woman continued to examine Dan.

"Guess it wouldn't hurt none. I don't wanna putcha out now. Sure ya don't mind?"

"No, ma'am. Just give me a moment to get off the road."

Dan pulled ahead of the Olds, parked on the shoulder, and turned on his flashers. He got out and walked around the passenger side of the car. The woman wasn't kidding. Her front right tire was flat and mangled. Dan figured she must have driven on it for a few miles before she realized something was wrong. By the time he reached the rear of the huge car, she had already popped the trunk.

The cavernous compartment was empty, but Dan saw some particleboard showing through what remained of the trunk's decayed vinyl floor. He lifted the warped piece of wood and couldn't believe his good fortune. A full-sized spare tire, complete with jack and tire iron, still remained in the compartment. He knocked on the tire with his fist and was surprised to feel that the spare probably had enough air to get to Palm Springs.

"It's your lucky day, ma'am. I think I can switch tires for you and get you back on the road in a few minutes."

"Are ya sure, young man? You two look like ya got some place t'go."

"We're in no big hurry," Dan replied. "I'm happy to help. I'm Dan Whitney." He nodded towards the car. "That's my wife, Chelly, in the car."

"Pleasure t'meet'cha both. I'm Stella."

Chelly glared at Dan from her window with a stern we're-going-to-be-late expression.

"It won't take more than ten minutes to get this changed," Dan shouted to Chelly. He hoisted the heavy tire out of the trunk and set to work putting together the old pump-style bumper jack. He climbed into Stella's car to make sure it was not in gear and the parking brake was on. Stella had the seat pulled up as far as it would go, since her elfish body required virtually no space for her scrawny legs. Dan's knee banged into the steering wheel, as he tried to wedge himself into the narrow space.

"Ow," he cursed. After setting the parking brake, Dan squeezed out of the car and set the jack up under the front bumper. He cranked the handle and lifted the car off the ground in no time at all. Five minutes later, he was cranking the jack handle in reverse to bring the old Detroit dinosaur back to the ground.

"There you go, Stella," he said, as he dropped the ruined tire into the trunk.

"I learned to drive on one of these babies, so I had lots of practice changing tires every winter and spring."

"I'm so grateful, Mr. Whitney."

She reached into her purse to look for some money.

"Can I give ya somethin' fer yer trouble?"

"Don't mention it, Stella. I'm just glad your spare was okay and I could help. Will you be alright now?"

"I s'pose so. I'll let you two be on your way now. Don't wanna slow ya down any more'n I have already." She extended a bony hand and shook hands with Dan. He was afraid Stella's wrist would crumble if he shook it too hard.

"Y'all drive safe, now," Stella called over her shoulder, as she wrenched open the heavy driver's door. Seconds later, the engine thundered to life. Dan watched the ancient Oldsmobile rumble away and walked back to the rental, where Chelly was wearing an impatient frown.

"Now look at you. Your clean shorts and shirt are all covered with dust," she said.

"It's okay. It took us less time than looking for a garage in Palm Springs. Besides, who cares about my clothes? I won't be wearing them this week any way!" he said, laughing.

Chelly cracked a smile. She finally saw some humor in their situation and managed to laugh along with Dan as he steered their car back onto the highway.

"Okay, then. Let's get naked! How much longer?" she asked.

"About 30 minutes. We just passed a sign that said 25 miles," Dan said.

"Speaking of getting naked," Chelly said. "I've been wondering. If your parents were so religious, how did a goody-two-shoes like you ever get into skinny-dipping?"

"Good question," Dan replied.

"Remember, I had older brothers who were teenagers. They were at that age where they were rebelling and experimenting. They were getting into anything that was taboo. You name it - smoking, drinking, making-out - even skinny-dipping whenever they got a chance. I went back down to Texas with them one summer to visit our cousins. All the guys would sneak down to the local swimming hole on hot days to skinny-dip. Sometimes some of the girls would sneak out and join us too. Everybody had fun. It just wasn't a big deal."

"That's it?" Chelly asked.

"Pretty much," Dan said. "Except for the things I learned from skinny-dipping at church camp with a girl named Judi when I was sixteen. But that's a story for another time."

"Dan!" Chelly squealed. Her voice jumped up an octave. "You're not going to leave me hanging like that, are you?"

"Yup," Dan chuckled. "I'll tell you all about Judi sometime over a bottle of wine. Maybe I can demonstrate some of the things she taught me!"

"I can hardly wait," Chelly joked. She may have been laughing on the outside. But on the inside, the reality of their destination was starting to register with Chelly once again. She felt a knot in her stomach and the tightness returned to her chest.

Part of her was looking forward to some romance and adventure. But another part was starting to feel fear as she pictured herself being completely naked and vulnerable in front of strangers. A wall started coming up in her mind. She became distant and quiet for the last half hour of the trip. She closed her eyes so Dan wouldn't see her anxiety. This time, she wasn't able to sleep.

CHAPTER 2

IT WAS just after noon when Dan and Chelly passed the sign welcoming them to Palm Springs. The rental car's GPS system guided them up Palm Canyon Drive, then onto a quiet, unassuming residential side street. After two blocks, the GPS announced they'd reached their destination: a white, Spanish-styled stucco wall topped with red terra cotta tiles. The wall was partially covered in vines, making it look more like a private residence than a hotel.

In the center of the wall was an arched doorway with a pair of heavy handcrafted pine doors set into the archway. The arch was painted a light gray and protruded about three inches, providing a subtle contrast to the clean white hue of the wall that was visible beneath the vines. The dark brown stained pine doors, each with a large black wrought-iron handle at shoulder height, gave the entrance a rich, sophisticated look. Above the door, on the curved portion of the arch, were large green-colored script letters spelling the words *Chateau Eden*.

Dan looked over at Chelly, whose face was a combination of excitement and apprehension.

"Well, here we are!" Dan exclaimed. "One week of total rest and relaxation! How do you feel?"

Chelly contemplated the pine doors from the car and took a long, deep breath. "Ready as I'll ever be, I guess," she sighed.

They exited the car and walked over to the entrance. On the right side of the arch was a black intercom with a white button. A small hand-written sign beneath the intercom invited visitors to *Push Button for Admission*. Dan pushed and they waited for a response. After a few seconds, a woman's voice with a distinct Spanish accent was heard above a background of static.

"Chateau Eden," she said. "May I help you?"

"This is Doctor Dan Whitney. I have a reservation for my wife and I."

"Señor Dan! Welcome back! I will buzz you in."

The intercom buzzed and the door lock clicked. Dan pulled on the handle and the door swung inward, revealing the bright aqua reflection of a pool in the center of a large courtyard. It was surrounded by a sun deck with neat rows of white lounge chairs. The courtyard was enclosed on three sides by long bungalows, and on the fourth side by the white stucco wall. Dan stepped through the doorway, with Chelly following timidly behind.

As the courtyard came into view for her, Chelly's cautious demeanor changed instantly.

"Oh, how sweet!" Chelly exclaimed, her voice rising into its upper register. Her eyes were drawn to the vine covered arbors that sheltered the front of the bungalows from the sun, giving a sense of charm to the courtyard. The bungalows themselves looked like they were built in the 1950's. Their white stucco siding with green trim and green shutters on the windows had a distinct European feel. The area was relatively small and private, giving it a warm, intimate feeling that helped Chelly begin to relax. The nearby mountains rose majestically above the roofs of the bungalows to her right. The sky above the mountains was an intense blue, with just a bit of haze and not a cloud to be seen.

Chelly's eyes returned to the courtyard. It was a beautiful Friday afternoon for this early in March, but the lounge chairs on the pool deck were not yet in use. *No signs of naked people yet,* she thought with relief.

Dan motioned Chelly to the bungalow on the left, whose open French doors welcomed visitors into the resort's lobby. A short, middle-age woman with brown skin and black hair appeared in the entrance to meet them.

"Carmen! So nice to see you again!" Dan said, as he reached down to give her a tight hug. As he released his hold on Carmen, he turned to introduce Chelly.

"Carmen, I'd like you to meet my wife, Michelle."

"Chelly, this is Carmen. She runs the place and sees to it that we have everything we need."

"Hello Señora. I am so happy to finally meet you. Señor Dan spoke kindly of you. We are pleased that you could finally join us!"

"Please come inside. I can check you in, and then I will show you to your room. We have the larger room beside the office available for you if you like," Carmen offered. "We thought you might prefer it, since you are staying with us for the week."

"Thank you," Dan said, then he turned to Chelly. "It's the same room I had when I was here at Thanksgiving. I think you'll really like it!"

As Dan filled out the check-in forms, Chelly's eyes roamed the lobby of Chateau Eden. The floor was tiled in glazed terra cotta, and the lobby was tastefully furnished with a large wicker sofa that easily seated four people, without being too bulky for the small room. Four other small wicker chairs were placed strategically off to the sides of the sofa, two on each side, creating a small conversation area. The sofa and chairs were upholstered in a rust fabric with a subtle tropical floral pattern. A glass topped rattan coffee table occupied the space in front of the sofa and chairs. Carefully placed plants added a warm, tropical feel to the room.

In the background, Chelly heard Carmen speaking to Dan. "Do you mind writing your car's license plate number at the bottom of the form?"

She heard Dan sigh. "I'm sorry, it's a rental and I don't remember the number. Mind if I run outside to get it?" he said.

"No problem," Carmen answered. "Please take your time."

Dan left the lobby and disappeared through Chateau Eden's double pine doors. Chelly's eyes continued taking in her surroundings.

"I love the light tropical feel of your lobby. It's so relaxing," she said to Carmen.

"Thank you, signora," Carmen answered. "We hope it is comfortable for you. There is a computer with Internet access at the other desk in the alcove. We also have an assortment of tea and coffee for your convenience, and the door to the lobby is open until eleven o'clock."

As Chelly saw Dan striding back into the lobby out of the corner of one eye, her gaze was captured by a large color photograph hung on the wall behind the sofa.

"This is beautiful!" Chelly exclaimed. "Dan, come and take a look at this beautiful portrait!"

Chelly pointed to the image of an adolescent Hispanic girl in traditional red attire, holding a tiny infant wrapped in a blanket. The young mother was sitting in an adobe hut with only a dirt floor.

"You can just feel the love she has for her baby," she said. "But there's also worry in her eyes. Whoever took this portrait did a beautiful job."

"Is the photographer local?" Dan asked.

"Ah, you like?" Carmen asked. "That is one of Francesca's portraits. We just put it on display last week. She is talented, is she not?"

"Francesca?" Chelly asked. "The owner?"

"Yes, it is me," came a melodic, lightly accented voice from behind Dan and Chelly. "I am pleased that you like it. It is one of my favorites. Wonderful to see you again, Dr. Whitney."

"It's great to be back again," Dan said, as they greeted each other with a hug.

Francesca then turned towards Chelly. "I am Francesca Capellini. My husband and I are the owners of Chateau Eden. I am so happy that you could come with your husband to visit us!"

"It's nice to meet you too," Chelly answered. "I'm Michelle Whitney, but just call me Chelly. Everybody else does."

Chelly's eyes surveyed Francesca discreetly. She noted the woman's casual but expensive attire, her short black hair, olive complexion, and slim figure. While she spoke with a slight Italian accent, she spoke English well. Her speech was formal and her choice of vocabulary was precise. Chelly immediately got the impression of a woman with style and grace.

Chelly motioned to Francesca's photograph. "You're very talented."

"You are too kind," Francesca replied. "It is what I do to be creative and to relax when I have some free time."

Chelly's face displayed her surprise. "You're kidding! You mean you don't do that for a living?"

"Unfortunately not," Francesca said. "I spend a great deal of time travelling between Europe and Los Angeles, helping Philippe in his art business. We also like to be involved as much as possible in running the Chateau here in Palm Springs. So, I am afraid it is difficult for me to find time to indulge my hobby."

"Well, we're glad you had openings at the Chateau this week," Dan said. "And we're even happier that you're both in Palm Springs while we're here. It's been a long cold winter in Detroit, and we've both been looking forward to a few days of sun and relaxation. You got my message about booking some massages for Chelly and I?" he asked.

"Yes," Francesca said. "We are fully booked with guests, but I managed to save times for both you and Chelly for this afternoon and tomorrow."

Francesca looked towards the registration desk. "Carmen, can you see which times I have reserved for Mr. and Mrs. Whitney?"

Carmen ran her finger down a page and found what she was looking for. "Ah, yes. We have times booked for two and three o'clock. It is warmer today, will you be setting up on the back patio?" she asked.

"I think so," Francesca replied softly. She turned towards Dan and Michelle. "It has been quite cool for the past couple of weeks, so I was having to set up inside. But I think we should be quite comfortable on the patio today. Is that okay with both of you?"

"Wonderful," Dan said. "We're looking forward to it. I think we're both carrying around a lot of tension in our necks and shoulders, so you'll have your work cut out for you. If you'll excuse me, I'll leave you and Chelly for a moment. I think Carmen wants me to finish with the registration."

He pulled out a small piece of paper from his pocket and completed the remaining paperwork for Carmen. She handed him two keys attached to a shiny brass tag with the number one engraved on it.

"The smaller key is for your room. It is the first room on your left as you leave the lobby. The larger key is for the front door, so you can let yourselves in at any hour. We only ask that you be respectful of the other guests if you come in late. There will not usually be anybody at the desk after seven o'clock. There is a telephone book in your room with emergency listings. The pool and spa are open only until eleven o'clock because they are very close to some of the rooms. Is there anything else we can do for you?"

"I don't think so," Dan said.

"As you know," Carmen continued, "we serve continental breakfast here in the lobby from seven to nine each morning. And we have wine and cheese on the patio at four thirty every afternoon to give you a chance to meet the other guests. If the weather is not so good, then the wine and cheese will be here in the lobby."

"Thanks," Dan replied. He turned to Chelly, who was still discussing photography with Francesca. "Chelly, is there anything you wanted to ask Carmen about the rooms?"

"I don't think so," Chelly answered, before returning to her conversation with Francesca.

"I was wondering what I should wear for the massages? Do you expect people to go nude?"

"This is your first visit to a clothing optional resort, is it not?" Francesca asked.

Chelly blushed pink with embarrassment. Like all redheads, her white freckled skin couldn't hide the increased blood flow and the redness in her face. "Yes, I'm afraid I'm a newbie at this," she said.

Francesca felt Chelly's anxiety and tried her best to make her guest feel comfortable. "That is quite alright. Most people feel nervous the first time. We like to describe our environment as *clothing optional* so you may dress any way that you feel comfortable inside the property. All we ask is that you cover yourself with a wrap or towel when you come into the lobby," she added.

"And for massages?" Chelly asked.

"Most of our guests feel most comfortable wearing nothing for their massages. But you are certainly welcome to wear panties or bikini bottoms if you feel more comfortable," said Francesca.

"Thank you," Chelly said. "I appreciate that. I think going topless, at least for the first day or two, will be a big enough step for me! But thanks for understanding."

Chelly was distracted by the sound of a door opening and closing from the office behind the registration desk. Seconds later, an average height, middle-age man with black-rimmed glasses and black hair emerged from the office. He was dressed in casual, but expensive, slacks and sport shirt that was open at the neck. An expensive gold chain hung around his neck. His hair was swept back and kept in place by ample amounts of hair product. Chelly saw some streaks of grey, partially hidden by patches of light reflecting off the hair product. There were lines of concern on his forehead and he appeared lost in thought as he moved beside Carmen at the registration desk.

The man's expression changed suddenly as he looked up and saw Chelly talking to Dan and Francesca. His eyes lit up initially as he noticed her, then became strangely distant for a few seconds, as if his mind had gone somewhere else. Suddenly, he became more animated again and his face transformed into a broad smile.

"Ah, Monsieur et Madame Whitney! You have arrived safely, I see," he exclaimed with a heavy French accent. He came around the desk and focused his attention exclusively on Chelly, extending his hand to hers, then raising it to his lips and giving it a delicate kiss. "*Enchanté Madame.*"

Michelle Whitney's romantic side practically melted inside as Philippe delicately kissed her hand. *Now this was a gentleman. And that French accent. No wonder Frenchmen had a reputation for being so romantic!*

"Your husband said such wonderful things about you when he last stayed with us," the man continued. "I am honored to finally meet you. My name is Philippe Morel."

PHILIPPE NOTICED Michelle blushing again. He watched with amusement as she struggled to speak. When she finally gathered herself together and found her voice, it jumped excitedly into her high register.

"So nice to meet *you*, Monsieur Morel," she said with obvious delight. "Dan has told me so much about you and your lovely hotel."

"Not so formal Madame! Please call me Philippe."

Philippe was flattered by Michelle's exuberant response to his greeting. At the same time, he also noticed her husband's cool, distant demeanor during the exchange of greetings. *I'll have to watch these two closely. They might do very nicely*, he thought.

Philippe finally turned to Dan and extended his hand. "I am pleased to see you again, monsieur. We are so happy that you could bring your lovely wife to visit us this time. Your bags are still in your car, perhaps? I will help you with them and show you to your room. Then perhaps we can give the Madame a short tour?" he asked, as he smiled at Michelle.

"Why thank you, I'd love that. I'll go help you carry some of our smaller stuff," she said.

As Philippe accompanied Dan and Chelly through the main entrance to their car, he turned to Chelly. "So you have just arrived in California? Did you fly into Los Angeles?"

"No," Chelly answered. "We were visiting my parents in San Diego for their fiftieth wedding anniversary last weekend. We just drove up from San Diego this morning."

"Ah, I see," Philippe replied. "So you have been on vacation already for a week."

"Well, not really," Chelly answered. "Visiting my parents isn't really a vacation, is it Dan? It's awful to say, but it feels more like a duty. We usually need a vacation after spending a week with them."

"I understand," Philippe said, recalling all too clearly the cold, distant relationship with his own parents in France. "It is the same for me when I go back to Paris. If there is anything I can do to make your stay more relaxing, please do not hesitate to ask me personally."

"Thanks. I'll be sure to take you up on that. I think that getting massages from Francesca will be a great start, but if I think of anything else, I'll be sure to let you know."

As they reached the car, Dan sprung the trunk open with the remote. They managed to get all of the luggage in one load. Chelly also managed to grab the bottles of white and red wine she had brought with her to keep her courage up.

The trio retraced their steps back through the main gate and through the courtyard to a set of French doors about 15 feet past the entrance to the lobby. Dan opened the door with their key and Philippe swung the doors open.

Chelly entered first, her eyes sweeping quickly around the room. The room was bright and mostly decorated in white, but accessorized with small bursts of color throughout. The large bed was covered by a fluffy, white duvet. The furniture was modern, and the walls were decorated with light pastel watercolors of Italian villages perched on cliffs overlooking the ocean. Chelly nodded her approval at the large mirror above the dresser. A small sitting area with a coffee table and two round chairs, upholstered in orange, occupied the other end of the room. Chelly poked her head into the small bathroom, which was also entirely decorated in white. The white floor tiles were accented with dark grey grout. There was a small but adequate shower in the corner. The European mood of the suite was made complete by the addition of a bidet.

"This is so lovely," she said to Philippe in her high register. "I love how it's decorated."

"Francesca decorated each room in the chateau differently," Philippe boasted. "As you can see, this one has a modern Italian appeal. Some of the others have more classical looks. But we tried to give them all a distinctly European style, so they don't feel like every other hotel room in North America."

"Well, she did a lovely job on this one," Chelly said. "Do you have time to show us around now, Philippe? I think Dan gets his massage in about half and hour."

"Certainly, my dear. Please follow me," Philippe answered.

Philippe led Chelly out of the room, with Dan trailing. He turned to the left, walking around the end of the bungalow that housed both Dan and Chelly's room and the office, then through a passage that separated their building from another bungalow set at right angles to theirs. They came upon a long, narrow patio area, about twelve feet wide, directly behind their room, where Francesca had already prepared her massage table. The white stucco wall continued around the entire perimeter of the property, and there were two trees casting shade over the patio.

"Here we have the patio and spa," Philippe said, with a sweeping gesture with his arm. "The citrus trees provide excellent shade for outdoor massages, and it is both quiet and private."

"As you can see, the spa can seat a dozen people easily. But, it has been known to fit up to 15 or 16 guests at one time, if you do not mind getting close to your neighbor!" Philippe chuckled, winking subtly at Chelly. "Just remember it turns off at eleven o'clock each night."

Chelly's eyes opened wide in excitement. "Wow, this is awesome," she squeaked in her high voice. "There's nothing I love more than a hot tub, friends, and a bottle of wine."

"This is going to feel like heaven after Francesca's finished working over my muscles," Dan said. "You guys are going to have to get a cart to wheel me back to the room afterwards!" he added, chuckling.

Philippe stood back, studying Dan and Chelly as they admired the hot tub area. Until now, he hadn't given much thought to his next project. But Chelly's enthusiastic response to meeting him had enticed him to start sizing them up as possible candidates.

There was something inexplicable about Chelly that captivated Philippe. She was dressed in shorts that showed off her muscular runner's legs. He estimated that she was probably only about 150 cm tall. She was short waisted, making her look slightly stockier than she was in reality. He found her ginger-red hair, tied into a ponytail, and her freckled white skin irresistible. But what he found most attractive was her enthusiasm and how easy it was to charm her.

Dan, on the other hand, made him feel uneasy. Recruiting the woman could be child's play, but he could see that the man could be a challenge.

He is a psychologist, Philippe thought. *I wonder what he is thinking about me? He is wary. I would not doubt if he is analyzing me right now. I must be careful with him. But, everybody has their weaknesses. If I am patient, I will find his.*

"Shall we move along *ma chère*?" Philippe said to Chelly. He touched her elbow subtly as he guided her back out to the pool and main courtyard area. He pointed to the arbors surrounding the courtyard as a slight hissing sound could be heard.

"The heat can be quite unbearable in the summer months, so we have small water lines and nozzles hidden in the vines," he said. "The jets give a spray of mist every few minutes to help keep people cool."

"That's awesome," Chelly exclaimed. "What a great idea." As her eyes followed the vines along one of the bungalows, another thought occurred to her.

"Philippe, you said that Francesca decorated each room differently. Do you think I could see some of the others before the other guests arrive?"

"Of course," Philippe replied. He was delighted that Chelly was showing so much interest. It gave him more opportunity to become better acquainted with her. "Let us look into this one over here. It is one of my favorites."

Philippe led Dan and Chelly to a unit in the far bungalow, opposite the main gate. Reaching for a ring of keys attached to his belt, he unlocked the door.

As he swung the door open, Philippe gave a sweeping gesture with his arm. "After you, *mes amis*," he said.

"Oh, it's beautiful," Chelly sighed as she passed through the doorway. "Look at the gorgeous canopy bed!"

"Ah, yes," Philippe said. "It was more difficult to decorate the rooms in this bungalow, since they do not get so much sunlight as the others. Francesca wanted a more classic French look, so we managed to find a few lovely antique pieces with dark red or brown stain, like that desk, the canopy bed, and those small chairs."

"She obviously spent a lot of time looking for the right antique pieces," Dan said.

"Yes," Philippe continued. "But at the same time, she chose a light cream color for the paint and wallpaper that still keeps the room bright. Then she found some lovely old landscape paintings that have some bursts of color in them."

"She did a beautiful job, didn't she?" Dan said. "She really is a creative lady."

"*Oui*," Philippe agreed. "I am lucky to have found her. She has learned much about art, fashion, and design from working beside me for the last twenty years. Shall we go back outside?"

As he finished locking the door of the unit, Philippe motioned across at the patio outside the entrance to the lobby.

"I hope Carmen told you about our wine and cheese gatherings, compliments of Francesca and myself. We find it is a delightful way for the guests to get to know each other, and for us to become better acquainted with our guests as well. I hope you will be able to join us."

"That's a great idea," Dan replied. "I'm sure we'll be here. By then, Richard and Pam and Tim and Shelley should have arrived, and Chelly can meet the people I met at Thanksgiving."

"We'll be there," Chelly answered. "I can't wait to meet the others."

"Philippe, I hope you don't mind if I go to our room," Dan said. "It's just about time for my massage and I don't want to keep Francesca waiting. Thank you so much for showing us around."

"The pleasure is mine, Monsieur. I will see you later then."

Dan walked the few footsteps to their room and unlocked the French door, then disappeared inside.

"So, Chelly," Philippe continued. "I understand you work in an emergency room. That must be very exciting. You must tell me all about it."

Philippe was only half listening to Chelly as she talked about the excitement and challenges of her job. Another part of him watched Dan as he entered the couple's room.

Yes, the psychologist could be a challenge, Philippe thought. *He is not as impressionable as his lovely wife.*

He was becoming excited by the prospect of another project. It would be dangerous starting another one so soon. But he was already thinking of possibilities for making it happen and the adrenaline was starting to flow. It was addictive and he was already hooked. At that moment, Philippe realized he couldn't turn his back on the thrill of another new project.

CHAPTER 3

CHELLY RETURNED to their room just as Dan emerged, totally naked, from the bathroom.

"Aren't you going to your massage?" she asked.

"Yup, but I was hot and sweaty after the drive up here, so I had a quick shower. I thought maybe Francesca would appreciate me being clean. What are you going to do now?"

"I thought I'd put on some sunscreen and catch a few rays until it's my turn," Chelly replied.

"Do you want me to do your back before I go?" he asked.

"Thanks, that would be great. Give me a few seconds, okay?"

Chelly pulled off her tank top, then unhooked and removed her bra. She searched her luggage until she found her yellow bikini and matching cover-up, setting them aside on the bed. She stripped off her shorts and panties, until she too was totally naked. She surveyed Dan's glistening body as he dried himself with a towel.

He was firm and muscular from swimming daily and lifting some weights in the gym. He still had a full head of hair at age 45, with only a touch of grey starting to show up on the sides. She still found him attractive and sexy. But she was also aware that other women found him attractive, and it sometimes made her feel a bit jealous and insecure. She desperately wanted to feel more intimate and romantic with him, but she often found herself holding back.

What can I do to make him more romantic? We just don't seem to be clicking physically lately. I wonder if he's seeing somebody else on the side while I'm working nights?

Her mind continued to wander as Dan finished drying. She couldn't put her finger on what she was looking for. But she just had a growing feeling that Dan wasn't romantic enough for her. She found herself pushing him away more often when he wanted to make love.

"Where's the sunscreen," Dan asked, as he finished drying himself. Chelly's mind came back to reality.

"Over here, in my cosmetic bag," she answered.

"How are you doing?" he asked. "I know you're worried about going nude, but you're going to do just fine. I think you're the most beautiful woman in the world, and you don't have anything to be ashamed of." He reached out to stroke her hair. "I love that red hair, and those little freckles, and how smooth your skin feels. You've got the tightest, sexiest butt and nice firm legs from all of your running. And I love the curves of your hips. You know you still drive me crazy, babe!"

I know. You've told me over and over. I'm voluptuous, like Cheryl Burke on Dancing With the Stars.

"I appreciate it, Dan, but I just don't see myself the same way you do. Thanks for trying to be encouraging."

Dan shook his head. "Okay, Chelly. I'm just trying to tell you that nobody else here is going to have a body that's better looking or more sexy than yours. Everybody has some flaws. Just go out there, get to know the others, and have some fun, okay? That's what you do best. Just be yourself, whether you're wearing clothes or not, and you'll do great!"

"Okay, okay. I hear you. I'll try! You'd better put that sunscreen on me now or you're going to be late for Francesca. Just get the spots I can't reach."

Dan squirted some of the white cream onto his hand, then spread it round and round a few times in a big circle in the area between Chelly's shoulder blades.

"You'll get to show off the new tattoo. I love the way the eagle's wings spread out from that little depression at the top of your butt. It looks hot on you, babe," he said. "There, all done."

He gave her a peck on the cheek. "See you in about an hour."

"Enjoy," she said. "I'll probably be out by the pool when you're done. Let me know when she's ready for me."

Dan threw a towel over his shoulder and hurried out the door. From the window, Chelly saw his firm butt and muscular body heading around the corner of their bungalow towards the back patio. As he disappeared, she looked at herself in the mirror. The loyal side of her began chastising her.

What's wrong with you, girl? You've got a guy who is intelligent, sensitive, caring, loyal and empathic. He'd never lay a hand on you or hurt you. He's got a great sense of humor and all your friends just love him! He's crazy about your body and still attracted to you. And it's not like he's bad in bed or anything. What more do you want in a guy?

As she looked into the mirror, she looked into her eyes. A part of her that sometimes felt lonely and rejected stared back at her, then answered back to her loyal part.

He's just so damn predictable and boring! It's like he's going through the motions. Just doing what he has to do because he's your husband. He never does anything exciting to show that he really loves you! He never does anything really wild or crazy or romantic. Like the guys on The Bachelor; why can't he be more like them? I just never feel like he really loves me. I feel like he's going to leave me tomorrow for somebody else.

An angry voice from even deeper inside Chelly's psyche continued.

And the thing that really drives me crazy. He's just so afraid of doing anything that's bad! I'll bet he never as much as rang somebody's doorbell and ran away when he was a kid! Sometimes he just makes me so frustrated and angry!

Sounds of laughter, coming from the pool deck, distracted Chelly. She went to the French doors and opened the curtains wide enough to see an African-American couple hugging and laughing with Francesca and Philippe.

Look's like everybody's starting to arrive, she said to herself.

Chelly remembered the things Dan told her about the people he met here last November.

That must be Richard and Pam, she thought. *Guess I'd better get ready to go out there and meet the gang.*

Chelly forgot about her conflicting feelings for Dan. Instead, she turned her attention to the naked body in the mirror before her. She began spreading sunscreen on her fair white skin, starting with her face.

He did a nice job, she said to herself approvingly, as she rubbed the creamy lotion over her nose and cheeks. She was referring to the recent cosmetic surgery she'd had done on her nose.

Nice and slim, and no more ugly bump that makes me look like an old hag.

She'd always felt self-conscious about her nose, ever since the kids in public school teased her about her red hair and the bump on her wide, turned up nose. She could still hear them chanting "wicked witch" at her until they made her cry.

Chelly rubbed the lotion into her neck and shoulders, reaching around to do her shoulder blades and upper back, then her lower back below where Dan had applied the lotion. She turned her gaze to her breasts.

The boob fairy must have made a mistake when she handed these out to the short girl, she remarked. She wore a 34C bra, but she looked more like a 36D because of her short five-foot stature.

And why did I get such huge nipples and areolae, anyway? I must remember to ask the doctor if there's anything he can do to make them smaller when I ask him about lifting the girls a bit. Another curse of the redhead, I suppose, she sighed.

She surveyed her stomach, hips, and thighs as she worked her way down her body with the sunscreen. *Tummy's still looking good, she thought. That would change if we had kids.*

Next, she twisted sideways to apply lotion to her butt and the back of her thighs, nodding with approval as she rubbed. *My thighs and butt are definitely my best features. They may be a bit chunky, but thank God I run to keep them in shape.*

Chelly stood back for a final look at her entire body and sighed. Her gaze was drawn to the only region she hadn't looked at yet. She chuckled to herself as she looked at the carrot red pubic hair.

I guess there's no doubt I'm a real redhead! She started feeling more anxious and self-conscious as she noticed her prominent outer labia showing through the thin patch of red hair.

Definitely wearing the bikini bottom! She concluded.

She heard more laughter as Philippe showed Richard and Pam to their room on the opposite side of the pool. She felt the tension growing in her body as the guilty part of her started planting seeds of self-doubt.

If mom and dad ever find out about this, Chelly, they'll disown you. And what would all your friends say!

She pulled on the vibrant yellow bikini bottom but left the top in her bag. Her sexual, romantic voice started talking back to her guilty side.

Oh well. They'll never know. Besides, you did it before at the spa in Germany and nobody ever knew. And if Jenny loved going nude, so will you. Who knows, maybe somebody will come onto us like they did to Jenny. That would make things interesting!

Chelly found the matching cover-up. It was transparent, showing her breasts and nipples, but it helped her to feel less naked and self-consciousness. She went into the bathroom and took a large white pool towel. Finally, she found the bag with the bottles of wine and a corkscrew.

How 'bout a glass of Chardonnay to calm the nerves, girl? She said to herself.

She found plastic cups on the coffee table in the sitting area and filled one of the cups to the top before collapsing in one of the room's two orange chairs. As she tipped the glass and took a large swallow, she felt the warmth from the wine settling in her stomach, and then slowly spreading outward to her limbs.

That feels better, she sighed. She sipped more slowly as the alcohol gradually took control of her body and she started to relax.

Chelly peeped through the curtains onto the pool deck, seeing a row of white plastic lounge chairs lined up in front of the wall that surrounded Chateau Eden. They were still empty. There was a small table with a clear glass top beside one of the lounge chairs, perfect for her to set down her book and her cup of wine. She rose from the orange chair and scrounged through her purse for her sunglasses. Her white Nike Fit running cap was still lying on the bed where she'd tossed it when they arrived. She donned the sunglasses and cap, reached for her book and wine, then took one last deep breath to collect herself.

Finally, Chelly opened the door and ventured out into the bright March sunshine and onto the pool deck, where she spread her towel and sat on the side of the lounge chair beside the small table. Hesitantly, she pulled the cover-up from her shoulders, exposing her milky white breasts to the warmth of the sun. *Here we go,* she said.

Chelly pulled her cap down low over her sunglasses, hoping nobody would notice her, but knowing that others would soon be seeing her partially naked body. She took another sip of wine, put her book down on the table, then laid back and closed her eyes, trying to enjoy the soothing heat of the spring sunshine on her bare skin. After a few moments, she drifted off into a light sleep.

THE SCRAPING of a plastic lounge chair beside Chelly wakened her from her nap. She was disoriented for a moment, then gradually remembered she was beside the pool at Chateau Eden. She turned her head to the right and noticed the totally naked backsides of a tall African-American man and woman. The couple was arranging the two lounge chairs beside Chelly so they faced the sun, and were spreading their towels over the chairs.

The woman turned around and noticed that Chelly was awake.

"Hello there. I'm so sorry if we disturbed you. I'm Pam and this is my husband, Richard." She extended her hand to Chelly, who reached up and shook it.

"Hello," Chelly replied, as she looked up at the taller woman. "I'm Chelly. Glad to meet you." Her eyes quickly surveyed the other woman. Pam had friendly brown eyes. Her black hair was shaved closely on the sides, while the remainder of hair on the top of her head was brought together into a short spiked look that gave Pam a funky, fun-loving appearance. Her skin was cocoa-colored, and not nearly as black as Richard's ebony skin. She appeared to be in her late thirties and had a good figure with a flat stomach and attractive waist and hips. Chelly noted that Pam wasn't muscular and probably not too fit, but was extremely curvy. She had large breasts with dark brown nipples and areolae, which Chelly observed, were starting to show some effects of gravity. Overall, Chelly found her to be quite attractive. The words voluptuous and Rubenesque came to mind as she summarized Pam in her mind.

"Hello," drawled the tall black man standing next to Pam. "I'm Richard. Pleased t'meet ya."

Richard's accent surprised Chelly. It had a backwoods sort of ring to it that made it clear he hadn't grown up in "the hood".

Chelly reached up to shake Richard's hand. She had to tip her head back to look up at his face. Her eyes were partially blinded by the sun that was shining from behind his head. She moved her head slightly to the side, using his head to shield her eyes from the sun. Unlike Pam, Richard's body was extremely muscular and fit. He had a pronounced six-pack and obviously spent many hours in a gym to keep it that way.

However, from her low vantage point in the lounge chair, it wasn't Richard's six-pack that first caught Chelly's attention. In her first ever encounter with social nudism, the part of Richard that she least wanted to find herself staring at, was right in front of her eyes. And that area of his body was at least as well developed as his abdominal muscles.

Chelly found herself feeling both shocked and aroused by the unexpected exhibition before her. She felt the blood flowing to her face, and she knew she was starting to blush. Even worse, she felt the blood starting to rush to her genitals. She was starting to get moist and was grateful she'd chosen to wear her bikini bottom. The moment seemed to last an eternity for Chelly, until Pam broke the silence.

"Excuse me. You wouldn't happen to be Dan Whitney's wife, would you?" Pam asked.

"Yes, I'm Chelly Whitney," she answered, relieved that the conversation moved away from Richard.

"Dan told us you were a redhead, so I thought it might be you. I'm glad you could join us! Are you going to be staying for the whole weekend?" Pam asked.

"Actually, we're booked into the Chateau for a whole week. We just spent the last week in San Diego with my parents, and now we really need some time to ourselves. We want to do a little hiking and shopping, but mostly lots of reading and relaxation by the pool.

"Where's Dan, anyway?" Pam asked.

"He's already getting his first massage from Francesca. How long are you guys staying," Chelly asked.

"Just until Sunday night," Pam answered. "Richard has to fly back to Iraq Monday. Things are always a little hectic before he goes back, but when Dan phoned to see if we could join you guys this weekend, we really wanted to see you."

"Iraq?" Chelly answered. She looked over at Richard, who had thankfully taken the lounge chair on the other side of Pam, and was arranging his towel on the chair. This time, Chelly was treated to the sight of his extremely tight, muscular legs and backside.

My God! She thought. *What a specimen. It doesn't get much better than that!* She took a deep breath to gather her composure and managed to refocus on the conversation.

"Uh … You're in the military Richard?"

"Not any more," he answered. "I spent fifteen years in the Marines, but I've been retired for six or seven. I do private security work now for large corporations all over the world. So I spend a lot of time travelling."

"That sounds exciting!" Chelly squeaked. Her voice was starting to rise into her higher register as the wine worked its magic and she started feeling more at ease with Richard and Pam.

"Dangerous would be a better word," injected Pam, with a hint of sarcasm.

"What's it like," Chelly said. "Is it really that dangerous?"

"Well, ya know I really can't tell y'all much about what I do. You know what they say. If I tell ya, I might have to shoot ya!"

Richard smiled at Chelly as they laughed together. "Say no more. I get the message," she said, winking in return.

"So, Chelly, Dan tells us this is your first time at a clothing optional resort?" Pam said.

The question reminded Chelly of her own naked breasts. For a few moments, she'd forgotten she was partially nude with two total strangers. She felt herself starting to flush slightly again.

"Well, sort of," she answered. "I went to a spa once in Germany when I was younger, with my old boyfriend. But it was mostly older people who went to the baths for medicinal purposes. It was interesting, but boring. This is the first time I've gone anywhere where I'll actually get to know the people and the lifestyle."

"Well, you came to the right place," Pam said. "It's easy to get to know everybody here."

"As you can probably tell from my red face, I'm a bit nervous," Chelly added.

"Y'all will really love it here," Richard said with his Texan accent. "Chateau Eden is our little oasis. The whole LA scene is so hectic, and our work is so stressful, we can't wait for our next visit. Y'all could say it doesn't look very exciting. But for us, that's the appeal. Most of us come here just to relax, visit, hang out, and recharge our batteries."

"I agree," Pam said. "I'm a realtor in Orange County and I'm constantly on-the-go when I'm back home in Placentia. The phone rings 24/7. When I come out here, I switch my cell phone to voicemail and have a colleague that takes turns covering weekends with me."

As Pam finished talking, the main gate opened and a middle aged man entered the courtyard.

"Tim!" Pam shouted. "Over here. Come and meet Dan's wife."

The ruddy faced man, who appeared to be somewhere in his mid-fifties, headed towards Richard, Pam, and Chelly. He was dressed in casual chino slacks and white dress shirt. A noticeable belly sagged over his belt.

"Hi guys," Tim said. He greeted Pam with kiss on the cheek, and then shook Richard's hand firmly. He turned to Chelly, and then reached for her hand.

"I'm Tim Jennings. Glad to meet you, Chelly. Dan's told us so many nice things about you. We're so happy you could join us for a weekend. Where's Dan?"

"He didn't waste any time gittin' into relaxin'," Richard answered. "He's laid out on Francesca's massage table right now."

"Nice," Tim said. "Fran was already booked, so Shelley and I see the other massage therapist tomorrow afternoon. Listen guys, I have to run to the airport. Shelley's coming in on the commuter from LAX in about 20 minutes. She's coming all the way from London, so she'll be jet lagged when she gets here. I shouldn't be long. We'll catch up to everybody at the wine and cheese, okay?"

"Looking forward to it. See y'all later," Richard answered.

Tim headed for the main gate and disappeared. Pam turned the conversation back towards Chelly as Richard settled into his lounge chair and opened a paperback.

"Chelly, I know you're feeling nervous about taking it all off. We've all been there and gone through that. Even though I was excited to come here and try it with Richard for the first time, I was petrified when I got here. I couldn't even take off my top right away."

"Y'all wouldn't know it," Richard cut in. "She's a regular exhibitionist now, aren't ya darlin'."

Pam rolled her eyes at Richard, and then winked at Chelly.

"Keep your comments to yourself, mister! We're having a little girl talk here," Pam said.

"As I was saying before we were interrupted. All the guests started coming out onto the pool deck without a stitch of clothing. Then I realized I was the only person in the place with any clothes on! I felt like everybody was staring at me. By the time Carmen set out the wine and cheese two hours later, I'd taken everything off! After that I just blended in. Once you get used to it, it just feels natural. You'll start resenting going anywhere else that isn't clothing optional. You'll see!"

"Thanks, Pam. I'm sure I'll be okay. I just need some time."

Chelly reached for the rest of her cup of wine, tipping it back and emptying the glass. She was feeling more of a glow as the wine continued to numb her body's anxiety response.

She was also starting to feel the heat from the midday sun, and felt beads of perspiration forming on her skin. She looked over at a large round thermometer, shaded by the vines just outside the door of the lobby. It showed 85 degrees, but it felt much hotter under the direct sun.

Suddenly, Chelly heard a soft hissing sound coming from above and slightly behind them. Seconds later, she felt a light, cooling mist start to fall on her hot flesh. She felt an electric tingle all over her skin from the sudden change in temperature, then looked down and saw goose bumps all over her skin. Her nipples were firm and erect. The sensation was both stimulating and refreshing, and she started to understand what Pam was saying. The sun, air, and water felt wonderful on her naked breasts.

"That felt great!" Chelly exclaimed. "What a great idea. I think I might just be able to get used to this place."

"That's the spirit," Pam said, deciding to change the subject. "Did I hear Dan say you're a nurse?"

"That's right," Chelly answered. "I'm an ER nurse at a major hospital in downtown Detroit."

"Wow," Pam said. "I'll bet there's never a dull moment in your line of work."

"You can say that again," Chelly said. "Lots of inner city violence and just plain weird stuff. Have you ever seen the reality show about the ER on cable?"

"Can't say I have," Pam answered.

"Well, that's my world when I'm at work!" Chelly said. "Just when you think you've seen it all, somebody comes in with something more bizarre. And we're always busy. It hardly ever slows down and it seems like we're always running. The stress is constant."

"Wow. I sure don't think I could do it!" Pam exclaimed. "I get faint and start feeling sick at the sight of any bodily fluid, don't I Richard?"

Richard looked towards Chelly, gave Pam a pitiful look, and shook his head in sad agreement.

"So how do you cope with all the stress?" Pam asked.

"I run," Chelly said. "As soon as I get home after my shift, I go for a nice long run. It gets me away from everything. I can just let my mind wander and do whatever it wants, instead of having to be on high alert, like I am for 12 hours at work. Until I get back from my run, I just can't stand any kind of noise or commotion. It helps that Dan is so calm and cool. He always gives me time to wind down."

"I know exactly what you mean," Pam replied. "I spend so much time trying to sell to clients, that my brain has to be switched on all day, every day. It's a good thing Richard is only around for a week at a time, because I love the silence when there's nobody else around. If he's home, he just makes noise, wants to hang out, and it takes me a lot longer to come down. Isn't that right, dear?"

"No kiddin'," he said. "I can't wait for the weekend so I can bring her down here to hang with friends, cut loose, and have some fun."

"Do you guys come down here every weekend that you're home?" Chelly asked.

She was trying to make eye contact with Richard to avoid feeling turned on by the sight of his body. She wasn't completely successful. She caught herself sneaking a couple of glimpses. Her face flushed.

"Pretty much," Richard replied.

Chelly knew he'd noticed her sneaking glances at his body, and also noticed her blushing.

"But I tell Pam she should try to get on down here at least one other weekend every month, even when I'm not home. Just to help her unwind. She sometimes comes down with Tim and Shelley."

Chelly realized Richard was admiring her breasts. He smiled and gave her a wink. He seemed to enjoy that she was having a hard time keeping her eyes off his body. Somehow, the wine was helping part of her to enjoy his attention. She smiled back timidly, blushed a bit, then looked back at Pam.

"It's not always possible for me to get away on weekends," Pam added. "They're my busiest times, with all the open houses. But I know how much it helps me to get away. I start feeling resentful if I have to go more than three weeks without getting to the Chateau."

Chelly was sure Pam noticed the non-verbal signals between herself and Richard. But she kept talking, showing no sign at all of being upset by the exchange.

Richard made eye contact and smiled at Chelly again.

"We just find the people we meet down here are more down to earth, more friendly, and more open minded. We feel so relaxed and have so much more fun with people at the Chateau. They aren't so uptight," Richard added.

Chelly saw Dan walking towards them from between the two bungalows on the other side of the pool, a towel over his shoulder. His skin was glistening in the sun from the massage oil.

"Hi guys," he called from across the pool. "Great to see you again!"

He walked casually around the pool and up to the lounge chairs, reaching out for Richard's hand as the big man got up from his lounge chair. He embraced Richard, and then turned to Pam, who planted a big kiss on Dan's cheek as he bent down towards her.

"Wonderful to see you, Dan! It doesn't seem like four months since you were here," she said, letting her hand linger on his shoulder for a few seconds.

"Likewise," Richard drawled. "We were just getting to know your pretty l'il wife, here. She's even lovelier than you led us to believe, you lucky fellow!"

He followed up the compliment by giving Chelly another big smile and another more obvious wink. Behind them, the main gate opened, and three more couples headed towards the lobby to check in.

"Looks like the Chateau is starting to fill up for the weekend," Dan observed. He turned to Chelly as he spread his towel and sat on the vacant lounge chair beside her. "Fran should be ready for you now. You can leave your stuff here while I catch up on things with Pam and Richard."

"Okay. How was your massage?"

"Heavenly," Dan replied. She's a magician with those fingers. You don't even have to tell her where to massage, or how hard to press. She just feels it and knows. You'll love it!"

"I can't wait," she said as she turned to Richard and Pam. "It was nice meeting you both. I'll see you later at the wine and cheese!" she said.

Chelly put on her cover-up without bothering to button the front. She threw her towel over her shoulder, then walked around the pool and disappeared between the bungalows.

AS SHE walked away from the rest of the group, Chelly was unaware that Richard's eyes were savoring the sight of her bikini-clad butt, her ginger-red ponytail, and her compact, shapely body disappearing into the distance. He appreciated seeing a woman who was fit like him, and he was imagining what she'd look like without the bikini.

Richard knew Pam was attracted to Dan's muscular swimmer's body. He saw her working her charm on him as they talked and laughed, always keeping her ample breasts in front of his face and often resting her hands on his arm or the bare skin of his shoulder.

This could be fun, he said to himself, smiling.

CHAPTER 4

DAN'S SENSES took in the delicate scent of orange blossoms from the orange tree beside the massage table. The fragrance enhanced the already peaceful atmosphere of Chateau Eden's patio as Dan relaxed on the massage table under Francesca's expert touch.

"It's so peaceful and quiet back here," he said. "And the temperature is perfect for being out on the patio."

"This is my favorite time of the year to be in the valley," Francesca replied. "When all the fruit trees are in bloom and the temperature is more pleasant."

She continued massaging Dan's calves, almost ready to have him turn over to do his front side. Dan's mind wandered back to his first glance of Francesca when he arrived at the patio. She was wearing a peach-colored cover-up with a floral pattern and an elastic waist. It hung loosely over her shoulders, her naked breasts, and torso. Its peach shade complimented the dark olive hue of her skin. The bottom of the garment ended just below her buttocks and revealed her shapely, muscular thighs.

The sound of Francesca's voice jerked Dan's mind back into the present.

"You do a lot of swimming Dan?" she inquired. "You have the muscles of a swimmer."

"You're very perceptive, Francesca."

"Please, you can call me Fran," she said. "No need to be so formal."

"Okay, Fran. You're right, I try to swim for about an hour, four days per week if possible. Being in the pool is my way of letting my mind relax completely. I feel really peaceful when I'm swimming."

"Much like me," Fran replied. "Sometimes it is difficult to find time with our busy schedule, but I make it my priority to get up early each morning to swim for an hour, if I can."

"I just wish there were places where I could go to skinny dip," Dan complained. "I just love feeling the water flowing over every inch of my skin. That's when I feel most relaxed!"

"I am fortunate," she said, as her experienced hands continued working, almost as if they were on autopilot. "We have a large pool at our estate that is perfect for swimming distances, and gives me the privacy to swim naturally."

"I remember …" Dan said, grimacing as Francesca pressed on a knot in his calf. " … when you and Philippe invited the guests from the Chateau to your home for Thanksgiving dinner last November."

"So when did you fall in love with swimming and skinny dipping?" he asked.

Dan noticed a palpable silence before Fran answered, as if her mind had gone someplace else for a moment.

"I used to like swimming in the sea, off the rocks in the little harbor in my village in Italy. I would get up early in the morning, before I went to school. If I was fortunate, sometimes I would see dolphins and they would play and swim around me. My childhood was not so happy. Swimming was a place where I could go to be by myself. But that is another story. And you are on vacation, so I will not burden you, Mr. Psychologist."

"I'm sorry," Dan said. "I won't pry. You look like you've managed to overcome whatever it was. You seem to be successful and have a wonderful life."

"Thank you," she said. "It has taken time, but I am thankful for everything we have. Philippe has done so much for me, taking me under his wing and making me part of his business."

"Time to turn over," she said. Fran politely raised the sheet, allowing him to turn his naked body over. She resumed massaging his legs and hips from the front side.

"How long have you been into photography?" Dan asked. "That portrait in the lobby is beautiful."

"When I was in school. What you call high school. I think I was about sixteen. I was working in a hotel in Monterosso. I did any job they needed me to do. That is actually where I learned massage too. During the busy tourist season, the massage therapist at the hotel had more business than she could handle, so she taught me to do massage to help her out. I also worked in the bar and restaurant."

"I remember seeing some black and white portraits at your estate when we were there at Thanksgiving. Were those yours?"

"Yes. People keep telling me that I should start selling them, but Philippe and I prefer to display them in our home. I think they have more meaning for me than they would for others."

"Well, I think you are much too modest," Dan replied. "From what I've seen, you seem to have a rare knack of seeing into your subject's eyes and capturing what they are feeling on film. You have real talent, Fran. Don't sell yourself short."

Fran had worked her hands all the way up the front of Dan's body, finally reaching his face where she would finish the massage.

"Thank you for your kind words. Now, time to relax your lips and face so I can finish your massage. Stop talking and relax everything."

Dan closed his eyes and let Fran gently knead the muscles in his face and massage his head. He dozed in and out of consciousness with Fran's relaxing touch. It was the perfect ending to a pleasant hour.

He heard Fran's voice and opened his eyes.

"I am finished. Please take your time getting up. By the time you get back to your room, I should be ready for Chelly. You can tell her to come over any time."

"Thank you, Fran. That felt awesome. I can't wait for another one."

"You are welcome. Will we see you later for wine and cheese?"

"Of course. It'll be fun seeing everybody again. Anyway, I should tell Chelly you're ready. I'll talk to you later."

That felt great! Dan said to himself, as he left the patio. *I can't believe how fast the time went. Nice conversation too. She's done a lot of different things in her life. She's quite a lady.*

He was surprised how much he looked forward to talking with her again.

FRAN LOOKED over at the small travel alarm clock on the patio table next to her massage supplies as she prepared the table for Chelly's massage.

She was surprised that Dan's massage had gone so quickly, but she was thankful. It had distracted her from all of her worries. But she was also puzzled.

That massage was strange. I talked much more with Dan than I ever do with most clients, especially men. Normally I do not trust them. But he is such a good listener. It is easier to relax around him.

She tried to shrug it off.

He should be a good listener. After all, that is what he does for a living.

But for some inexplicable reason, Fran wasn't able to shake the need to know more about this intriguing man.

FRAN MASSAGED Chelly's back, using much the same progression she had used for Dan's massage. She rolled down the top of Chelly's yellow bikini to expose her lower back, revealing the soaring bald eagle tattoo at the top of her buttocks.

"What a beautiful tattoo," Fran said, as she continued kneading the muscles in Chelly's back. "When did you get that?"

"Before I met Dan," Chelly replied. "I'd just got myself out of a bad relationship with a guy named Derek. I was starting to get my self-confidence back and I vowed I'd never give up my independence like that to any man again. I figured it was my time to soar. So I thought a soaring eagle would be the perfect design to help me remember my vow. How about you? Do you have any ink?"

"I do," Fran answered. "In almost exactly the same place as your eagle. I was telling Dan about times when I was swimming in the sea back in Italy, when I was fortunate enough to have dolphins swimming and playing around me. They were so beautiful and so free in their own natural environment. And like you, I have also had some difficult situations in my past and I had to work hard to free myself from them. The dolphins remind me of what I want to be, but they also remind me of where I come from. So I have a tattoo of a breaching dolphin on my lower back."

"Oh … That's so beautiful!" Chelly exclaimed in her higher voice. "You'll have to show it to me later."

"I noticed that Dan did not have any tattoos," Fran observed. "That is unusual these days."

"I know," Chelly answered. "I've been trying to talk him into getting one since I met him. He's such a nice guy, but sometimes he's such a stick-in-the-mud. It's so frustrating. There are days when I just want to scream at him to take a walk on the wild side. You know - do something wild and crazy."

"Perhaps we should get together and take him for his first tattoo while you are here," Fran suggested impulsively.

"What a great idea!" Chelly remarked, her voice back in her high range again. "Would you really do that with me? Maybe we could get some of the other guests to come along with us too. He'd have a tough time saying no to everybody."

"Let's talk with him about it tomorrow," Fran said. She covered Chelly's back with the sheet, and then lifted it again to expose her legs and the yellow bikini-covered buttocks.

"That would be awesome," Chelly said. She was enjoying the massage and was feeling much more comfortable with Fran. She didn't even have much of a glow from the wine any more. Her bikini suddenly felt like it was getting in the way.

"Here, let me make this more convenient for you," Chelly said. She grabbed the sides of her bikini bottom, lifted her butt off the table and wiggled it out of the tiny piece of yellow fabric. She reached down and slid the garment downwards until it slipped over her feet.

"Thank you, Chelly. Are you sure you feel comfortable taking it off?"

"I think so. I don't want anything to get in the way of enjoying this massage. I'm a runner, you know. And my butt has been tight as hell for the past week. So, give me the best butt massage you've got, girl."

The two women laughed and Fran did her best not to disappoint Chelly, who dozed off after a few minutes. After she finished doing the legs and buttocks, Fran nudged Chelly's shoulder.

"Time to roll over."

She held the sheet up discreetly while Chelly rolled over onto her back, then she covered Chelly's fair-skinned upper torso and genitals.

"Chelly, I have been working out here for more than an hour, and I am starting to feel hot. Do you mind if I take off my top while I finish your massage. If it makes you feel uncomfortable, I will understand."

"Don't worry about me," Chelly answered. "Make yourself comfortable."

She watched Fran as the other woman removed her cover-up. She was wearing a white string-bikini bottom that left little to the imagination. The brilliant white fabric stood in stark contrast to her well-tanned, olive-colored skin. Her breasts were smaller than Chelly's. From the side, they looked like two small pears suspended on Fran's chest. Her nipples and areolae were much smaller than Chelly's, but were much darker brown in color. The contrast between Chelly's fair white freckled skin and Fran's heavily tanned Mediterranean coloring could not have been more dramatic.

"This massage feels sooooo good," Chelly sighed. "I wish it would never end."

Her ponytail wasn't fitting properly in the headrest and was digging into the back of her head. She lifted her head and unwound the elastic, releasing her full head of shoulder length red hair. "There, that's better," she said.

Fran took the elastic from Chelly and began working on the front of Chelly's muscular legs and thighs. "That feels wonderful," Chelly remarked.

"Dan seems to be a nice man. How long have you been together?" Fran asked.

Having already revealed her naked body to Fran, Chelly was feeling more comfortable about sharing more about herself to the other woman. She liked her.

"We've known each other for over ten years. We met in the hospital where I work in Detroit. I noticed this good-looking psychology intern in the cafeteria one day. He started talking to me in the food line a few days later, and asked me out by the time we'd finished eating lunch. I'd been single for about a year and figured the time was right to start dating again. By the time he finished his internship at the hospital, things were pretty serious and we knew we wanted to live together. Nine years later and we're still together."

Fran finished massaging Chelly's legs, then pulled the sheet down to cover her from the hips down. She listened as Chelly continued to talk, and started some light massaging of Chelly's abdomen and rib areas.

"Sometimes it hasn't been easy," Chelly continued, "but I guess every marriage has its ups and downs. I'm sure you know what I mean," she said.

Fran nodded slowly, but didn't say anything. Chelly's mention of marital stress triggered Fran's mind to start drifting back to the current chaos in her own marriage to Philippe. She started sliding back into the darkness that began three weeks ago.

Chelly felt Fran's hands moving gradually upwards towards her neck and shoulders. Her eyes were closed and she had no idea that Fran's hands were now on autopilot, while the rest of her brain was lost in her recent traumatic life events. Chelly was completely unaware that Fran was struggling to keep up her protective walls and to keep herself present.

The part of Fran's brain that was on autopilot saw Chelly's red hair covering her neck, getting in the way of her massage. Instinctively, Fran leaned and reached all the way over Chelly's naked torso to push the hair away from her neck. She didn't feel her own nipples brushing across Chelly's breasts as she reached out for the hair.

Chelly was partially awake at that moment, with her eyes closed. She was completely relaxed. It was one of the rare times that she ever let her guard down completely. She was unaware of anything but the sensual, relaxing pleasure of the massage. Dan was right. Fran's fingers were like magic.

Suddenly, Chelly felt a tingle of electricity coming from her breasts and nipples as something brushed ever so lightly across her naked skin. Then she felt Fran's fingers gently moving the hair away from her neck. It was a gentle touch, unlike anything she'd ever experienced before. Not like when a man is trying to fondle and stimulate her breasts. It felt soft and innocent, yet electric. She felt the current of electricity spread slowly down through her abdomen and into her genitals, feeling the blood slowly building down there. Her genitals started feeling warm and she started to feel the entrance of her vagina becoming moist.

Chelly kept her eyes closed. Fran continued to massage her neck and shoulders, as though nothing had happened.

Chelly started wondering. *Did Fran just make a pass at me? It doesn't feel that way. But what if she did? What will I do if she does it again?*

She felt confused. Any other time in the past, the thought of a sexual encounter with a woman would have been foreign to her. She had never thought for an instant that she was anything but heterosexual. Yet somehow, the thought of having an encounter with Fran right now was causing her to feel increasingly aroused.

Even more confusing to Chelly was how quickly she was beginning to trust this woman with both her naked body and intimate thoughts about her husband.

Why do I feel so close to this woman? I hardly even know her! Chelly knew that it usually took a long time before she warmed up to people and started trusting them. Yet within a couple of hours of meeting her, Chelly felt a different sort of closeness developing with Fran.

It seemed like the sensual touch and state of relaxation from the massage had synergized with the empathy and vulnerability Chelly was feeling from their conversation. It was much like mixing alcohol and drugs. Each one separately had a pleasant effect. But the combination was intoxicating for Chelly.

Something was happening inside her. The romantic, sexual part of her identity was awakening from a long slumber. Whatever had just happened, that part of her suddenly knew it wanted more. She was confused. She didn't know exactly what it was she wanted sexually. But that part of her was realizing for the first time that she wanted much more, both sexually and romantically, than what she'd been getting from Dan.

In her dissociated state, Chelly was unaware that Fran had managed to bring herself back into the present and was once again fully focused on Chelly's massage. She finished kneading Chelly's neck and shoulders, and then started massaging her head as though nothing had happened.

Chelly was nudged back into reality by the change in Fran's touch from her shoulder to her head. She tried to let the confusing thoughts go and managed to allow herself to enjoy the pleasure of having her head and face massaged, knowing that the massage was winding down and coming to an end.

After a few more moments, Chelly felt Fran gently remove her hands from her face, leaving her entire body craving the pleasurable sensations to continue.

"Take your time getting up," Fran said. "There is no rush because you are my last massage for the day. How was that for you?"

"It was just divine!" Chelly answered. "I'll be going for a long run tomorrow morning, so I'm sure I'll be asking you to spend a bit more time on the legs tomorrow. But this was perfect. Thank you."

"You are most welcome," Fran replied. "I look forward to seeing you again tomorrow. Will you be joining us for wine and cheese? I believe it will be starting in a few minutes."

"For sure. I may be a bit late, though. I think I'll have a shower and do something quick with my hair. But I should to see you there shortly."

"Wonderful, I will see you later then," Fran replied.

She opened a back door to the bungalow and entered the office, leaving Chelly lying by herself on the massage table. Slowly, she pulled the sheet away, revealing her completely naked body. She pushed herself up and sat on the edge of the table, her feet dangling over the side.

Chelly sighed and started talking to herself. *That was amazing!* She paused for a moment, then continued her self-talk.

Too amazing! What's got into you girl? First you start getting all hot and bothered when you meet Richard today. Then the same thing happens when Fran touches you. What would you do if they actually made passes at you? Geez! You're a married woman. What would your friends and family say if they ever found out you got the hots for every naked person you saw? What would they think if they found out you had sex with another woman? Or had sex with anybody besides Dan?

Get a grip, girl! She commanded herself. *You're being bold enough just being here for the week. Listen to what Dan said. Just get to know the others and have fun!*

She hopped down from the side of the massage table and donned the yellow bikini bottom and her cover-up.

Chelly tried hard to believe her little pep talk. But something inside left her feeling unsettled. It was a sense of restlessness. But it was also a sense of foreboding. She couldn't put her finger on where the feeling was coming from or what was causing it.

She continued to feel unsettled and distant as she walked back around the corner of the bungalow. She opened the door to their room, lost in thought, not even noticing the guests who were gathering on the patio outside the lobby, only feet away.

CHAPTER 5

FRESHLY SHOWERED, her hair almost dry, Chelly peered through an opening in the blinds to see what people were wearing for the wine and cheese gathering. Everybody was completely naked. Dan was sitting in a cluster of lounge chairs, talking with Richard, Pam, Tim, and another dark skinned woman.

That must be Shelley. She's beautiful!

Their small group had all taken wine and snacks back to their lounge chairs on the pool deck, while other guests sat on chairs under the arbor outside the lobby, just feet away from her. As Chelly watched all the nude bodies before her, she felt the tension returning to her muscles and butterflies in her stomach again.

She reached for the yellow bikini bottom, and slid her feet into her flip-flops. She reached for her cover-up, and then decided against it at the last second.

No sense taking it if you're not going to wear it, she said to herself. *You don't need a security blanket*!

Chelly opened the door, stepped out onto the patio, and headed straight for the wine and cheese table. Carmen had set out a selection of red and white wines, and an assortment of cheeses, crackers, taco chips, dips and some salsa.

"Hello signora," Carmen said. "Did you enjoy your massage?"

"Oh yes," Chelly replied. "It was awesome! I can't wait to have another one tomorrow!"

"I am so pleased you enjoyed it. Would you like some wine? We have three choices of white and red, all from California. Please take a plate and have some food too," Carmen said.

"I'll have some Pinot Grigio, please," Chelly said.

She loaded an assortment of cheese and crackers on her plate, and took her glass of wine from Carmen.

"Thanks, Carmen," she said, and then walked over to where Dan and the others were talking.

Pam was the first person to notice her and waved. "Pull up a chair. How was your hour with Fran?"

Dan turned around to greet Chelly as she joined the group. "Hey, how'd it go?" Dan echoed.

"Wonderful," she said. "Thanks for the recommendation everybody."

"Chelly, I'd like you to meet Tim's wife, Shelley Paul," Dan said, as he motioned to the brown skinned woman in a lounge chair between Tim and Pam.

"Pleased to meet you," Chelly said, chuckling at the similarities in their names. "I think I'm going to have to go by Michelle instead of Chelly this weekend, just to avoid confusion!" The two women laughed as Chelly, alias Michelle, reached out to shake Shelley's hand.

Michelle was in awe of Shelley's beauty. She guessed the other woman was in her mid-to-late forties. She was fit, her muscles were well toned, she had shapely legs, and Michelle figured she probably looked five years younger than her true age. Both her skin and eyes were brown, and she had short black hair. Michelle admired the woman's perfectly clear complexion and smooth skin.

"Pleased to meet you too, Chelly. No need to change your name because of me," Shelley laughed. "I'm sure we'll manage to keep things straight."

Chelly's eyes continued to scan Shelley's physical attributes. Her breasts were large and firm, and Michelle noticed some slight scarring beneath both breasts from implant surgery.

Now those are the boobs I want, Chelly thought, as she brought her mind back to the conversation.

"Tim tells us you had a long flight from Europe," Chelly said. "Do you travel a lot for your work?"

"Yes, it's a necessary evil," Shelley answered. "Our head office is in Switzerland, and one of our subsidiaries is headquartered in London. I usually work out of our North American headquarters in San Diego, but I can do quite a bit of work from home. When Tim and I decided to move in together, his work didn't have any flexibility, so I moved up to Placentia to be with him."

"Ohhh, how romantic," Chelly cooed, her voice rising into her upper register. "That's so sweet! What line of work are you in?"

"I work for a major pharmaceutical company. I oversee all of our North American clinical research trials. I need to go to Europe every two or three weeks for meetings to review all of the research results and to organize future trials."

"Wow, that sounds interesting. You trained as a pharmacist?" Chelly asked.

"Actually, I didn't. I started off as a nurse, but ended up falling in love with research," Shelley said.

"How cool," Chelly exclaimed. "I'm a nurse too. But I'm still working in an ER back in Detroit."

Tim moved from his lounge chair to sit beside Shelley and join the conversation.

"And what do you do, Tim?" Michelle asked. "Shelley told me you work in L.A., and that she moved up to Placentia so you guys could be together."

"That's right," Tim said, as he put his arm around Shelley's waist, giving her a loving squeeze. "When we got together a few years ago, I was just finishing up my social work training. I found my dream job working with inner city kids in a really rough area where I grew up. Shelley knew how much it meant to me. So she moved here, rather than ask me to move." He put his arm around Shelley's shoulder and planted a kiss on her cheek. "And we've been together ever since," he added.

Chelly looked at Tim and Shelley. They seemed an unlikely couple. While she looked young and fit, and in her mid-to-late forties, he had a ruddy red face, a noticeable belly, and looked to be ten to fifteen years her senior.

"So how did you guys meet?" Chelly asked, "With you working in the inner city and Shelley flying around the world."

Richard overheard Chelly's question.

"Pam and I have to take credit for that," he interrupted. "I met Tim while we were both volunteerin' for a veteran's charity. I'd been in the marines and he'd been in the navy. Well, not really in the navy. He was just a cook, ya know," he drawled, winking at Tim.

"Anyway, we hit it off and got ta be friends. One weekend the charity had a fundraiser and Pam got involved with helpin' us find some corporate sponsors. She managed ta get Shelley's company on board."

"So I came up for the day with my PR rep," Shelley added. "We all had a great day, raised plenty of cash for the vets, and Tim tried all day to get my phone number. He was pretty persistent, so I finally gave in. And the rest, as they say, is history."

"That's the sweetest story," Chelly squeaked in her high register. "I'm such a sucker for romance. You guys just brought tears to my eyes!" She sniffled and giggled at the same time. Everybody else in the group laughed along with her.

"She's not kidding," Dan added. "You know the TV show, *The Bachelor*? She *TiVo*'s every episode. One minute she's yelling and screaming at all the characters for being so stupid, then the next minute she's got the tissues out because it's so romantic. Sometimes it's like she thinks she's one of contestants in the show!"

The group laughed loudly this time. The wine was beginning to loosen everybody up, and everything seemed funnier.

Chelly wasn't laughing. She narrowed her eyes and glared at Dan, sending a clear non-verbal message that enough was enough.

Just then, a loud voice came from behind the group. Chelly turned to see Philippe and Francesca coming over to visit the group.

"You Americans," Philippe scoffed, shaking his head from side to side. "You would all do well to be as romantic as this beautiful young woman! Compared to Europeans, you have all forgotten the art of romance!"

Chelly felt his eyes making contact with hers, and she smiled back.

"Take the Italians, for instance. Where Francesca comes from in Cinque Terre, there is the Via Dell'Amore - the Way of Love. Lover's lane, I think you would call it in America. On this path between Manarola and Riomaggiore, lovers from everywhere come to attach small locks with their names onto the guardrails and fences along the path, to seal their love for eternity. There are thousands of locks along this romantic trail. At night, it is truly magical, with the moonlight shining on the sea and lighting the way!"

Chelly gave Philippe a smile of gratitude for coming to her rescue. He nodded imperceptibly to acknowledge.

"But, to really see and feel romance, you must go to France; especially Paris. Everywhere you go, you see young lovers. In the beautiful museums and gardens, the restaurants, and all along La Seine … *il est magnifique*!" he exclaimed.

Philippe took Michelle's hand in his, raising it to his lips and kissing it. "Everybody in America should be as romantic as you, Madame!"

In a graceful gesture, he bowed to Michelle, and then transferred her hand back to Dan. "You are a lucky man, monsieur!"

"Wooooooooh," swooned the group. They applauded Philippe's grand gesture. Chelly felt her ears and face flushing at all the attention, both from Philippe and from the rest of the group.

"I see that Madame has no more wine. Come with me, I will get you a refill," Philippe said. He took Chelly's hand and helped her up from her lounge chair. He placed his hand gently on her back and guided her towards the table with the wine.

THAT WAS a little over the top, Dan thought. He watched Philippe guide his wife towards the wine and cheese table, his hand still on her bare back.

A typical Frenchman - the perfect match for Chelly's romantic side, I guess.

Dan let go of his thoughts as he noticed Fran standing by herself behind their group. He got up from his lounge chair and made his way towards her. "You don't have any wine, Fran. Can I get you some?" he asked.

"No, thank you!" she replied. "I have to drive home after the wine and cheese hour is over. But, thank you anyway."

"I want to thank you again for the massage and the pleasant conversation today. It was totally relaxing," Dan said.

"You are quite welcome. I am glad you enjoyed it."

Dan was struck by Fran's beauty: her dark smooth skin, her muscular physique and the gentle curve of her hips. He could barely make out the round contours of her bare breasts through the translucent material of her cover-up. The melodic lilt of her accented voice was immediately calming.

But it was Fran's deep brown eyes that captured his attention. They were friendly, yet somewhat distant, at that moment. There was much more going on in her eyes than Dan could see on the surface. It lured him further into them, and left him needing to find out more about her.

"I still can't get over how natural your photographs are, Fran. I've tried taking portraits of people, and mine always turn out just looking like snapshots. How do you do it?"

"I am not sure really. I just enjoy the times when I can be alone with my camera and have the freedom to roam at my own pace. Those times are rare. When we travel, Philippe usually wants me with him when we are searching for new artists and entertaining them. But, when it comes to talking business, he usually does not need me. At those times, I usually hire a driver and go to places where the tourists do not go. I like to see people being themselves in their own environment."

Dan noticed Fran's eyes look nervously in Philippe's direction, then quickly back towards him.

"And I am patient," she continued. "I spend a lot of time watching people. I try to capture their mood and what they might be thinking in that situation. Are they enjoying their work, or are they just doing what they must do to survive? Are they feeling hopeless or helpless about their future? Can I see the love they have for others in their eyes? Then I try to capture their feeling in the camera."

It was Dan's turn to steal a quick glance in Philippe's direction. He and Chelly were engaged in animated conversation. Dan's eyes returned and reconnected with Fran's.

"I try to get the shots from a distance, without them seeing me," she continued. "That way, my presence does not contaminate the mood. I am fortunate to have a large telephoto lens and steady hands. If they have not noticed already that I have taken their photo, I always introduce myself and offer to pay them something. Often they are thankful for the money. Other times they refuse. Sometimes they offer to pose for more formal portraits. So I get a lot of different shots that way."

"Well, they certainly are beautiful," said Dan. "I'd sure like to see more of them sometime. Do you have some smaller prints you could bring to the hotel sometime this week? I would seriously consider buying one or two of them from you if Chelly and I see something we both like."

"I do. Are you really interested in seeing them?" she asked.

"Absolutely," Dan replied.

There was an uncomfortable moment of silence. They both glanced over towards the wine and cheese table, where Philippe and Chelly were still engaged in animated conversation. The sun was just disappearing behind the mountains, and the air was cooling down noticeably. Some of the naked guests on the far side of the pool, who were now in the shade, were starting to gather their things and make their way to their rooms.

"Perhaps I should go and start cleaning things up," Fran said. "It is past five o'clock already."

"It's been nice talking with you," Dan said. "I'd better tear Chelly away from Philippe so he can help you. Anyway, we need to talk with the others about what we're doing for dinner tonight."

They made their way towards their spouses. Chelly was beaming broadly, deep in conversation with Philippe.

PHILIPPE SAW Francesca and Dan walking towards him. He let Chelly's high-pitched voice fade into the background as his wife approached with the handsome American.

"Hey, Chelly!" Dan said. "What's up? We should let these two people get back to work. I'm sure they want to get things cleaned up so they can go home too."

"Not to worry, my friend," Philippe said. "I was just telling Michelle some of my story. She wanted to know how I became involved in the art business. It is really not very exciting."

"What do you mean? It's fascinating!" Chelly exclaimed. "You get to fly all over the world, discovering bright new artists!"

"That does sound interesting," Dan replied. "I'd be interested in hearing about it too, but it's getting late. I think we'd better go talk to the others about dinner. The wine and snacks just made me realize how hungry I am!"

"Me too," Chelly said. "Thanks for indulging me, Philippe. I hope I didn't keep you from your work!"

"Not at all, Madame," he replied and smiled. "It will not take Francesca and myself long to clean up, will it my dear?"

Philippe's eyes bored into his wife's. He waited while Fran nodded in passive agreement. Satisfied, he turned his attention back to Dan and Chelly.

"I trust you and Mr. Whitney will have a pleasant evening, and I hope I will have the pleasure of talking with you both some more."

"I'll look forward to it," Chelly said. Philippe felt the warm touch of her hand on his shoulder as she spoke. He felt a charge of electricity rush through his body in response to her touch.

"Have you made any plans for dinner yet?" Philippe asked. "If you like, we could make some suggestions."

"We haven't talked to the others yet. But I'm sure we're all open to any ideas," Dan said. "Let's go and see if they've made any plans."

"After you, my dear," Philippe said, once again guiding Chelly's bare shoulder with his hand. The two couples joined Pam, Richard, Shelley and Tim as they were picking up their belongings from the lounge chairs.

"So, everybody. What should we do for dinner tonight?" Pam inquired.

"Do you all like Mexican food?" Fran volunteered.

Dan and Chelly looked at each other and nodded in agreement. "We both like it," Chelly replied.

"Well, there is a new family-owned Mexican restaurant only a few blocks from here on Palm Canyon," Philippe said. "You could walk there in ten minutes."

"That's a great idea," Pam said. "We can drink lots of wine with dinner and we don't have to worry about driving home,"

"We were there just a couple of weeks ago," Shelley said. "The food's terrific. It's our new favorite restaurant, isn't it Tim?"

"Absolutely. You'll have to try the *Chicken Molé*. It's the best I've ever had!" Tim exclaimed.

"Comin' from a former chef, that's mighty high praise," Richard said.

"Looks like it's unanimous," Dan said. "Mexican it is. Thanks for the suggestion, Philippe."

"It is nothing," Philippe said. "Anything we can do to make your stay more pleasurable."

"It's about five-fifteen now," Richard said. "Can y'all meet here about six-thirty and we'll walk on over together?"

Everybody indicated his or her agreement.

"Okay ladies," Pam said. "Now for the worst part of the day. Time to put on those tight old bras again!"

The women groaned and the group burst out laughing. Even Chelly, who was starting feel at home without her bra, wasn't looking forward to putting hers back on again.

"See you guys at six-thirty!" Chelly said, as she and Dan headed towards their room.

Philippe watched the delightful sway of Michelle's hips and buttocks from behind as she and Dan walked away from him.

Back inside the lobby of Chateau Eden, Philippe and Fran continued cleaning up after the wine and cheese gathering.

That went well, Philippe said to himself. *That hot little redhead can't get enough of my French charm. And her psychologist husband seems to be quite taken with Francesca. This might work out very well.*

Part of him was feeling nervous about moving forward with a new plan. *How can I do this without anybody else knowing? How can I trick them both so they will not even realize they are trapped?* He asked himself.

Until it is too late, of course! Growled another voice, emerging from somewhere deep inside. As it continued to creep over the walls in his mind, the internal growl transformed into a low, sinister laugh that echoed through the silence of the deserted lobby.

THE SUN had disappeared over the San Jacinto Mountains and the desert air already had a chill to it. Dan and Chelly emerged from their room to find Richard and Pam on the patio outside the lobby.

"Hi! Don't y'all look perty when you're all cleaned up," Richard remarked, winking at Chelly. "Are y'all hungry?"

"You bet," Dan replied. "I'm looking forward to this. We haven't had a good Mexican meal for a long time, have we Chelly?"

"No. After a week with my parents, I'm looking forward to some good food, wine, and laughs!"

"Well, I'm sure we can make all three happen for you," Pam laughed. "Here comes Tim and Shelley."

The three couples passed through the large pine door, emerging from Chateau Eden onto the quiet Palm Springs side street. As the gate closed behind them, Dan turned to Tim and Pam.

"Do you know how long Philippe and Fran have owned the hotel?" he asked.

"I think they bought it just about the time we started coming here, didn't they Richard?"

"That's right. It's only been a year or two. They bought it from another couple that tried to turn it into a nudist resort. But the place was pretty run down," Richard answered.

"We saw the advertisement for Chateau Eden in the LA Times Lifestyle section when all four of us were sitting on our patio one night about a year ago," Pam said. "I saw the ad first and was curious. I was a bit nervous, but for some strange reason I felt like I had to ask the others if they thought they'd like to try it."

"You did?" asked Chelly, surprised. "I thought you were the nervous one who wouldn't take her clothes off!"

"Yeah, I know. I got cold feet once I got here," Pam explained. "Just because I was curious doesn't mean I wasn't scared to try it. It seems Richard, Tim, and Shelley were all curious too, so we decided to come down and see what it was like. Best decision we ever made, right guys?"

"Without a doubt," Shelley answered. "Like Richard says, it's our little oasis away from home."

"Well, they seem to have done a great job of turning the place around," Dan observed. After they'd walked another block, Dan turned to Tim. "What do you think of Philippe?"

"Umh … sometimes I think he tends to be a bit full of himself. But I'm not sure that isn't just being a French male. What do *you* think?" Tim asked.

"Pretty much the same," Dan answered. "He really seems to think he's a real lady's man, but he seems harmless."

Chelly, who was walking with Pam and Shelly, just ahead of Dan and Tim, overheard their conversation.

"Well, I think he's just charming," Chelly shouted, looking back over her shoulder as she walked. "You heard him. You North American guys could learn a few things about romance from the French."

Dan and Tim looked at each other and shrugged. "Maybe you're right, Chelly," Dan replied. He wasn't about to challenge her for a second time today.

The group emerged from the dark side street into the brighter lights, shops, and restaurants of Palm Canyon Drive. They spied the Mexican restaurant's sign about a block ahead and quickened their pace, spurred on by their substantial appetites.

The restaurant was large, simply furnished, and had many tables packed closely together, all covered with red-checkered tablecloths. The staff put two square tables together at the back of the restaurant for their group of six.

The men sat towards one end of the table, with the women at the other. Chelly ended up sitting next to Richard, while Pam was next to Dan on the other side of the table.

A young Hispanic-looking man approached their table. "May I start anybody off with a beverage?" he inquired politely.

"Let's order a couple bottles of wine," Pam suggested. "Who wants red and who wants white?" She asked around the table, finding an even split in preference.

"Anybody object if we start with Chardonnay and a Pinot Noir?" she asked. There were no objections, so Pam selected two bottles from the wine menu, and the waiter disappeared behind the bar.

Dan noticed two separate conversations developing almost immediately. Tim and Dan started talking about their shared interests in social work and psychology. Chelly was getting to know Shelley and Pam better. Richard was caught between the two conversations, but he seemed more interested in the women than in Tim and Dan's discussion.

"So Chelly, how was your first day at Chateau Eden?" Shelley asked. "Pam tells me this is your first nudist experience."

"Not bad," Chelly admitted. "I'm doing a lot better than I expected. I want to thank both of you for being so understanding. I thought I was going to feel really uncomfortable baring my boobs in front of the guys. I don't know what I expected, but everybody just sort of acted the same as they usually do when they're wearing clothes."

"What did I tell you?" Pam answered.

"To tell you the truth, I think I was more nervous seeing the guys naked than I was about them seeing me." Chelly felt her ears and face getting flushed as she admitted it.

Pam laughed and gave Richard a salacious look.

"Well, my dear. The first sight of Richard's body can be a bit intimidating for *any* woman!" All three women and Richard exploded in laughter. Chelly felt her anxiety starting to ease.

Richard nudged her on the shoulder and smiled broadly. "What can I say? I have that effect on the ladies! You know what they say about 'once you've tried black'!"

The wine and laughter were definitely suppressing Chelly's inhibitions. This time, instead of blushing, she felt the blood starting to pool between her legs again. Instead of feeling embarrassed, she found herself fantasizing about putting Richard's attributes to good use.

Pam picked up on Richard's flirting, as she did earlier this afternoon. Once again, instead of showing any signs of being upset, she leaned over to Chelly.

"To be honest, dear," Pam said in a sultry voice, while winking at Richard, "This is one of those times when the product more than lives up to the packaging!"

They burst into even louder laughter, helping Chelly to relax even more with her new friends.

DAN AND TIM were distracted by the roar of laughter across the table. Dan hadn't seen or heard Richard flirting with Chelly. But he was glad to see her relaxing and being herself with her new friends.

I hope she'll start to feel more comfortable with her body this week, he thought. *Hopefully, she'll relax and we can have more quality time for ourselves over the next week.*

At that moment, the waiter appeared with the two bottles of wine, pouring everybody a glass. "Are we ready to order?"

"You'd better start at the other end with the men. We've been too busy talking!" Shelley laughed.

Both Dan and Tim ordered the *Chicken Molé* that Tim had recommended earlier. "Do you want to share a guacamole salad, Chelly?" Dan asked.

"Sure," she said. "And I think I'll have the *Shrimp in Pipian,*" she said to the waiter.

"Certainly, signora," the waiter replied. "And the other signoras?"

"I'll have the *Chicken in Pipian,*" Shelley replied. "Could we please have a pitcher of water too?"

"Of course. And you signora?" he said to Pam.

"How about the *Carne Asada*? I've never tried that yet. Is it good?"

"Si, it is one of my favorites, signora," he answered.

"Okay, I'll trust you," she said

"And finally, you signor," he said to Richard.

"I'll try *Chicharron in Salsa*. And can y'all bring a plate of nachos for us while we're waitin' for our meals, please?"

"Certainly signor. Will there be anything else?"

"I don't think so. That should be all for now."

"I'll be right back with your water and the nachos," the waiter said, excusing himself and disappearing into the kitchen.

Chelly picked up her glass of wine and held it up for a toast. "To new friends. Cheers, everybody!"

A chorus of *Cheers* and clinking glasses broke out around the table. Then Richard's loud voice emerged over the din.

"To nude friends!" his voice boomed. The group roared with laughter as their glasses clinked again in the air.

WITH DINNER over, separate conversations had resumed at both ends of the table.

"Shelley, how did you manage to go from nursing to working for the big pharmaceutical company?" Chelly asked.

"Well, it's a long story, but I'll try to make it short. As you can likely tell from my dark skin, my dad is from India. My mom is English and they met while dad was attending university in London. His first degree was in medicine, but he liked research more than clinical practice. Mom was a nurse, and she always thought it would be the ideal career for me too. Dad eventually took a research position in Baltimore, so we moved to the States. A few years later, he took a position with a lab out in San Diego, so that's how I ended up there."

"So you followed mom's wishes like a good girl and went to nursing school?" Chelly asked.

Shelley nodded and took a sip of Chardonnay, while Chelly followed suit.

"I guess I didn't have any better ideas," Shelley continued. "Dad helped me get a summer job as a research assistant in his lab, and I was fascinated by the work. So when I graduated from nursing, I went on and got my Masters degree in epidemiology."

"Cool," Chelly said. "So you never even worked as a nurse?"

"No, I didn't. While I was still in grad school, I got a summer job at a state mental hospital where they were doing a lot of drug trials. I made contacts with some of the drug reps while I was working there, then landed my first job with my current employer and never looked back. I realized that doing research was my first love. So I guess in the end, I'm more of a daddy's girl."

"That's so interesting," Chelly said. The pitch of her voice was getting higher as she felt the warm glow of the wine, and as she felt increasingly at ease with Pam and Shelley.

"So, how about you? Do you enjoy working in the ER?" Shelley asked.

"Yeah, I do," Chelly answered. "Some people think I'm crazy, but I love doing the front line clinical work. It's hectic and there's always a lot of stress. But I feel like I make a difference in the ER. At the end of the day, when we've saved some lives, that's the payoff for me."

"That's awesome," Shelley answered. "I'm glad you love it. After all, that's what's really important. We have to love what we're doing, right?"

"That's for sure," Chelly said. She turned to Richard, who was sitting beside her and listening in on their conversations.

"How about you, Richard?" Chelly asked. "You must love what you're doing to stay in such a dangerous line of work."

"I can't say I love it," he answered. "But I can't turn my nose up at the pay - not now, anyway. If I work hard for a coupl'a more years, Pam an' I'll have enough invested in properties, an' I probably won't need t'a work anymore. That's our goal, anyway.

Then I can stay home an' spend more time with my gal! Right, Pam?"

"Oh great!" Pam groaned in mock horror. "That's all I need. Having you around making noise and making a mess all the time. It's a good thing you're so loveable!" she giggled, then wrapped her arms around him.

"Anybody for another glass of wine?" Chelly asked, as she picked up the nearly empty bottle of Chardonnay.

"None for me," Shelley said. "I think the jet lag and the wine are starting to hit me. Why don't you finish that off, Chelly."

"Pam, do you want some more?" Chelly asked.

"What the hell," Pam answered. "You finish that off, and we'll order another bottle. Richard, ask the guys if they want another bottle of red."

AS THE WOMEN and Richard continued talking about work, Dan noticed Shelley in the middle of a wide yawn. Their eyes met and he smiled to acknowledge her fatigue. She responded with a tired smile.

"Shelly's pretty tired tonight," Dan said to Tim. "How do you guys manage spending so much time apart when she travels? You both still seem really happy."

"Shelley's the best thing that ever happened to me," Tim replied. "She's the most well-balanced, healthy person I've ever met. I've learned so much about life from being with her. She's confident and independent, but at the same time she's the most genuinely empathic person I've ever met. She doesn't have a defensive bone in her body. No matter what, she isn't afraid to sit down and work through things with me. I've never known anyone like that."

"I know what you mean," Dan agreed. "Even in the short time I've known her, I've seen how confident and genuine she is. I'm glad you guys managed to find each other."

The waiter appeared with two new bottles of wine, serving everybody at the table except Shelley. Dan and Tim continued to enjoy both the wine and the conversation.

"I met my first wife on a shore leave in Vietnam, you know," Tim revealed. "I got her pregnant, married her, and brought her back here to the States, away from her family and her way of life. She was so resentful about being left alone every time I went back to sea. So every time I came home, the arguing got louder and louder. She got pregnant again, and got even angrier. And the louder she complained, the harder I tried to avoid spending time at home, even when I was on leave. I had two small kids and they never got to know their dad," Tim admitted. His eyes were red and starting to water.

Tim swallowed hard. Dan took a sip of wine, then leaned closer to Tim as the older man gathered himself and continued his story.

"I just didn't have the skills for being a dad. I had no role models. My own dad was an alcoholic and left my mom when I was only two. He just disappeared from my life. Mom had a few boyfriends over the years. They were all drinkers and there was lots of arguing. Some of them physically abused mom. But she never let any of them move in. She protected us from them and worked long hours to support my brother and me. My brother and I were pretty much on our own as we grew up, and we started getting into a lot of trouble in the neighborhood. Alex ended up getting caught stealing a car and did some time. I was heading in the same direction too," he added, shaking his head sadly.

Tim paused. Both men relaxed and enjoyed more of their Cabernet in silence before Tim continued.

"Then one day, I got my draft notice. The navy probably saved me from going to jail. It kept me out of trouble and taught me some discipline. It wasn't a bad life. But it cost me my wife and kids. There came a time when I finally wanted to grow up, do something with my life, and make amends for my past."

"So you retired and decided to go back to school to be a social worker?" Dan asked.

"Yes, I wanted be able to give something back to my old community if I could. Maybe save just one young kid from going to jail like my brother, or save one from wasting his marriage or his relationship with his kids like I did."

"Shelley helped me to reach out to my kids. They're both adults now, with their own lives. But they're good kids, and they've gradually opened up and made a bit of room in their lives for me. Shelley's taught me how to let people into my life, and how to love. I'm so grateful to her for that," he concluded. He was getting choked up again as he finished telling his story.

Dan reached over and put his hand on Tim's shoulder. "She's just bringing out the good qualities that were always inside you Tim. There's always been a great guy in there. But I guess we both know from our line of work that sometimes it takes a special person to bring out the best in us, doesn't it?"

Tim was having difficulty speaking. He nodded his agreement with Dan, and then they each finished another glass of wine.

Dan leaned closer and lowered his voice to Tim.

"I really envy what you and Shelley have," he said. "One of the reasons I brought Chelly here this week is because we need to spend more time together - just the two of us. She hasn't been happy lately, and I'm worried. I really want to try to get back some of the fun and intimacy we had when we first got together."

At that moment, they were interrupted by Pam's loud voice from the other end of the table.

"I'm passing the check around the table so you all can settle up. Then we can head back to the Chateau. There's lots of time for more wine and soaking in the spa before it shuts down at eleven. It's only about eight thirty now, so the night's still young!"

Moments later, as they prepared to leave the restaurant, Tim and Dan lagged behind the others. This time, Tim put his hand on Dan's shoulder.

"I hope you find what you came here for," he said to Dan. "Chelly seems like a really nice girl. I hope you guys have a great week and I hope it works out for the two of you."

"Thanks, Tim. I appreciate it," Dan replied. He and Tim followed the others from the restaurant. The door swung closed behind Dan. He felt a shiver surge through his body as he emerged into the cool desert night.

CHAPTER 6

BACK IN their room, Dan stripped off his clothing, wrapped a pool towel around his waist, and slid his feet into some flip-flops.

"Hey, Chelly! I'll take a bottle of wine and a couple of cups over to the spa for us," he shouted to Chelly, who was in the washroom. He opened the bottle and re-inserted the cork loosely, then took two plastic wine glasses from the coffee table.

"Just go ahead without me, Dan. I'll be over in a few minutes," she answered.

"Okay, I'll save a spot for you!" he shouted back.

He opened the room's French door and immediately felt the crisp desert air on his skin. Rounding the corner of their bungalow, Dan saw that none of their group was in the spa yet. Three other couples were sitting quietly at one end of the giant hot tub, sipping wine from plastic cups.

Dan peeled his towel away and let it fall to the concrete deck, feeling the cool night air on his entire body. As he climbed down into the hot water, his skin tingled from the rapid change of temperature. The heat began penetrating his muscles and he immediately felt his body start to relax.

"Hello," he said to the other three couples. "I'm Dan. How are you all doing? Beautiful out here tonight, isn't it?"

The other couples politely exchanged introductions then resumed their conversation.

Dan leaned back and looked up into the cloudless black sky. It was difficult to see any stars in the west because of the light pollution from Los Angeles. Toward the east, however, Dan saw a number of twinkling stars and constellations suspended in the black sky over the desert. He detected the faint fragrance of orange blossoms in the evening air as his body surrendered to the warmth of the spa's soothing waters.

Before long, Dan heard voices coming from across the courtyard and recognized Pam, Richard, Tim, and Shelley as they came through the gap between the bungalows.

"Whoa, is it ever cold out here tonight! How's the water Dan?" Pam shouted. Her booming voice was showing the effects of the substantial amount of wine she had consumed so far tonight.

Dan saw Shelley shiver as she dropped her towel and quickly stepped down into the hot water. "You're not kidding, Pam. It's freakin' cold out here!"

Richard and Tim dropped their towels on the deck and slid their naked bodies under the bubbling hot water.

"You Californians are just soft," Dan teased. "You need a winter or two in Michigan to appreciate how beautiful tonight is! Can you smell those orange blossoms in the air? It doesn't get much nicer than this."

"I agree," Shelley answered. "It's a nice time of year, even if it is chilly at night."

"Anybody want some red wine?" Dan asked. He sat up on the edge of the spa, feeling his skin chill quickly as the hot water quickly evaporated from his body. Tim and Richard passed their plastic wine glasses for Dan to fill. Pam poured herself a tall glass of the white wine she'd brought with her.

The group of five laid back in the water, enjoying the soothing flow of water and bubbles around their muscles. The warm glow of wine was spreading through their body. Shelley wasn't drinking, but still looked like she was ready to fall asleep. The other three couples in the spa, their quiet gathering interrupted by the five newcomers, climbed from the spa and returned to their rooms.

"How are you doing, Shelley?" Dan asked. "You're looking awfully sleepy over there."

"I'm fading fast, Dan. But I want to stay up a bit longer so I can get my body clock back in sync with Pacific Time. I'll be a lot better tomorrow."

"Here comes Chelly!" Pam interrupted. "Come on in girl, the water's great!"

Chelly had her ginger-red hair up in a ponytail. Her body was wrapped in a beach towel from above her breasts down to her thighs. She took a deep breath, and then dropped her towel, revealing her totally naked body. She blushed as she made an embarrassed curtsy to Dan and the rest of the group.

Dan was surprised, but felt proud of Chelly as he took her hand, helping her as she stepped down into the spa.

"There, I did it! I'm one of you now!" she said, laughing.

Dan smiled to show her how proud he was of her courage. He planted a quick kiss on her lips. Richard raised his wine glass in the air for the others to see.

"To Chelly!" they chanted in unison.

"Thanks guys," she said. "If my family and most of my coworkers knew what I was doing right now, they'd be so shocked."

"Well, they don't know what they're missing," Shelley responded. "Your parents must be pretty strict. Are they quite religious?"

"Oh yeah," Chelly sighed. "You don't know the half of it. Just this morning at breakfast, Dan and I got the big lecture about a woman's place being at home, barefoot and pregnant in the kitchen. Then dad told Dan there wouldn't be any need for psychologists if everybody had faith that the Lord will take care of them! Now you know why we needed to come here this week to relax!" she said, laughing.

"Ouch," Tim said to Dan. "How did you come back to that zinger?"

"Well, I tried using logic on him. That was a mistake! I told them I'd seen a couple of preachers over the years that both had severe cases of Post-traumatic Stress Disorder. I pointed out that they were both men of great faith, but were still struggling with their PTSD and needed help badly. I didn't convince him, so I diplomatically dropped the subject."

"Tim was telling me that you really enjoy working with people with PTSD," Shelley said. "That sounds like difficult work. What's it like?" she asked.

Dan looked into Shelley's dark brown eyes. Despite her fatigue, he saw her genuine interest and empathy.

"Well," Dan said, "if you've ever heard people say that somebody has 'fallen apart', that's a pretty good analogy. Trauma victims have often learned to block things out, or keep their memories and emotions locked up behind big walls in their minds."

Dan paused for a sip of wine, and then continued his explanation.

"The big problem occurs when they get hit with one big traumatic event. When that happens, the walls come down and they can't keep their emotions separate. Everything comes rushing out at them all at once. When the walls come down, everything falls apart for them."

Dan's eyes strayed momentarily from Shelley's face, unable to avoid noticing her sculpted brown breasts. Embarrassed, he quickly lifted his eyes and gulped more wine.

"My job," he continued, "is to try to find all the important traumatic memories - sort of like a detective finding all the pieces to their puzzle. The tough part is figuring out how to put all the pieces back together."

"Wow, that does sound difficult," Pam added. "How long does it take to help people with PTSD?"

"It depends on a lot of things," Dan replied. "For some people who've had many traumas in their lives, it can take months or even years."

"I can see that it's very satisfying work for you," Shelley reflected.

"So, Chelly," Pam interrupted. "What's it like being married to a shrink? Is he always trying to psychoanalyze you?"

"Oh God," Chelly answered. "He'd better not!"

She rolled her eyes, looked sideways at Dan, and then continued.

"It happens sometimes. I made the mistake of asking him to interpret a couple of my dreams. Once I got him started, I couldn't shut him up!" she said.

"She's right," Dan added. "It's a tough balancing act, isn't it Tim? We spend the whole day listening to people, being empathic, and trying to teach them how to solve their problems. It's tough to stop analyzing and to be a good listener at home after a long day at work."

"That's for sure," Tim added.

"I can tell when Tim's had a long day of listening," Shelley added. "Some nights he's just all listened out and I can tell his mind is somewhere else."

"It's hard," Dan added. "I just have to try to take my psychologist hat off and be like any other husband when I get home."

Dan decided it was time to stop talking about work.

"But, if any of the rest of you want to be analyzed," he chuckled, "bring your nickels and I'll hang up my *Doctor Is In* sign!"

The group broke into laughter at Dan's *Peanuts* cartoon reference.

"More wine, anybody?" he asked. "I've got a bit left in this bottle."

"I'll have some," Richard replied. "Then I've got 'nother one we can start on over here. Tim and Shelley, do you want some?"

"No more for me," Tim said. He looked at Shelley who shook her head. "And I think Shelley's just about ready to call it a night before she falls asleep on us!"

"I'll have some more," Chelly chirped.

"Comin' right up, perty lady," Richard said to her with a smile.

"So, what's everybody got planned for tomorrow?" Dan asked.

"I'm getting up early to go for a run," Chelly said. "Anybody else want to come too?"

"I probably should," Tim laughed, "but I wouldn't be able to keep up. Shelley and I usually go for a hike up the mountain before breakfast, before the sun gets too hot. Are you and Richard going to join us, Pam?"

"We'll see," Pam hedged. "I will unless Mr. Holloway here decides to get amorous!"

"Oh sure, blame me," Richard said, laughing. "You know you just can't keep your hands off me when I'm home!" The rest of the group laughed along with the couple's suggestive banter.

"I'll join you and Shelley for a hike," Dan said. "I'd normally go for a long swim every morning at home, but the pool here is too small for serious swimming. I feel like getting some exercise, if you don't mind me tagging along."

"Not at all," Shelley said. "We'd love to have you join us. We can cool off in the pool when we get back. It's going to be hot tomorrow."

"Anybody feel like doin' some dancin' tomorrow night?" Richard asked.

"Yeah," Pam added. "We could go to that awesome club on Indian Canyon with the two dance floors. One of them usually plays a mix of music us older farts can dance to. How about it everybody?"

"That sounds awesome!" Chelly exclaimed, her voice jumping in pitch. "We haven't gone dancing for ages, have we Dan?"

"You're right. Sounds like fun!"

"How about you guys, Tim?" Dan asked.

"We'll have to see," Shelley said. "We'll join you all again for dinner, but I'll have to wait until tomorrow night to see how much energy I have, if that's okay with you guys." She looked over at Tim and gave him a nod, indicating it was time for her to go to bed.

"Sorry to break up the party," Shelley added. "But I think I need to get some sleep now."

"I think we'll both call it a night," Tim said. Both he and Shelley sat up on the edge of the spa to cool off. Before long, they picked up their towels and dried off. "See you all tomorrow morning!" Shelley said. "Is seven o'clock too early for hiking, Dan?"

"That should be perfect," he answered. "That's about when Chelly usually goes for her run. I'll see you guys then. Have a good sleep!"

Dan, Chelly, Richard and Pam all sat up on the edge of the spa for a while to cool down after being submerged in the hot water for so long. Steam rose from their naked bodies, and everybody felt their skin tingling as the cold night air confused the overheated temperature receptors in their skin.

Richard laughed as he looked at himself and his three companions.

"Sure can tell it's a cool night from lookin' at y'alls nipples right now!"

Goosebumps and beads of water covered everybody's skin. Both Chelly's and Pam's nipples were firm and erect. Dan noticed immediately that Richard's eyes were drawn to Chelly's large, reddish-colored nipples. Dan had to admit that both women looked voluptuous and sexy in their current state. He felt a stirring in his genitals and decided to slide back down into the water to avoid embarrassing himself.

Dan watched Chelly. Her eyes were locked onto the sight of water droplets glistening all over Richard's black skin and muscular body. The signs of attraction were obvious: her face and ears were flushed. Dan caught her stealing a look down at Richard's genitals, his penis also showing the first signs of arousal. The sexual and romantic side of her was obviously aroused by Richard's hot-looking body and his flirting, but Dan could also tell from her blushing that she felt guilty about feeling aroused. A serious look came over her face. It looked like her guilty side was taking charge.

"I think it's time for a visit to the lady's room," Chelly announced nervously. "All that wine is just going right through me!"

"Good idea," Pam said. "We'll be back in a few minutes, guys."

Pam and Chelly dried off, quickly covering their breasts and upper bodies to keep warm.

"Chelly seems to be takin' to being nude like a fish to water," Richard said, after the women had left.

"Yeah, I'm really proud of her," Dan said. "I know it's tough for her. She's self-conscious about her looks, even when she's fully dressed. So it must be even harder for her when she's totally naked."

"Hard to believe she doesn't like how she looks," Richard observed. "If you don't mind me sayin' she's one hot little lady. You're one lucky fella."

"Well, thanks Richard. I have to admit they both looked pretty damned hot sitting up there on the edge of the spa like that. We're both pretty lucky, I'd say."

Part of Dan wondered if Richard was starting to come onto Chelly. But then he started imagining Chelly's response to such a suggestion.

For Pete's sake, Dan. Stop being a psychologist for a few days! Lighten up and have some fun! You're at a nudist resort. We can't help seeing and talking about our bodies!

She's right, he said to himself. *Lighten up and have some fun, Dan. You're on vacation!*

"Want to finish off this bottle of red, Richard?" he asked.

"Sure thing. Ain't this the life?"

"Absolutely," Dan replied "Cheers!"

Pam returned to the spa first. Seeing the space next to Dan, she dropped her towel and put her hand on Dan's shoulder to steady herself, and then she stepped down into the spa and sat beside him. She felt the tingle as her cold skin met the hot water.

"Oooh, my hands are cold from being out of the tub. Feel them, Dan!" she said, as she leaned closer to him, placing her cold hand on his exposed neck and shoulder. She let her hand linger, then ran it through the hair on the back of his neck before slowly removing it. She leaned back and stretched her legs out, letting her body rise to the surface. Her legs floated to her left and were above Dan's lap. Her breasts floated on the surface, presenting a visual feast right in front of Dan's eyes.

"Ahhh. That's so relaxing," she sighed. She put her left arm around Dan's shoulder and lowered her legs, so she was now sitting across his lap.

Dan was taken completely by surprise by the move. *Just relax, Dan. It's just the alcohol talking. She's just being friendly.* Part of him couldn't deny he was enjoying the new seating arrangement. His face turned red as Chelly arrived back from the washroom. He saw a surge of jealousy flash across her face for an instant, and then saw her contemplating the empty space beside Richard. Her dilemma was only fleeting. She put her hand out for Richard to help her down into the spa.

"I hope you don't mind me borrowing Dan for a few minutes to help me warm up," Pam said to Chelly, a coy smile on her face.

Dan felt his penis stirring beneath her leg. Pam looked at him with a knowing smile and a wink, and then slid her legs off his lap and back in front of her. She let her arm linger around his neck for a few more seconds before patting his neck and bringing her arm back around in front of her.

"No problem," Chelly answered, returning Pam's coy smile. "My hands and feet feel like icicles too!"

"Over here, sweetheart" Richard said to Chelly. "Swing your legs over and I'll massage your feet to warm them up."

"Oh, would you please?" she squeaked, her voice clearly in her excited, higher pitched voice.

Dan tried to ignore watching Richard, as he began massaging the sole of one of Chelly's feet. Chelly leaned back into her seat, looking up at the starry sky and letting a jet of water and bubbles massage her back. After a few moments, Richard picked up her other foot and gave it the same treatment.

"Ohhh, that's wonderful. You can do this all night!" Chelly sighed.

"Is that an invitation, my dear?" he said, as he chuckled, then looked and winked at Pam and Dan. The wine was clearly taking its toll on everybody's inhibitions. They all laughed at Richard's suggestive comment.

Dan noticed Chelly glancing nervously at him. He was enjoying the playful flirting, and was curious to see how his wife was going to deal with Richard's flirting, so he said nothing.

Realizing that Dan wasn't going to say anything, she grinned back at Richard, summoned up some courage, and countered with her best Scarlett O'Hara imitation.

"Why Richard! What kind of lady do you take me for? I'd have to know you for at least another day before I take you up on that kind of offer, kind sir!"

They all laughed again. Having had her fun, Chelly pulled her legs back in front of herself again. "Thanks, Richard. That felt great!"

"Well, everybody," Dan said. "Looks like we've run out of wine. I know I'm going to be paying for this when the alarm goes off before seven tomorrow morning." He looked across at Chelly to see if she was ready to call it a night, when the light suddenly went out in the spa and the jets turned off.

"Damn," Pam said. "Looks like it must be eleven."

"Yeah," Chelly said. "I guess it's 'pumpkin time'. Running isn't going to feel very good tomorrow morning after all this wine. Oh well, you only live once."

Both couples climbed out of the spa and dried off quickly in the chilly night air before wrapping up in their towels to keep warm.

"Good night you two," Pam said, as Chelly and Dan opened the door to their room and disappeared inside.

"Thanks for a fun day!" Chelly said to Pam and Richard. "Thanks again for making me feel so welcome! We'll see you both tomorrow!"

PAM TURNED to Richard as they walked back to their room.

"They're certainly a hot little couple, aren't they? Do you think they might be up to a little swinging if we get them all heated up on the dance floor?"

"They sure didn't seem to mind a bit o' flirtin' now, did they?" Richard answered. "Guess we'll just have to shake our booties, keep the wine flowin' an' see what happens."

He winked salaciously at Pam, gave her a squeeze on the butt, and then put his arm around her waist.

"Until then, darlin', I guess we'll just have to party by ourselves, won't we?"

DAN WAS lying in bed, waiting for Chelly to join him and thinking of the day's events. He thought back to how pleasant and relaxing his massage and conversations with Fran had been. Then his mind drifted to the flirting with Richard and Pam in the spa, and the sexual tension that had started to build near the end of the evening. He felt himself growing harder as he recalled the image of Chelly and Pam sitting on the edge of the spa with beads of water glistening on their skin, and the nipples erect on their full breasts. He remembered the sensations of Pam sitting in his lap, with her arm around his neck. He was definitely feeling the need for sexual release as Chelly climbed into bed beside him and set her alarm for six thirty.

Dan rolled over, putting his arm over her stomach and letting his hand rest against the side of her breast.

"I'm really proud of you, Chelly," he said tenderly. "You make friends so easily. I just knew you'd like the rest of the group. I'm glad you felt relaxed enough to go completely nude tonight. How do you feel?" He leaned over and planted a tender kiss on her cheek.

"I'm surprised," she replied, rolling over onto her back and looking up at the ceiling as she spoke. "It wasn't as big a deal as I thought it would be. Fran helped a lot. She made me feel so relaxed during my massage that it just felt right to take everything off while she was massaging me. It also helped when she felt comfortable enough to go topless too."

"Fran went topless?" Dan asked in surprise. "While she was giving you a massage? That's unusual."

"Maybe. But it is a nudist resort, Dan. It was a hot day and she was feeling hot and sticky after giving you your massage. Why shouldn't she be able to take her clothes off too? I told her I didn't mind. I just loved the sensation of having my legs and butt massaged without her having to work around my panties or my bikini bottom. Thanks for bringing me here, Dan. It's been fun so far."

"You're welcome," he said, as he leaned over and gave her another gentle kiss, this time on the lips.

"What do you think about the others?" Dan asked.

"Shelley and Tim are really nice," she answered. "I really like Shelley. She's so warm and friendly. And I like Richard and Pam too. They're a ton of laughs. I'm really looking forward to going out dancing with everybody tomorrow night. It should be a lot of fun."

Dan propped himself up on one arm and began stroking Chelly's breast as he leaned forward and kissed her softly on her lips. He was completely unaware that Chelly's mind had already started to drift elsewhere at the mention of Richard's name.

WHILE DAN kissed her lips and stroked her breast, Chelly was remembering the spectacular image of Richard sitting on the side of the spa. His bulging pecs, well-defined abdominals, and his black skin were glistening with beads of water, and his penis was starting to show signs of growing larger.

Chelly started feeling ashamed at the arousal she was feeling - not from Dan's stroking and his kisses, but from the fantasy that was taking over her mind. All she could think of now was taking Richard's muscular body in her arms and taking him inside her.

Dan's tender probing touches were making her feel confused and guilty. The loyal part of her was trying to tell her that Dan was her husband, and she should be making love back to him right now. But it wasn't working. The fantasy was too strong and it wouldn't surrender to her loyal and guilty voices.

"I'm sorry, Dan," Chelly said out loud. "I've had too much wine. My head's spinning and I've got a headache. Do you mind if we wait 'til the morning or tomorrow night?" She gave him a quick, dismissive kiss on his lips. "I promise I won't drink so much tomorrow. Thanks for understanding. I love you!" she said, rolling onto her side and pushing him away with her butt.

CHELLY ROLLED over onto her side, her back towards him, before Dan could say anything. An ominous silence hung in the air.

Dan felt rejected and frustrated again. He knew there wouldn't be any sex again tomorrow morning if she were getting up early to go for a run. She'd been so relaxed and playful today. He was hoping she might bring some of that playfulness back into their bed tonight. But now, he was starting to feel a sense of hopelessness. *Will this week really bring us any closer together? Is there anything I can do to help her feel closer?*

He looked over at Chelly's clock. It was eleven forty. He knew he'd have a hard time falling asleep if he kept worrying. He forced himself to start thinking about happier thoughts: about today's massage and tomorrow's activities. The memory of Fran's massage and her firm, but relaxing touch, helped to slow down his thoughts. It wasn't long before both he and Chelly were sleeping soundly.

DAN WAS wakened from his sleep around 2 a.m. Chelly was cuddled up closely beside him and was stroking his limp penis, which was starting to respond to her stimulation. She started kissing his chest as she massaged his quickly hardening organ.

"That feels beautiful, Chelly. I love you!" he said softly, as he ran his hands through her hair. There was no response from Chelly. She pulled the blanket back from Dan's body and her kisses inched slowly and methodically downward towards his now fully erect penis. She teased him by moving past the throbbing organ, which was starting to yearn for more attention. She skillfully alternated kisses, licking, and nibbling on the insides of his thighs. An occasional flick of her tongue on his shaft heightened his longing for more touch.

Dan was puzzled. He usually had to coax her to go down on him. When she did, she only seemed to be doing it from a sense of duty. She told him she didn't enjoy it and made him promise to warn her if he felt himself starting to come. She gagged even at the thought of his semen in her mouth. Yet, at this moment, she was on a methodical mission to drive his senses crazy by fellating him.

She took him in her mouth. She closed her lips on his rim, and slid them all the way down to the base of his shaft in one smooth motion. Dan groaned in ecstasy at the sudden intensity of the sensations. Her lips loosened their grip and slid back up the shaft, circling his rim again. This time, small flicks of her tongue gently circled the most sensitive part of his organ, stimulating him, but also teasing him, at the same time.

Chelly changed position, this time straddling Dan's body. She positioned her sexual parts and lowered them onto his lips and mouth. She started rubbing her labia and clitoris roughly over his lips, starting to moan as she did so. Dan's tongue moved up to lick them as they circled rapidly over his mouth. Her juices were flowing freely, tasting both sweet and salty. The taste and odor of her sex were driving Dan crazy. He needed to be inside her. But she was far from finished with using him yet.

She slowed the circular motion of her pelvis, and then moved off Dan's body. This time she came at his throbbing penis from the front. The glans of his penis was now hypersensitive. The flicking of her tongue resumed around the glans and rim. Then he felt her teeth, just barely touching and gently scraping his glans. By now, the nerve endings in his shaft were unable to tell if he was hurting or feeling ecstasy. Then it all stopped for a few seconds. Her tongue moved back down and began licking his testicles. She alternated kissing and nibbling the inside of his thighs, then kissing and licking his balls, then gently sucking them into her mouth and swirling her tongue around them. The feeling was sensual, but was a diversion that also allowed the throbbing in his penis to abate slightly.

Dan's brain was spinning. "Where did she learn this? She's never done any of this before? He was speechless. He laid back and let himself go on this roller-coaster of sexual ecstasy."

Chelly released his balls gently from her mouth. Her tongue slowly flicked its way up the shaft until she came to the focal point, the most sensitive point on his organ. She sensed exactly where it was from his breathing. She held the tip of her tongue gently on that spot, much like a massage therapist holding pressure on an acupressure point. Then, she reached all the way down to the bottom of one of his legs.

Dan felt a slow, scratching sensation. Chelly was using all five fingernails to slowly and gently scratch the inside of one leg, moving slowly upwards from his ankles towards the tops of his thighs. Dan felt like an electric current was being generated and was being funneled directly towards the trigger point on his shaft, where Chelly's tongue was focused. The effect was electrifying. She moved her hand to the opposite leg and used the same scratching motion to focus a new current of energy directly into his penis. His ecstasy continued to grow and he moaned loudly.

Dan felt the urgency rising gradually from his testicles into the base of his shaft. He knew he was getting close to ejaculation. He was about to warn Chelly when she seemed to sense it, lifted the tip of her tongue from his shaft, and went back to nibbling on his thighs and balls. Dan felt himself relaxing slightly as the urgency eased. Chelly turned herself around again and repositioned herself over Dan's mouth and lips. Her pelvis began to circle slowly and she moaned loudly again as Dan's tongue found her inner labia and clitoris. She circled faster and pressed harder on Dan's face. His face began to hurt as the pressure and speed increased.

Just when he thought he couldn't stand it anymore, Chelly raised her pelvis and quickly moved to one side of his body. Without warning, she turned to face him and straddled his pelvis with her own, taking his penis and guiding it easily into the entrance of her moist vagina. Then, with one sudden thrust of her hips, she had him deep in her vagina and the gyrations gradually picked up speed. The volume of her moaning increased with the speed of the pelvic rotations.

Dan stared into Chelly's eyes. They stared blankly right through him, as though he wasn't even there. Her body was on autopilot, going through instinctive reproductive acts that were programmed into her brain, but Dan had never seen her use before. He reached out and fondled her large breasts, which hung right in front of his eyes. It suddenly dawned on Dan. It was like Chelly was sleepwalking! Only instead of walking, she was going on a wild sexual ride in her dreams!

Chelly slowed the gyrations, and then raised herself slowly so that Dan wasn't so deep inside her. She began to slowly rise up and down, her muscles now tightly clenching and massaging the entire length of his phallus. They both began to moan loudly. Dan heard himself calling her name in rhythm to the rise and fall of her muscles on his shaft. The gyrations of her pelvis steadily picked up speed.

Dan felt the urgency rising again from his balls into the base of his shaft. This time, the speed of Chelly's pumping action kept increasing and her moans began to increase in pitch, quickly turning into squeals of ecstasy. Dan felt the urgent sensation keep moving up his shaft, knowing he had reached the point of no return. His organ was urgently craving release.

Dan felt himself go rigid, then felt the rhythmic explosions of his semen shooting into Chelly's vagina. He felt his body starting to relax from the release of sexual tension.

But Chelly was only beginning to close in on her own climax. She resumed the wild circular gyrations of her pelvis again. Her body needed to take advantage of his hard penis before he started to shrink. Suddenly, Chelly's movements became more focused. He felt her grinding the front of her vagina against the glans and rim of his penis. The focus of her gyrations narrowed to stimulate her G-spot.

At the same time, Chelly leaned forward and pressed her pelvis harder against Dan's to increase the pressure on her clitoris. The two sets of nerve endings in her clitoris and G-spot were now fully in sync. Dan felt Chelly's need for release growing more urgent. She urged her pelvis to move faster and harder against Dan, increasing the stimulation until she finally went rigid, finally obtaining her own intense release.

Dan felt the contractions surging through her vagina. She screamed in ecstasy. "Oh, Richard. Don't stop, honey. Please don't stop. Keep moving! Keep loving me!" she moaned. She started gyrating wildly again.

Dan was stunned by the words that had just escaped from Chelly's mouth. He felt his penis being bent in all directions. It was no longer feeling pleasant for him. *She's dreaming that she's fucking Richard's brains out!*

Dan was confused. Strangely, however, he didn't feel angry. Chelly's gyrations picked up speed until he became afraid that his penis was going to snap off. He had visions of being that guy you hear about on the news who shows up at emergency to have his penis sewn on again!

Then she came again. Her body tensed. Once again, Dan felt the rhythmic contractions wracking her vagina. He fondled both of her full breasts as she leaned back and arched her back for that final surge of ecstasy. She was beautiful when she let herself go. Her breasts lifted high into the air. Her eyes closed. He knew she had it in her. He'd seen glimpses of her powerful sexuality in their early lovemaking. But it quickly disappeared once they were married. He knew she was holding back for some reason and he'd been trying to find a way to help her release it for a long time. Rather than feeling angry, he was curious.

Chelly leaned forward and put her head on Dan's chest, resting peacefully as her body came down slowly from the intense climaxes she had just experienced. Dan's penis had shrunk, but he let himself enjoy the pleasant sensations of being surrounded by the softness and warmth of her moist vagina. She didn't say a word. Dan realized she was fast asleep again. He stroked her back for a while as he continued to think.

Maybe we need to spend more time talking about each other's sexual fantasies, he thought. *Maybe even finding ways to play and act them out in our lovemaking.*

Rather than feeling hurt or angry, Dan started to feel a bit more hopeful. He was starting to see a door of opportunity opening for them.

He nudged Chelly gently. "Time to roll over and go back to sleep," he said softly.

He guided her body and an unconscious part of her lifted herself automatically off him. She rolled over onto her side of the bed, not opening her eyes once during the process. He looked at her lovingly. He couldn't wait for morning to talk with her about what had just happened.

CHAPTER 7

THE RELENTLESS beeping of Chelly's alarm was dragging her mind back into a state of semi-consciousness. Her eyes opened just wide enough to see the glowing green digits showing 6:30. Her mouth was dry and her head was pounding with a wine hangover. It took a moment to remember she wasn't in San Diego any more, but was now in the quaint European-styled room at Chateau Eden. Bits and pieces of an erotic dream started to seep into her consciousness, followed by a vague sensation of tenderness in her genitals.

Was I dreaming, or did I really have sex last night? She reached down and felt her pubic region. The telltale sign of dried sexual fluids told her she'd been doing a lot more that just dreaming. She was confused. Any fragmented images remaining from her dream seemed to involve Richard. Yet, here she was lying on her side with Dan spooning her, his body's shape molded perfectly to hers. His arm was curled around her waist, with his hand gently cupping one of her breasts. She felt a kiss on her back and felt his penis stirring against her.

"So how'd you sleep?" Dan asked. "Feeling any effects from the wine?"

"Not bad," she lied. "I'm glad I was drinking white instead of red. That probably saved me. Actually, I had a great sleep!" she exclaimed. "Didn't even wake up once. Not even to go to the bathroom."

Chelly rolled over onto her back and stretched her arms above her head, exposing her breasts from beneath the covers.

Dan leaned over and gently kissed one of her nipples.

"So, did you have any interesting dreams last night?"

The unusual question came out of the blue and caught her off guard. Chelly started feeling panicky. *Where's he going with this?*

"I don't think so. Why are you asking?" she answered.

"Just wondering," Dan said. "There was quite a bit of drinking and flirting going on in the spa last night, and you saw a lot of naked bodies yesterday - some pretty hot looking ones too. I wouldn't have been surprised if you'd had visions of Richard dancing in your head last night! Do you find him attractive?"

Michelle's face turned crimson at Dan's suggestion. *How did he know about that?* She was still oblivious to her wild antics during the night.

"Maybe, a bit," she confessed. Her blushing face was giving her away and she knew she couldn't hide it. "You have to admit he's got a pretty amazing body, even from a guy's perspective."

"Absolutely," Dan agreed. "What guy wouldn't want to have a body like that? Do you mind if I ask you a question? Don't take it personally. I'm just curious."

"I guess not, why?" Chelly asked.

"Do you ever have any sexual fantasies? You know - like dreaming of having sex with somebody else? It's perfectly normal and healthy, you know. Almost everybody does. I just wondered if you ever do."

"Why? Do you fantasize about having sex with other women?" she demanded.

"Well, sure," Dan admitted. "Like last night, when I saw you and Pam sitting there on the edge of the spa in the cold night air. You looked like a couple of hot mermaids - both of you with goose bumps and your nipples standing straight up. What guy wouldn't be having a fantasy of being in bed with two hot sexy women like you and Pam? I'm sure Richard probably was too!"

"Are you telling me I'm not sexually attractive enough by myself?" she pouted.

"No, that's not what I'm saying," Dan answered. "I'm just saying that research has shown it's perfectly normal for both men and women to have sexual fantasies. Sometimes it's about having sex with different partners. Sometimes it's just fantasizing about doing different things in different places with your own spouse."

"I don't want to talk about it," Chelly said, frowning. She pulled a sheet up to cover her breasts, feeling embarrassed by the topic.

"It's normal for couples to talk about their fantasies, and even to find ways of acting them out within the marriage," Dan continued. "I'm not going to judge you for having a fantasy. I just want to know if you ever have them. It might suggest something we can use to liven up our sex lives. That's all!"

"So why are we having this conversation all of a sudden!" Chelly demanded. "Is it because you want my approval to get it on with Pam?"

"No!" Dan shouted, his frustration starting to get the better of him. "It's because you woke up in the middle of the night and did some pretty amazing things to me with your mouth that you normally don't like doing. Then you got on top of me and rode me so hard I was afraid you were going to break my penis off! And when you came, you were moaning Richard's name over and over again. So I just wondered if maybe you didn't have Richard on your mind, just a little bit, yesterday!"

Chelly was stunned. From the burning sensation in her face, she knew her face was crimson. She sat up, with her knees tucked up to her chest, pulling the sheet up as high as it would go in an unconscious attempt to cover her embarrassment.

"And do you know what?" Dan continued. "I don't even mind. In fact, I'm glad! Because it tells me there's a normal woman hiding in there, who has a much healthier sex drive than I've been seeing for a long time. And I'm wondering how I can get you to show that sexual side of yourself more often - because I think it's a beautiful part of you, and I love you!"

The conflict was building between Chelly's romantic, sexual side and the loyal and guilty parts of her conscience. She went back on the offensive again.

"Well, I'm not some little bitch in heat, running around looking to have sex with every man who gets a hard-on when he sees me, if that's what you mean!" Chelly yelled. "I think you were probably just having your own wet dream last night, after having your little mermaid fantasy. I think you just came all over me!"

"I didn't say anything like that, so stop putting words in my mouth," Dan insisted. "And I didn't have a wet dream. I'm just saying it's normal for both of us to have fantasies. It shows we're both alive and have some curiosity about new ways to express ourselves sexually. It helps couples add spice to their marriage and to keep things feeling new! Fantasies are only a problem if we start keeping them from our partner or start exploring our curiosity behind our partner's back! I'm not accusing you of anything!"

"Well, thank you at least for that!" Chelly pouted.

"In fact," Dan said. "I saw something about fantasies on TV last week. Some researchers were saying it's extremely common for women to daydream about making love with a younger man, or a man of a different race. Or having quickie sex with a total stranger in some strange place, like a plane or train. Believe it or not, it's even common for heterosexual women to fantasize about experimenting with having sex with other women."

Chelly found herself blushing again, as she remembered the arousal she felt after feeling Fran's breast brushing against her own. She hid her head in the sheet so Dan wouldn't notice. She was deeply confused. Her guilty and loyal parts were struggling with the idea that her fantasies about Fran and Richard could possibly be healthy. Those were values she'd learned well from her parents. On the other hand, her romantic, sexual side was afraid of what she might find out about herself if that side was turned loose, as Dan suggested had happened last night.

"So now you're telling me I should be encouraging you to have homosexual fantasies or fantasies of having sex with younger women?" Chelly shouted.

"No!" Dan shouted, his frustration showing again. "The research just says that men's fantasies are different from women's in some ways. We're more likely to want to be dominant with a more submissive woman, or want to get kinky and have our women tie us up! But some of our fantasies are similar too. Men also fantasize about having quickie sex in public places. Apparently, that's a common fantasy for both men and women!"

Chelly hated arguments like this one. They always made her feel afraid that Dan was rejecting her. She saw his frustration growing by the minute. And she knew he was frustrated with her distant, rejecting behavior lately. Her loyal side was so afraid that he might give up on her. But, as much as she desperately desired more sexual adventure, the romantic, sexual part of her identity was too afraid to let go with him.

"Well, I have a tough time believing it. You know how I was raised. If my holier-than-thou parents ever thought I was dreaming of having sex with a black man, they'd think I'd burn in hell forever. Can you understand how hard it is for me to be more sexually open and expressive?"

"Absolutely, Chelly. And I want to help you if I can, without trying to push you. I'm never going to suggest that you try something if you're not comfortable with it. But if I see you showing some interest in exploring something that's a bit different, can I bring it to your attention? Even if it's something you showed me in a dream?"

The room was silent as Chelly thought things over. She let the sheet drop away from her breasts.

Dan's probably more afraid to explore sexual fantasies than I am. He's too afraid to do anything bad. In fact, Pam and I would probably have trouble persuading him to do anything as kinky as a threesome or swapping partners.

"Okay, Dan." Chelly said. "I promise I'll tell you if there's anything I want to explore. And I promise to listen if you have any fantasies. But it doesn't mean I'll automatically agree to act them out with you."

"That sounds fair," Dan said.

"But the same goes for you," Chelly added. "If I agree to act out your fantasies with you, you have to do the same and 'take a walk on the wild side' for me. Have we got a deal?"

"Sure. You know I love you, babe. I just want us to be happy."

"I know," she replied. She held him close and gave him a long, passionate kiss. He immediately started feeling aroused.

"Good Lord, she exclaimed. Are you that starved for sex?"

He grinned back at her and shrugged. "What can I say? You know what guys are like in the morning. Want to have a quickie before you go for your run?"

"After how I allegedly rode you last night? If what you say is true, your dick must be too sore to have sex. I wouldn't want to risk any further injury," she mocked. "Besides, I need to go running before it gets too hot."

With that comment, Chelly hopped out of bed and disappeared into the bathroom, closing the door behind her.

ONCE IN the bathroom, Chelly stood for a moment, looking at herself in the mirror. She had goose bumps again and her nipples quickly popped out. *Brrrr, it's cold in here!* She heard the sound of birds singing, turned her head, and saw the wide-open bathroom window.

No freakin' wonder I'm cold, it must have been open all night, she thought, as she slid the window down and closed it tightly.

Chelly looked back at herself in the mirror. Her hand moved slowly down to her genital region and into the curly red thatch of pubic hair. She caught her breath as her fingers felt large amounts of dried vaginal fluids and semen.

Shit! He wasn't making it up, she said to herself. *What did I do? What's wrong with me?* She was struggling to accept Dan's explanation that her fantasy of Richard was normal.

Okay, girl. Give your head a shake and pull yourself together. Your bladder is about to burst. Take a pee, then get dressed and go for your run. You'll feel better once you get running.

Moments later, she emerged from the bathroom, quickly pulled on her running attire, then disappeared out the door.

She left without saying another word to Dan, leaving him alone and lost in thought about the events of the past few hours.

ON THE PATIO behind Dan and Michelle's bungalow, Philippe was doing early morning maintenance on the spa. He heard the sounds of arguing coming from the open bathroom window. He went quietly to the window and knelt down, putting his ear close as he dared.

...No, that's not what I'm saying Chelly. I'm just saying that research has shown that it's perfectly normal for both men and women to have sexual fantasies ...

Philippe's ears perked up. *They are arguing about fantasies. How interesting!* He listened as the couple continued to argue.

... you woke up in the middle of the night and did some pretty amazing things to me with your mouth. Then you got on top of me and rode me so hard I was afraid you were going to break my penis off! And when you came, you were moaning Richard's name over and over again. So I just wondered if maybe you didn't have Richard on your mind just a little bit yesterday! ...

Philippe's mind raced to fit this new information into some sort of a plan.

... But the same goes for you. If I agree to act out your fantasies with you, you have to 'take a walk on the wild side' and do the same for me. Have we got a deal? ...

Perfect! Philippe said silently. *Absolutely perfect! I've got them now, right where I want them! I must tell Francesca right away. There is much to do in a short time.*

He felt a rush of sexual energy surging through his body. It always happened whenever a plan started coming together. There was no feeling in the world like it for Philippe.

DAN WAS just finished dressing when there was a knock on their door.

That must be Shelley and Tim, he said to himself. He went to the door and swung it open, ready the greet them. Instead, he found himself face to face with Philippe.

"Philippe! I was expecting Shelley and Tim. You caught me off guard."

"Please excuse me, Dr. Whitney," Philippe said. "I am so sorry to bother you. May I have a word with you?"

"Sure, is something wrong?" Dan asked. Philippe's eyes were only making fleeting contact, and he was fidgeting with the ring of keys that hung from his belt.

"I am afraid I have some bad news for you and the Madame. We have a problem with the sewer line running from the street to the office and your room. We have been waiting for weeks for the contractor to tell us when they are going to do the repairs. We heard nothing from them until late yesterday. Suddenly, they are ready to start digging things up on Monday morning. Unfortunately, it will cause some damage to your room. I am afraid I am going to have to ask you and Michelle to move."

Dan sensed something different about Philippe this morning. He seemed nervous. He dismissed his premonition, knowing Philippe must be upset by the last-minute notice from the city.

"I'm sure that's not a problem," Dan said. "Chelly's out for a run right now, but I'm sure she won't mind changing rooms. Which room are you moving us to?"

"Ah, but that is the problem. We are fully booked for the next week. There are no other rooms here at Chateau Eden we can move you to. I am so terribly sorry. I do not know what to say."

"That's too bad," Dan said. His shoulders slumped initially in disappointment, but within seconds, his brain was in problem-solving mode. His muscles tensed, his shoulders straightened, and his pulse quickened, ready to deal with the challenge.

"I guess we'll have to get a room at one of the other naturist resorts. That's so disappointing. We were looking forward to this holiday so much. Chelly will really be upset."

"I understand completely," Philippe said. "But there may be something else I can do for you," he added quickly. "You remember visiting our estate with the other guests for Thanksgiving dinner in November?"

"Of course," Dan said. "We all had a great time. That was over in Palm Desert, wasn't it?"

"That is correct. I have talked to Francesca and we have thought of a solution for you and the Madame. We have a guest room in our estate that we use for clients who come to visit our office in Los Angeles. It will be empty this week. We would be grateful if you would accept our invitation to be our guests at the estate for the remainder of your stay. Free of charge, of course, to compensate you for your inconvenience."

Dan was caught off guard by the offer. "That's most generous, Philippe. But we can't take advantage of you and Fran like that. I'll phone around to the other resorts to see if they have any rooms.

"That is the other big problem, Dr. Whitney, especially at a nudist resort. Spring break is starting this week and most hotels in the city are heavily booked. I'm afraid you may not have many options."

Dan saw the look of concern on Philippe's face, unaware that it was a mask the Frenchman was wearing to disguise his lies about the alleged repairs to Dan and Michelle's room. The mask of concern also hid exaggerations about spring break, since the city was nowhere near as popular now for spring break as it was in the 1980's. The mask convinced Dan that they would have difficulty finding another room somewhere in the city at this busy time of year, especially if there was only one other nudist resort in the city.

Dan realized that Philippe was offering an attractive solution to his dilemma. He was tempted by the invitation, but he didn't want to accept without talking it over with Chelly first. He ran though the choices available to him in his mind, trying to see if there were any others he hadn't considered. He couldn't see any other good options, yet something was nagging at him, making him reluctant to accept.

Conflict of interest? As a psychologist, I wouldn't think of having a social relationship with a client if I could avoid it. Is there any problem with Chelly and I getting to know Philippe and Fran on a personal level?

Dan couldn't think of any obvious conflicts at the moment, but something still nagged at him. He noticed a smile on Philippe's face, realizing that the Frenchman didn't seem nearly as nervous and fidgety as he was a few minutes ago. He was waiting for Dan's decision with a look of cool confidence that was unsettling.

"You're sure we wouldn't be inconveniencing you and Fran?" Dan repeated.

"Nonsense, my friend," Philippe answered quickly. "We spend much less time at the Chateau during the week when Carmen and her husband manage the office, housekeeping, and maintenance. We drop in occasionally to take care of any large issues that come up. We love entertaining, and we would be honored if you would share our estate with us."

Stop being a psychologist. Why waste all that time trying to find another hotel when we have an offer like this, Dan said to himself.

"Okay, Philippe. I'd love to stay with you and Fran, as long as we aren't causing you any inconvenience, and as long as Chelly says yes. We'll still have our rental car if we want to drive somewhere to go hiking or shopping. So there isn't much reason why we have to stay here in Palm Springs. We were mostly going to be doing some day-hikes and hanging out by the pool anyway," Dan reasoned.

"Then I think we have the perfect retreat for you!" Philippe exclaimed.

"Just one more thing," Dan said. "Are there some good places where Chelly can go running in the morning?"

"Of course," Philippe replied. "There are some quiet roads winding gradually down the through the hills into the town. It is quite flat down there, if that is what she prefers. Francesca tells me that you are a swimmer. I am sure she would love to have some company in the pool!"

"Sounds ideal," Dan answered. "I'm looking forward to it already!"

Dan noticed that Philippe had lost any trace of his prior anxiety and was looking calmer - almost too calm. Something about the other man's behavior was still bothering Dan. Yet, he still couldn't identify why he was feeling so uneasy.

Tim and Shelley emerged from their room and caught Dan's eye. "I'm going for a hike with Tim and Shelley, but I should be back by about nine o'clock. Chelly should be back by then too. When would you like to hear back from us?"

"As soon as possible, since Francesca and I will need some time to get things ready," Philippe replied.

"We'll come into the office and confirm with you as soon as I've talked with Chelly."

"Wonderful. I'll talk to you soon, my friend," Philippe said. He reached out with both hands to confirm their deal with a sturdy handshake, then turned and disappeared in the direction of office.

Dan locked the door of their room, then walked across the pool deck to greet Tim and Shelley. The three hikers opened the large pine door and disappeared outside the walls of Chateau Eden.

AS THE main gate closed behind Dan, Tim, and Shelley, Philippe beamed with pride at his accomplishment. He rubbed his hands eagerly, like an excited young boy, as he walked back towards Chateau Eden's lobby. Everything was falling into place nicely. He joined Francesca, who had been setting out the continental breakfast.

"Good news, Francesca! Dr. Whitney and Michelle will be joining us at the estate for a few days. There is much for us to do tonight and tomorrow to prepare for our guests!"

Francesca remained silent. She turned her back to Philippe and retreated into the office. Nothing made Philippe angrier than being ignored. He bolted after Francesca, his face turning red with rage.

"Francesca! Did you just hear what I said? We can go ahead and get ready for our guests!"

"Lower your voice, Philippe!" she replied in a loud whisper. "Do you want all the guests to hear you? This is *your* project, not mine. You do not have to do this, Philippe. I beg of you! These people are not idiots. What happens if something goes wrong again? What if we get caught this time?"

Anger raged in Philippe's eyes. His lips were pursed tightly and the muscles in his crimson face were straining. He pushed her roughly against the wall, his hand compressing her throat. She was gasping for breath as he gradually increased the pressure on her windpipe.

"Don't you ever challenge me again, you ungrateful little bitch!" he rasped, his face so close she could feel his hot breath searing into her face. "You had nothing until you met me. And you will have nothing if I decide I don't need you anymore! You will do exactly what I tell you to do to please our guests, do you understand? You will do anything to make their stay and my project a success. And I mean *anything*!" he commanded. "Do you understand?"

Francesca's lungs were burning. She was unable to speak. The walls were crashing down in her mind and she was starting to panic. Philippe saw the distant look in her eyes. He slapped her face to bring her attention back to his face. Her eyes blinked in shock and were full of fear. Philippe knew she would not dare to challenge him again.

"I said, do you understand?" he repeated, whispering hoarsely.

She nodded her head slowly up and down. Philippe slowly released his hold on her throat. She collapsed to her knees in front of him, gasping for breath and submitting to his will.

He smiled sarcastically at her, as if nothing had happened between them, kneeling so his face was level with Francesca's. "Now you put a smile back on that beautiful face, *ma chére*, and get back to work. Immediately!" he hissed. "The guests will be looking for breakfast any minute and we must not disappoint them. *Oui?*"

Francesca nodded more quickly this time. She rose to her feet, and Philippe allowed her to slip out from between him and the wall. She hurried back to preparing breakfast for the guests.

Philippe was feeling confident that everything would work out perfectly this time. The wheels were in motion, and he felt like nothing could stop him.

A part of his brain that needed to compete, to control, and to win was taking charge now. It began speaking to another side of him - the side that could usually hide his anger behind a wall, and could charm and manipulate people into doing anything he wanted them to do. Normally, the manipulative, charming side was able to control his anger. But today, he had lost control. He couldn't let that happen again. He needed to stay in control of the situation.

Soon, Philippe, soon, he said soothingly.

"One or two more days and that stupid couple will be under your control. Your plan is both simple and elegant. They will do all the work for you, and they won't even notice until it's too late!"

Once again, he felt the rush of sexual energy surging through him. He was feeling more powerful and more invincible by the minute.

WALLS

CHAPTER 8

IT WAS only a short walk for Tim, Shelley, and Dan from Chateau Eden, then across Palm Canyon Drive until they were at the base of the hills. From there, a small trail ascended into the heights above Palm Springs.

It was a clear, cloudless Saturday that promised to be even warmer than the previous day. The hikers felt the heat from the sun already, even though it was still low in the sky. There were no trees. The scruffy, low desert vegetation still retained some green color from spring rains, but was quickly becoming bleached brown. Tim, Shelley, and Dan were fully exposed to the sun's penetrating rays, which were reflecting off the hillside and quickly heating the trail. After a few minutes of hiking, Tim began lagging behind Dan and Shelley.

"Hey, guys. I need to stop and catch my breath. I'm not in the same shape as you two billy goats."

All three hikers stopped to drink some water and to gaze over Palm Springs and the valley, allowing Tim's breathing to become less labored. The view was stunning on this clear day, even from a short distance up the hill, as they looked out through the morning haze at the distant desert. As Tim caught his breath, Shelley turned to Dan.

"Tim said that you and Chelly are having some problems. I'm sorry to hear that. Anything you want to talk about?" Shelley inquired.

"Thanks for asking. If you're wondering if we're in crisis at the moment, I don't think so. It's sort of a chronic problem that isn't going away," Dan replied.

Having caught his breath and had some water, Tim rejoined them. The trio resumed trekking up the series of switchbacks that zigged and zagged their way up the mountain.

"You mentioned last night that Chelly seems unhappy," Tim said. "What's the problem?"

"Well, I think she has a real fear of intimacy. She doesn't feel comfortable confronting issues with me at all."

"That's pretty common for people with negative, critical parents like Chelly's folks, isn't it?" Tim asked.

"You don't have to answer this if you don't want to," Shelley added. "Is it affecting your sex life too?"

"Yeah, I'm afraid that's part of the problem too. On one hand, she's a hopeless romantic. She loves romance novels and shows like *The Bachelor*. She has a romantic fantasy of what she thinks love should be like. On the other hand, I don't think she has any concept that real love is sharing and confronting all the ups and downs of everyday life. I've tried everything to put more romance into the marriage, but it never seems to be enough. I don't know what else I can do anymore!" Dan said, shrugging his shoulders in frustration.

"Well, I understand what she's feeling," Tim said. "I'm the poster-boy for men with fear of intimacy. But I guess I'm lucky. I met somebody who was patient enough to teach me that she wasn't threatening." He reached out and held Shelley's hand as he finished talking.

"It's hard to notice fear of intimacy in somebody when you first meet them," Shelley said. "I didn't suspect Tim had issues until we started talking about moving in together. That's when we started having communication problems."

"Shelley made me sit down and face the problem," Tim added. "It was scary. But she was so patient with me, it just got easier. Now that I'm not afraid to talk, it seems like our problems are all so much smaller."

"Mind if I change the subject?" Shelley asked. "What was it about Chelly that really attracted you to her?" she asked.

"To be honest," Dan answered. "I think it was her looks. When I first saw her from a distance in the lunchroom in the hospital, she looked just like one of my old girlfriends from Vancouver who cheated on me."

Tim was starting to lag behind Shelley and Dan again, and was falling out of the conversation. They stopped to let Tim catch up, and to drink some more water. They were sweating freely as the sun rose higher. Shelley handed the water bottle to Tim, who managed to take small sips between gasps of breath. A small gecko darted across the path in front of them. It was one of the few visible signs of animal life in the parched landscape, which was taking a direct hit from the morning sun.

"So tell me more about this old girlfriend," Shelley continued. "It sounds like she really messed you up."

"You're not kidding," Dan said. "I met Brenda while I was still in med school in Vancouver, before I changed and went into psychology."

"You were in medical school first? I didn't know that. What happened, did you change your mind?" Tim asked.

"Well, it actually had a lot to do with what happened with Brenda," Dan continued. "So I'll tell you the whole story. I met her one day while I was playing touch football with a bunch of the guys from med school. I was the smallest guy in the game, so it turned out that Brenda and I played *man on man* against each other all afternoon and had a lot of fun. I was stupid and didn't get her last name or phone number at the time. I thought she was with one of the other guys."

"I saw her around campus once or twice, but didn't give her much thought. Then one Friday night, I went with some of the guys to a dance on campus. She bounced up to me and asked if I remembered her. I called her by name and told her how much fun I'd had playing football against her. We danced all night, she took me home with her, and we were inseparable for about eleven months. As far as I was concerned, she was the love of my life, and I was planning to spend the rest of my life with her."

Tim stopped once again to catch his breath and to sip some more water.

"C'mon Tim," Shelley said. "Just a couple of hundred more yards. We can rest in a couple of minutes."

Shelley and Dan continued talking as they continued up the path to the lookout.

"So what happened after eleven months," Shelley asked.

"Well, one weekend she told me she'd gone home to visit her parents. It turns out she stayed in the city and didn't tell me. I just happened to be in the wrong spot at the wrong time and saw her kissing another guy. I phoned her and told her what I'd seen, so she broke down and admitted everything. She said she was sorry, but she didn't want to see me again. I was shocked. I didn't have a clue that anything was happening."

"Oooh, that sucks!" Shelly said. "I'm sorry you went through that. You must have hurt for quite a while!"

Tim finally caught up with Dan and Shelley at the lookout, about half way up the mountain. His chest was heaving as he tried to gulp enough oxygen into his lungs. He took slurps of water between his deep gasps for air.

"Thanks, Shelley," Dan said. "Looking back on it now, I'm pretty sure I was depressed. I'd already been struggling with not liking med school. I'd been having a hard time pushing myself through that term anyway. And I went on some of the worst dates you could ever imagine over the next few months!" Dan said. He laughed as he recalled some of the bad memories. "I think my self-confidence was at an all-time low. I was really down on myself."

Dan and Shelley relaxed as they drank from their water bottles and looked out over the valley and the city, waiting for Tim to catch his breath. After a few minutes, the trio finally started walking back down the path towards Palm Springs at a slower pace. It was easier for Tim to join in the conversation as they descended.

"So, how did you pull yourself out of it?" Tim asked. "Was this when you switched from medicine to psychology?"

"Well, both sort of happened at the same time," Dan answered. "I went back home to Calgary to visit my parents and friends after exams were over. While I was home, I went out for coffee one night with a girl who was my best friend all through high school: her name was Anika. The funny thing is, we didn't even go to the same school. Our families both went to the same church, so that's how I knew her. Even though we were best friends for years, we never dated or got serious. She always told me she didn't have time for dating guys because she wanted to focus on getting into med school. To be honest, I was a bit intimidated by her and didn't want to scare her off, so I just stayed friends with her. We always talked when we had problems and gave each other advice about everything."

"She sounds like a good friend," Shelley said. "So how did that date go?"

"It was awesome," Dan recalled. "We talked about everything, just like old times. I felt my confidence coming back, even while I was talking with her. When I told her I didn't like med school, she looked me straight in the eye and asked me if there was anything else I enjoyed. When I told her I was thinking about psychology, she told me to go for it, if that's what I really wanted. So, when I went back to Vancouver, I went straight to the dean of medicine and dropped out of med school. Then I walked across campus to switch to psychology."

"Anika sounds like a special person. Did you keep in touch?" Shelley asked.

"We did for a while. But we drifted apart over time because we'd both moved away from Calgary. She was in med school in Edmonton and I was in Vancouver. Neither one of us had much reason to go to either city, I guess," Dan replied.

Tim shook his head. "Did you ever think about going just to visit her?"

"Yeah, a few times," Dan said sheepishly. "Looking back on it now, I can see I was stupid. I've wondered a lot over the years about what might have happened if I'd really tried to take our friendship further. I guess that's one thing I'll never know."

"Anyway," Dan continued. "I was really down about women and relationships after Brenda dumped me. I had a few short relationships and a lot of meaningless sexual encounters while I was in grad school. I think I was still looking for another Brenda and nobody else seemed to compare with her."

"Until you saw Chelly in the hospital cafeteria," Shelley concluded.

Another gecko darted onto the path in front of Dan, causing him to stop. Iridescent spots of color shimmered on the tiny creature's brown back in the bright morning sun. The creature scurried into the brush as Tim walked up behind Dan.

"Exactly," Dan said, bringing his mind back to the conversation. "Then I saw Chelly in the cafeteria. She looked so much like Brenda; I couldn't stop myself from introducing myself to her, then asking her out. Now that I think about it, I've probably always been trying to make my relationship with Chelly be like I wished it could have been with Brenda!"

"So maybe you're both looking for a fantasy romance - something other than what you've got," Tim concluded.

"You're probably right," Dan admitted. "But, I'm committed to staying with Chelly. I'm not going to give up on her. I think I really do love her, despite our problems."

"What if it just isn't meant to be, Dan?" Shelley asked. "What if you're just not compatible or she's looking for a fantasy romance to make herself feel loved and complete? What then?"

"I guess that's one of the reasons I brought her here this week," Dan answered. "I'm hoping she learns to feel content with what she has, whether it's her looks, her body, or her marriage. I guess I thought if she can learn to feel more comfortable with her naked body, it might help her to feel better about herself on the inside. I know it's not going to be an instant solution, but maybe it could be a step in the right direction."

"Well, she seemed to be getting more confident as the day went on yesterday," Tim said. "Let's hope it helps her self-acceptance. I hope you guys have a great week at the Chateau, and I hope it brings you both closer together!"

"Me too," Shelly added. "She's a really nice girl, and you guys are a nice couple. I hope it works out."

"Thanks," Dan replied. "I appreciate your support. By the way, it looks like there's been a glitch at the Chateau. Chelly and I won't be able to stay there for the rest of the week. That's why Philippe was talking to me when you came out of your room this morning. Something about contractors having to come in and dig up our room to get at the sewer line."

"That's odd," Tim said. "He never said anything about sewer problems when we stayed in that room a few weeks ago, did he Shelley?"

"No," she answered, a puzzled frown on her face. "Maybe it's something that just came up recently. What are you guys going to do?"

"Remember Philippe's and Fran's estate in Palm Desert?" Dan asked. "He and Fran felt so bad about inconveniencing us, that they invited us to stay in their guest room at the estate for the rest of the week. Free of charge, no less!"

"That sounds like an offer that's hard to refuse," Tim exclaimed. "You can live the lifestyle of the rich and famous for a few days."

"That's nice of them," Shelley added. "Does it matter if you're in Palm Desert rather than Palm Springs?"

"Not really," Dan answered. "I feel a bit odd accepting the invitation, since we don't know them very well. I haven't been able to tell Chelly yet, because she'd already left for her run. But I'm betting she's going to be really thrilled"

The three hikers fell into a steady stride as the path leveled out and they re-entered Palm Springs. Within a few minutes they'd crossed back over Palm Canyon Drive and down the side street towards the large pine entrance to Chateau Eden. They were all sweating profusely as they opened the gate and entered the courtyard, since the day was heating up quickly as the sun rose higher in the cloudless sky. They went directly to the lounge chairs on the pool deck, stripped down to their skin, then rinsed under a shower on the pool deck before plunging into the pool."

"Ahhhhh, Dan sighed," as he felt the cool shower hitting his hot skin. "That feels good. How's the water, guys?" he called to Tim and Shelley, who were now floating in the pool.

"Awesome!" Shelley answered. "You're going to love it!"

Dan jumped into the pool and immediately ducked under the water, swimming smoothly below the surface until he was at the far end of the pool. He summersaulted and twisted his body in one smooth movement to reverse his direction and swam back towards Tim and Shelley. The cool refreshing water slid gently over every part of his body as he glided smoothly through the pool. He surfaced and took a deep breath of fresh oxygen for his lungs.

That's what I've been missing all week! He said to himself. He was glad to be back in a pool, even if it was too small for a decent swim.

The Chateau's main gate opened and Chelly walked into the courtyard and pool area, her skin glistening and her tank top drenched with sweat. "Hi everybody," she called, when she saw Tim, Shelley, and Dan in the pool. "What a great idea. I think I'll join you."

"Come on in! The water's great!" Dan said.

Chelly slipped out of her running gear and was naked in no time. She didn't appear to be the least bit uncomfortable with her second day of social nudity, looking like she'd been a nudist all of her life.

"How was your run?" Dan asked.

"Awesome," she answered. "This city is so flat and so peaceful at this hour, I felt like I could have run forever. But, it was getting hot and I was running out of water, so I had to come back. I'll have to take more tomorrow. How was your hike?"

"Terrific," he replied. "It felt good to get some exercise and fresh air."

Dan spotted Fran setting breakfast out in the lobby and it reminded him about the problem with their room.

"By the way," Dan said. "Philippe came by our room just after you left for your run. There's a problem with our room for the next week. Apparently, they've been waiting for contractors to do some sewer repairs under our room. They contacted him late yesterday to say they'd be here first thing Monday morning."

"What?" Chelly exclaimed. Her forehead creased, her voice lowered, and her serious side took over. "Are they going to move us to another room?"

"That's the problem," Dan answered. "All the other rooms are fully booked this week, but ..."

"That's just great!" Chelly interrupted. "Just my luck to have my vacation ruined! So what are we supposed to do now?"

"Whoaaah, slow down! Relax." Dan said calmly. "Philippe came up with solution. How would you like to spend the next few days relaxing at Philippe and Fran's estate in Palm Desert as their guests? No charge!"

The frown on Chelly's face disappeared. Her eyes opened wide. A look of surprise and happiness instantly replaced her frown. Her voice transformed into a high-pitched squeal.

"Their estate? As their guests!" she exclaimed. "The mansion with the huge pool and the incredible view? Are you kidding me, Dan?" She could barely contain her excitement. Then her serious look returned and her voice lowered.

"You did say yes, didn't you?" Chelly asked.

"Well, I didn't want to inconvenience them. And I feel a bit uneasy because we're their customers and we hardly know them, but ..."

"Are you crazy, Dan?" she exclaimed. "They offered to put us up like royalty for the rest of the week, and you're feeling uneasy because you feel some conflict? Would you stop being a psychologist for just one minute? Did you say yes?"

Chelly's face glared at Dan, waiting for his reply.

"Yes, I did," Dan admitted. "It seems like a wonderful opportunity, and I told them we were grateful for their offer."

A look of relief swept over Chelly's face. Her voice became excited and raised in pitch again. "Ohhhhh, I can't wait!" she squealed. "I'm so excited!"

"No kidding," Dan remarked. "I thought you'd be thrilled. I think I'm ready to dry off and put on some clothes for breakfast. Are you coming?"

He turned to Tim and Shelley, who had been watching quietly while he and Chelly argued. "You guys ready for breakfast too?" he asked.

"Yup," Tim replied. "You and Shelley wore me out on that trail. I'm starved!"

"Me too," Chelly said. "My stomach didn't stop growling at me while I was running. I hope there's lots of food left."

The two couples climbed out of the pool, their skin glistening and goose bumps forming on their skin. They dried themselves quickly, and then headed for their respective rooms.

AS PHILIPPE heard Chelly's excitement about the unexpected change in plans, then watched the two couples drying themselves with towels, his face broke into a broad grin.

I wouldn't want to let my little redhead down, he thought, laughing silently. *I'm sure I can make this an experience she will never forget!*

Philippe's face was beaming. He felt new energy and excitement surging through his body. Like Michelle, he too couldn't wait until Sunday evening for their experience to begin!

CHATEAU EDEN'S nude guests were congregated around the pool deck, worshipping the warm March sunshine. The sun was reaching its zenith, just after noon on this peaceful Saturday. Some were relaxing or dozing in their lounge chairs. Others were sitting along the edge of the pool, carrying on conversations and dipping their feet in the cool, refreshing water. Yet others were floating on foam pads on the pool's surface or dunking in the water to refresh themselves. Every ten to fifteen minutes, the gentle hiss of cooling mist could be heard amongst the arbors surrounding the pool deck. The atmosphere was one of serenity and relaxation.

Dan and Chelly were both reading. Dan was devouring a suspense-filled espionage novel. The fast-moving pace of the book was a welcome escape from the steady diet of tedious psychological reports and research he was accustomed to reading. Chelly was lying on her stomach on her lounge chair, lost in a romance novel. Shelley was sitting up and reading the Saturday *LA Times*, while Pam was scanning through the latest *People* magazine. Richard and Tim had a chessboard between their chairs and were engrossed in strategy.

The serenity was disturbed by the opening of Chateau Eden's large pine entrance gate. A man and women entered the courtyard, pausing briefly to study the collection of nude bodies around the pool. The man was dressed in a poorly fitting navy suit. The woman was smartly dressed in light-gray slacks and matching suit jacket, with a cream-colored camisole beneath it. Their serious, businesslike demeanor and dress gave them away immediately as police detectives.

Detective Beverly Dixon was a ten-year veteran of the Palm Springs Police Department, who had been driven to make detective, succeeding after only five years on the force. She was about five-foot-10 with long legs, a short waist, wide hips, and shoulder length blonde hair. Dixon was highly intelligent, perfectionistic, and refused to admit there was any case she couldn't solve. She was thirty-two years old, married, and had two little girls at home.

Her partner, Detective Kelvin McKnight, was forty-five years old. He made detective at the age of thirty-five, and had remained in his current position for the past ten years. He was African-American, over six feet tall, balding down the middle of his head, and beginning to show a belly rolling over his belt. Unlike Beverly, he had little motivation to rise higher than his current station in life. He was content with his quiet life in this tranquil retirement community.

Shelley lowered her newspaper to see who had entered the courtyard. She raised her eyes to survey the visitors, just as they turned and disappeared into the lobby. Shelley lost sight of them in the dark shadows of the building's interior. She reached over and tapped Tim on the shoulder.

"Did you see that?" she asked. "A couple of cops just walked into the lobby. They looked like detectives. What's that all about?"

Tim shrugged his shoulders. "Who knows?" he said. "Some heinous crime committed in this lazy retirement town, perhaps?"

Shelley laughed and went back to reading her paper. Tim reached out and made his next move in the chess game. Richard grimaced. He hadn't seen that one coming at all.

INSIDE THE lobby, Beverly Dixon gave the metal bell on the desk a single sharp ring. Philippe was in the office. He gave a furtive glance towards the back patio where Francesca was setting up her massage table and preparing for work, glad that she wasn't aware of the police presence.

Philippe emerged from the office, his face smiling at the two unidentified people standing before him.

"Hello. Detectives Dixon and McKnight, Palm Springs Police Department," Dixon said pleasantly, as the two flashed their badges at Philippe.

"Are you the manager or owner?" Dixon inquired, making it clear that she was the lead detective on this matter.

"I am," Philippe replied. "Philippe Morel at your service. How may I help you today, officers?" he answered with his French accent, still wearing the polite smile on his face.

"Do you mind if we ask you some questions?" Dixon continued.

"Of course not," Philippe answered.

"We've been asked to do some follow-up by LAPD regarding a missing-persons report they're investigating," Dixon said. "The people involved are Columbian nationals who were supposed to be vacationing in the LA or Palm Springs areas. When they didn't arrive home, as expected, their family in Bogota reported them missing."

Dixon motioned to McKnight. He produced two photographs from his pocket and handed them to her. "Have you ever seen these two people: Diego and Juanita Alvarez?"

Philippe looked carefully at the photographs before answering. "I do not believe I have, officer."

"Please take a closer look," Dixon said. "Are you sure?"

Philippe once again examined the photos. "No, detective. I'm quite sure I have never seen these people. Do you think something suspicious has happened to them? Perhaps they decided to vacation somewhere else. Perhaps somewhere in Mexico?"

"Well, we know they boarded the plane in Bogota and arrived at LAX," Dixon said. "They rented a car at the airport, then disappeared. Nobody has seen or heard from them since."

"Hmmm. That does indeed seem strange. I hope nothing terrible has happened to them," Philippe said.

"Do you ever remember being contacted by anybody named Alvarez about making reservations at your … uh, hotel, Mr. Morel?" Dixon said.

Philippe paused, giving the impression that he was doing his best to remember.

"I cannot be sure, detective. I have so many inquiries that it is difficult to remember all of them. Do you have a time period?" Philippe asked. "That would make it easier to check my records."

"Probably somewhere between late December and mid-February. Does that help?" Dixon asked.

Philippe guessed that the woman knew Alvarez had contacted him, so he knew he must be careful.

"Merci, Detective. I will have a look for you. Would either of you like a cup of coffee while you wait?" he asked.

"No, thank you," McKnight responded. "Mind if we have a look around while we wait?"

"Not at all, Detective. I should only be a moment," Philippe said. He disappeared into the office and opened up *Outlook* on the office computer, quickly finding what he was looking for. Philippe delayed for a few minutes, making it seem like he was still searching. After a few moments, called out to the detectives. "Ahhh … I do have something here."

Philippe printed out an email inquiry from Alvarez, as well as his reply, and then emerged from the office with the two pieces of paper, which he handed to Dixon.

"Detective Dixon, it seems Mr. Alvarez did contact me about a reservation for the middle of February. It was quite short-notice. Unfortunately, we were fully booked for the weekend he requested. You can see in my reply that I referred him to the other nudist resort in Palm Springs. He thanked me for the reply and I did not hear from him again."

Dixon wasn't convinced. "You say it was short-notice. If it was important for him to find something quickly, did he contact you again in any other way? Did he phone the hotel again to check for cancellations?"

"Not while I was here. You see, I am only in Palm Springs some of the time. I happened to be here when he emailed the hotel about the reservation. However, I was in Paris and London the following week. If he phoned the hotel that week, my manager, Carmen, would have been the person to take the call. She is not working this weekend, but she will be here on Monday if you have any questions for her."

Dixon continued her questioning. "They didn't happen to drive down here from LA on impulse? Maybe take a chance that you had a cancellation?" she asked.

She's like a bloodhound searching for a scent. She just won't let it go, Philippe thought.

"Not while I was here," Philippe repeated, irritation starting to creep into his voice. "This is not the type of resort where people tend to come impulsively. Most people usually think about this for a while. They usually phone or email for more information. If they are already clients, they know they have to book a couple of months in advance. Is there anything else, detective?"

"Do you have any other employees who might have responded to emails or a phone call, Mr. Morel?" Dixon asked.

"Only Carmen's daughter; she usually works for us on weekends. If she had replied to an email, it would still be in the 'Sent' mailbox. When I just checked, there was only this one reply in that mailbox. She could have answered the phone if Mr. Alvarez had called. Would you like me to talk to her when her family returns on Monday?" he inquired.

"No, thank you, Mr. Morel. You've been most helpful," Dixon said. "I think we're finished," she pronounced. "If we have any further questions, can we reach you here, Mr. Morel?"

"I'll be here next week, but my wife and I will be going back to Europe for two weeks after that."

Philippe took one of Chateau Eden's cards and flipped it over, writing his business email address and mobile number on the back.

"You can reach me any time I'm in the US on my mobile number. This is my business email account. I check it when I'm outside the US, so you can always email me if you have a question."

"You've got a business email account too?" Dixon asked. "Is there any chance Mr. Alvarez would have contacted you through that account Mr. Morel?"

"Not unless I gave him that address. I use the other account only for my other business. I am an agent and art dealer. This hotel is merely a hobby for me. I only give my business email to business clients and people I know well. I do not use it for hotel business," Philippe concluded. He handed the business card to Dixon.

"Thank you, Mr. Morel" Dixon said. A smile appeared on her face and her businesslike demeanor vanished. "I think that's all for now. If we need you, we'll be in touch."

"You're more than welcome, detectives. I'm always happy to help your department," Philippe added.

"C'mon Kelvin. Looks like we have bad news for LAPD," Dixon said.

The two detectives exited the lobby onto the pool deck. They stepped into the bright sunlight, and then stood for a moment while their eyes adjusted to the bright light, surveying at the crowd of nude bodies sprawled in the sun or in the pool. Dixon looked at McKnight and shook her head. "I don't get it, Kelvin. What's the appeal to walking around naked in front of other people? Do you get it?"

"Nope. I'm with you," McKnight said.

They turned and walked through Chateau Eden's main gate, then to their unmarked car.

"So what do think?" McKnight asked.

"I don't know," Dixon answered. "There's something about that guy that isn't sitting right with me, but I just don't know what it is. Do you know what I mean?"

"Yeah, I feel it too. He wasn't nervous at all. Almost everybody's nervous when we interview them. He was too calm and cool," McKnight added.

"You're right," Dixon said. "I think that's part of it. He was pretty helpful too. Almost too helpful, don't you think?"

"Yup. I think we need to keep an eye on Monsieur Morel," McKnight said.

"I agree," Dixon replied. "Trouble is, his email records from his Internet provider match what he gave us. He wasn't lying about the phone calls, cuz we've gone over both the hotel's phone records and his cellular records. I didn't see any security cameras, inside or out, so we've got nothing there. I get the feeling we're missing something, but I just can't think of what it could be!"

The car was sweltering. Dixon started the engine to get the AC going.

"Let's keep digging, Kelvin," she continued. "I want you to start turning over stones to find out anything you can about Mr. Morel. Maybe that'll kick start our brains and we'll see something we missed. Meanwhile, I'll get back to LAPD and tell them it's a dead end here for now."

"Sounds like a plan," McKnight replied. "I'll see what I can dig up."

The black car backed out of Chateau Eden's parking lot, and then disappeared at the end of the street as it turned onto Palm Canyon Drive.

SHELLEY LOWERED her newspaper as the two detectives emerged from the lobby. She watched as they surveyed the guests, then shook their heads and departed through the gate. She went back to reading the paper. A few minutes later, a small article caught her attention.

"Hey you guys, did anybody else hear about the couple from Columbia that disappeared somewhere around LA? Apparently, they landed at LAX, rented a car, and then just disappeared into thin air."

She thought silently to herself for a moment, and then wondered out loud to her companions.

"I wonder if those two cops had anything to do with the missing couple? Maybe they're checking all the hotels in the area," she said.

"Well, they have their work cut out for them," Pam suggested. "There's a hell of a lot of hotels in the greater LA area to check out. Good luck if that's what they're doing."

Pam's eyes returned to her *People* magazine and Shelley continued reading her newspaper. Dan was engrossed in his suspense novel. Chelly's eyes were closed as she napped in the warm sun.

"Checkmate," Tim announced.

"Dammit, Jennings," Richard cursed. "One'a these days ah'm gonna figure this game out. Wanna go again?"

Tim and Richard reset their respective chess pieces on the board and were soon lost in strategy. The atmosphere of serenity and relaxation resumed behind the sheltering walls of Chateau Eden, the brief intrusion of the two detectives much like the blip of a skipped heartbeat, barely noticed by the congregation of sun worshippers.

CHAPTER 9

FRAN'S MIND was preoccupied and distant as she adjusted the sheets on the massage table. She was unaware that Chelly had just appeared from between the bungalows.

"Oh!" Fran gasped, her body recoiling with fear as she found Chelly suddenly standing just a few feet away.

"I'm so sorry. I startled you!" Chelly apologized.

"It is not your fault," Fran said, trying to slow her heart and catch her breath. "My head was someplace else. So good to see you again. Did you and Dan have a nice evening last night?"

"We did," Chelly confirmed. "The Mexican food was great, then we came back and soaked in the spa 'til it turned off at eleven. It was a lot of fun. We had a little too much wine, but what the heck, we're on vacation, right?"

"Of course. What else are vacations for," Fran replied.

Unlike yesterday, Chelly was totally naked, except for the flip-flops on her feet and the towel over her shoulder. She reached up to remove the elastic from her ponytail, releasing her ginger hair to hang down to her shoulders. She felt a light, warm breeze caressing the nerve endings in her skin. Fran was once again working topless in the afternoon heat.

"Do you want me on my stomach again?" Chelly asked, as she moved towards the massage table.

"Yes, thank you," Fran answered. "What will it be today? Any areas you would like me to focus on, or would you just like another relaxation massage?"

"Well, I went for a long run this morning. I'd really like you to spend most of the time on my legs and butt. I have to tell you, the work you did there yesterday was the best massage I've ever had. I'm so glad I went totally nude so you didn't have to work around my bikini. I could really feel how deep you were able to work on my gluts. It felt great!"

"I am glad it helped," Fran said.

Chelly pulled back the sheet and climbed onto the table. Fran covered her legs and buttocks, warmed some oil between her hands, and then began working on Chelly's back.

"Oh, that feels good," Chelly sighed. "Before I forget. Thank you so much for offering to put us up in your home while they're repairing our bungalow. That's so generous of you and Philippe to inconvenience yourselves for us!"

There was a long delay before Fran answered.

"It is nothing, really," she replied. "We are delighted to have you. We hope you enjoy your stay."

Fran was having difficulty keeping her mind focused on Chelly's massage. The walls in her mind were being assaulted by images and thoughts of the young Columbian couple. Even worse than the images and the thoughts, there was fear. She was tense all over her body. Her stomach was feeling ill. Her hands went on autopilot, relying on her procedural memory to guide her through the massage. The screams and images of the young Columbian couple were blurring together with disturbing images of Dan and Chelly. She felt a chill shoot through her body as a flood of images and emotions continued to seep over, under, and around the walls in her mind.

Fran became vaguely aware of Chelly's voice, seemingly far away, working its way back into her consciousness.

"I hope we'll have time to get to know you and Philippe better," Chelly was saying. "He's so charming. You both live such interesting lives. It will be nice to spend more time with you both!" Chelly's voice was muffled as she spoke downwards through the hole in the middle of the headrest.

"Are you feeling okay today, Fran?" Chelly asked, aware that Fran seemed somewhat distant. "You seem quiet today. Is anything wrong?"

"Nothing to worry about," Fran replied. "My stomach is a little unsettled. I will be fine, but thank you for asking."

Fran had finished working Chelly's upper legs and was now working on her buttocks and hips.

"I noticed you reading a book earlier today," Fran said, trying to keep the conversation going to keep her mind present. "Do you mind me asking what you are reading?"

"Oh, it's just a Nora Roberts romance," Chelly answered. "It's light reading, but I just love them. I'm a sucker for a good love story. How about you, Fran? What do you like to read?"

"I like to read biographies and history," Fran said. "The lives of famous people are so interesting."

She lowered her voice and leaned closer to Chelly as she continued massaging. "But I have what you Americans call a *guilty pleasure*," she admitted. "Sometimes I like to read romance novels too. Philippe thinks it is ridiculous. He thinks it is beneath a lady of my class to read such trash. So I read them sometimes when he is not around. I love happy endings. They make me cry happy tears!"

The two women laughed together.

"That's so cute," Chelly said. "I cry at the endings too. I'm surprised Philippe has such a strong opinion, though. He's such a gentleman and seems so romantic. He'd make the perfect character in a romance novel. I can see it now. Philippe sweeping a common American girl like me away with his romantic French accent and charm. What do you think?"

Fran started feeling panicky. She had to be careful what she said in return. She hated lying and wanted to tell Chelly how wrong she was about Philippe. But, if she ruined Philippe's plan, he would never forgive her. She forced a laugh, trying to push back her fear.

"Well, for me the perfect character would be a tall, intelligent American man, sweeping a poor Italian girl off her feet, then taking her back to America to be happy forever!"

The two women laughed at their different fantasies.

"That's hilarious," Chelly said. "Our husbands will have a good laugh when we tell them that one!"

At the mention of the two couples being together, Fran's mind started racing, uncontrolled, into the future. First, she imagined Philippe charming his guests and giving them a false sense of security. Then she saw much more disturbing images that brought back the wave of fear that grew steadily in the pit of her stomach.

Fran heard her own voice, the independent, businesslike part of herself, calling to her from a distance.

Come back, Fran! She pleaded. *Stay here. Feel your hands. Feel Chelly. Do your work. Breathe slowly. Stay calm.*

She gradually regained control of her mind and managed to orient herself to the present moment. The businesslike part of her searched desperately for another topic of conversation.

"You said yesterday that you were in a bad relationship before you met Dan. Do you mind me asking you about it?"

"Not really," Chelly said. "It's been a long time now and I've dealt with it. He seemed like a nice guy when I first met him. He was in medical school. I was going to be a nurse. He came from a family with lots of money, so he got everything he wanted."

Chelly winced as Fran's fingers found a tender spot.

"Oh, keep pushing down deep in my butt with your thumb," Chelly said. "That hurts so good!" She continued the story of her relationship with Derek.

"We had lots of fun for a while. He took me to Europe with him one summer. It started off being exciting, but I started seeing a dark side to him. He started taking control of deciding where we were going to go. Whenever I tried to give my opinion, he'd get angry. Then he began putting me down and calling me stupid. I couldn't figure out what I was doing to cause him to be that way, so I just worked harder to try and please him."

Fran moved the massage from Chelly's butt and hips, down to her legs.

"Oh, that feels amazing, Fran. Especially my knees. I didn't realize they were so tender."

"So you started blaming yourself for not making him happy?" Fran asked.

"Yes, How did you know?" Chelly asked. "I started trying to find new ways to please him. We weren't having as much sex as when we first met, so I started suggesting different things to get him more turned on. It was actually my suggestion to take him to the nude spa in Germany, but I was pretty naive. I didn't realize there was nothing erotic about going there. It was mostly older people sitting around naked and soaking in the hot springs."

"Okay, Chelly. Roll over. Time for the front of your legs," Fran said. She lifted the sheet while Chelly turned over onto her back. Once she was settled, Fran's fingers started kneading Chelly's muscular thighs.

"Go on. What happened next?" Fran asked.

"When we got back from Europe I started dressing up in sexy lingerie and kinkier outfits to get him more excited. Then I suggested some harmless bondage. It started to work. He was paying more attention to me and seemed to be more turned on. But then he started getting rough. I pretended to like it at first, but he started getting rougher and hurting me more. When I asked him to stop, that seemed to turn him on even more. It seemed to make him feel more in control. He started demanding sex more and more during the day when we were together. Then one day I found the drugs in his coat pocket. I realized why his personality had changed."

Chelly's eyes were turning red, and tears started running from the corners of her eyes. Fran's massage strokes slowed. She noticed Chelly growing more distant, realizing the other woman's mind was slipping into a dark abyss. She knew the feeling well and knew what to do.

"Chelly," she called. "Wake up! Come back to me." Fran put both hands on Chelly's shoulders and jiggled her body back and forth gently.

Chelly opened her eyes and looked up at Fran.

"I'm sorry. I must have been someplace else," she said. She knew she had to finish the story quickly, before she lost control.

"I knew I had to leave Derek, but it took me a long time to get enough courage to actually do it. Could I have a drink of water, Fran? I'm thirsty."

Fran handed Chelly a bottle of water, placing her hand gently on the other woman's shoulder as she helped her sit up and drank. As Chelly lowered the bottle from her lips, Fran looked into her eyes, sending her a silent message.

"Thanks for listening," Chelly whispered to Fran. "You understand, don't you?"

"Lay back down," Fran whispered, purposely avoiding the question. "Close your eyes. Breathe slowly. I will do your face and head to finish things off today. Don't talk. Concentrate on feeling my fingers on your skin and focus on how they feel. Just relax."

Fran's head was starting to spin from her own torrent of emotions that were triggered by Chelly's story: empathy, fear, loneliness, and helplessness. Her hands were back on autopilot again, her brain trying to reinforce the walls that were being tested by the surging emotions. The businesslike, professional side of Fran concentrated on feeling Chelly's skin beneath her fingers. She smelled the fragrance of the orange blossoms and tried to connect with the gentle, warm breeze blowing across her skin at that moment. She managed to bring her focus back on Chelly's massage, and on helping Chelly keep her mind in the present. She knew too well what had just been happening in both of their minds.

"Keep taking nice slow breaths, Chelly. Feel my fingers on your face. Smell the fragrance of the orange blossoms all around you. Feel the table beneath you. As I lift my fingers from your face, keep taking those slow breaths. Keep looking at my face. There you go. You are safe here. You know that?"

Chelly nodded back at Fran. "Thank you."

She paused briefly then repeated her previous question to Fran. "You've been hurt before too, haven't you?"

This time Fran nodded back in agreement. There was a huge lump in her throat that wouldn't allow her to speak. Her emotions were in danger of overpowering her. She struggled to keep herself present long enough to finish with Chelly.

"Just take your time, Chelly. There is no hurry. Get up when you are ready," she said, desperately trying not to let her emotions show.

"Thanks again, Fran. I really mean it. I guess we'll see you sometime tomorrow afternoon when we go to your place."

"We will see you then," Fran answered. "Do you think you could you tell Dan to give me ten or fifteen minutes so I can have short rest?"

"Sure, no problem," Chelly answered. She lay on her back, gradually letting her mind come back fully into the present.

Fran gave Chelly one last pat on her shoulder, and then walked quickly towards the rear office door. Thankfully, Philippe was not in the office when she entered. Fran closed the door behind her. She peered out of the window, watching Chelly get up from the table, slip her feet into her flip flops, and put her hair back up into a pony tail. She picked up her towel, and slowly left the patio. Fran moved away from the window. She let the weight of her entire body slump back against the door, and then closed her eyes. She let out an enormous, long breath.

My God, what have I done! What am I getting myself into?

FRAN'S MASSAGE table was covered neatly with fresh sheets as Dan arrived at the back patio. Still topless, Fran took a deep breath and opened the office door, stepping onto the patio to greet him.

"Hi, Fran. Did you have a long enough rest?" Dan asked.

"Yes, thank you," she replied. "Are you enjoying this lovely afternoon with the other guests?"

"Definitely," Dan answered. "I just want to thank you and Philippe again for offering to let us stay with you this week. I'm looking forward to it!"

"It is our pleasure," Fran said. "So what will it be today?"

"My legs aren't feeling too bad. I think I'd just like to have another relaxation massage today. Is that okay?"

"Of course," she said. Fran pulled back the top sheet as Dan draped his towel over a chair, then he slid his naked body face down onto the massage table.

Once again, Fran warmed some massage oil between her hands, then she set to work kneading Dan's back, gradually increasing the intensity of her stokes so he could adjust to the pressure.

Fran was distant. She couldn't stop her mind from racing ahead to the following evening, when Dan and Chelly would be joining them. Her hands slipped back into autopilot, and her distant mind had trouble engaging in conversation. Fortunately, Dan let himself go with the relaxing touch of her massage strokes, and he was having trouble staying awake. Fran lost track of time as her hands went through the motions. Before she knew it, she had finished massaging the backside of Dan's torso and legs.

She tapped Dan's shoulder gently. "Okay Dan, time to roll over onto your back."

As he propped his upper body up with his arms, Fran lifted the sheet to allow Dan to roll over on his back. She then lowered the sheet to cover his torso and genitals while she resumed massaging his legs and feet. Dan surrendered to the sensuous pleasures of

Fran's expert hands, continuing to cross in and out of consciousness as she worked.

As her hands continued to move automatically down one leg and foot, then over to Dan's other leg, Fran continued to be plagued by the flood of images, thoughts, and emotions of Philippe, the Columbian couple, and also of Dan and Chelly. She felt her intense fear gripping her entire body.

Fran was still in a state of disbelief over the recent escalation in Philippe's anger and violence. Although he had become increasingly manipulative and emotionally controlling over time, he had never become physically violent until Alvarez provoked him. He had never been physically violent towards Fran until today. He had always protected her and kept her safe - until now. In addition to panic, she felt sadness at the loss of her sense of safety and security. She felt like she had lost the Philippe she had always known. She was feeling increasingly lost and afraid.

More importantly, Fran was starting to feel an emotion she had always been able to keep safely behind her walls. She was beginning to feel anger towards Philippe. The same anger she had felt towards her brother-in-law and the other men who had abused her as a teen.

Fran finished massaging Dan's legs. She expertly unfolded the bottom half of the sheet to cover his legs. Then she pulled down the top half of the sheet to expose Dan's torso, while covering his legs and genitals. She did all of this without being aware that she was doing any of it. Her eyes were focused on Dan's face as she continued to massage, yet she continued to struggle with her fear, sadness, anger, and guilt. Dan's eyes were closed. His lower jaw hung loosely, his lips slightly apart, with the hint of a contented smile on his face as he soaked up the relaxing sensations from the nerve endings in his tissues.

At that moment, Dan crossed back over the boundary between sleep and consciousness and opened his eyes. His eyes locked onto the distant gaze in Fran's eyes. Their eyes remained locked, and

Dan developed an intense empathic connection with Fran's emotions. The sudden eye contact jolted Fran abruptly back into reality.

As Dan gazed deep into her eyes, she saw him recognize and understand the fear, loneliness, and sadness that had managed to emerge from behind the walls in her mind. She felt completely vulnerable and emotionally naked. She felt herself starting to blush with embarrassment, not from her almost naked physical appearance, but from knowing that Dan was seeing right through her and into her soul.

Fran's fear intensified. She never let anybody see what she was feeling inside, especially men. At the same time, she felt a conflicting emotion; a deep and primal longing to be understood, loved, and accepted by another person. While she feared Dan's understanding of her, it was also the one thing she had always craved, without knowing it.

The connection between Dan and Fran deepened as their eyes remained locked. Time felt like it was standing still for both of them. Fran finally broke the silence.

"What do you see in my eyes?" she asked quietly. Strangely, she realized that her emotions were subsiding. The part of her that had longed for intimacy was tentatively emerging from behind her walls, managing to push her fear aside for the moment.

"I see sadness and loneliness," he answered. "You must be good at hiding that, because I haven't noticed it before. Up until now, you've seemed confident and happy to me. Do you have anybody else in your life besides Philippe? Any family, friends, or activities in the community?"

Fran didn't answer. Instead, she turned her head away, giving away her answer with her body language. She was feeling increasingly uncomfortable again as Dan started probing her life. He continued exploring what he had seen in her eyes. More than the sadness and loneliness he saw in Fran, he was most worried about the fear.

"You're afraid of something," he continued. "Some terrible things have happened to you in the past, haven't they."

As soon as Dan uttered the statement, Fran felt herself becoming more restless and agitated. She avoided making any further eye contact with him. Now that she was no longer massaging Dan, her hands were fidgety and she didn't seem to know what to do with them. She felt the muscle in her face and jaw tensing.

Realizing he had struck a nerve with his question, Dan sat up on the massage table, swinging his legs over the edge of the table. The top sheet slid off him and onto the patio, leaving him completely naked.

"What is it, Fran? What's happened to you? Has somebody abused you? Tell me," he pleaded in a low whisper.

Fran felt even more agitated and distant. Her eyes were red, but no tears were forming. Her mind was drifting back into the past again. He instinctively reached out and touched her bare shoulders, shaking her gently, hoping to bring her attention back into the present.

As she felt Dan's touch and the gentle shaking of her shoulders, her mind managed to jump back to reality. Her eyes once again met Dan's worried gaze.

Fran felt his empathy, and felt the deepening emotional connection between them. As their connection quickly intensified, she became aware that Dan's penis was restless and growing slowly. He blushed and averted his eyes away from hers. He moved his hands to shield the rising organ from Fran, but her eyes had already seen the source of his embarrassment.

"I'm sorry," he said. "This shouldn't be happening."

"Do not be embarrassed," she replied. She reached down and picked up the sheet from the patio, handing it to Dan so he could cover himself.

"You're vulnerable right now," he said sheepishly. "It's not right in my profession to take advantage of your vulnerability. I'm supposed to feel empathy, not get turned on sexually. I'm sorry. It won't happen again."

"Is it wrong if you do not follow through, and nothing comes of it?" she asked in return.

"Well … no … I don't know," Dan answered. There was a long pause while he considered Fran's question. "We're supposed to be aware of what we're feeling, so we don't act on it."

"So you did not act on it. And I am not your client anyway, am I? So you did nothing wrong. Correct?" Fran asked.

"I suppose you're right," Dan admitted. "But it's still embarrassing. Anyplace else but here, I'd be able to cover it up with clothing."

Fran realized they were both shaken by the sudden, intense emotional connection between them, and by Dan's sexual arousal. An awkward silence invaded the patio and time felt like it was standing still again. Fran glanced over her shoulder at the small clock she had placed on the patio table beside her massage table. Dan followed her glance and realized that his hour had almost run out. He ended the uncomfortable silence by confirming what the clock was telling them.

"It looks like I've almost used up my hour, Fran. It was amazingly relaxing again, as usual. I'm sorry I didn't let you finish things up properly," he apologized.

"Just one more thing," Dan added. She felt him make eye contact with her once again as he spoke. "The fear I saw in your eyes. It's not all from the past, is it? It's also here in the present. What's making you so afraid right now, Fran?" he asked.

She felt his eyes pleading with her to share her burden with him. As soon as the words were out of his mouth, she knew she couldn't hide her fear from him. He'd seen it in her eyes, and he seen her mind struggling to put her defensive walls back into place, and to protect herself from the fear. She quickly averted her eyes from Dan to cut off the empathic connection. It was becoming too much for her.

Fran's mind was struggling to keep in touch with the present, looking around her desperately for something to say or do that would help. She saw Dan's towel draped over the back of the patio chair beside her.

"Here, Dr. Whitney," she said curtly, as she placed the towel in his lap. "Make sure you wash the massage oil from your body before you go into the pool or spa."

Dan was at a loss for what to say next.

"Oh, … for sure," he replied nervously. "I guess we'll see you and Philippe tomorrow evening sometime. You know. To check out of the Chateau and then follow you over to the estate."

"Yes. Tomorrow evening. We will see you both then," Fran replied, absent-mindedly.

Not knowing what else to say, Dan turned his back and walked away. Fran watched, lost in thought, as he disappeared between the bungalows on his way back to his room.

DAN DIDN'T even notice Chelly and the others on the pool deck as he entered their room and went straight to the bathroom to run water for a shower. He was deeply disturbed by the intensity of the connection and the arousal he'd just experienced. Different parts of his brain started arguing back and forth as he stepped into the shower.

What just got into you, Dan? You came here with Chelly to work on getting closer with her, not to start coming-on to other women!

The parts of Dan that were loyal and logical, and the responsible side of him that was so afraid of doing anything bad, were all chanting their disapproval of what had just occurred. He didn't want to upset Chelly, Fran, or Philippe by appearing to be making a move on Fran.

Yet, deep down inside, part of Dan still felt the hurt and rejection from Brenda in Vancouver many years ago, and it still longed for a deeper, intimate, romantic connection. That part of him still felt that same rejection and hurt on the occasions when he felt Chelly pushing him away. But today, it was that same rejected part of him that felt exhilarated and aroused by the intensity of the sudden connection with Fran.

The conflicting parts of Dan's brain didn't want to acknowledge each other.

Dan's responsible and loyal sides managed to win the struggle for now, bringing his focus back to the present: to enjoying his vacation with Chelly, and to enjoying their time with their new friends at the Chateau this weekend.

AS DAN disappeared around the corner of the bungalow, Francesca Capellini struggled to make sense of the intense connection she had just made with Dan. It wasn't like her to let her walls down and to let anybody see her emotions. It was especially unlike her to allow herself to feel vulnerable again to a man. She was angry with herself for letting her guard down.

Yet, at the same time, a dormant, inquisitive part of her was emerging. It was strangely curious about the man who had just made such a sudden impression on her life. That inquisitive side of her could see there was something different about Dan. Unlike most of the men she had known, he seemed to be gentle, empathic, and caring. He cared more about what he had seen in her eyes, than about making sexual advances, unlike all the other men she had ever known.

Her distant, untrusting, businesslike part of her identity was shouting at her not to trust Dan. But deep inside, a part of her that secretly longed to be loved and understood, had just been roused after a lifetime of hiding behind walls in the depths of her mind. The inquisitive side of Fran wondered what it would be like to feel that kind of love and understanding more often.

PHILIPPE HAD been watching Francesca's encounter with Dan from the office window with intense interest.

Rather than feeling jealous or insecure at the connection he had just witnessed, he once again started feeling the surge of energy and strength growing inside him as he realized how well this would fit into his plan. His mind became obsessed with manipulating this piece of good fortune into the final operational details of his new project. Time was short. He hadn't planned on involving the Whitney couple. But they were perfect, and he couldn't waste the opportunity. This time, fate appeared to be breathing life into his most perfect project yet, seemingly without Philippe having to do any of the work. To Philippe, it felt almost too good to be true.

CHAPTER 10

CHELLY AND DAN had just finished dressing. Dan noticed that Pam and Richard were already outside on the pool deck, talking loudly.

"Are we ready to go?" he asked.

"I think so," Chelly answered. "You go ahead and join them. I'm just trying to decide which shoes to wear to go dancing."

Dan left Chelly in the room while he went out to greet Pam and Richard.

"Hi guys," he said. "Everybody in the mood for dinner and dancing?"

Dan felt Pam's eyes scanning him from head to toe, as Chelly emerged from the room. Pam looked at Chelly, and then back at what Dan was wearing.

"Chelly, did you see what your husband is wearing for a night out on the town? He looks like he's dressed to visit his parents instead of going clubbing. Tell me you didn't approve of this!"

Chelly shook her head sadly.

"No, I'm afraid that's Dan's idea of dressing up. I keep trying to tell him he looks like an old college professor in his Van Heusen chinos and patterned shirts, but that's his idea of fashion!" Chelly said.

Pam frowned, took one more disgusted look at Dan, and then turned to Chelly. "C'mon girl, we've got to do something about this. Back into your room you two! Let's see if we can fix this up while we're waiting for Tim and Shelley! Richard, you wait here and tell them we'll just be a couple of minutes!"

Pam grabbed Dan by the hand as though he was a small schoolboy and dragged him back towards their room. Chelly couldn't stop herself from laughing as she trailed behind.

Back inside the room, Pam inspected the room for Dan's luggage. "Okay, Chelly. Where's his suitcase so I can see what we have to work with? Help me see what he's got in here!"

Chelly pointed it out, and the two women started tossing clothing back and forth, with Pam giving the occasional roll of the eyes and shake of her head.

"My God," she exclaimed. "You couldn't dress more conservatively if you tried, Dan! Come on! You're a sexy looking guy, so I want you looking hot tonight! Damn, do we ever need to take you clothes shopping!"

She spotted a white dress-shirt, but no pants that were any dressier than the chinos Dan was wearing. Then a new pair of new slim-fitting blue jeans caught her eye. "That's got some potential, Chelly. Does he have any shoes besides those lace-up Bass specials he's wearing?"

"He's got a pair of good Italian leather loafers over here that might look with the jeans," Chelly answered.

"That'll have to do," Pam said. "Okay, Dan. Strip down and put on the jeans and this white shirt."

Dan stripped down to his boxer shorts and was putting one leg into the jeans when Pam frowned and rolled her eyes.

"For God's sake, Dan, take off those boxers. You can't go stuffing them into those tight jeans. Hurry up! We've already seen each other naked, so no need to be shy."

The two women laughed as Dan sheepishly followed instructions, stepping out of his boxer shorts.

"Can you toss me a pair of briefs, Chelly?" Dan asked.

"Briefs!" Pam exclaimed in horror. "You're going commando tonight, my friend. We wanna see that tight little butt and sexy package in these skinny jeans, right Chelly?"

The two women smiled and joined each other in crude laughter. Dan did as he was told and pulled the jeans over his bare skin. He felt rough denim rubbing against the sensitive skin of his genitals. To his surprise, he didn't find the sensation unpleasant.

After climbing into the jeans, Dan donned the white shirt and began buttoning up the front of the shirt and the sleeves.

"Wait a minute," Pam interrupted, before Dan could finish. "Leave the sleeves and don't you dare button that thing up to the collar!" She unfastened two buttons, making sure that Dan was showing some chest hair. Then she partially rolled up the sleeves to give the shirt a more casual look. She continued to rifle through Dan's suitcase, finally finding a good black leather belt.

"Here, this will add a touch of class to the jeans. Okay, now get your shoes on!"

Dan waited as Pam stood back and surveyed him from a distance, a look of satisfaction on her face. "There! Now you look hot! What do you say, Chelly? Do you think we can take him out in public now?"

Chelly looked at Dan, giving him her best *I told you so* look. "Yeah, I think it's safe! Oh, I see Shelley and Tim out there. Let's go!"

The trio exited the room and greeted Shelley, Tim, and Richard outside the lobby. Dan looked sheepishly at Richard and Tim, who grinned back at him, chuckling at his new fashion makeover.

"Not dressing-up tonight?" Pam asked as she looked at Tim and Shelley.

"No, sorry guys," Shelley answered. "I'm still tired, so we decided to pass on going out to the club. We're just going to come back to the Chateau after dinner, have a quick soak in the hot tub, then get to bed early. You four can still go to the club if you want. Don't let us hold you back."

"Ah, that's too bad," Chelly said. "We'll miss you guys!"

"We'll still have lots of time together before we head back home tomorrow," Shelley said. "We'll drive all of you to the restaurant in our SUV if you like. We can fit all six of us. You guys okay with taking a cab to the club?"

"Yup. That's probably a good idea, ain't it y'all?" Richard answered. "That way we can let loose and not worry about the cops, eh Dan?"

"Sounds good to me. Is everybody still okay with Italian tonight?" Dan said.

The rest of the group chattered in agreement as they filed through Chateau Eden's main gate, making their way to Tim and Shelley's vehicle for the short ride to the restaurant.

TWO HOURS later, the three couples emerged from the Italian Restaurant amidst boisterous laughter, much of it induced by liberal quantities of wine. The cab that Pam had ordered was waiting outside. First Dan and Chelly, then Pam and Richard, all gave Tim and Shelley a hug as they parted for the evening.

"Have fun you guys," Shelley said. "See you all tomorrow morning if you don't drink too much. Are you coming hiking with us again tomorrow, Dan? You're welcome too, Chelly, if you don't go running!"

"Thanks for the invite," Chelly answered. "I think I'm going to run a bit longer tomorrow. But Dan can join you if he likes."

"How about you, Richard? Are you two going to come with us?" Tim asked.

"Nah," Richard answered. "I think we're goin' ta be lazy. Maybe share a little skin, eh darlin'?" he said, winking at Pam.

Pam exaggerated rolling her eyes at Richard. "Thank God you're getting on a plane on Monday! Then I can finally get some sleep! Don't you ever get enough?"

Richard, Pam, Dan, and Chelly laughed freely at Pam's mock exasperation with Richard's need for sexual release after spending weeks in Iraq. Shelley and Tim waved, and then climbed into their

SUV. Richard held the back door of the cab open for Pam, Chelly, and Dan, and then slid into the front seat beside the driver.

"Zenobia's Night Club," Richard said to the driver, who nodded in acknowledgment as the vehicle pulled away from the restaurant.

The two couples joked and laughed all the way to the club. Dan noticed that Pam seemed to enjoy being packed tightly into the back seat, pressed closely against Dan on one side. With each joke and subsequent wave of laughter, she leaned more closely against him, pressing her breast closely against his chest. Her left hand frequently dropped and brushed against the inside of his right thigh. Dan tried to ignore it the first few times it occurred, attributing her touches to their close proximity. But it was soon apparent to him that her touches weren't accidental. At one point, she smiled and a winked at him as her hand fell close to his crotch.

As far as Dan could tell, Chelly was enjoying the social outing and laughter. She seemed oblivious to what Pam's left hand was doing. Richard spent the entire trip leaning over the back seat, engaging Chelly in conversation and charming her with his humor and his Texas drawl.

The couples entered the central lobby of Zenobia's just after eight p.m. The music was already pounding two different rhythms on either side of them.

"The club on the right plays mostly Hip Hop and Electronic for the younger crowd," Pam said. "This one on the left plays Rock and Alternative. Are you guys alright with that? We'll stay for about an hour and a half, so we have time to go back and spend some quality time in the spa before it shuts down."

Dan and Chelly nodded their agreement. Richard led the way into the club. It was early, and Dan noticed there were only about fifteen couples so far. They had no problem finding a booth. A waitress quickly took their drink orders, and then Richard grabbed Pam's hand, pulling her onto the dance floor.

"Shall we join them?" Dan shouted across the table.

Chelly jumped to her feet and started wiggling to the beat. She and Dan found their way onto the dance floor to where Pam and Richard were already gyrating in time to the pounding rock rhythm. Dan noticed that his own white shirt glowed brightly under the club's black lights.

Chelly's looking hot tonight, Dan said to himself, as his eyes roamed approvingly over every curve of his wife's body. She was wearing a short, tightly fitting white skirt that showed off her waist, muscular thighs, and her firm butt. A backless halter-top, tied around her neck and cut low in the front, emphasized her ample bust. A large silver and emerald-colored necklace drew people's eyes down towards her cleavage. The halter-top was also mostly white, with a light green and pastel floral pattern that contrasted against the brilliant white background under the black lights. She let her red hair out of the ponytail tonight, letting it hang down to touch her shoulders. Dan gazed lovingly at her, turned on by the sight of her swaying hips and the movement of her breasts as she danced.

Dan turned his attention to the Holloways. Richard was dressed in a perfectly fitted pair of grey slacks with white pin stripes that glowed under the black light. Like the slacks, his light-yellow shirt also fit perfectly. A number of white buttons, left open and glowing under the black lights, created a v-shaped glow that drew attention to his muscular black chest. Dan watched with fascination as Richard gyrated his hips to the music. His muscular body, expensive clothing, and elaborate dance moves drew attention from both men and women alike on the dance floor.

Dan's gaze drifted from Richard to Pam. Not to be outdone by her husband, Pam was decked-out in stylish white capris that also glowed and hugged her body tightly, showing little or no evidence of panty lines except for a hint of a thong at the top of her buttocks. Like Chelly, she wore a halter-top tied around the back of her neck. It was pure white and adorned with rhinestones, so that it glowed, but also sparkled under the multi-colored lights in the club. From the swaying of her large breasts as she danced, and the two distinct bumps that pushed thru the halter, it was clear to Dan that Pam wasn't wearing a bra. One other thing was also clear. She was totally aware that she looked hot.

As the two couples danced close together on the dance floor, Pam deliberately bumped her hips and butt into both Richard and Dan at every opportunity, smiling seductively at Dan whenever she connected with him.

After a few dances, both couples retreated to the washrooms, and then returned to their table to catch their breath and converse over drinks.

Richard smiled at Dan, and then looked admiringly at Pam and Chelly.

"So whatta ya think, Dan?" he began. "Are these two not the hottest looking gals in the club tonight? We gotta be the luckiest guys here, eh?"

As he finished complementing her, Richard winked and smiled lasciviously across the table at Chelly.

Her face flushed in embarrassment.

"Yeah, I have to agree with you there, Richard!" Dan agreed.

Pam reached across the table and rested her hand on Dan's to get his attention.

"Look around the dance floor, Dan. What do you think looks sexier? All these half-dressed people on the dance floor, swinging their hips and doing pelvic-thrusts, or a bunch of nudists lying in the sun reading? Women in string-bikinis versus nudist women?"

"No contest," Dan replied. "The dancers and the bikinis. The thrill is all in the anticipation of what we want to see, but can't. That's what turns people on. Once you see the forbidden fruit under the string bikini, it loses its attraction over time, wouldn't you say?"

"Absolutely!" Pam agreed. "The excitement is all in unwrapping the package, if you'll pardon the pun!"

They all burst into laughter at Pam's innuendo. She followed up her joke by reaching across the table again and grabbing Dan's hand.

"Hey, Chelly! Mind if I steal your man for a few dances?" Pam shouted.

"Go ahead!" Chelly shouted over the music. "Do you mind if I borrow yours?"

"Not at all," Pam shouted, giving Chelly a suggestive wink. "Take him out for a test drive. But, like I told you last night, dancing's just a sample of what those hips can do, girl!"

"C'mon Richard," Chelly shouted. "Let's see if those hips live up to the hype!" She grabbed his hand and started moving her hips to the music, enticing him to follow her out onto the dance floor.

Once Pam reached the dance floor with Dan, she broke into a flurry of activity, her hips undulating and her breasts swaying up and down, then back and forth, in front of Dan's eyes. As she began heating up, he noticed beads of perspiration running down the inside of her cleavage.

Dan silently agreed that Pam looked extremely sexy on the dance floor, clothed in her halter-top and tight capris. With her breasts swaying and bobbing as she danced, he found her even more appealing now than when she was relaxing, completely nude, at Chateau Eden.

"Katrina and the Waves!" Pam shouted. "I haven't heard *The Game of Love* for years. I use to love this song!" She moved her gyrating body even closer to Dan's.

Richard and Chelly gradually danced their way over so they were right beside Pam and Dan. The alcohol was clearly loosening up the inhibitions of all four dancers. Even Dan, who was normally stiff as a board when he danced, was limbering up in response to the intensely sensual aura being exuded by Pam's dancing.

Richard moved closer to Dan and shouted to him. "Hey, Dan! Ya dance perty good fer a white guy!"

"I'll take that as a compliment from you!" Dan shouted and laughed, as the couples continued to dance with each other's partners.

The movement of Richard's pelvis was becoming even more provocative than Pam's swaying breasts. Dan noticed that Chelly was responding with increased movement of her hips, pelvis, and breasts. She turned her back to Richard, who moved close to her butt and began rotating his hips suggestively.

"Woooh, you two!" Pam shouted. "Get it on, Chelly and Richard!"

Pam followed suit. She turned around and backed into Dan. She pulled his arms up around her stomach and rotated her butt against his groin. She looked back over her shoulder, smiling seductively as she pressed her body closer to his.

Dan was starting to feel confused for the second time today. The loyal side of him, the part that always feared being bad, was struggling against his basic male urges. On one hand, he was feeling turned-on by his own wife's sexy body and her movements on the dance floor. His intention for bringing her to Palm Springs on vacation was to bring them closer together. But on the other hand, he had been distracted twice today by other women: first by the sudden emotional connection with Fran, and now by the arousal he felt in response to Pam's not-so-subtle flirting. He was afraid to admit his attraction to both Fran and Pam, although he was attracted to each of them in very different ways.

This isn't at all how I planned things, he said to himself.

Dan felt a sense of relief when the music ended, and some space opened between him and Pam. However, his relief was short-lived as the music transitioned into a slow ballad.

"Ahh, a slow one," Pam remarked. "You okay with another dance, or would you rather go back to the booth and talk?"

Dan's loyal side thought it was best to go back to the booth. But it was no contest. His male urges easily won the battle over his conscience.

"I'm good to keep on dancing," he said hesitantly. "We can talk and have some more to drink after a couple more dances."

He held out his arms rigidly to take Pam into a dance hold.

Instead, Pam wrapped her arms around Dan's neck and drew him close to her. She buried her head on his shoulder. He felt her lips breathing softly into his ear. Her large warm breasts squeezed tightly against his chest, and one of her thighs pressed closely between his legs. At the same time, one of his thighs was fitting closely between hers. She sighed in his ear as their thighs mutually massaged each other to the rhythm of the music.

"This feels so nice," she whispered into his ear.

Pam's hands dropped down onto the small of his back, then to his behind. She pulled him more firmly towards her. The mixture of her perfume and natural pheromones, plus the movement of their bodies against each other, was more than Dan's body could resist. He started to feel embarrassed by his arousal and began to blush, wondering what Chelly was going to say if she saw them dancing so closely.

He looked over at Chelly as she clung to Richard. Her head was looking away from him. She was either totally unaware of what was going on between himself and Pam, or she wasn't the least bit concerned. Her head rested comfortably on Richard's exposed chest because of their significant difference in height. Dan saw that she had surrendered herself completely to the slow rhythm of the music and Richard's muscular body.

Surprisingly, Dan didn't feel jealous either. He was too distracted and confused by his unexpected attractions to both Fran and Pam today.

"Richard and Chelly look cute together, don't they?" Pam whispered into Dan's ear.

"They're quite a contrast." Dan said nervously. "She looks like a dwarf compared to him. And her skin couldn't look any whiter against his dark skin. Same thing with her red hair and his black!"

"Yeah," Pam observed. "But they seem to have a lot of fun together. I'm glad you brought her to the Chateau this time so we could meet her. And it's so good seeing you again." She squeezed her arms, bringing their bodies closer together, just as the ballad was drawing to a close.

The tempo of the next song picked up and the music was much louder. Dan spoke into Pam's ear. "Thanks for the dances, Pam. That was fun. Let's go back to the table so we can finish our drinks and talk some more, okay?"

They arrived back at the table at the same time as Richard and Chelly. Pam slid into the booth beside Dan, leaving space at the other end of the booth for Richard and Chelly, ensuring that they would sit together.

"This is so much fun. You guys are awesome dancers." Chelly squeaked in her high, excited voice. "This club was a great idea. Thanks for bringing us along!"

THE COUPLES ordered another round of drinks, guzzling the cold refreshments quickly, and then returning to the dance floor with their spouses. Pam and Richard were watching Dan's and Chelly's bodies moving to the beat of *Billie Jean*. Richard leaned down to talk in Pam's ear.

"Chelly and Dan didn't seem to get jealous seein' each other slow-dancin' with us, did they darlin'?"

"Not at all," Pam answered. "In fact, I'd say they both really enjoyed flirting with us. I know Dan liked it. At least one part of him was enjoying it, if you know what I mean!" She and Richard grinned at each other, and then exchanged salacious laughter.

"That Chelly's one hot little redhead, darlin'," Richard sighed. "I get turned on by the way she gets so excited when she's havin' fun. Why, I get excited just thinkin' about gettin' inside her and makin' her squeal. How 'bout you and mister square britches over there?"

"That's just the thing," Pam answered. "He's going to be a challenge. I know there's a hot, sexy guy inside. I see it when he's been drinking and lets his guard down. And he's got such a great body! I just want to see if I can teach him how to use it properly!"

"How about switchin' partners for one or two more dances, then gittin' those two back to the spa so we can all get naked again!" Richard suggested.

"Okay," Pam said. "You keep working on making sure Chelly keeps wanting to have more fun. I'll keep working on mister responsible. I'm going to make him so horny he'll be begging Chelly to let me screw his brains out tonight!"

"Sounds like a plan!" Richard agreed. He and Pam casually danced closer to Chelly and Dan. As the song ended, they subtly switched partners again, turning up the heat and continuing to build up the sexual tension in their naive victims.

CHAPTER 11

"FEELS GREAT to be naked again, eh guys?" Pam said, as Dan and Chelly joined them on the pool deck outside their room.

"Another chilly night, though!" Richard added. "Just look at all those goose bumps'n hard nipples!"

All four of the guests were completely naked except for their flip-flops and the towels over their shoulders. Chelly noticed Pam sliding right away between her and Dan, while Richard moved in beside her and took her by the arm. Richard was carrying a bottle of red wine for the guys, while she had a bottle of white to share with Pam.

"I have an idea," Dan said. "Why don't we all stay out in the cold air for a while to chill down our nerve endings - sort of like when we roll around in the snow in Michigan, right Chelly? Then when we get into the hot water, it feels like pins and needles all over!"

"I'll try anything once," Pam said, as she took Dan's arm. "But I don't want you guys staying out in the cold too long, or your men-parts will shrink up and disappear. We wouldn't want that, would we Chelly?"

The group of four burst out laughing again, feeling increasingly comfortable with the banter and innuendo that had been going on within the group since yesterday. Surprisingly, there were no other hotel guests using the spa at this hour, leaving the patio completely to the two couples. They milled around on the patio, joking and shivering, for about five minutes until Pam couldn't stand it anymore.

"Okay, time's up. I've had enough," Pam said. "C'mon, Dan. Let's wake up those nerve endings!" She grabbed him by the hand and dragged him to the spa, waiting only for him to help her down into the hot water. Noticing that Pam had seated herself beside Dan, Chelly allowed Richard to help her into the spa, then sat close beside him.

"Wow!" Pam said. "This feels awesome. Every nerve in my body is tingling right now. I can't even feel the hot water - just the tingling. What a great feeling! Almost as good as an orgasm, eh Chelly?"

Chelly blushed at the mention of sex. She was immediately reminded about Dan's story of last night's erotic dream. She glanced sideways at Richard, who saw the red flush on her face before she could turn away.

"No need to be shy, li'l lady," he said to Chelly. "It's a perfectly natural part of bein' a woman. Right, Pam?"

He grinned and winked knowingly at Pam, then turned his attention back to Chelly.

"Remember yesterday mornin'? You were blushin' for bein' partly naked, right? But tonight, bein' naked seems natural, doesn't it?"

"Yeah, I suppose," Chelly answered. "But talking about sex and orgasms is different. It feels a lot more personal."

The conversation was getting too intimate for Chelly. She caught herself twirling her hair nervously with her fingers. She needed to do something to calm her anxiety, and she had to do something else with her hands. She remembered the bottle of white wine sitting on the patio behind her.

"Richard, would you pour a lady a glass of wine, please? Anybody else want some while Richard's pouring?"

"I'll have some. Hey, I've got an idea everybody!" Pam blurted. "I haven't played *Truth or Dare* for ages. How about we all drink up a glass o'wine, and have some laughs?"

"Awesome idea!" Chelly squealed, picking up on Pam's exuberance. "I can't remember when I last played! I'll bet I was in high school! How 'bout it Dan?"

"Sure, I'm game. But I don't think I've ever played. Anybody want to explain the rules to me?"

"No way!" Chelly and Pam shouted in unison. They looked at each other in dismay, rolling their eyes.

"Don't forget," Chelly said in a sarcastic tone, "Dan's always been a good boy. The only naughty thing I've ever heard him admit to was skinny dipping with his cousins! Okay, let's do it. Are you in Richard?"

"Wouldn't miss it for the world, darlin'," Richard answered. "Wanna tell Danny boy the rules, girls?"

"Sure," Pam answered. But first we all gotta empty our glasses. We'll have way more laughs that way!"

Richard opened the bottle of red wine for himself and Dan, filling their glasses. Everybody tipped up and quickly drained their glasses. Then Richard poured a round of refills for the players to drink during the game.

"Okay, Dan," Pam began. Her arm was now permanently around his neck. "We'll play with two teams: Richard and I against you and Chelly. Each person will take turns asking one of the other team to choose between answering a question, totally truthfully, or doing a dare. The question or the dare has to be embarrassing for the other person, or it's no fun, right Chelly? It's easy. You can start, Dan. You ask either Richard or me to answer a question or do a dare. What's it gonna be?"

"Okay, Richard," Dan said. "Truth or dare?"

"I'll make it easy for you," Richard said. "I'll pick *truth* this time. Anythin' y'all wanna know, just ask away!"

Dan thought for a moment, but he hadn't quite caught the spirit of the game yet.

"Okay, Richard. I think I've got one. I've been wondering ever since I met you. Your accent doesn't seem right. How did a brother like you end up with a backwoods Texas accent? If someone heard you talk, but didn't see your skin, they'd probably think you were a redneck instead of a brother. So how'd you get the accent?"

"Oh, Dan!" Pam groaned. "Can't you ask him anything more embarrassing than that?"

"Boring!" Chelly added.

"Take it easy on the poor guy," Richard said. "This is his first turn. He'll do better next time around, once he's seen us in action, eh Chelly?"

"As for your question," Richard continued, "My dad was in the air force. Ever heard of the Tuskegee Airmen?"

"Yeah, I think so. Weren't they the first all-black squadron in the air force in the second world war?"

"Right. After the war, he was one o'the few in the squadron who stayed in the military. He was assigned to pilot trainin' at Lackland, in San Antonio. After all the controversy 'bout lettin' colored people into the military, dad wanted t'prove he belonged. He decided it was 'mportant t'integrate his family into air force culture, much as possible. We were one of the few colored families t'live on base, surrounded by a lotta redneck Texan's an' southern boys. So I grew up surrounded by good ole' white boys and picked up their accent. When I was old enough, I wanted to fly just like my ole man, so I joined up for the air force too. Does that answer your question?"

"Absolutely," Dan said. "Your dad was a real trailblazer. You must have been really proud of him."

"Yeah, he was a pretty tough ole' dude. He had t'be tough t'survive. But 'nuff about me, who goes next darlin?" Richard asked.

Chelly felt Richard's arm draw her closer. She was enjoying herself and it felt good.

"It's Chelly's turn," Pam said. "What's it gonna be, girl? Truth or dare?"

"I'll say truth. Who asks me a question this time?" Chelly asked.

"I've got one for ya, darlin," Richard said. "Now don't ya'll go blushin' again. An' remember, y'all gotta tell the whole truth now! Are ya ready?"

"Of course. Bring it on big guy!" Chelly dared.

"Okay then. Have ya ever had a fantasy or a dream 'bout havin' sex with 'nother person besides Dan?"

Chelly felt herself turn bright red almost instantly, feeling like her face was burning up. She felt trapped. Her mind was scrambling to figure out how to answer. She couldn't possibly tell Richard that she dreamt about fucking his brains out, especially in front of Pam! She saw Dan sit upright, suddenly much more interested in the game.

"Woooh, Chelly," Pam squealed. "Look at you blush! Looks like we got somethin' here! Come clean, girl!"

Chelly's eyes pleaded with Dan not to say anything as she started to answer.

"Well," she said. She felt herself swallowing hard. "Dan told me once that I must have had a pretty raunchy dream the night before. It seems I woke him up and started making some pretty hot love to him. He told me the next morning that I rode him so hard, he was afraid he was going to end up in emergency. You know. As one of those guys who has to have it sewn back on in the ER?"

Richard and Pam burst into laughter.

"So who were ya' ridin', girl?" Richard pressed.

"Sorry to disappoint you," Chelly said. "I didn't remember the dream, so I can't tell you who I was fantasizing about." She glared at Dan, once again begging him not to say anything more.

"Well, Chelly. You naughty thang, you! Who'da thought a sweet l'il girl like you could be so raunchy! Too bad we don't know who the lucky guy was, eh Pam?"

"Yeah, but now we know she's human, don't we?" Pam said, smiling.

Chelly's ears were still burning. She quickly turned the attention back towards Pam.

"Yes, Pam. But now it's my turn, so you'd better be careful. What's it going to be? Truth or dare?"

"I'll say truth," Pam answered. "What do you wanna know?"

"Tell us who you lost your virginity to and how it happened! You gotta tell us everything!" Chelly said.

"Oh, Lord," Pam groaned. "You would ask that one, wouldn't you. That was so long ago! I was a sophomore - sweet sixteen. I got asked out by Michael Washington, captain of the basketball team. He was such a hunk and I was so excited! I did not want to make a bad impression on that boy! No sir! He coaxed me into the back seat his car. I was terrified, but no way I was goin' to admit it was just my first time. I went along with him, thinkin' he was an experienced stud. But he must've been more nervous than I was! He came the second he got inside me!"

Pam reached for her wine glass and took a sip, letting the cool liquid slide down her throat.

"So I thought to myself: *That's it?* It was such a letdown. And he was so embarrassed he couldn't even bring himself to talk to me or even make eye contact again. It was like I didn't exist. I think I wanted to join a convent after that! Good thing I didn't, eh dear," she said to Richard.

"Yes, ma'am!" he exclaimed. "You must'a got back into the saddle with somebody who taught you real good!"

"Why, thank you my dear. Did you hear that, Dan? I come highly recommended. No pun intended, of course!" she joked. She grinned at Dan as the others all chortled at her innuendo.

Chelly reached for her wine glass and took another sizeable gulp. She was starting to enjoy the raunchy humor. She noticed a warm feeling growing between her legs as more blood started flowing into the area.

"Okay, Dan. I get to ask you now," Pam said. "What's it gonna be? Truth or dare? Better be careful. I'm not going to pull any punches!"

"Everybody else picked *truth*, so I'll do the same. Give me your best shot, Pam. I can take it, can't I Chelly?" he said.

"Oh, you think you're so smart," Chelly laughed. "Give him a good one, Pam. Make him sweat."

"Very well, then. Dan, I wanna know if women of other races turn you on. Do you ever have fantasies of hookin' up with them? An' if you do, you gotta tell me which women really turn you on - in addition to your favorite redhead, of course," she added, nodding in Chelly's direction.

"Good one, Pam!" Chelly said. "I hear it's healthy to have fantasies, Dan. So what are yours?" Chelly narrowed her eyes and zeroed in on Dan's, waiting for his answer.

"Look, he's starting to blush!" she squeaked to Pam. "Looks like you hit a nerve!"

Chelly was enjoying seeing Dan squirm. Secretly, she was just as interested in finding out if he had any secret fantasies too.

"C'mon, Dan. Out with it, or you're gonna have to do a dare instead!"

She saw Dan hang his head while he tried to decide what to say. He was having trouble making eye contact with Pam and Chelly.

"Well," he began, lifting his head. "I guess I'd have to say that I get turned on by other races: Asian and Indian women. But probably most of all by African-American women."

Chelly saw his face turn a deep crimson. "Ooooooh!" the others shouted in unison. All three broke into laughter after they finished razzing Dan.

"How sweet, my dear!" Pam exclaimed. She turned her body sideways and draped her feet over Dan's thighs, both arms now encircling his neck, so that she was now sitting sideways on his lap. "I'm flattered, of course!" She kissed Dan on his cheek.

"We better watch those two, Chelly," Richard teased. "They may just leave us sittin' here to party by ourselves if we're not careful! Your turn to ask Chelly now, Pam. Let's see if you can put the perty redhead on the hot-seat!"

"Truth or dare, Chelly? What'll it be?" Pam said.

"Dare!" Chelly challenged. "Bring it on. Let's see what you got, Pam. You're playing with the sleep-over Truth or Dare champion of Michigan, you know!"

"Okay," Pam said, defiance in her voice. "I dare you to sit in the lap of somebody on the other team, and to French kiss that person for a full minute. So who's it gonna be? Me or Richard?"

Chelly's mind started racing. A small part of her felt guilty about enjoying the sexual flirting with Richard. But she'd feel even more guilty if she didn't play by the rules and let the others down. Her romantic, sexual part was definitely attracted to Richard, and was incredibly tempted to take things further with him. But right now, she was too timid to admit it openly. She saw only one way out of her dilemma. She got up and stood in front of Pam.

"I'm borrowing your friend for a minute, Dan. I'll give her back when I'm done!"

"Ooooh," Pam said, once she realized Chelly had out-maneuvered her. "We'd better not get too steamy, or we're going to make a couple of guy's fantasies come true here!"

Pam swung her legs away from Dan's, sliding off his lap. She reached out towards Chelly, pulling her closer. Chelly sat sideways across Pam's lap. She put her arms around Pam's neck, and then placed her lips tenderly on Pam's. Pam gently returned the kiss. Chelly was surprised to find herself enjoying the sensations again, as she was yesterday when Fran's naked breasts touched hers during her massage. Her lips became more active against Pam's, and her tongue began to make quick flicks and explorations into Pam's mouth, with each woman occasionally finding each other's tongues. Pam responded eagerly to Chelly's probing, and their lips pressed more closely together. Then, Chelly felt Pam's hand searching for her breast, gently fondling it as their kissing became more intense. She felt the blood racing into her genitals as she became more aroused.

"Okay ladies," Richard interrupted. "I'd say that was an enjoyable minute all around, wouldn't you say Dan?"

"Oh yeah!" Dan exclaimed. "That was one incredibly hot dare. So far, you're the winner, Chelly."

Chelly stared into Pam's eyes while she lingered on her lap, her arms still around the darker woman's neck. Pam looked stunned by the unexpected pleasure she'd just experienced.

"I really enjoyed that, Chelly," Pam said. "I mean it. I'd say we just opened up a whole lotta different ways this li'l party could go."

Chelly let go of Pam's neck and swung herself confidently off her lap. Pam swung her legs back over Dan's thighs, and then snuggled up to his chest while Chelly returned to the other side of the spa and cozied up beside Richard.

"Chelly, it's your turn to ask Richard," Pam said. "What do you choose, Richard?"

"I liked what I just saw from Chelly. You got spunk, girl," he said in admiration. "I think I'll try a dare from you."

"Okay, Richard," Chelly said. "I want to see what that spectacular body can do."

"Wooooh," Pam squealed. "So do we all!"

"Sorry, Pam. That's not what I have in mind. Richard, I want you to get out onto the deck. Then I want you to spend the next minute doing bodybuilding poses that show off every part of your body. Starting right now. Let's go - out into the cold!"

"Sheesh. Good one," Richard admitted. "I'll see what I can remember from the gym. Here goes nothin'!" he announced, as he climbed out of the spa onto the patio.

Richard started doing his best Arnold Schwarzenegger imitations, with the other three bathers convulsing with laughter and cheering him on. To everybody's surprise, he did a credible performance, ending it with flare by throwing in a pelvic thrust for emphasis. Dan, Chelly, and Pam were laughing hysterically.

"Awesome!" squealed Chelly. "Encore!"

"Sorry," he answered. "It's gettin' cold out here. I think ya need t'warm me up!" he said, stepping down briskly into the spa beside Chelly again.

Richard effortlessly lifted Chelly up and set her down so she was now sitting across his lap, just as Pam had been sitting on Dan. She put her arms around his waist and leaned her torso and one of her large breasts against his chest.

"Your turn now, Pam," Dan said. "Pick your poison pretty woman. Truth or dare?"

"I pick dare too," Pam replied. "I'll bet you can't think of a dare as good as Richard's last one!"

"Maybe," Dan answered, a twinkle in his eye. "But I think I'd like to see you get out onto the deck to entertain us with some belly-dancing for the next minute! How 'bout it Richard and Chelly?"

The three of them hooted at Pam until she finally clambered out of the spa.

"It's damn cold out here, you guys!"

"Well," Dan answered. "Then you'd better get that body moving to keep you warm. One minute - starting now!"

Pam was like a fish out of water. But the entertainment value of her attempt, given the amount of alcohol everybody had consumed tonight, produced howls of laughter.

"Time!" Dan cried. He was almost in tears from watching. "Excellent attempt my dear. Come back down here and I'll warm you up again."

Chelly watched as Dan helped Pam back down into the spa. Her wet skin was glistening and covered in goose bumps and her dark nipples hard and erect. She saw one of Dan's hands graze one of Pam's breasts and nipple as he guided her into the spa. His face reddened and he glanced nervously towards her. Chelly looked away and leaned against Richard's chest, pretending not to notice.

"Brrrrrr," Pam said, her teeth still chattering. Whose turn is it now, anyway?"

"I get to ask Dan now," Richard replied. "What do you say, bro'? Truth or dare?"

"Everybody else is doing a dare this round, so I guess I'd better not jam out," Dan said. "I guess it's a dare!"

"Well, now. This should be interesting," Richard chuckled. "Chelly, what'ya say we ask Dan to French kiss Pam, just like you did. Then maybe we'll get Pam to tell us which one of you is the best French kisser!"

Chelly saw Dan look at her with panic in his eyes, pleading for her to intervene. She grinned back, enjoying his moment of panic. She saw the *good boy* in Dan fighting against doing something bad.

Poor guy. He's so loyal too, Chelly thought.

"Come on, Dan. What are you afraid of? She's not going to bite. You know you want to do this!" Chelly teased. She saw the seductive smile on Pam's cocoa-colored face. Her lips were parted and waiting in anticipation, ready to receive Dan's lips.

Finally, Dan realized Chelly wasn't going to save him. He caved in to both the peer pressure and his male desires. Chelly watched as their lips met. Pam took control. Her kiss was gentle, yet passionate. One of her hands stroked Dan's neck and head as her lips and tongue tenderly searched Dan's lips. Her mouth pressed more firmly against Dan's lips, her tongue starting to make quick explorations of his. Chelly saw Pam's hand slip downwards to where Dan's manhood was more than likely rising to the occasion beneath her genitals. The intensity and speed of the mutual probing of their lips and tongues increased. Pam started grinding her butt in a slow circle in Dan's lap.

Chelly settled into Richard's arms. She was so intent on watching Dan and Pam, she was barely aware that her fingers had been lightly stroking one of Richard's thighs. As she watched her husband and Pam locked in pleasure, and as her fingers continued to softly stroke Richard's thigh, she recalled the sweetness of her own long, intense kiss with Pam. Her own sexual response was rapidly coming alive again. She felt Richard's organ growing beneath her, coming into contact with her genitals. The romantic side of her brain joined with her sexual desire, creating a force that was oblivious to any objections that may have been on her mind only moments before. She looked up into Richard's dark face and their lips moved together eagerly, their spouses quickly forgotten in the midst of their own sudden passion.

Dan and Pam opened their mouths for air. Pam looked over at Richard and Chelly, who were now lost in their own embrace.

"They look beautiful, don't they Dan?" she whispered in his ear. "Almost as beautiful as I feel with you right now …"

Suddenly, the patio and spa were plunged into darkness and silence. It was eleven p.m. - quiet time at Chateau Eden. The four guest's faces were now dimly illuminated by only a single light bulb outside the back door of the office.

"Shit," Pam muttered. "Wouldn't you know it? Just when things were starting to get good! Richard, what do you say to inviting this fine looking man and his beautiful wife back to our room to continue the party? It would be such a shame to ruin this moment."

"We'd both be honored if y'all would join us," Richard agreed.

Dan sat up straight, and Chelly saw the serious, responsible side of him take over. The transformation from sexually aroused male to loyal spouse occurred like a switch had been tripped in Dan.

"I'm sure we're both really flattered by your invitation, and I have to admit it's incredibly tempting to join you. But this is really sudden. It's something Chelly and I have never discussed with each other. I don't want to disappoint you. You're both charming and sexy people. It might be something that we'd both be open to trying with you another time, after we've had some time to discuss it some more."

Chelly's eyes narrowed and her forehead was furrowed into a deep frown. She glared at Dan, giving him the look that wives reserve only for when they are beyond angry with their spouses.

Pam reacted to the tension that was rapidly building between Dan and Chelly. She knew that the mood and timing for any further romantic activities had just evaporated. She nodded to Richard to indicate that the evening was over.

"We understand, Dan. It's a big decision," Pam said. "I'm sure we'll be seeing you guys again at the Chateau in the future, and we'll have plenty of time to get to know each other better then, won't we Richard."

Richard nodded his agreement. Pam lifted herself off of Dan's lap and gave him a parting kiss on the lips. Richard did the same with Chelly, and then he took Pam's hand and helped her out of the spa.

Dan rose to his feet, reaching for Chelly's hand. She refused to take it, turning her back to him, and then climbing out of the opposite side of the spa by herself. They stepped into their flip-flops, grabbed their towels and quickly wrapped their bodies to insulate themselves from the cool night air.

Chelly's romantic, sexual side was frustrated beyond belief. An angry part of her, that she rarely ever allowed to show, had exploded to the surface. Within microseconds, she was seething with anger. She stomped the short distance to their room, leaving Dan trailing behind her, without uttering a word. The tension between the couple cut the crisp, silent desert night like a freshly sharpened knife. The door to their room slammed behind Chelly. Dan stood by himself outside the door, the patio and courtyard of Chateau Eden silent, except for the distant hum of traffic. He felt helpless, guilty, and completely alone.

PHILIPPE WAITED for a long minute after both couples disappeared from the patio before quietly slipping out the back door to the office. He crept to the open bathroom window of Dan and Chelly's room, crouching with his head low and his ear as close to the window as possible. As Dan entered the room and the door latch clicked quietly behind him, the silence was shattered as Chelly released a torrent of pent-up frustration and rage.

"What the hell was that out there, Dan?" she screamed. "Who gave you permission to speak for both of us? You just shut down everybody else's fun!"

"Chelly, calm down. It was pretty obvious they were coming-on to both of us and wanting more than just drinks and laughs, wasn't it? Out of consideration for you, I didn't want to say yes to wife swapping without talking it over with you first! I'd never want to say yes and just assume it was okay with you."

"Coming-on to us? Don't be ridiculous, Dan. We were just playing a harmless party game and having fun. Stop jumping to conclusions and don't ever speak on my behalf again, okay?"

"Harmless party game? You've got to be kidding, Chelly! In case you didn't notice, there were four adults in that spa, not kids. And you can't deny that everybody was getting pretty hot and horny with each other. If that isn't coming-on to us, I don't know what is! And the fact that you think it was just harmless fun just confirms to me that I had to slow things down until we had a chance to talk about it!"

Outside the bathroom window, Philippe smiled and leaned closer so he wouldn't miss a word.

"Right!" Chelly continued shouting. "Even if they were seducing us, you just assumed I wouldn't be okay with it. So you barged ahead and thought it was okay to put words in my mouth and say no for me! What's the difference, Dan? What you did was just as bad as going ahead and saying yes without asking me! I thought we had this conversation this morning. You promised you'd stop being such a square and cut loose and have some fun sometimes, if there's something I want to do!"

"Yeah, but we didn't talk about swinging. And we didn't talk about doing it with Pam and Richard. So how did I know you might have wanted to go back to their room? How was I supposed to know you might be okay with swapping? I don't ever want you to feel like I'm pressuring you to do something against your will. "

"You didn't know what I was thinking or what I felt because you jumped right in and answered for me, Dan! You didn't give me a chance to say yes or no! You didn't even give them a chance to say what they wanted to do in their room. Maybe they just wanted to play cards! I guess we'll never know what they were going to say, will we?"

"Okay, Chelly. Then let's have the discussion right now. What would you have said if they did ask us to swap with them? Would you really have wanted to play out your fantasy of having sex with Richard?"

Philippe's heart was racing as he overheard the argument. His legs were cramping, so he shifted position. He strained to hear every word. The success of his plan depended on it. As he heard Chelly growing more confident and becoming angrier with Dan, Philippe's own confidence grew. *They do not know it, but they are telling me everything I need to know about their weaknesses!*

"Would I want to make love with Richard? Hell, yes!" Chelly screamed. "He's charming and funny. He's romantic. And what woman wouldn't want to test drive that beautiful black body!"

Chelly paused, and then pointed a finger in Dan's direction. She was only getting started.

"But what about you, Dan? Let's forget what I would have done for a moment. It seems I'm not the only one who has a fantasy of making it with somebody black, eh? What would you have done, mister goody two shoes? Wouldn't you like to live out your fantasy with Pam too? What a terrible dilemma for your poor conscience. You're just dying to be with that sexy black body, and bury your face in those big boobs. And your dick is just dying to be inside her, isn't it? But we wouldn't want Dan to do something naughty now, would we?"

"Alright!" Dan said. "Let's say I wouldn't mind being with Pam. Wouldn't you feel jealous about me being with her?"

"No, I wouldn't. I was getting hot seeing you two together," Chelly answered. "What about you, Dan? Would you be jealous?"

Dan paused for a moment to think.

"I don't think so," he answered. "I just want to see you happy. I want to see the real Chelly not being afraid to come out. You're a really hot, sexy woman, and it turns me on to see you turned on. Even if it's with another guy. Or even with another woman, like when you were kissing Pam tonight. Both Richard and I were getting hard watching you two together!"

Philippe's legs were growing numb. He needed to stretch badly, but didn't dare move. He couldn't afford to miss a word.

"Well, if you want to see me happy," Chelly shouted, "then let me make up my own mind about what I want to do. Don't ever speak out for me again, do you hear me! Speak for yourself and I'll speak for me, okay?"

"Okay, I hear you," Dan conceded. "All I ask is that you don't rush into something without us talking about it first. There's a lot to consider. Did you ever stop to think about having safe sex? How do you know if Richard and Pam are clean? Would you just take their word for it? What if they didn't have any condoms? We don't have any right now!"

"I would've asked if they had protection. I'm not stupid, you know. I am a nurse!" Chelly said.

"And there's another even more important issue," Dan added. "I brought you here so I could share this place with you and meet the friends I met here last time. I did it so we could spend time with each other - to reconnect and get closer, and maybe find ways to re-energize our sex lives. The idea was to do it together, with each other. Not to spend the week sharing ourselves sexually with other people."

"Well, you're the one who said it was healthy to explore our sexual fantasies, Dan. You're the one who brought it up in the first place. Why is it a big issue all of a sudden? What if my fantasies are to have sex with strangers, or with men of a different race, like Richard? Don't you still want to encourage me to explore my fantasies, Dan? You said they were common fantasies for women. That means I'm just following up on my natural urges, doesn't it?"

"Sure," Dan admitted. "But can't we find ways to explore some fantasies within our marriage first? Maybe we could make sex more exciting by doing it in different places. Hell, let's join the *Mile High Club* and do it in the lavatory on the flight home! There are so many more emotional risks to exploring fantasies outside a marriage. I see people all the time at work who've tried swinging. But they're usually coming to see me because their spouse ran off with the neighbor, or because their partner is coercing them to have sex with people when they don't feel comfortable doing it! I see the damage it causes, Chelly!"

"Maybe that's true," Chelly admitted. "But don't swingers say it helps them build trust in their partners? Don't they say it helps them to communicate better by talking about their different sexual experiences?"

"Yeah, some do," Dan agreed. "But those people need good communication and trust before they get into it. If they don't already have good relationships with good communication, having sex with strangers isn't likely to improve it. And to be honest, given the difficulty we're having in communicating right now, I question whether our relationship is stable enough to survive swapping partners."

Philippe continued to eavesdrop on the unsuspecting couple, feeling the ominous silence in the room while Chelly's anger percolated. He waited for the inevitable eruption that was sure to follow, but wasn't able to stay in the same position any longer. He tried to shift his weight to his other leg, almost losing his balance. He barely managed to keep from falling over.

"There you go again!" Chelly screamed. "Who says you get to be the judge of how strong our marriage is! Did you think to ask me if I thought our relationship was strong enough to survive swinging? I get sick and tired of being treated like my thoughts and feelings don't matter, just because you're supposedly an expert and I'm just an ignorant emotional woman!"

"That's not what …"

"Furthermore," she continued. "I'm sick of you getting to decide what we should or shouldn't do because you're the one who allegedly knows what's healthy! Can't you take off your fucking psychologist's hat long enough to have some fun like the rest of us? It's ironic, but I often think you psychologists are the most anally retentive bunch I've ever seen! And I'm sick of it! I've just about had enough!"

Chelly was so angry her voice was shaking by the time she finished. Philippe was starting to feel increasingly anxious.

Their arguing is starting to endanger my plan. I can use some small disagreements - it will be easy to make either one of them feel guilty. But they are both pushing each other away. That could be a disaster.

"I think it would have been fun to continue the party with Richard and Pam in their room," Chelly said. "Especially if I got to play out my fantasy with Richard and you got to play out yours with Pam. Who knows, it might have been fun watching each other have sex with somebody else, and then talking about what it was like for both of us. But I guess we'll never know, will we Dan? Because mister 'I'm a psychologist and I know everything' decided he knew what was best and decided to be a big party-pooper!"

"Okay, Chelly. I get it. I made a lot of assumptions I shouldn't have made. You're right. I'm sorry. What do you want me to do?"

"I want you to forget being a psychologist when you're with me, and just try being a regular guy. Quit overanalyzing everything. Take a chance on making a mistake once in a while. And most of all, I want you to trust me enough to make some of the decisions, and to go along with me once in a while. If you want to build trust and bring us closer, trust me once in a while!"

"Alright, I suppose I can try doing that," Dan said. "What can I do to make it up to you?"

"You owe me after tonight," Chelly said. "You'd better remember that! The next time we're ever in a situation where we have to make a decision as a couple, I get to make my own decision, and you have to trust my judgment and try going along with me. I might be making a mistake, but I deserve the chance to make that mistake. Can you manage to do that for me?"

Philippe realized he was holding his breath as he crouched beneath the open bathroom window. His legs were both numb from lack of movement and oxygen. He was praying for Dan to agree with Chelly. It would make his plan a *fait d'accomplet* for Philippe. The brief silence between Chelly's demand and Dan's response seemed like an eternity for him, until he finally heard Dan clear his throat and speak.

"Sure, I guess I can do that. You have my word. I'll start letting you make decisions and start trusting you. But it's hard to stop being a psychologist completely. I live it every day, you know."

"Fine!" she huffed. "But once you've given me your input, you have to trust me to decide whether I want to consider it or not. Do we have a deal, Dan?"

At that moment, Philippe lost his balance. His shoulder and head bumped against the back wall of Dan and Chelly's room. His legs were so cramped, he struggled to get back on his feet, moving as quickly as his semi-paralyzed legs could carry him.

They must not know I have been listening to them!

"WHAT WAS THAT?" DAN asked, hearing a loud thump from the direction of their bathroom. "I'll go and check it out," he said, as he hurried into the next room.

"Hey, Chelly," he called. "Did you leave the window open today? It's damn cold in here!"

"That's weird," Chelly answered. "It was open all last night too, so I closed it this morning. How did it get open again?"

"Maybe housecleaning opened it up earlier in the day when it was hot," Dan reasoned. He heard more sounds from outside the window. He turned off the bathroom light so his eyes would adjust, and then looked out onto the patio. All he saw in the dim light was Philippe putting the cover over the spa. He closed the window and rejoined Chelly back in their room.

"Nothing to worry about," he reported. "It was just Philippe closing the spa."

"Is that all? I'm exhausted. I'm getting ready for bed," Chelly said. She headed for the bathroom and closed the door behind her.

Dan sat on the end of their bed, his face in his hands, trying to make sense of the night's events. Everything had been so much fun. He and Chelly both seemed to be having a good time at dinner and at the club. Sure, there was some flirting going on, but everybody had been drinking and having a good time.

What went wrong? Why did I keep encouraging Pam's flirting? I want to be getting closer with Chelly, so why didn't I set some boundaries with Pam? Even worse, why don't I feel jealous of Chelly and Richard's flirting? Do I have a fantasy of watching my wife fuck another man? Do I want to see if everybody else turns her on more than I do? Am I second-guessing whether I can satisfy her, or any woman for that matter?

Dan's head was spinning. There were so many questions and he had no answers. The responsible and loyal parts of him were beginning to feel increasingly ashamed of himself for his desire for Pam, not to mention the deep connection and arousal he'd felt for Fran this afternoon.

Why are things going so wrong, when I'm trying so hard to do everything right?

It felt as though Chelly was slowly slipping away from him. The old feeling of rejection from his past was starting to surface again, and he couldn't block it out. Dan made a promise to himself.

I'll do whatever Chelly wants to keep her happy. I can't lose her. I can't let it happen to me, ever again!

CHAPTER 12

EARLY SUNDAY morning found Dan in a deep REM sleep. The recurring dream had chosen this morning to make an appearance. He didn't have it often, but it came out of the blue without warning every few months. He was in Calgary and was back in high school again. He and his friend Anika were sixteen. They were best friends, but they had never taken their friendship to a sexual level. In the dream, they were always on the verge of consummating their relationship sexually for the first time.

He slowly unhooked her bra and let it fall to the ground. His trembling hands explored every curve of her freshly exposed breasts. He marveled at the silky smoothness and the milky glow of her skin in the dim light of his bedroom. His parents were gone for the weekend, leaving the two teens undisturbed and alone with their youthful passion.

Anika was stroking the hair on his bare chest, slowly moving downward towards his belt. She unfastened the buckle as Dan's fingers continued tracing gentle curves around her breasts. She opened his pants, and then crouched towards the ground, lowering them enough for him to step out of them. They pressed their bare chests together, feeling the warmth of each other's skin. Anika's hand ventured into Dan's briefs, getting her first touch of his warm, hard penis. She was surprised by how soft the skin on the outside felt, despite how swollen and hard it felt on the inside. Her fingers began exploring the long hard shaft, the softness of the head, then she stroked downward into the furry softness of his hair, finally feeling the swollen, hard sac suspended below his organ. Anika pulled down his briefs, leaving him completely naked. Her hands followed the back of his legs upwards, reaching and exploring the firm curves of his buttocks.

Dan's hands worked their way down over Anika's youthful, flat stomach. One hand worked its way gently inside her panties on the front, gently teasing her pubic hair and brushing over her labia. Then, both of his hands worked their way inside the elastic at the back of her panties, pulling them down to expose the smooth skin of her backside. His hands circled round and round each cheek, then gradually pulled her last piece of clothing down towards her ankles. She stepped out of the panties, and the pair pressed their naked bodies tightly together. The two young lovers felt their genitals coming together for the first time. Their lips merged into a long, passionate kiss, their hands gently stoking each other's backs and necks, or running their fingers through each other's hair.

Anika's hand moved downward and resumed exploring Dan's penis, while he started stroking the inside of her thighs, then gently traversed over her pubic hair and labia, He felt her lubrication flowing freely from between the smooth, rounded folds of skin. Their kisses increased in intensity and the tension in their genitals increased synchronously, causing both virgins to start feeling an escalating need for release.

"Do you have the condom?" she whispered. After a brief silence, she heard Dan tearing the package and discarding the wrapper.

"Lay down beside me, Dan. I love you so much," she said. When the couple was lying together, she took the condom from his hand and placed it over the head of his penis. She unrolled it until it covered the entire organ.

"I want to feel you inside me," she whispered. She slid next to him and he moved his body over hers.

Dan felt her fingers taking his penis and guiding it towards her vagina, gently pushing until he felt her labia being pushed aside. She was letting him take control, waiting for him to slide deeper inside. Dan felt her labia move apart, and felt him starting to slide inside her …

Out of nowhere, the peace and serenity of the dream's lovemaking was shattered by a rude beeping sound - like the sound of a truck's back-up signal, only right beside them in the bedroom. Dan's eyelids popped open. He was disoriented, struggling to make sense of what was happening. There was no truck backing up. He looked around the bedroom, realizing he was no longer in Calgary. He noticed the modern European styling and furnishings in the room, the pastel shades in the Italian watercolor landscapes decorating the walls, then cast a quick glance at the body lying next to him in the bed. The red hair brought his mind back quickly into reality. He heaved a frustrated sigh as he realized he was at Chateau Eden in Palm Springs, lying next to his wife, Chelly. It wasn't 1981. He wasn't sixteen years old and making love for the first time with Anika. It was March 2006.

The dream ended as it usually did - suddenly. Every time it happened, he and Anika were at the point where he was just entering her, with Dan expecting them to take each other to their first mutual sexual ecstasy. But every time, something unpredictable happened, either within the dream or in his external reality, that interrupted his fantasy lovemaking. Laying in bed, Dan felt frustrated and alone. He started wondering why he and Anika had never become lovers, even though they'd been best friends for many years. Then he wondered about how things got so out of control last night, and why things were going so terribly wrong with Chelly.

He gazed at Chelly. She had stirred briefly to hit the snooze button after the alarm went off, then rolled over for a final ten minutes of sleep. Dan exhaled another long, slow breath as he watched her rest. He knew her routine. She would pop out of bed with the next alarm, quickly dressing herself for her ritual morning run. She rarely let herself linger in bed long enough to kiss or cuddle on mornings when she went running. He heaved another long sigh, feeling just as frustrated and alone with his current reality as he did with the abrupt ending to his dream.

THE ROOM felt silent and empty after Chelly left for her morning run. Dan continued to lay in bed, his mind ruminating over the events of the last two days and the argument with Chelly last night. He was still struggling with his surprise emotional connection with Fran, and the excitement he felt in response to Pam's flirting. In both cases, his behavior was completely out of character. He usually thought of himself as a responsible person with good boundaries. He was at a loss to explain yesterday's events and his lapses in character.

He heard Tim and Shelley come out of their room onto the pool deck, where they talked and waited for a few minutes for Dan to join them. He didn't get up, opting instead for some more time to think by himself. When he didn't emerge from his room, he heard them open Chateau Eden's gate and continue without him.

Dan needed to swim. It was where he did his best thinking, and it had been eleven days since his last long swim back in Michigan. He couldn't stand it any more. He grabbed a pool towel from the bathroom, opened the door and headed for Chateau Eden's small pool. He slipped into the cool, invigorating water, submerging his head and allowing himself to delight in the sensual pleasure of the cool liquid flowing over his skin, before surfacing for air. After catching his breath, Dan did a shallow dive, swimming effortlessly under the surface until he reached the end, where he did a graceful turn. He continued underwater to the other end of the pool.

As he surfaced, he was greeted by the sounds of lovemaking drifting from Richard and Pam's room. Pam's moaning was reaching a crescendo as she moved closer to orgasm. Finally, she uttered a long, loud sigh that was half way between a whimper and a cry, as she reached her climax. Dan began wondering what last night might have been like for him if he hadn't turned down

Richard and Pam's offer to continue partying in their room. He laid back and lifted his feet off the pool floor, floating on his back, breathing slowly, and gazing up into the clear blue morning sky. His breathing slowed and he gradually gained more control over his thoughts.

Dan alternated between floating on his back and swimming lengths underwater for about half an hour, before pulling himself up onto the edge of the pool. The cool morning air brought his skin alive. He sat on the edge for a few moments to enjoy the sensations, then stood up and dried himself before returning to their room to shower, then heading to the lobby for breakfast. He was reading in the lobby when Chelly and other guests trickled into the lobby for breakfast. Dan and Chelly didn't speak once to each other, instead sitting across from each other in awkward silence while Chelly read the newspaper and Dan continued reading his book.

After breakfast, the naked guests once again flocked to the lounge chairs, spending the rest of the morning and early afternoon catching a few more hours of spring sunshine before most of them had to return to the reality of their lives in the Los Angeles area. The mood was much less playful than the previous two afternoons, as the departing guests began anticipating their return to reality. Pam and Richard said nothing about the sudden end to the previous evening's activities. Shelley, Pam, and Chelly alternated between reading and casual conversation about their books or Pam's *People* magazine. Tim and Richard played a couple of games of chess, then Tim and Dan talked psychology and social work for a while. As the afternoon sun sank closer to the mountains, Shelley, Tim, Richard, and Pam gathered their things from the pool deck and retreated towards their rooms to pack. Chelly quietly followed suit, having barely spoken to Dan all day.

Dan spotted Philippe in the office. He wrapped himself with his towel and entered the lobby to discuss arrangements for going to the estate tonight.

"Ah, bonjour Doctor Whitney," Philippe said, his face beaming a broad smile as he entered the lobby. "I have checked you and the Madame out and have your paperwork ready for you now, if you wish."

Dan noticed at once that Philippe was in an exceptionally good mood.

"Thanks Philippe. I was wondering when you and Fran wanted us to be ready to move to the estate. Do you have directions for how to get there?"

"I am glad you asked," Philippe replied. "I will be busy here at the Chateau until all the new guests are checked in. I should be finished by about seven o'clock unless we have late arrivals. Fran has been preparing for you and will return to take you back to the estate. She should be here around five o'clock. Will that be satisfactory to you and the Madame?"

Dan checked his watch, noticing that it was about four o'clock.

"That should give us plenty of time. Thanks again for everything you and Fran are doing for us, Philippe. We'll bring our bags out to the lobby when we've finished packing."

"It is our pleasure, monsieur. I look forward to your visit with us!" the Frenchman replied, his face covered by a broad smile and his eyes sparkling behind the thick black frames of his glasses. Philippe whistled happily and carried on with his work. Dan picked up his paperwork and exited the lobby. He returned to their room to find Chelly with her body and hair both wrapped in towels after her shower. She was hovering over her suitcase, deciding what to wear and what to repack.

"I just talked to Philippe," Dan said, finally breaking the icy silence between them. "Fran will be here about five o'clock to take us back to the estate. We'll both be ready by then, right?"

"Yup. I just need to decide what to wear," Chelly snapped. Dan came up behind her and put his arms around her waist. He gave her a penitent kiss on her neck. She remained stiff in his arms.

"I'm sorry again for last night," Dan said. "I was out of line and won't speak up for you again. I promise. Do you forgive me?"

"I don't know, Dan," Chelly answered. "It's easy to say sorry. But I guess I'm going to have to take some time to see if you can prove you mean it."

She took his arms and firmly removed them from around her body.

"Now, what in the world do you wear for a casual visit to somebody who is rich and famous?" she thought out loud. "Dan, you'd better shower and get yourself packed if we're going to be ready to say goodbye to the others and meet Fran!"

Dan undressed for his shower, his mind continuing to churn over last night's events, Chelly's icy response to his apology, and the growing distance between them. He was distracted, showering and packing his things with his body on autopilot. His mind continued to ruminate about how to make up for his recent blunder, and how to bring himself and Chelly closer together.

Dressed and packed, Dan carried their bags to the lobby and left their key with Philippe. Shelley and Tim, and Pam and Richard were just coming out of their rooms. He and Chelly met the other couples just inside the large pine gate at Chateau Eden's main entrance. Shelley and Tim reached out to embrace Dan and Chelly.

"It was great meeting you, Chelly," laughed the other Shelley. "Looks like our names didn't cause too much confusion. We're so pleased you could come to the Chateau with us. When are you and Dan going to come back and spend some time with us again?"

Dan was tempted to answer the question, but looked at Chelly and wisely decided to defer to her instead.

"You guys are all so friendly. I never dreamt of going nude with other people before. Who knew that I'd enjoy it as much as I did! But you all made it feel so natural! I can't wait to come back sometime," Chelly said.

"When would be a good time, Dan?" Chelly asked, looking in his direction. "Sometime in the fall?"

Dan noticed that Chelly was acting as though there was nothing wrong between them.

"How about Thanksgiving again?" Tim suggested. "None of us have family in the area to visit, and we've already reserved rooms along with Pam and Richard for that weekend. What do you say, Chelly?"

"Sounds like a great idea, doesn't it Dan? I'll just have to check the vacation schedules for the ER to see if I can take the time. But even if I'm scheduled, I'll find a way to call in some favors and switch with everybody else! Let's say it's a plan, okay Dan?"

"If you want to do it, then I'm in!" Dan answered. "Great to see you again," Dan said, as he shook Tim's hand and the two men embraced one last time.

Dan was happy they would be coming back again to visit their new friends, and was relieved that Chelly appeared to be willing to return the Chateau Eden with him.

Dan and Chelly turned to Pam and Richard, who also bid farewell with warm embraces.

"Great to meet you, li'l lady," Richard said to Chelly. "Can't wait to get t'gether with y'all again in the fall." He gave Chelly one last wink and his signature smile.

"Take care," Pam whispered in Dan's ear. "Can't wait to pick up where we left off. Make sure you and Chelly have a good talk and patch up whatever happened last night. We want to see you guys here together again, is that a deal?" She and Dan exchanged kisses on each other's cheeks.

"It's a deal," Dan reassured her quietly. "I'm glad Chelly wants to come back, and so do I." They exchanged smiles and one last embrace before separating.

The couples exchanged their final farewells, and then Pam, Richard, Shelly, and Tim disappeared from sight, with the pine gate closing behind them. Dan and Chelly were left standing alone in front of the gate.

Dan felt some sadness and emptiness as silence descended over the pool area. He turned his thoughts to Fran's imminent arrival. For the moment, he managed to put the increasing tension in his marriage out of his head. Instead, he started to feel some nervous anticipation about the opportunity to visit with Fran and Philippe at their luxurious estate.

Maybe sharing this little adventure and having some fun together this week will finally help to turn things around, he thought hopefully.

THE SILENCE in the car on the short trip between Palm Springs and Palm Desert was almost unbearable for Dan. Fran had driven Philippe's Mercedes back to Chateau Eden, leaving the car for him. She was riding back to the estate with Dan and Chelly, giving Dan directions as he drove. Chelly was still hardly speaking to him. Fran didn't say a word, apart from giving directions, and she avoided making eye contact with either Dan or Chelly. Dan couldn't tell whether she was self-conscious about her unexpected intimate encounter with him on Saturday, or whether she was nervous about something else. He hoped she wasn't embarrassed or anxious about having him as a guest at the estate.

Dan's responsible side was still feeling guilty, both about the intensity of the closeness with Fran yesterday and his argument with Chelly. As for Chelly, he knew she was still angry with him after their fight. But he also knew it was better to leave her alone for a while to let her cool off in her own time.

IN THE deafening silence within the car, Chelly was still confused by the myriad of emotions she had been feeling since her argument with Dan. She had felt unheard and invisible when Dan spoke on her behalf in the spa last night. The independent side of her was still furious at him. Her sexual, romantic side was frustrated, and continued to wonder what it might have been like for her and Dan to swap partners with Richard and Pam for the night. On the other hand, she was also feeling guilty about wanting to take those romantic and sexual risks. What would her family and friends think of her? The loyal aspect of her identity was also feeling some shame for wanting to step outside her relationship with Dan to fulfill her romantic and sexual fantasies.

FRAN'S MIND raced as Dan drove towards Palm Desert and the estate. She was having difficulty keeping herself focused on the being present in the car. She couldn't force herself to make eye contact with either Dan or Chelly. If she did look at them, she was unable to stop the haunting images. Either she was reliving the gruesome events of Diego and Juanita Alvarez at the estate and in the darkness of the desert night, or her mind was jumping ahead into the future, to images of what she knew was going to happen with the unsuspecting couple riding in the car with her. She was overwhelmed by fear, shame, and worthlessness.

On the other hand, the newly rediscovered sexual, romantic side of her was trying to rise into her consciousness. It was struggling to imagine, even if only for a few seconds at a time, what it might be like to know Dan more intimately. But just as quickly, an overwhelming fear swept over her. A fear of what could happen if things went wrong again this time, like they did with the Columbian couple! Then the flashbacks intruded again. She felt so overwhelmed that she just wanted to run away and hide, someplace where nobody could find her.

THEY WERE getting closer to the estate now. Dan guided the car along a road that climbed and wound its way up the mountain above Palm Desert. The neighborhood was relatively new, with sprawling luxury estates nestled safely behind security walls and gates. Palm trees could be seen over the security walls, part of the carefully manicured grounds surrounding the ostentatious homes. Dan drove around a final switchback, the road finally straightening out for a hundred yards before ending in a cul de sac.

"We are the last gate ahead on your left," Fran said, her emotionless voice finally breaking the sterile silence.

As they approached the last gate, Dan realized that the security wall surrounding the last estate was at least two feet higher than any they had seen on their drive up the mountain. Unlike any of the others, this wall was topped with razor wire. It became increasingly imposing and ominous as their car approached closer to the wall, and to the heavy wrought iron gate that interrupted the expansive enclosure. This wall was not only much higher, but also much longer than any belonging to the nearby estates. It became clear to Dan that Philippe's and Fran's estate was considerably larger and more secluded than any on the mountain.

"Boy, that's quite a wall," Dan exclaimed.

"Philippe is conscious about security," Fran answered curtly. "We have some expensive pieces of art displayed or stored in the house and it is important that we protect it."

"That makes sense," Dan said, not giving the question another thought.

"Wow," Chelly sighed, as she caught her first look of the low, sprawling Mission style home. She started coming alive as she realized the expanse and luxury of their accommodations for the next few days. "This is beautiful, Fran!" she exclaimed.

Fran pulled a remote control from her purse. The gate parted and began to swing open in two slow, wide arcs until there was enough room for Dan to drive through. The grounds were impeccably contoured and landscaped with natural desert vegetation, interspersed with mature palm trees. Another press of the remote control resulted in a garage door opening on one end of an expansive four-car garage, as the huge wrought iron gates slowly swung closed behind them.

"You can just pull the car into the garage, Dan. Welcome to our estate."

"It's stunning!" Chelly squeaked with delight. "And we've hardly seen anything yet. I can't wait to see inside."

"Follow me and I will show you around," Fran said. "If you like, you can leave your bags here for now, until you know where your suite is."

Dan and Chelly followed Fran through a doorway from the garage into a long hallway. They walked down the hallway past a laundry room and two large, separate washrooms for men and women. On the other side of the corridor, an open door revealed an enormous, well-equipped kitchen. It was filled with industrial-sized stainless steel appliances and expansive countertops and work areas. Dan looked at Chelly, who was awed by the spectacular kitchen that was clearly capable of catering to the needs of large gatherings.

Fran led them further into the building until they emerged from the hallway into a large open central area of the home. Dan was impressed by the expansive vaulted ceilings, heavy wooden beams, and wood ceilings of the home's Mission architectural style.

"I love the architecture, Fran," Dan said. "I usually find the Mission style has a heavy, dark feeling. But whoever designed your home opened it up with all these windows. It's so light and bright,"

Through those windows, Chelly saw the large custom-designed swimming pool for the first time.

"Look at that pool!" Chelly exclaimed. "I know you told me it was big, Dan. But this is amazing."

The pool had an oval-shaped central area with a long narrow arm coming off one side that was designed for swimming longer distances. A waterfall cascaded gently into the pool from a large berm at the far end of the pool's narrow arm. The landscaped grounds sloped downward from the pool and out of sight, revealing a breathtaking panoramic view northward and eastward over the entire Coachella Valley.

"You are very observant, Dan," Fran said. "We wanted an open and spacious feeling to balance the warmth of the wood and the

Mission style. Before us, you see the large, open living area. We have a number of conversation areas spread through the room so we can easily entertain many clients and business associates. To your left, you can see our dining room, also in the Mission style, but we opened up the side overlooking the yard with wall-to-wall glass to keep it bright."

Dan's eyes roamed to the remaining two walls of the immense room, which were tastefully decorated by a few carefully selected paintings, as well as sculptures and ceramics that were either displayed on pedestals, or carefully placed on top of buffets or tables. The pieces of furniture were all modern variations on the Mission style. Rather than being crafted from large, heavy pieces of wood, each piece of furniture was crafted from smaller, slimmer pieces of lumber. They were stained with medium tones that gave them a lighter, warmer, and more pleasing appearance than heavier, more traditional Mission furniture.

"This is beautiful," Dan exclaimed. "You've done a great job of creating the mood you wanted." He was turning his body to take in the areas behind him, when he noticed a number of black and white photographs carefully spaced on the walls.

"Are those more of your work, Fran?" he inquired. "They're just as beautiful as the ones back at Chateau Eden."

"Thank you," Fran replied. "Philippe and I chose some of my best portraits for that wall. We change them occasionally to give us some variety."

Dan was particularly attracted to one of the photographs. It was a portrait of a homeless woman on an urban street, staring blankly into Fran's camera. There was a mixture of emotions in the woman's eyes. There was much loneliness and despair. But Dan also saw that the photo was snapped at the exact moment that the woman realized she was being photographed. He noted that the woman's eyes were opening wider, as though she was afraid of whatever she was seeing.

"What about this one, Fran?" Dan asked. "Where did you take this?"

"In Los Angeles," Fran answered. "One day when Philippe was doing business with some customers, I took my camera into the city for the day. This woman was doing some begging, but was mostly just sitting and watching the world around her. There was something about her that was different from the other homeless people. I do not know what it was, but it was in her eyes. She seemed observant and intelligent. She was dressed like the others, but she did not seem to belong there. It seemed to me that she might be hiding from the rest of the world. On one hand, she seemed to be longing to be somewhere else. On the other, she also seemed afraid to be anywhere else."

"That's incredible. That's what I see too," Dan agreed. "Your eye is drawn to the photograph because of the dissonance between the setting and what you see in her eyes. But it's so beautiful because of that dynamic," he added.

"Oh, look!" Chelly exclaimed, as she poked her head in one of the doors along the back wall of the living area. "There's an art gallery in this room." The room was behind a short expanse of glass that interrupted the rear wall, and appeared to be a quiet place where people could sit to view the art, or perhaps just sit and read.

"Yes, rather than having a library like many older homes, we decided a small gallery with some of our nicer pieces would be more appropriate for us."

"It's a beautiful idea," Dan said. "What's the other door next to that hallway over there?"

"That is Philippe's home theatre," Fran answered. "He enjoys films and wanted to have a nice theatre space where he could watch them in the comfort of our home." Dan noticed Fran was afraid to make eye contact again. He wondered why she was suddenly more anxious.

"What's in the wings on both sides of the pool and patio?" Chelly asked. She was on the other side of the living space, gazing out the window overlooking the pool area and back gardens.

"The wing on the left has our master suite and Philippe's office," Fran answered. "The wing on the right has two guest suites. You will be sleeping in the one at the far end. It has windows overlooking the valley, the pool, and the rest of the grounds. Would you like me to show you to your room now?" Fran asked.

"Oh, I can't wait!" Chelly squealed, unable to conceal her delight. "This is so beautiful!"

Fran led them down a hallway, which was entirely glass on the left side, facing the pool. There were two doors at the end of the hallway.

"The other smaller guest suite is on your right. The one on the left is yours," Fran said. She swung open the door to a large bright guest suite that also had the Mission style vaulted ceiling. Unlike the modern European look that Fran had given their room at Chateau Eden, this room continued the modern Mission theme of the rest of the house, but was bright, airy, and relaxing.

Chelly walked into the bathroom, decorated with marble floors, a large Jacuzzi, and a large glass-walled shower enclosure with showerheads that could spray the occupant with water from all sides.

"This is so luxurious," Chelly sighed. "Thank you again for taking us in this week!"

"Please do not mention it," Fran replied. Once again, Dan briefly noticed her looking away from Chelly and avoiding eye contact. As he gazed over the valley from the bedroom window, he detected the corner of a large two-story shed on the property beside the estate.

"What's that larger building beside the house?" he asked.

"That is Philippe's studio," Fran said. Her reply was curt, and once again she was avoiding eye contact. "He does some photography and film work out there in his free time."

Fran quickly changed the subject. "Would you two like to go outside and see the pool and spa?" she continued.

"Oh, I'd love to!" Chelly said. She followed Fran through a sliding glass door, with Dan following closely behind.

"Here is the spa, just outside your room," Fran gestured with her hand. "And here is the pool, Dan. I hope you enjoy some nice long swims while you are here. Tonight, after Philippe is home, perhaps we can come out to the spa, share some wine, and enjoy the view. The grounds and the waterfall are illuminated and it is really quite beautiful out here in the evening. Would you like that?" she asked.

"We'd love to," Dan said, looking to Chelly for confirmation.

"Please feel free to go without clothing when you are outside on the patio, in the pool, or in the spa, just as you would at Chateau Eden," Fran explained. "The grounds are quite private, since we are the highest property on the mountain. We only ask that you cover up in the house just as you did at the Chateau."

"Oh, I almost forgot," she continued. "I have prepared a light dinner with some cold wraps and salad. It has been a busy day and Philippe will not be able to cook dinner tonight. I hope that will be enough for you," she apologized.

"Definitely," Chelly replied. "But you don't have to feed us while we're here. We can go out to restaurants. We'd also like to take you and Philippe out for a meal some night this week - just to say thank you. Would that be alright?"

Dan caught a glimpse of panic in Fran's eyes before she answered.

"Oh, we do not mind at all!" Fran replied quickly. "Philippe loves to cook for guests. He does not often get a chance, and he is an incredible chef! He would be offended if you did not let him cook the dinners this week!" she added.

"That's kind of him," Dan said. "Let us know if it's a problem, because we don't mind eating out. We would have been going out to restaurants every night if we'd been staying at the Chateau."

"It is Philippe's pleasure," Fran repeated. "Just be sure you tell him if you have any food allergies. Do you have any more questions?" she asked.

"I don't think so," Dan said. Chelly nodded her agreement. "I think I'll go back to the car and carry the bags in now."

It took two trips for Dan to finish moving their luggage to the guest suite. Fran was showing Chelly the master suite in the other wing when Dan put down the last bag and looked out the window to survey the estate. There was no doubt that the home and the grounds were beautiful. But Dan continued to have an unsettled feeling in his guts.

I wonder what's wrong with Fran today? She seems really nervous and distant.

His eyes were drawn repeatedly to the ominous ten-foot barrier with the razor wire that surrounded the property. It was dark when he had been here last November, and he hadn't noticed the wall at all. In the daylight, however, it felt ominous.

Somehow, things didn't feel quite as idyllic here as they seemed to be. He couldn't put his finger on it, but something just didn't feel right. His eyes returned to the wall again and he found himself having a random thought.

It must be just as hard to get out of this place, as it is to break in. It's a good thing we can open that gate from the inside.

Dan turned his attention to the inviting waters of the swimming pool. He decided to get naked and try it out. *I need a good swim to clear my mind,* he thought. *I'm just being paranoid. And I need to relax and have a good time with Chelly this week. This place will be really good for us. Nice and isolated. No distractions.*

He walked out onto the pool deck, with only his towel over his shoulder and his flip-flops on his feet. The stamped concrete pool deck seared his feet as he kicked off the flip-flops. He quickly walked down the steps into the oval shaped area of the pool. He felt the refreshing water over his entire body as he let himself slip under the surface of the water. Then he surfaced and started swimming towards the end of the long arm of the pool. Dan's body was reluctant to do as his brain initially instructed, but his muscles started to loosen up gradually and his stroke became smoother after one or two laps. He tried to relax his mind, but the nagging feeling in the pit of Dan's stomach just wouldn't leave.

What could possibly be wrong? Maybe it's just the arguments I've had with Chelly, he thought. Then Dan remembered his intimate encounter with Fran yesterday. He started feeling ashamed of his unexpected attraction to his host. *How can I want to make things right with Chelly, but also feel attracted to Fran at the same time?* He asked himself.

He tried with little success to just swim and let his mind relax. Something continued to bother him. This wasn't just about the arguments with Chelly or his encounter with Fran. Something was trying to warn him that the recent arguments with Chelly were the least of his problems.

Dan's arms continued to pull him swiftly through the water while he gathered his thoughts. He finally came to a resolution.

Chelly and I have a week together here in paradise before we have to go home. Stop worrying about what happened with Fran. It was just one of those awkward moments. Stop being so paranoid! He said to himself.

But, short of being a fortune-teller, Dan had no way of knowing that fate was conspiring to tear down the walls of his organized, responsible, and predictable world.

PART TWO: THE END OF INNOCENCE

CHAPTER 13

TEN-YEAR-OLD Philippe Morel sat at a table in the kitchen of his parent's opulent home, situated on a nine-hectare country estate outside Paris. He was carefully sketching the middle age woman who was cooking dinner for him. The massive house was empty on this April afternoon, apart from Philippe and his nanny, Isabelle. Philippe's hand slowed to a stop. He gazed through the kitchen door at the empty dining room where his parents, Christian and Hélène, so often entertained his father's business associates and prospective clients. He conjured images of those gatherings, when he was usually paraded into the room at the beginning of the evening, and presented to the guests as if he were a little trophy. He imagined his parents embracing and greeting guests with the customary kiss to each cheek, and he saw himself shaking hands with the important guests, as he had been instructed to do by his parents. He saw his immaculately dressed mother warmly charming the guests, while his father watched his dutiful trophy-wife with approval.

Philippe's resentment grew with each image of his parent's warm and charming behavior towards their guests. He resented that they spent more time entertaining guests than they did with him. He resented each warm embrace that the guests received. It was more than he ever got from Christian and Hélène Morel. He resented that his parents were so frequently away from home, leaving him in the lonely, empty house, with only Isabelle to keep him company.

As the CEO of a major French bank, Christian Morel often travelled to the major cities of France and Europe for business.

When it suited her, Hélène accompanied her husband on those trips. When it didn't suit her, she often elected to take extended vacations, spending time on the Riviera or on the couple's yacht, socializing and meeting friends at exotic Mediterranean and Adriatic ports. While she was warm and charming with her friends and with Christian's associates, Philippe despised that his mother was so cold and distant towards both himself and his father.

Philippe brought his mind back to his pencil-sketch and looked up at Isabelle. He tried his best to capture the warmth of her constant smile, the gentle curves of her middle-age figure, and the flowing red hair that brushed gently over her shoulders.

Isabelle had been a teacher when she was young, before she married. Her husband, Pièrre, had been a miserable, controlling alcoholic. He forced her to stop teaching after they married, even though the couple had no children and there was no need for her to remain at home. He did his best to isolate Isabelle from her family and former friends. She had loved teaching children, and she was devastated when she discovered she was unable to bear children of her own.

Isabelle gained her freedom at the age of thirty when Pièrre inevitably wrapped his Renault around a hydro pole after one of his late-night drinking binges. Needing to find employment, she focused on looking for situations where she could satisfy her urge for working with children. Her search led her to reply to Christian and Hélène's advertisement for a nanny for their infant son. She bonded instantly with the infant Philippe, and the two had been like mother and son ever since.

"Isabelle," Philippe said, looking up from his drawing. "Can we do some reading when you are finished? I'm tired of sketching."

"Not this afternoon, my little man. I must do some laundry before your *maman* and *papa* come home tomorrow. What will they say if I send you to school in dirty clothes?"

"They won't even notice," Philippe answered. "They never do. When are you going to take me to the Louvre? You promised."

"We must wait for the next time your parents are away. Perhaps I can tell them you were ill for a day and had to miss school. You and I will get up early, make a picnic lunch, and take the train to Paris. We will have the whole day to ourselves for our adventure. It will be our secret! Would you like that?"

"You promise?" Philippe shouted. He grabbed Isabelle's hands and the couple danced around each other. "I can't wait! Merci, Isabelle. I love you!"

"Okay, okay. Now go back to your drawing and let me get back to my work."

Philippe sketched a few strokes, and then put down his pencil. "May I go out and help Henri until dinner time?"

"*Oui*," she replied. "But make sure you are back by six o'clock for dinner."

"I will. *Merci*!" Philippe shouted. He ran to Isabelle and threw his arms around her neck, giving her a giant hug. Then he sprinted out the back door into the gardens surrounding the estate, the door slamming behind him.

Isabelle marveled at Philippe as he disappeared out the door. *That boy's thirst for knowledge is unquenchable. If he is not reading, he wants to learn how to draw or paint or take photographs. Or he wants Henri to teach him about gardening and nature. I must plan to take him into Paris more often. There are so many wonderful places in the city for us to explore together, and for him to learn.*

Out in the yard, Philippe scanned the gardens behind the estate. "Henri! Henri! Where are you?" he shouted. Henri was nowhere to be seen. He stood perfectly still and listened. Soon he heard the cracking of twigs and branches in the distance.

The woodlot, he said to himself.

Philippe dashed towards the grove of trees at the rear of the property. The cracking sound grew louder as he reached the first trees, and it wasn't long before he saw a grey-haired man in overalls and a heavy red felt shirt, hard at work in the woodlot.

The elderly man was dragging deadwood into a pile of brush behind the small wooden cottage he inhabited between April and October each year. It was early April and the leaves were not yet out on the trees. Henri was just getting started on cleaning up the vast amount of last year's growth from all over the estate, including the trees that had fallen in the woodlot over the winter. It was an unusually warm day for April, even in the partial shade of the woodlot. Sweat was running down the old man's forehead and dripping off the end of his nose.

"Henri! It's me, Philippe! Can I help?" the boy shouted, running towards the man. Henri put his large, calloused, dirty hands on the boy's shoulders, surveying him from top to bottom.

"My word! How you've grown over the winter. I almost did not recognize you, *mon ami*.

"Isabelle says I've grown three centimeters since last summer!" Philippe boasted.

"Before we know it, you will be a handsome young man," Henri observed. "You must have many girlfriends at school now, *c'est vrai*?" he teased.

"*Non!*" Philippe exclaimed. "All they do is talk about their clothes, their hair, and kissing boys! They are just little girls, not like Isabelle. Isabelle teaches me about grownup things like history and music and art! She is *my* girlfriend!"

"Ah, I see," Henri replied. "Well, until those little girls grow, up you can spend as much time as you like with Isabelle and me. You may come out to visit me in the woods anytime. We can listen to the birds singing, or watch the birds and animals in the woods."

"Look over there," he whispered, as he put his arm around the boy's shoulder. "Do you see those two pheasants strutting about? The brightly-colored one is the male and the brown one is the female."

As Philippe and Henri watched, the male pheasant mounted the female, completing their courtship ritual.

"What are they doing?" Philippe asked innocently. "Are they fighting?"

"*Non*, Philippe," Henri laughed. "They are mating. They are coming together to make babies, just like your *maman* and *papa* came together to make you! Have your parents not told you about the birds and the bees yet?"

Philippe gave Henri a puzzled look, and then looked back at the colorful male atop the female. She had become quiet and passive, accepting her mate's advances.

"*Non. Maman* and *papa* never talk with me. What does this have to do with bees?" the confused boy asked.

Henri smiled and laughed, then patted the boy on the backside.

"Come back to my cottage. I think I have some soda. I will tell you all about it. What do you say?"

"Isabelle doesn't allow me to have soda. She says it will rot my teeth. And it is almost dinner time. She'll be angry with me if I spoil my dinner!"

"Well, we do not have to tell Isabelle everything, do we? It can be our little secret. You may visit me any time and I promise I will have soda for you. How would you like that?"

"You promise you won't tell Isabelle or my parents?" Philippe insisted.

"On my honor," Henri promised, raising his right hand as an oath. "Let's hurry back to my cottage so you are not late for dinner."

The older man put his arm around Philippe's shoulder once more, smiling as he guided the boy back towards the small cottage. Philippe loved that the older man was willing to take time to explain things to him. The warm touch of the man's arm on his shoulder gave him a feeling of closeness he only ever felt with Isabelle. He felt special because the older man was willing to share his soda with him, and because they would share their secret together. Philippe wore a broad smile on his face as the pair walked together towards the privacy of the secluded cottage.

SITTING ALONE in his bedroom two years later, shortly after his twelfth birthday, Philippe was confused. He tried to remember when he began hating Henri. On one hand, there was a part of him that still felt needed and accepted by the old gardener, and still wanted to admire him. But that part of his identity had learned how to erect walls in his mind to block out the molestation. The walls helped turn his memories of the past two years of Henri's abuse, and his feelings of fear, disgust, shame, and self-loathing, into little more than dark shadows in the recesses of his mind. The walls helped him to forget and to endure each day. Yet there was no part of Philippe that was strong enough to stop himself from sneaking out of the house to continue meeting Henri again and again at the cottage.

He had grown more somber and depressed over time. His grades had fallen in school and he was more withdrawn. He had overheard Isabelle talking with *maman* and *papa*, expressing her concerns to them.

"There is something wrong with the boy. He is not his normal, happy self. Please take him to talk to somebody," she had pleaded.

"Nonsense!" his *papa* answered. "The boy just needs to stop daydreaming about art and start applying himself! There is no need to take him anywhere."

Philippe was also struggling with his hatred. He remembered Isabelle wagging her finger at him when he talked back to her. He recalled her scolding him when he became angry.

"Those who are angry are seldom content, Philippe. Remember that! You are too good a person to be angry," she said.

Not wanting to disappoint Isabelle, and not wanting to feel the rage that was slowly coming to a boil inside him, Philippe managed to push his anger behind barricades within his mind. But as his rage slowly approached the boiling point over time, Philippe was struggling to find ways to keep all of the painful emotions from flooding out from behind his dissociative barriers.

Nightmares of dark memories from the past two years flashed through his mind every night.

Two pheasants mating in the woodlot. A bottle of soda.

Just our little secret. More soda. Henri drinking from a bottle of wine.

Just touch it gently. See how it grows? Another bottle of soda. More wine.

Remember. Nobody must know our secret! More soda.

Horrible tastes. Horrible pain. Humiliation.

Here, boy! Have some soda, and get me some more wine.

Don't ever tell me you don't want to do it anymore. What would your maman and papa say? What would the boys at school say? What would your precious Isabelle say? Have another soda and do as I say you little prick!

Henri passing out from drinking wine.

Sneaking back into the house on the fire escape. Climbing into his own bed. Shaking with fear and pain.

Helpless. Unable to see any light in the dark shadows.
More nightmares.

Images of maman drinking wine with papa's guests. Reaching into her purse for a small pill and washing it down with more wine. Maman passing out on the floor in front of the guests.

Philippe woke suddenly. He blinked, feeling confused, trying to make sense of what had brought him back into the present. Then it came to him. A bottle of wine. Little white pills. A dark, shadowy figure toppling to the ground. A small light flickered in the darkness. Philippe smiled to himself for the first time in almost two years. A feeling of hope washed over him. The images became clear and the light became brighter. His brain started working out the details of a plan, and a feeling of peace came over him in his dream. There were no more nightmares this night. He rolled over, closed his eyes, and fell into a deep sleep.

THE FOLLOWING day was Saturday, and *maman* and *papa* were due to arrive home later in the day. For the first time in months, Philippe was out of bed at dawn, long before Isabelle had to come and waken him. He went over his plan again, making sure he remembered the details.

Philippe went to work quickly. He dressed in the clothing he had worn the previous day, leaving only socks on his feet. Then, he crept quietly downstairs to the laundry room to look for a pair of Isabelle's rubber gloves. After locating a pair of light blue laundry gloves, he made his way silently back upstairs and down the hallway to his mother's empty bathroom. Philippe searched through her medicine cabinet until he found some almost-empty bottles of old prescriptions. He carefully read the labels until he found what he was looking for. With surprisingly nimble fingers, he opened the two bottles while still wearing the rubber gloves. He removed one glove and poured four blue Xanax tablets into his palm, followed by four yellow Valium tablets. He pocketed the eight small pills, wiggled his hand back into the glove, and then slipped out of the bathroom. He crept quickly down the long staircase to the main floor. Moving stealthily, he entered the kitchen, opened a drawer and retrieved a corkscrew, making barely any sound in the process.

Philippe made his way to the doorway to *papa's* wine cellar, opening the door then cautiously closing it behind him. He turned on the light and scampered down the stairs to the racks of vintage wines. The cellar before him was lined with racks of wine on three sides: the wall in front of him and both sidewalls. In addition, there were three rows of similar racks, parallel to the two sidewalls. To Philippe, it looked like a library, except that bottles of wine took the place of musty old books. The wines were first sorted by type and then by year.

He scanned the racks for anything that was older - something that might be one of *papa's* favorites - something he was more likely to miss. His eyes caught a label with the year 1956 embossed on it - a *Chateau Laffite Rothschild Pauillac*. The label looked grandiose and expensive. Philippe lifted the bottle carefully off the rack, unwrapped the lead foil from around the neck, slipped the foil in his pocket, and then went to work with the corkscrew, extracting the cork from the bottle.

Philippe carried the bottle from the wine cellar to the utility room where he found an old washtub. He poured a few milliliters of wine from the bottle, carefully washing it down the drain with water. Suddenly he froze. The musty old ceiling joists creaked overhead. His chest tightened and his heart began racing as he listened. Then the old house fell silent again. *It's just the house creaking,* he thought. *Hurry, there is little time!*

He jumped back into action, reaching into his pockets for the eight small tablets, dropping four of each color into the bottle of wine. He pressed the cork back into the bottle and swirled the liquid impatiently for a minute or two, until he was satisfied that the pills were dissolving.

Philippe carefully climbed the stairs from the cellar, carrying the bottle of wine with him. He turned out the light, and then slowly opened the door a crack. He looked and listened to make sure Isabelle was nowhere near. When he was sure the way was clear, he scurried back into the kitchen, where he returned the corkscrew to its drawer. Then, quickly and silently, he hopped back up the stairs in his socks, passing dangerously close to Isabelle's bedroom suite, then slipping unobserved into his own room.

Philippe's body sagged against his bedroom door, letting the air escape from his lungs in a long, slow sigh of short-lived relief. There was much more to do and no time to relax yet. With a renewed sense of energy, he hid the bottle and the piece of lead foil in a paper bag at the back of his closet, and then quickly peeled the rubber gloves from his sweaty hands. He changed into fresh clothes, gathered up his dirty clothes and the rubber gloves, then slid silently back down the stairs to the laundry room, where he threw the dirty clothes in the dirty laundry, then replaced the gloves where he found them.

Suddenly, he heard movement upstairs. This time, it was the sound of human footsteps.

Isabelle!

He heard the door to Isabelle's suite open, recognizing her footsteps descending the staircase. Philippe scampered back into the kitchen, sliding to a stop in his socks in front of the refrigerator. He threw open the door and stuck his head inside. As Isabelle entered the room, she saw Philippe pulling a bottle of juice and a grapefruit from the refrigerator.

"My Lord, Philippe! What has possessed you today? This is the earliest you've been out of bed in months."

"The birds woke me up," he lied. "I couldn't sleep anymore, so I came downstairs for some food."

"Well, drink up your juice, take a croissant and run along. I'll make you a big breakfast. Then we must get this house cleaned up before your *maman* and *papa* return this afternoon. I'll call you when it is ready. Run along, now!"

Philippe let another long sigh escape as he left the kitchen. He cursed himself for almost allowing himself to get caught. But everything was in place now. He smiled a sinister smile, feeling a growing sense of confidence as he looked forward to executing the final part of his plan.

The part of Philippe that loathed Henri so much - the angry part that he had managed to push behind the walls in his mind for so long - was starting to emerge from the dark shadows, growing larger by the moment. As it did, he saw a blur of images from the past - images of the old man, then images of bottles of wine and soda. Soon all of the other painful emotions were also pouring out - fear, sadness, helplessness, and loneliness - until he could no longer contain them all. The angry part of Philippe screamed out silently over all the other parts of his being.

Nothing will stop me now! Nothing!

AFTER SCHOOL on Monday, Philippe took his schoolbooks up to his bedroom, and then came down to the kitchen, as usual, to have a snack with Isabelle. He was less talkative than usual, choking his food down quickly and nervously.

"May I take a walk through the woods and visit Henri for a while before dinner? I have almost no homework tonight."

"Okay," Isabelle said. "Be back by seven o'clock, though. Remember, your parents are home and dinner must be served on time. Please don't keep them waiting."

"I'll be back by then. I promise," Philippe said, with little emotion showing in his voice.

He slipped out the back door, then walked slowly along the path that wound its way through the gardens to the rear of the property, looking furtively over his shoulder to make sure nobody was watching. He lifted the top from a decorative Japanese-style urn in the garden, grabbing the brown paper bag and a large stone he had carefully concealed there the previous night. Moving quickly, he stopped by the fishpond and placed the large stone underwater, just inside the pond wall. Finally, he ambled the short distance to Henri's cottage, brown bag in hand, stopping in front of the cottage's weathered door. He slowed his breathing, feeling the pounding of his heart straining against his painfully tight chest. He steeled himself, and then knocked with three distinct, slow knocks.

"*Entrez*!" Henri's surly voice growled from inside the cottage.

Philippe's hands were clammy as he turned the handle to open the door. The old man's form was a shadow in the back of the darkened cottage. The dark silhouette of a wine bottle was raised to his lips.

"Wha's in the bag?" Henri demanded, his voice already slurred from wine.

"I …I brought you something," Philippe stammered. "It was left after *papa's* last business dinner. I thought you might like it.

It's expensive. They had already opened it, and they were going to waste it."

"A gift from my young friend, eh? On the table," he ordered. "So what other gifts do you bring me today? What else can you do to please me?"

Philippe felt his entire body shudder in response to the question. He struggled to keep his composure and searched for the right words.

"Whatever pleases you, Henri. You know I only want to make you happy."

"Of course you do, boy!" Henri answered gruffly. "*Venez ici!*"

Philippe felt the mask descending over his face. To Henri, he always appeared willing, submissive, and almost loving. On the inside, he struggled to keep the rage and revulsion from flooding out from behind his invisible mask. His body moved mechanically toward the old man, his movements, his actions, and the painful emotions all hidden precariously behind the walls that he had built in his mind over the past two years.

One last time, he told himself. *Then never again!*

"MAMAN AND PAPA. May I please be excused? I need to study for my history exam."

"Of course, Philippe," *Maman* replied. "You will come and say goodnight to us before you go to bed?"

"Yes, *Maman.*"

"Run along then," she replied, her hand waving him away dismissively.

Philippe climbed the staircase to the second floor and his bedroom, closing the door behind him. He looked out the window, confirming that it was dusk. He opened his history textbook and left it on his desk. Philippe went to his closet and reached inside for the large torch that he had concealed under some shirts. He pulled a pair of gumboots from the back of the closet. The boots were clean and shiny. He slid his stocking feet into them, and then carefully slid the window upwards enough to make an opening through which he could squeeze his young body. The window squeaked loudly in it's casing.

Merde! He cursed silently.

His heart pounded, his muscles tensed, and he held his breath. He paused and listened carefully to see if Isabelle or his parents had heard the loud squeak. He counted slowly and silently to himself as he waited.

... 14 ... 15 ... 16 ... 17 ... 18 ... 19 ... 20.

After what seemed like an eternity without any sound, Philippe took a slow, deep breath and began moving again. He squeezed carefully through the open window, maneuvering his feet onto the fire ladder outside. Once his feet were firmly planted, he started moving deliberately. He scampered down the ladder and stepped into the shadows, moving under the cover of bushes, flowerbeds, and darkness. Philippe didn't turn on his torch. His eyes gradually adjusted to the darkness as he dashed furtively from bush to bush, making his way slowly towards Henri's cottage. Finally, he stood before the door. His heart was pounding with fear, but he was now driven by a purpose. He sucked in a deep breath, and then knocked timidly on the door.

No response.

He knocked three more times, louder and more deliberately this time. *Still nothing.* He looked around, took a deep breath, and then gave three more loud knocks.

"Who izh it?" Henri mumbled, his words heavily slurred.

Philippe turned the handle and pushed the door open. He peered into the cottage's single room. Henri was sprawled on the floor, his back propped up against a large stuffed chair in the corner. His head drooped and rolled from shoulder to shoulder, as he tried unsuccessfully to look up at Philippe.

Philippe nodded to himself with satisfaction as he watched Henri struggle to stay conscious. *The wine and pills are doing their job.*

"Huh … what …?" Henri mumbled to Philippe, trying without success to make sense of the situation.

"There is some kind of large animal roaming around in the woods, Henri! Down near the fishpond. It was howling. Did you hear it?"

Henri's eyes narrowed. His brain churned slowly.

"*Non*," he replied, struggling to find even that single word.

Philippe knew he had to work quickly. If Henri passed out, he would never be able to move him. He looked around the room, spotting the empty wine bottle on the table. He removed the last four of *maman's* pills and the previously removed lead foil from a small plastic bag, then scattered them on the table beside the bottle. He turned his attention back to Henri.

"Come, Henri. You must come and listen. *Papa* and *maman* will not be happy if they knew you didn't take a look."

He took Henri by the arms and pulled with all of his strength. Henri didn't budge.

"Come on, Henri. You must help me. Try to stand and I'll pull your arms. Ready? *Un, deux, trois* …"

Henri leaned forward and struggled to get to his knees, but his legs buckled as he tried to stand.

Philippe felt desperation and panic setting in.

"Come on, Henri. Try again. You're almost there!" he pleaded. Once again he counted to three, summoning his body's adrenaline to pull mightily on Henri's arms. This time the old man wobbled to his feet. Philippe moved quickly to put his arm around Henri's waist. Then, he put Henri's arm around his own shoulders to support the old man. They took a tentative step forward, and Henri lost his balance. Philippe's knees threatened to buckle. It took every ounce of his strength to hold himself upright, stabilizing the old man as he did so. They took two more steps. Henri seemed to find his legs enough to remain steady. Cautiously, Philippe helped Henri through the door onto the cottage's porch. He made sure to leave the door slightly ajar.

"Be careful on the steps," Philippe said. "One foot at a time, Henri. You can do it. Put your hand on the railing. Good. One more step. There, you did it!"

It felt to Philippe like it took forever to help the old man down the two small steps onto solid ground.

"Did you hear that? I heard something growling," he said to Henri. The old man tried to listen. A puzzled expression came over his face, when all he could hear were the usual sounds of the night.

"Come on," Philippe urged. "It's not far to the fish pond. We'll hear it better there. Just lean on me." Philippe kept to the crushed gravel path that led from the woodlot onto the lawns of the estate. He knew they would leave few traces on the dry gravel. Step, by agonizing step, he helped Henri cover the thirty meters to the fishpond. Philippe's mind was racing.

What if he falls? What if somebody sees us from the house?

The night was clear, and the crescent moon provided enough light for them to see the path, yet not enough to for others to see them unless they were watching closely. Philippe was thankful that he didn't need to use his torch.

It seemed like an eternity before Philippe and Henri finally reached the pond. It was surrounded by a low concrete wall, only about thirty centimeters high.

" … hear nothing." Henri mumbled.

"Look, Henri. Over there! On the far side of the pond! Move closer to the wall!" Philippe said, in an urgent whisper. He guided Henri to the edge of the pond, removed his arms from around Henri's waist, removed the old man's arm from around his own shoulder, and then pointed out into the darkness.

The old man tottered precariously on unsteady legs, looking bewildered. He strained his eyes to look beyond the pond, to the deserted lawns of the estate. He looked even more bewildered when he heard the sound of twelve-year-old feet running at him from behind, followed by silence as Philippe launched himself at Henri's back. Henri tumbled forward, tripping over the short wall of the pond and lurching headfirst towards the water. The last thing Henri would see was a dark shape rushing towards him, on a collision course with his head.

Philippe grabbed for the stone that he had hidden in the pond that afternoon on his way to Henri's cottage. He raised it over his head, ready to smash it down on Henri's head. But the old man did not move. Philippe waded further into the shallow water in his gumboots and nudged the body with his foot.

Nothing, Philippe thought.

Henri remained motionless, face down in the water. Only then did Philippe notice that the old man's head was resting against a large, jagged rock in the pond. In the dim moonlight, he thought he saw blood trickling from Henri's scalp. Philippe stood, barely breathing, making sure Henri's face remained under water. After a few minutes, he knew it was over.

He climbed carefully over the wall and out of the pond. He stuffed the handle of his torch back into the pocket of his pants, and then picked up the large stone. He carried it back to the place in the garden from which he had taken it, and carefully set it back in place.

Philippe crept back towards the house, once again being careful to stay in the darkness behind bushes. He wiped the bottom of his boots in the grass as he walked, making sure there was no mud or dirt left on them. He reached the bottom of the fire ladder, and carefully removed his boots. He placed his torch in one boot, and then climbed the ladder, wearing only his socks on his feet. As he reached the top of the ladder, he slowed himself, and then stopped. He listened until he was satisfied that he heard nothing. He raised his head and quickly glanced around his room. His muscles were taught and he held his breath.

When Philippe saw that the door was still closed and the room was empty, he let out a sigh of relief. He reached through the window and placed his gumboots gently on the floor. Then, he scampered up the last couple of steps, squeezed back through the window, and quickly replaced the boots and torch in his closet. He looked at the open window, realizing he almost forgot to close it. He leapt into action, sliding it back down into the closed position. He stood beside the window, his heart pumping and his breathing still rapid.

Philippe started taking slow, deep breaths to calm him and to slow his racing heart. He was just beginning to feel relaxed when he heard footsteps, then a knock at his door. His body went rigid. His heart and breathing quickened again.

"Philippe, may I come in?" It was Isabelle.

"*Oui. Entrez*," he replied.

"You look flushed. How are your studies going?" she asked.

Philippe gathered his wits and took one more breath before answering.

"Very well," he replied calmly. "But I'm getting tired. I think I'll have a bath, then say goodnight to *maman* and *papa*."

"Good idea," she answered. "Just leave your dirty clothes outside the door in your basket and I'll put them in with the laundry. Have a good sleep, Philippe."

Isabelle put her arms around Philippe and embraced him as she kissed his cheek. They held themselves in a close embrace that lasted many more seconds than usual. Philippe felt her warm body and bosom pressing against him. He felt a stirring in his groin. Isabelle stepped away, a look of confusion on her face. Philippe's face turned crimson with embarrassment. Isabelle turned and left his room.

Philippe was exhilarated by the closeness of the embrace, and by the outcome of the night's events. He waited until he no longer heard any footsteps in the hallway. He went to his bureau and removed a pair of pajamas, brought the gum boots out of the closet, then pulled the door open a crack, enough to see the staircase and Isabelle's bedroom door. The way was clear. He quickly stepped out of his room and ran down the hallway to the bathroom, locking the door behind him. He leaned up against the door, once again slowing his racing heart and rapid breathing.

Philippe turned on the faucets and began filling the tub as he removed his clothing. He meticulously washed the gumboots to remove any remaining signs of dirt or dust, leaving them as shiny as they had been before he left the house. He dried them with a towel and stood them on the floor. When the tub was full, he climbed in and reclined. He immersed his body and let the hot water soothe his tense muscles.

Only then did a sinister smile start to appear on his lips. It spread slowly across his entire face. Then, a feeling of elation started spreading through his inner core. Everything had gone just as he planned.

It's over. I'm free!

There would be no more degradation and humiliation at the hands of Henri. An electric current of pride and power was now surging through his body. He looked down and saw himself becoming aroused. He started stroking the shaft of his growing penis. The pace of his strokes increased, becoming faster and faster until finally, his body went into spasm. The milky fluid spurted into the air, then splashed into the bath water, leaving the adolescent boy feeling spent and exhausted. An overwhelming sense of peace came over Philippe. At that moment, he made a pact with himself.

Never again will I be controlled by anybody else! It is I who will make sure that people do as I wish, just as I did with Henri tonight. And may God help anybody who gets in my way!

THAT NIGHT, for the first time in months, there were no nightmares. Philippe awoke Tuesday morning feeling refreshed and happy, ready to restart his life. He went to school as usual. Then, part way through the morning, *Maman* and *papa* came to the school with somber faces and took him out of class. Isabelle had found Henri. He had drowned in the fishpond. The police found one of *papa's* bottles of wine and some of *maman's* pills in Henri's cottage. He must have been stealing wine and pills from the house. He must have gone for a walk and passed out from the mixture of alcohol and drugs. Accidental overdose, they said. He fell into the pond and struck his head on a rock, then drowned in the shallow water. A tragic accident! Philippe made himself look sad. He forced tears to flow from his eyes.

The police file was closed. *Papa* and *maman* hired a new gardener and resumed their travels. Philippe became more confident and happy than ever before. He took more "sick days" from school when *maman* and *papa* were away. He and Isabelle spent those magical days visiting museums in Paris to study art and history, or to watch the artists and people along the banks of the Seine. Philippe practiced sketching the sights of Paris, using them as inspiration for paintings, and improving his skills as an artist.

The visits to Paris were their little secret. Isabelle and Philippe grew closer with each clandestine adventure they shared, and with every day they spent together in their mutual solitude in the Morel estate.

CHAPTER 14

PHILIPPE FELT inspired as he and Isabelle emerged from the *Galeries Nationales du Grand Palais*. Their day had started early on this crisp autumn morning, riding the train into Paris and jostling with the crowds who flocked into the city to earn their living. Unlike the multitudes of commuters who either were sleeping, reading, or wearing the blank stares of minds that were only half awake, Philippe was energized. He was full of anticipation for sharing another precious day in the city with Isabelle.

They had visited the museum together before. But Philippe was eager to see a new exhibition, *The Nude in Art History,* that had opened recently. Their previous visits to galleries in the city had introduced him to a variety of themes and historic styles, but Philippe quickly grew bored of drawing and painting landscapes or still-life objects. Instead, he wanted to embrace the challenge of capturing the essence of people in portraits. Now that he was fifteen, his interest in capturing the human figure was increasing in proportion to the levels of testosterone in his body.

"That was exquisite!" he exclaimed to Isabelle, sounding much more mature than his fifteen years. "Is there anything more majestic than the muscular physique of a man or the gentle, flowing curves of a woman? I so wish that I could paint like that!"

"You can do anything you set your mind to," Isabelle said. "Just look at how much your painting and photography have improved over the past two years. All you need now is more practice. Remember how frustrated you were with your landscapes two years ago? Then remember the many hours you spent, watching and talking to the other artists beside the Seine, then practicing what you learned."

"But this is different," he argued. "Renoir, LeBasque, Enjoiras, Patko and the others all had studios and models to pose for them. Before that, they studied the human figure in art classes with live models. Where am I going to do that? I can't wait until I'm eighteen. But *maman* and *papa* would never hear of it. Do you think they would let me be in the same room as a naked woman? They would only tell me to stop dreaming and wasting my time on art, like they always do!

Isabelle sighed, seeing the look of pain Philippe always showed when he was disappointed.

"I understand your frustration, Philippe. Perhaps we could ask them again to let you register in some art classes. We just wouldn't tell them any details. They've seen some of your work, and I think they were impressed by some of your landscapes, even if they won't admit it. They might give their approval."

Philippe was silent as he and Isabelle continued walking towards the *Champs Élysées*. He had a plan, but he was nervous. He needed to choose the right words for revealing it to Isabelle.

"Isabelle, you could help me hire a model to come to the estate when *maman* and *papa* are away. I have some money saved!" he added enthusiastically.

"Absolutely not, young man! I would lose my job if your parents knew I allowed a naked strangers into their home, and allowed a fifteen-year-old boy to be with her!"

Philippe's face turned into a pout, making sure Isabelle noticed. They walked on in silence as he considered how to sell the potential solution to his problem. After a few moments, Philippe looked at Isabelle and broke the silence.

"You could model for me. It would not be like I was drawing or painting a stranger. We know each other. We wouldn't have to bring anybody else into our home. Only you and I would know."

Isabelle's mouth dropped open. She was caught off guard completely by Philippe's suggestion. He saw her struggling with the dilemma. He knew she loved him and wanted to help him in any way she could. He also knew her sense of responsibility for taking care of him. But he knew she would have great difficulty saying no to him. He implored her with his eyes to help.

"Philippe, you must not ask me to do this. You know I would do almost anything for you. You are like a son to me. But it would not be proper for a grown woman to show herself to a boy your age! Your parents would never forgive me if they found out! There must be something else we can do."

Philippe's face turned into an even larger pout and his eyes continued to implore Isabelle to reconsider.

"Isabelle, please! I must learn to capture the human figure now. If I wait until I am eighteen, it is another three years! You are my only hope. I beg you. Please help me. You are such a beautiful person. I want to learn to capture all of your beauty in my paintings and photographs. It is the only way I can learn to take my art to a higher level. It would be our secret. Nobody else would ever know."

"I'll have to think about this carefully, Philippe. But enough for now! Let's find a nice place to eat our lunch. Then we can walk around and enjoy the beauty of the city on this wonderful autumn day. You can take some photos. Perhaps we can find some artists to observe or some galleries to explore. Come, we mustn't waste this beautiful day."

PHILIPPE WENT to his closet and brought down the carefully hidden box containing all of the photos and drawings he had made of Isabelle over the past few months. He looked with pride at the first nude busts of Isabelle. She had, of course, not been able to refuse him, and conceded to bare her breasts to see how his drawings and photographs turned out. He remembered the look of pride in her eyes when she looked at the fruits of their first collaboration - Philippe's first attempts at capturing her semi-nude figure.

"They are beautiful, Philippe!" she remarked, her voice and her eyes showing their sincerity and her pride in him. "I know you have talent, but these … They surpass anything I expected from you. I am so proud of you. You make this old matron look far more beautiful than I could ever be in real life!"

"Nonsense," he had replied. "You are the most beautiful woman in the world to me! Thank you so much for helping me, Isabelle." He remembered the gentle kiss he had planted on her cheek, and the warmth of her hands as she held his hands in hers. He remembered how easy it was to get her to take the next steps. He showed her books with photographs of some of the classic nude poses he wanted to attempt.

"Would you just try doing one?" he said. "Perhaps just sitting by a window reading a book, or sitting by the fire so I can practice showing your curves with natural lighting."

Philippe looked at the full figure photos and drawings, not just with pride, but also with a sense of power and control. It had been so easy to manipulate Isabelle, once he understood her weaknesses. He saw the loneliness and longing in her eyes. He knew that he was the closest thing to a child that she would ever have. He knew how much pain it caused her to see him disappointed. It had been so easy to feign disappointment, to pout, and to look longingly at her like a small child or puppy, and to see her squirm with discomfort. He loved the feeling of victory he felt when she finally succumbed to his pleading.

He felt his full erection as he looked through the photos. He admired Isabelle's flowing red hair, her slightly freckled, alabaster skin, her full breasts, the gentle curves of her waist, the fullness of her thighs, and the roundness of her buttocks. Yet it wasn't the sight of her body that was arousing him. It was the power. It was the anticipation of the next step in exerting his will over Isabelle. He felt no anxiety or apprehension as he put down the photos on his desk. He closed his eyes to envision today's photo shoot in Isabelle's suite. His camera was already set up on his tripod, and the room was arranged to his liking. His thoughts were interrupted by a knock at his bedroom door.

He opened the door to see Isabelle standing in the hallway, wearing her slippers and a bathrobe. His eyes travelled to her hair. She had let it down from her usual matronly bun on the back of her head, so that her red hair flowed freely to her shoulders. In contrast to her simple bathrobe, her face was immaculately made up. He reached out to take her hand, guiding her back down the hallway to her suite.

"You look magnificent," Philippe exclaimed. "I've been looking forward so much to this afternoon. You were beautiful in the classical poses. But I can't wait to see you in some more contemporary and modern positions. How are you feeling?"

"I'm excited too," she replied. "I can't wait to see how this shoot turns out. I was so nervous the first few times I posed for you. But now, instead of fear, I'm thrilled to help you! I put the satin sheets on the bed, just liked you asked. They look elegant and romantic!"

Philippe smiled and nodded his approval as they walked into her room. He saw Isabelle's careful attention to the details he had asked her to prepare for their shoot. It was midday, and the white room, with its high cathedral ceiling, was brightly illuminated with an even midday light that reflected off the white furniture and every wall in the room. It created a space that was perfect for Philippe, who had no professional lights or reflectors to aid him. He had learned to use whatever natural lighting was available to him, and it had greatly enhanced his ability to see contrast and shading in his photographs and paintings.

"You've studied the types of poses I want?" Philippe inquired. "I want these to look modern and seductive. I want you looking at the lens as if it were your lover. Like you are doing a dance, seducing your lover to join you in bed. I want to see that on your face and in your eyes, Isabelle. Do you think you can act the role?"

Isabelle nodded in agreement and opened her robe, revealing her large breasts and Rubenesque figure. Her attention to detail did not stop with her makeup. Her red pubic hair was neatly trimmed and her toenails and fingernails carefully painted a deep red shade. Without a word, she climbed up onto the bed.

Philippe went to work. They started with some poses of Isabelle kneeling and sitting on the bed. Next, he asked her to lay on her back on the bed. He climbed a tall stepladder they had brought upstairs for the purpose, taking shots downward from the ladder. Isabelle's white skin blended with the white sheets, which were carefully placed and wrinkled to create shadows and texture. He used a diffusion filter over the lens to provide a soft, mysterious feeling to the images.

"That's good, but must look more seductive, Isabelle. Can you cross your arms in front of you, and then put your hands on your breasts. Make it look like you are caressing your breasts and nipples. That's right. Excellent. Now look at the camera. Let me see the desire in your eyes!"

Isabelle slipped into her role naturally. He saw the sensual, sexual Isabelle emerge. It was the part of her that had always craved the touch of a loving partner, and had always wanted children. He knew that those needs had been frustrated by her late husband. It was easy for that part of her to come alive. It took little effort from Philippe to encourage her sexuality to take over, and to live out the fantasy that he was creating through his lens.

"Wonderful, Isabelle. Now, can you let one hand lay on your private parts? Like you are pleasuring yourself and teasing your lover." He climbed down the ladder, pushing it aside. Then, he moved himself and the camera closer to the bed, taking a lower, more direct angle to look provocatively up Isabelle's legs at her genitals.

Isabelle paused momentarily to look at Philippe. He saw the responsible Isabelle wondering how far to go in front of him and the camera's lens. He felt that side of her trying to regain control. He countered it by appealing to Isabelle's unfulfilled romantic side, as well as to that loving part of her that couldn't stand to disappoint him. He spoke slowly, softly, and deliberately to her.

"You look absolutely beautiful, Isabelle. Show me what it is like for a woman who is in love. I want to see what you look like, how you move, and understand what you feel. Close your eyes. Imagine your lover taking you and making love to you. Don't disappoint me now!"

Isabelle closed her eyes. Her fingers began gently brushing her pubic hair, circling her outer labia. Gradually, the circles grew smaller, focusing on massaging her clitoris with light strokes. Her breathing quickened and Philippe sensed her arousal. He moved closer to the bed so that she was within his reach, leaving the camera unattended on its tripod. He spoke to her again.

"Isabelle. May I touch you? You are so beautiful. Show me how it feels."

He gently touched her hand and started guiding her movements. She opened her eyes, looking at him through eyes of romantic longing and loneliness. The responsible, motherly part of Isabelle was nowhere to be seen. Her body and mind had completely surrendered to her long-repressed feelings of loneliness, longing, and lust. She reached down with her free hand, took his hand, and then placed it gently over her vaginal area, showing his hand how she wanted it to move. She was moist and Philippe started to feel intoxicated with the power he felt over her. His erection returned, straining to find freedom from the confines of his clothing.

Isabelle's eyes found his growing manhood. She sat up and swung her legs over the side of the bed so that Philippe was standing between her legs. She slowly unzipped his pants and unhooked his rigid penis from beneath his underwear, lowering the clothing out of the way. He felt her hand close on the firmness of his shaft and he groaned. Then she gently stroked his length. She reached out and pulled his head towards hers, until their lips touched. Her tongue searched longingly for his and her lips pressed eagerly against his mouth. She stopped kissing him long enough to remove the rest of his clothing, and then helped him onto the bed.

The two lovers lay side-by-side, facing each other. Isabelle guided his hands, instructing him on how her womanhood felt and how it worked. Finally, she brought him close and guided him inside her. As he filled her up, he felt himself become engulfed by her warmth and softness. He felt the ecstasy as she continued to massage him and squeeze him from the inside with her vaginal muscles.

Philippe felt a surge of power and electricity shoot through him. It was exactly the same feeling he felt on that dark night three years ago, when Henri was laying outside in the fish pond, face down in the water - when Philippe was soaking in the bathtub, reliving the sense of power and control he had felt at ending Henri's life - the night he had taken back control of his own life.

Philippe ejaculated quickly. He read Isabelle's eyes as he felt himself pulsing rhythmically inside her. He realized that she was feeling the closest connection she had ever felt with another person before. It was all she had ever wanted and needed. And he knew she would need to feel this close again, despite the distant protests from her responsible side.

Isabelle looked up into Philippe's eyes.

"You know how much I love you, don't you," she said to Philippe. "I never want you to leave me."

"I need you too," Philippe replied. He was basking in the post-coital afterglow, and in an immense sensation of power, control, and grandiosity at that moment.

How can life get any better than this?

Philippe and Isabelle lay peacefully beside each other, his head nestled between her two large breasts. Neither one of them had a care in the world at that moment.

ISABELLE'S MIND was startled back into reality by the sound of angry, raised voices coming from downstairs. In the distance, she heard Hélène Morel's voice screaming her name. Helplessness and terror started spreading through her body. She had been lost in worry. She was almost two months pregnant and would start showing soon.

The cruel irony of her pregnancy had brought her to tears. It was the one thing she had always wanted most in this world. Now it had happened, and she had no idea what she was going to do. How could something she had wanted so much for all of her life, now be the cause of her ruin? Abortion was out of the question. If she left the Morels now, where would she go? Where would she work? How would she survive? She had nowhere to go. She felt completely trapped and helpless.

"Isabelle!" Hélène Morel screamed. "Get down here immediately!"

Isabelle descended the staircase slowly. Her footsteps felt like she was in a funeral procession. An ominous weight was bearing down on her shoulders. She shuffled dutifully into the sitting room, where her employer sat waiting impatiently. The cleaning woman, whose regular cleaning chores had taken her into Philippe's bedroom and closet today, was standing at attention beside her outraged employer. Hélène's face was scarlet, and her eyes and the veins in her neck were bulging. She was seething with anger. Her eyes felt like lasers to Isabelle, searing holes through her as she entered the room. On the coffee table before her sat an open box. Philippe's drawings and nude photographs of Isabelle were scattered all over the table and the floor.

"How could you!" she screamed at Isabelle. "After all these years! I thought we could trust you! You whore! You child molester! You are finished here. And I will make sure you never work anywhere with children again! I want you to pack your things and to be out of here tomorrow. Do I make myself clear, you bitch!"

Isabelle stared blankly at Philippe's mother. Only part of her mind was present. Another part deep inside was overcome with feelings of insurmountable shame and humiliation. And Hélène did not even know she was pregnant yet. Isabelle nodded blankly, turned, and then plodded from the room. She ascended the stairs to the second floor in a zombie-like trance. She was overwhelmed by a flood of loneliness, shame, sadness, and an incredible sense of hopelessness. She slowly closed the door to her suite behind her, feeling isolated and alone. It was more than she could bear.

PHILIPPE JUMPED out of the taxi that transported him too and from school each day, then burst excitedly through the estate's grand front entrance. In his book bag, he had an envelope with his most recently developed rolls of photographs, the ones showing him and Isabelle making love in various positions. He couldn't wait to get them upstairs so he could conceal them in his secret chest. He was stopped in his tracks by an angry scream from *maman* as he passed the entrance to the sitting room. His feet slid to a halt on the polished marble floor.

Philippe's eyes were drawn to the open box and the scattered photos and drawings. His eyes widened and a surge of terror ripped through his body, as he realized what was happening. At the same time, his senses were unconsciously aware of the distant scraping of furniture on a floor, somewhere else in the house.

"Philippe Morel!" his mother screamed. Her words were filled with venom. "You ungrateful little bastard. How could you do this to me? How could you do this to your *papa*? Do you have any idea what people will think of us now? When your father comes home tonight, you are going to show him this obscene pornography, and then you are going to burn each piece and the negatives, one by one, until we are certain they are all destroyed. Then, we are going to discuss sending you far away to a private school, where you can learn some discipline and responsibility, and start focusing on a serious education. With any luck, perhaps you can salvage yourself and become something respectable someday!"

Philippe had an unsettling feeling that something was terribly wrong. His mother's words registered with his inner ears, but his brain was preoccupied and wasn't processing the sounds.

"I want you to go upstairs and say goodbye to that tramp. She is leaving here tomorrow and you will never see her again! Do you understand?" she screamed.

Philippe was stunned as he stood in front of his mother. His mind was reeling. He felt his world coming unglued and quickly spiraling out of control. He felt weak and impotent, a feeling he had not experienced since the days of abuse from Henri. It was the feeling he vowed he would never feel again. The anger began to build inside him, gradually re-energizing his brain and muscles and bringing him back into the reality of the moment. His eyes burned at his mother and he finally found his voice.

"This is all your fault! You're nothing but a cold, selfish bitch! You've never been a mother to me. All you care about is yourself! Isabelle is the only person in the world who has ever cared for me. She may as well have been my mother, because she's a better person than you will ever be. If you send her away, I'll never forgive you!"

Philippe turned on his heels. His anger propelled him out of the room and up the stairway to the second floor. He went directly to Isabelle's door and knocked quietly.

"Isabelle, it's Philippe. May I please come in?" he whispered urgently.

There was no response. He waited for a moment, feeling impatient talk to her. He knocked again, this time more loudly.

"Isabelle! Open the door! I need to talk to you!" he pleaded. Still no response. He couldn't hear a sound from inside the room.

Philippe tried the handle, finding it unlocked. He opened the door a crack and peered in. Through the slight opening, he saw the chair from Isabelle's dressing table lying on its side on the floor. He threw the door open, fearing she had fallen and that he would find her lying helpless on the floor. He saw nothing on the floor except the misplaced chair. An irritating creaking sound emanated from the ceiling above him. He started to sense that something was wrong. Isabelle's dressing table was no longer against the far wall. It was standing directly in front of him at the foot of her bed. He remembered the distant sound of scraping furniture.

That damned creaking sound.

Suddenly, a chill ran through his entire body. His eyes lifted slowly upwards toward the high ceiling. An involuntary scream sucked the remaining air from his lungs. The grotesque image of Isabelle, her head swollen and purple, her eyes bulging from her head, her corpse hanging by a belt from the light fixture high above him, completely overwhelmed Philippe's senses.

Unable to process the flood of sensory and emotional input that he was experiencing at that moment, a barricade slammed shut in Philippe's brain. His mind went blank. He was enveloped by a merciful, numbing darkness as he collapsed to the floor.

CHAPTER 15

"CIAO, MAMMA!" Shouted ten-year-old Francesca Capellini. The wiry, dark haired young girl knew she was late. She ran into the restaurant and dropped her book bag to the floor.

"You're late, Francesca!" bellowed the harried-looking woman behind the restaurant's bar. "What took you so long to walk home from school? You know your sister is waiting for you so she can come to work! Hurry up!"

"I'm hungry, *mamma*. Can I have something to eat before I go?"

"You can find something to eat at your sister's," insisted the older woman. "Now hurry! I need her here right now. It's high tourist season and we'll be run off our feet tonight!"

"I don't like going there, *mamma*. Why can't Giulia find somebody else to babysit?" Francesca complained.

"Because you are family, you ungrateful girl! Family helps family. Someday you will need help with your babies, and you will be grateful for your family. You will see."

"I'm not having any babies!" Francesca insisted, stamping her foot and crossing her arms defiantly. "I don't even want to live here in Manarola. I want to move far away from this awful place and never come back!"

"Don't talk like that!" *mamma* shouted. "You should be happy that you have a good home and family. Why would you ever want to go away?"

"Because I don't have a good home or a good family!" Francesca shouted. "*Papa* is a God-damned drunk and hardly ever comes home. I don't even know him. You are always working at this damned restaurant. I never see you and you never spend any time with me! All I ever do is look after those crying babies. And I don't like being at their apartment. Paolo is creepy. I don't like him."

"Stop your cursing and don't talk about Paolo that way! He is family," *mamma* shouted. She crossed herself, as if apologizing for her daughter's insolence. "It's not my fault that your *papa* is a sailor. You have no idea how much I've had to sacrifice to raise you on my own for ten years, you self-centered brat! And Paolo is a good Christian man. He is like a father to you. I don't ever want to hear you saying bad things about him. Do you hear me?"

"Yes, *mamma*," Francesca mumbled. She bowed her head in defeat. She knew from experience it was useless to argue with *mamma*.

"Now off you go, girl!" *mamma* insisted. "Don't forget to take your books with you. Go!"

Francesca picked up her book bag and slung it over her young shoulders. She grabbed a couple of breadsticks from a basket on one of the tables as she shuffled dejectedly out of her mother's restaurant.

Outside, the Via di Corniglia wound its way gently downhill towards the village's tiny marina. The late spring days were becoming hot and Francesca wished she could be swimming after school, like many of the other children in Manarola's small elementary school. A variety of small restaurants and cafes, their patios overflowing with tourists, graced both sides of the street. Small shops sold souvenirs or local wines and liqueurs, made from the terraced vineyards and orchards in the hills above Cinque Terre's small villages. Small fishing boats, nestled on trailers, were parked at irregular intervals along the side of the street, causing bottlenecks of tourists wherever they were parked.

In the opposite direction, the road sloped gradually uphill for about one hundred meters, where it met a three-meter high wall. Two staircases ascended, one on each side of the wall, to the town's small piazza, which was elevated above the street. The piazza served three functions. In addition to being a meeting place for local villagers, it was home to *Aristide*, a restaurant housed in a huge gazebo. Finally, the piazza also acted as the roof for one of the tunnels on the local Cinque Terre railway line. The trains, which arrived and departed from the bustling little station on the edge of town, wound their way through a series of tunnels in the coastal hills, including the one beneath Manarola's piazza.

Francesca walked directly across the street to a steep and narrow stone staircase, nestled between two shops. The stairs wound their way uphill into the maze of pastel-colored, terraced buildings that perched on the steep hillsides. She hopped nimbly up the stairs, even with her book bag on her shoulders. Her sturdy young legs were accustomed to the ups and downs of living in Manarola.

As she climbed the stairs, Francesca's mind drifted back to the encounter with her mother, just moments ago. She hated her life with *mamma* and Giulia. She barely knew her *papa*, a disenchanted and bitter man, who had served briefly in the Italian navy at the end of the Second World War. He married Francesca's *mamma* in the euphoric afterglow at the end of the war. The honeymoon was short-lived. Disenchanted and unable to find work in Cinque Terre, *papa* signed onto a merchant vessel in Genoa and spent most of his time at sea, drinking and womanizing between voyages with prostitutes in the dark, narrow passages of old Genoa. Occasionally he remembered that he had a wife in Manarola, on the coast to the south of Genoa. He would venture home in his drunken state, long enough to lay a beating on Francesca's *mamma* and to force himself on her.

Francesca's sister, Giulia, was born in 1950. *Mamma* took care of neighborhood children during the day, then waited tables in the local restaurants at night to make ends meet. At the same time, she saved money in the hopes of someday having her own restaurant. By 1964, she managed to have enough money to buy a tired-looking restaurant from an elderly couple that had no family to inherit their enterprise.

Mamma and fourteen-year-old Giulia began working hard to carve a new life for themselves. They lived in a cramped apartment above the restaurant. Soon after opening their establishment, *Papa* made one of his rare visits home, impregnating *mamma* with Francesca before he went AWOL again for another two years. *Mamma* became increasingly bitter and resentful for having to raise another child from infancy. She made sure to regularly remind Francesca of the sacrifices that she and Giulia had made for her over the years, and how difficult Francesca had made life for both of them.

Francesca was lonely. She spent countless hours occupying herself in the restaurant with the few toys that *mamma* and Giulia left for her, while they tended to the restaurant and only occasionally checked on her. Even when Francesca was left in Giulia's care, the older teenaged sister was resentful for having to care for her baby sister, when all she really wanted to do was spend time with friends and talk about boys. Francesca never felt close to either *mamma* or Giulia. She desperately longed to be held and to sit and cuddle on somebody's lap, like the other children she saw. She longed to feel loved. To keep the feelings of loneliness at bay, she built walls in her mind. She learned to occupy herself, to be independent, and to rely on only herself whenever possible.

Francesca also built protective walls of distrust. After all, if you couldn't trust your *papa, mamma,* or sister to love you or make you feel wanted, whom could you trust? When she was old enough for school, she kept her classmates at a distance, partly because she had never learned to socialize much with the other children, and partly because she found herself unable to trust anybody to get close to her.

Francesca zigged and zagged upwards through the stairs and passages until she reached an alley about midway up the hillside, emerging into a small piazza that looked out over the

Mediterranean and the small railway station below. A handful of local villagers were relaxing in the piazza, some playing cards and some looking on. Four other elderly women sat beside each other on a bench, knitting in the late afternoon spring sunshine. She stopped for a moment to catch her breath.

"Ciao, Francesca!" the four women chimed in unison, as they recognized her and took a break from their knitting. "How is your *mamma*?" one of them asked.

"She is fine, thank you," Francesca replied. "The restaurant is keeping her busy these days. Excuse me, but I have to go to Giulia's apartment now," she said brusquely. Then she was gone, skipping up more stairs to a narrow alley that sloped steadily up the face of the hillside. The rooftops of buildings on the downside of the hill were on her left. The right-hand side of the alley was lined with two story apartment buildings that lined the hillside rising above her. Francesca stopped after about one hundred meters, turned right, then climbed another twenty steps between two buildings. At the top of the stairs, she came to a landing with an apartment door on each side. She knocked quickly on the door on her left, and then opened the door's latch without waiting for a response.

Francesca was greeted by the sound of wailing two-year-old twins. Her nephews, Guido and Maurizio, were clinging to Giulia's legs as she tried to ready herself for work. Francesca attempted to divert their attention and separate them from their mother, but the decibels increased to a deafening level. To make things worse, Giulia was screaming at her too.

"What kept you, Francesca? Did you crawl home from school today? Don't you know that *mamma* needs me at the restaurant? I don't know what we're going to do with you. You're hopeless! I left food on the counter for the boys. All you have to do is feed it to them. Do you think you can manage that?"

"Yes, Giulia," Francesca replied. "And I'll make sure to get them to bed by eight o'clock so they won't be grumpy all day tomorrow," she continued, mimicking the orders that Giulia repeated every night. Francesca picked up little Maurizio to stop his screaming, but Guido became angrier at being ignored.

"Paolo should be home by nine tonight," Giulia continued. "He's on the Cinque Terre train this month, so he'll be home early, as long as he doesn't stop for a beer. Make sure you don't go running home until the apartment is clean!" Giulia shouted over the wailing twins.

"Yes, Giulia," Francesca repeated. There was no expression in her voice.

Giulia grabbed her purse and a sweater, and then ran out the door, slamming it behind her as she fled the menagerie in her apartment.

Strangely, Guido and Maurizio stopped crying within seconds of their mother leaving. Francesca put Maurizio back on the floor, and then she began playing with her two nephews. She quickly transformed their distress into chuckles of laughter. Even at the age of two, the young boys felt the difference between Francesca's affection and Giulia's cold, distant attitude towards them. In return, the twins made Francesca feel like somebody needed her. The evening passed quickly for Francesca. She expertly fed and bathed her two young nephews, then read to them until they were both sleeping soundly.

Francesca lost track of the time. She set to work, washing the dishes then cleaning up the boy's toys and sweeping the floors. She heard the front door handle rattle. Looking up at the old clock on the wall, she was surprised to see it was already nine thirty. Paulo must have exited the tunnel from the train station and gone directly to the pub that beckoned to him from directly across the road from the tunnel's exit.

Paolo was only in his late twenties, but he looked at least five years older. He had a well-developed belly hanging over his belt. His *ItalRail* conductor's uniform fit him badly. The shirt was baggy in order to accommodate his belly. His pants were large in the waist, and were too large and baggy for his atrophied buttocks. Large rings of sweat extended downwards from his armpits. He had dark rings beneath his tired, inebriated eyes. He reeked of sweat, cigarette smoke, and beer.

"So, Francesca. How is my little sister tonight? Do you have a hug for Paolo?" he asked. He leaned down unsteadily to hug her.

Francesca immediately felt uncomfortable. The walls of distrust became activated instantly within her brain. She ducked from Paulo's large arms as he tried to encircle her. She gave him a token hug around his large waist, and then slipped quickly from his grasp as she felt his warm breath and the stale smell of beer coming towards her. Francesca felt the conflict growing inside her. On one hand, all she ever wanted was to be held and to have a family that loved her. On the other, Paolo felt creepy and she knew instinctively that she should fear his hugs.

Paulo reacted with anger as Francesca eluded his embrace.

"You little bitch," he shouted. "What do you think you're doing? We're all family here. I'll teach you some manners and show you how to respect me!" He raised his hand to strike her. He watched as she cringed and readied herself for the blow. He stopped himself, then started laughing hysterically. He turned away and walked to kitchen, looking for his dinner and feeling proud of himself. Scaring the little bitch was enough fun for one night.

CHAPTER 16

"BRAVO, FRANCESCA! That's how it's done!" Signora Pecunia applauded. "The rest of you girls should watch and learn from Francesca! She is as graceful and effortless in the water as a dolphin!"

Signora Pecunia's group of twelve-year-old Middle School students were gathered on the rocks that formed a breakwater for the village of Riomaggiore's tiny harbor. She was attempting to give swimming lessons to her physical education class. Most of the girls had already taken lessons and knew how to swim. Thus, most of the girls were much more interested in whether each other's swim wear was fashionable or not, and weren't the least bit interested in swimming.

Francesca, on the other hand, had never taken swimming lessons before. Signora Pecunia was amazed at how quickly she learned. It seemed like she was born in the water. She was a natural swimmer.

As Francesca climbed out of the water, she elicited a mixture of reactions from her classmates. Some of the girls stared at her resentfully, jealous of the adulation Francesca was receiving from their instructor. Others were pointing and giggling at Francesca's old-fashioned, hand-me-down swimsuit that had once belonged to Giulia almost fifteen years ago in the mid 1950's. The suit was far too small, drawing attention to her budding breasts, and riding up into the crack of her buttocks, revealing large areas of flesh. She was well aware of how ridiculous the suit looked, and how tight and sticky it felt on her. When she was in the water, she wished she could shed the skintight costume and feel the cool Mediterranean waters flow freely over her real skin. When she was out of the water, she wished she could crawl under a rock and become invisible.

"Girls! That will be enough! Pay attention. Remember, your swimming test is in three weeks. It will be part of your grade in this class. If you want to pass the exam, I recommend that you all pay more attention to your swimming, like Francesca, and less to each other's swimwear! That will be all for today. Make sure you all have everything you brought with you!"

Wrapped in towels, the group of girls paraded up the main street of Riomaggiore, through the tunnel under the train tracks, then back up onto the main street to walk the rest of the way uphill to the school. Signora Pecunia led the way, followed by two distinct cliques of girls. Francesca trailed behind by herself. Her towel was wrapped tightly around her to shield herself from embarrassment.

Francesca noticed Signora Pecunia looking at her. She could tell that her teacher felt sorry for her. The teacher often praised Francesca and encouraged her to find her own strength and self-confidence, and to develop her independence from the other girls. Francesca liked her and responded to her praise and encouragement. She knew Signora Pecunia had spoken to the other teachers, making sure they were all aware of her intelligence, drive, and determination. Francesca was beginning to find herself. She knew she was artistic and creative, and was developing a passion for art.

As the students approached the school, the teacher dropped back and fell in beside Francesca.

"You're a talented swimmer, Francesca. Have you ever thought about joining the swim club in La Spezia?"

"Grazie, Signora. Yes, I thought about it. But it isn't possible. My *mamma* is busy with her restaurant, and my family depends on me to help with my two nephews after school and on weekends."

"That's a shame. But I understand how important family is too," the teacher added, nodding her approval. Unfortunately for Francesca, Signora Pecunia had no idea how dysfunctional the young girl's family really was in reality.

LUCA ROLLANDI was waiting for Francesca outside after school. He was an awkward looking boy with blonde hair and acne, but Francesca found that he was good company, and he made her feel more safe on the walk home during the winter months, when the late afternoon light was poor. Like Francesca, Luca was also an outsider with his classmates, who also didn't feel like he fit in with any of the cliques in their small school. He and Francesca understood how lonely and isolated each other felt. They had become as friendly as Francesca would allow them to become.

She had changed out of the grotesque swimming costume and back into her school uniform: a knee-length grey skirt, white knee-socks, white blouse, and the school's navy tie with white diagonal stripes. Luca wore his grey slacks, a navy blazer, white shirt and an identical tie. They both carried canvas book bags on their backs.

"Are we taking the train to Manarola, or do you want walk?" Luca asked.

"Let's take the Via Del Amore," Francesca answered. It's a nice day for walking and we can save the train fare."

They walked past the Riomaggiore train station, taking the scenic walkway that hugged the cliffs and looked out over the Mediterranean, instead of taking the train. They talked intermittently about their day at school, but the conversation was stilted and difficult for the self-conscious youths as they traversed the walkway.

The Via Del Amore, as local villagers called it, wound its way around the base of steep coastal cliffs, taking about twenty minutes to walk from Riomaggiore to Manarola. As the pair of adolescents neared Manarola, they came upon thousands of small padlocks, attached to the cables of safety barriers and the chain link fences that kept the pathway safe from small rockslides. The padlocks had been locked in place over the years by thousands of young lovers to signify the bonds of love between them. Each lock had the names of the lovers and a date or a short note that was either engraved into, or attached to each lock for posterity.

Barely a word was spoken between the two youths as they nervously avoided gazing at the symbols of young love. Suddenly, Luca's hand searched for Francesca's and he entwined his fingers with hers. She stiffened immediately, taken completely by surprise by Luca's gesture. But she didn't let go. The warmth of Lucas' hand felt so good to a part of Francesca that longed for love and connection to another person. In contrast, alarm bells were going off in other parts of her mind, immediately putting up her barriers of distrust. She was confused and unsure how to react.

"I like you," Luca said to Francesca. "Maybe someday one of those locks will be ours." He squeezed her hand tighter as he spoke.

"Maybe," she replied stiffly. In her state of confusion, she was no longer aware of the touch of Luca's hand, or the words that were coming out of her mouth. Her mind was someplace else, unable to give any more of a response to his warm, non-verbal message of friendship. She walked the rest of the way home in silence.

FRANCESCA SAID a stiff goodbye to Luca, just outside the tunnel that carried people from the Via Del Amore and Manarola's train station, into the village proper. Rather than turning left and walking over the piazza to *Mamma's* restaurant so she could change out of her school clothes, Francesca turned to her right for a few paces, then took a switchback pathway uphill towards Giulia and Paulo's apartment.

Paolo didn't like it when she changed out of her school uniform. Her pace slowed more and more as she climbed higher and drew nearer to Giulia's apartment. She stood still and looked out over the village. Below her to the right, the main street wound its way uphill until it turned left and disappeared around a bend in the road. She sighed, and then turned her head forward, looking up the hill towards her destination. Her legs started to turn limp, and a feeling of resignation and dread descended upon her. She had difficulty forcing herself to walk the rest of the distance to the apartment.

Once inside, Francesca's ears were deaf to Giulia's usual barrage of commands. After Giulia left, Francesca's mind went on autopilot. She played with the boys, who were now four years old, and then she fed them their dinner, ran their baths, and cleaned up the dishes. She forced herself to read to the twins, put them to bed, and then resigned herself to waiting numbly for the sound of Paolo's hand on the door handle. Part of her mind was telling herself to run and never come back. Yet another part of her felt completely helpless. That part was telling her that if she ran, she would have no place to go, and no hope of ever having a family that loved her. Yet another part of her secretly craved the attention that Paolo gave to her. In a twisted sort of way, it felt better than no attention at all.

When the sound of his hand on the door handle came, she went numb. Paolo came into the room and smiled knowingly at her.

"Bona sera, Francesca. Do you have a kiss for your brother?" Dutifully, she walked to him, wrapped her arms around his belly to hug him, and then kissed him on his cheek.

"Bona sera, brother," she replied mechanically.

"Brother?" Paolo questioned. "Don't you mean *master*?"

"Yes, bro …master," Francesca said, lowering her head to avoid making another mistake.

"You're being a bad girl, aren't you? Look me in the eyes, girl!" he commanded. "Now, what do you say to me? Say it like you mean it."

"I've been a bad girl, master!" she stated.

"That's better. Are the boys asleep?" he asked.

Francesca nodded affirmatively, without speaking. Paolo put out his hand. "Come with me," he ordered.

Paulo led her to the bedroom, locking the door behind them.

"So what should I do to such a bad girl, Francesca? What do you think would be a fitting punishment for a girl who doesn't show the proper respect for her sister's husband?"

"Bad girls deserve to be spanked, master!" she replied.

"That's right. Come here, then!" he ordered. "You know what to do. Don't disappoint me, you bad girl. Bend over!"

Francesca went to a chair that sat in front of Giulia's dressing table and leaned over the back of the chair. Paolo walked towards her slowly, and then knelt down. He deliberately ran his hands slowly up the outside of Francesca's legs, lifting her skirt as he did so. He flipped the skirt up over her back, exposing her thighs and the panties covering her buttocks.

Francesca held her breath. She stared down at the chair, trying to send her mind back to swimming in the harbor in Riomaggiore. She called upon her mind to remember every possible pleasurable sensation from her swim in the Mediterranean earlier in the afternoon. She became oblivious to Paulo, who was now running his hands over her buttocks, caressing them while he met his own perverted needs for power and sexual release.

"What do we have here, Francesca? You know these aren't the panties I like you to wear for me. I'm afraid your punishment must be harsher. What do you think I should do about this?"

Francesca was silent. Her mind was far away and unaware of Paolo's increasing anger.

"So, you're ignoring me, are you? It looks like I need to do something to get your attention!" he muttered angrily. His eyes darted around the room. His muscles quivered as he became more agitated. He started loosening the buckle of his belt. Without warning, he leaned over and grabbed her face with both of his hands, twisting it around so he was face to face with her, trying to get her full attention.

"Take off your panties and your skirt!" he ordered. Part of Francesca heard the words in the distance, acting upon them as if she was a robot. Behind her walls, she felt a sense of humiliation and worthlessness overwhelming her consciousness. She stepped out of her panties and undid the button that allowed her skirt to drop to the floor, exposing all of her private parts.

Paolo roughly pushed her down over the back of the chair again. Then he set to work with the buckle end of the belt on Francesca's bare flesh.

Francesca felt a distant pain searing through her bare flesh. The walls in her mind were holding. They kept her mind and body numb to the excruciating sensations of the belt buckle as it tore into her flesh. Her walls were less successful at holding back the feelings of humiliation, the feelings of worthlessness, and a growing rage inside her. The independent, resourceful part of Francesca's mind that had always managed to take care of herself, was starting to take over. It was gathering strength from her anger. The independent part of Francesca was resolving to never let herself feel humiliated again.

After five brutal lashes, Paolo had had enough. Francesca's buttocks and upper thighs were slashed. Blood was dripping from the wounds and running down the back of her leg. Paolo was breathing deeply, feeling intoxicated with the power and control he had over the girl. The violence was starting to escalate. Francesca knew that touching her, spanking her, and having her pleasure him was no longer enough. It was the first time he had ever used the belt-buckle on her. It terrified Francesca that Paolo was so exhilarated by the experience.

"Dress yourself!" Paolo commended. "And when you come here tomorrow, what do I expect you to do?"

"Anything you wish, master!" Francesca said instinctively.

Paolo's eyes left Francesca for a few seconds as he re-threaded his belt back through the loops of his pants. Francesca quickly slid her panties under Giulia's side of the bed with her foot. They were out of Paolo's sight, but still slightly visible from Giulia's bedside. The resourceful part of Francesca's brain prayed that Paolo wouldn't remember the panties.

Paolo looked up again and stared into Francesca's eyes as she finished buttoning her skirt.

"That's right. You will do whatever I wish! Now get out of here! And I don't need to tell you what will happen if you tell anybody about this, do I?

"No, master. I would never say a word to anybody. May I go now, master?"

"Get out, you little slut. Make sure you clean yourself up on the way out. And don't be late tomorrow," he snarled.

Francesca adjusted her skirt delicately over her wounded flesh. Gingerly, she slipped her feet into her shoes. Almost any movement caused the pain to burn in her open flesh. She opened the bedroom door, limping slowly and painfully into the hallway. She heard Paolo follow her out the bedroom door, and felt his eyes lusting after her. She held her breath. Finally, she heard Paolo closing the door absent-mindedly behind him. He hadn't noticed the panties peeking out from under Giulia's side of the bed. Francesca went across the hallway to the toilette to clean herself up, closing the door behind her. Only then did she allow herself to start breathing again.

MAMMA'S RESTAURANT was crowded with tourists the following night. There were lineups at the front door and *mamma* was frustrated.

"Giulia! We need tables! What's the problem? Why is everything moving so slowly tonight?"

"I don't know, *Mamma*. The kitchen screwed up a couple of my orders and we had to wait for them to make things right. I think we have more people than usual."

"Well, speed things up! We don't want people walking away or spreading the word that our service is slow!"

"I'm doing the best I can, *mamma*. I've got a vicious migraine. I can't go any faster!"

Giulia didn't tell *mamma* that the mistakes with the food orders were her fault. Her mind was someplace else. She couldn't shake the image of the young girl's panties she had found under her bed this morning. Giulia's head was pounding. She couldn't concentrate and was starting to feel nauseous. In the distance, she heard the chefs pounding on their bell, her signal that more orders were ready.

As she got closer to the kitchen, the cacophony of noise became more than Giulia's brain could tolerate. She felt her stomach convulsing, its contents starting to move. She abruptly changed direction and raced for the toilette. Surges of nausea rapidly emptied her stomach, and then continued as waves of dry heaves. When it finally ended, she was weak and trembling. Giulia burst into tears and sobbed, her head hanging over the edge of the porcelain bowl. After a few moments, she flushed, and then filled the sink with water to freshen up and gather her composure. She looked in the mirror, noticing that her normally olive complexion was now pasty and white, and she had black rings under her eyes. She decided she had to leave.

"*Mamma*, I'm sick to my stomach and have to go home. You can get one of the hostesses to take over my tables. Christina has done it before and knows what she's doing. She'll do fine. I'm sorry to let you down, *mamma*!"

Mamma threw her hands in the air and heaved an impatient sigh.

"What can I say? If you're sick, you're sick. We'll find a way to manage. Go home and get Paolo to take care of you. He's a good man. I'll call you tomorrow to see how you feel. Go on, now. Pronto!"

Giulia stepped into the cool evening air, sucking a huge gulp of the fresh air into her lungs, and then letting it out slowly. She looked at her watch. It was almost nine o'clock and Paolo should be home soon. She recalled *mamma's* words.

He's a good man.

She crossed the street and started ascending the stone staircase into the maze of buildings, taking frequent breaks to catch her breath. She ducked into a narrow alley about thirty meters from the stairway to their apartment and waited patiently. The evening air was comfortable, and she would wait as long as she needed.

Giulia didn't have to wait long. Within ten minutes, she heard a set of heavy footsteps coming towards their apartment from the other direction. She peered around the corner from her hiding spot and confirmed it was Paolo. She recognized the distinctive shape of his body, even in the dim light. She listened to his footsteps as he climbed the stairs to their apartment, and then heard the sound of the door slam behind him.

Giulia crept silently along the alley, and then up the stairs to their apartment, keeping her head below the window beside the front door so she could listen, yet remain unobserved. She heard Paolo's angry voice, but couldn't make out what he was saying. She also heard Francesca's timid voice. Her voice was so weak that Giulia couldn't hear anything the young girl said. Then it went silent. Giulia waited for what seemed like an eternity. In reality, it was only a couple of minutes by her watch. She carefully raised her head and peered through a crack in the curtains that partially covered the window. The living area of the apartment was empty.

Giulia removed her shoes and left them outside the door. She turned the door handle, finding that Paolo had left it unlocked. The handle clicked as she turned it. She held her breath and froze, desperately fearing that Paolo might had heard it.

After a long pause, Giulia started breathing again, but it was now rapid and her heart was racing. Nobody had heard her opening the door. To Giulia, her breathing sounded like a howling windstorm, and she was afraid it would give her away. But gradually, breath by breath, she brought her respiration and heart rate back to a more normal rate. She heard Paolo's voice rising in anger again, this time coming from the direction of their bedroom. She couldn't see Francesca anywhere. She moved her stocking feet slowly in the direction of the bedroom until she was outside the door, then put her ear close to the door and listened.

"So what is your punishment going to be tonight, you bad girl? Tell me what you would suggest!"

Giulia was confused. Why was Paolo disciplining Francesca? What had she done? And why were they in the bedroom? She remembered the panties she found on the floor in her bedroom this morning, and the answer came to her. She felt the nausea growing in her stomach again.

Giulia placed her hand on the door handle and turned it, but it stopped in her hand. Paolo had locked the door from the inside. She reached into her hair and pulled out one of the bobby pins that were holding her hair in place. She waited until Paolo raised his voice again, and then pushed one end of the bobby pin firmly into the lock. As it clicked, Giulia turned the handle, threw the door wide open, and burst into the room.

Paolo wheeled around. His jaw dropped open as he saw his wife standing in the doorway.

Giulia's mouth was agape at the spectacle in front of her. Twelve-year-old Francesca, wearing only her panties, was kneeling on the floor in front of Paulo. His trousers were down around his ankles, with only his boxer shorts covering an obvious erection.

Everybody in the room froze. Paolo's eyes were wide and frantic as his mind raced to come up with an explanation. Francesca stared at Giulia, trembling with fear and pleading with her eyes for her older sister to rescue her. It was Giulia who broke the silence. She looked down at her terrified little sister, and tears began to roll down her face.

"You little slut!" she screamed. "How could you tempt my husband like this? How could you do this to me! After all I've done for you, you ungrateful little tramp. Put on your clothes, and then get out. I don't ever want you to step foot in this house again. Get out!" she shrieked.

Francesca picked up her clothes, piece-by-piece, and slunk down the narrow hallway into the living room to dress. The twins were wide-awake and bawling in their room. She heard Giulia and Paolo arguing loudly behind her as she slowly dressed herself. Her thighs and buttocks still throbbed from the previous night's beating. She found her book bag on the floor by the front door, and then hoisted it over her shoulders and onto her back.

Francesca stepped into the darkness and paused briefly on the landing. She drew in a long breath, and then emitted a long, slow sigh of relief. She set off into the darkness for home, determined to keep her promise to Giulia: that she would never return to that apartment again.

FRANCESCA slept fitfully night. Even after a full day, the pain in her buttocks and thighs was still excruciating. She couldn't get comfortable, even lying on her sides. But the physical pain was hardly noticeable, compared to the feelings of humiliation and shame she was still feeling. She felt dirty and worthless. Outside, the first light of dawn was beginning to leak through the cracks around the edges of the yellowed, threadbare curtains covering her bedroom window.

Francesca pulled back the covers. She carefully swung her legs around, while pushing her body into the air at the same time with her muscular arms, managing to keep her backside from touching the bed as she moved. She hopped off the bed onto her feet. Her wounds were crusted and stinging. She pulled on an old pair of sweat-pants, a thin pair of socks, a t-shirt, and an old sweater to keep away the morning chill. She picked up her sneakers and crept out of her room, then into the bathroom to void herself. On her way out, she took her bath towel, carefully rolling it and tucking it under her arm.

Francesca skulked through the dark apartment, sliding out the door and closing it gently behind her. She descended the stone stairway to the street below, moving as if she were a ghost. Only when her feet were on the street, did she bend down to slide her feet into the sneakers and tie her laces, wincing as her clothing brushed over the angry nerve endings in her raw wounds. She set off like a ghost in the shadows, down Via di Corniglia towards the marina.

Francesca saw the eastern sky growing lighter. The horizon gave off a gentle pink glow that transitioned into soft violet, then into a deep cobalt blue as she scanned the sky from east to west. A handful of fishermen were readying their skiffs for another day's work. She ignored them, and none of them paid any attention to the slim, dark figure scurrying down the boat ramp and up over the dark rocks that separated the tiny harbor from the open Mediterranean.

Once on the other side of the rocks and out of sight of the fishermen, Francesca quickly peeled off her sweater, and t-shirt, and then gingerly lowered her sweatpants until she was entirely nude. Her bare skin responded with goose bumps, and the tiny hairs on her body all stood at attention in a futile attempt to keep her skin warm.

She stood quietly for a moment, her arms folded tightly over her budding breasts to keep herself warm. She gazed out over the calm, glassy water, preparing herself for the shock that was to follow. Then she lifted her arms, held them out in front of her, and launched herself out over the water, barely causing a ripple as her slender body knifed through the surface into the dark waters below.

The seawater was only slightly more frigid than the cool morning air. Francesca felt it flowing gently over every square centimeter of her body, caressing it gently as it washed over her skin. The salt water stung initially, then the cool liquid helped to numb the pain from her wounds. She surfaced from her dive, feeling exhilarated and energized.

A feeling started growing inside Francesca - something she couldn't ever remember feeling before. It was a pleasant, positive sensation. It was the feeling of freedom - freedom from the grotesque, skintight swimsuit she was forced to wear for swimming classes, and freedom from the physical pain in her buttocks and legs. But most of all, she felt the cool Mediterranean waters washing away, for the moment, the feelings of worthlessness and shame. It cleansed her of the dirty feeling she had every time Paulo leered at her, demeaned her, threatened her, touched her with his sweaty hands, struck her, or forced her to touch him over the past two years.

Francesca's arms stroked silently and effortlessly through the water along the coastline of Cinque Terre, heading towards Corniglia. After about ten minutes, she turned around for the return swim back to the rocks at Manarola. She paused to float on her back, looking back toward the cloudless eastern sky. The sun had peeked over the horizon, the soft pink color gradually giving way to a soft blue in the east. The sky overhead was turning a deep azure as night slowly gave way to daylight.

Suddenly, a pair of dolphins breached the surface about twenty meters from Francesca, startling her and focusing her attention back into the present. They surfaced again, this time standing upright and clucking at her, as if they were laughing and heckling her feeble human attempts at swimming. Francesca laughed along with them. She realized she was feeling the same sense of freedom as these two beautiful marine creatures. They swam circles around her and she tried to swim with them, smiling and laughing each time she stopped to breathe. The creatures disappeared beneath the surface. The next time she saw them, they breached about one hundred meters toward the west. They clucked and chuckled at her again, as if saying their goodbyes to her. Then they slid beneath the surface and disappeared.

Francesca felt totally exhilarated. The walls in her mind were down completely. She was fully present and taking in all of the pleasurable sensations and emotions of the moment. She felt parts of herself emerging from deep inside for the first time, no longer kept prisoner by her defensive barriers. They were the parts of her that were resourceful and independent. These newly discovered aspects of herself were gradually taking over and energizing her.

Francesca rolled over and started stroking smoothly back toward the village to get ready for school. A new day had dawned. Francesca Capellini now felt free, and she decided it was time to start living life on her own terms.

CHAPTER 17

SUSAN KEANER'S patience was wearing thin. She had been hired to take family portraits as part of a First Communion celebration at a hotel and restaurant in Monterosso. The adults had quickly lost control of the large group of children, once the young ones had eaten their fill.

I didn't come all the way from La Spezia to Monterosso to be somebody else's babysitter, she muttered to herself.

Suddenly, Susan heard a young female voice rise above the commotion, addressing the adults in the restaurant.

"I'll watch the children while you grown-ups have your pictures taken. Then I'll bring the children in as you need them." She nodded in Susan's direction. Susan nodded her thanks in return.

Susan had noticed the young teen helping to serve meals while she was setting up her equipment for the portrait session. The girl was slim with short dark hair and an olive complexion. Susan noticed that she was efficient and pleasant. She was good at her work, but didn't smile very much. Susan guessed that she was about sixteen years old.

When the portraits were finally finished, Susan busied herself with packing up her lighting equipment and cameras. She didn't notice the young woman approaching her until she stood up and found the adolescent standing directly in front of her.

"Ciao! I hope you did not mind me interfering with your work," the young woman said. "I thought you might need some help with the children."

"Not at all, young lady. My name is Susan - Susan Keaner. And yours?" she asked in fluent Italian. Susan reached out to shake the teenage girl's hand.

"I'm Francesca Capellini," the girl said.

"I'm grateful to you for helping, Francesca. You're good at your work. Have you worked in the restaurant for long?"

"About a year. I started in the restaurant, but sometimes they ask me to help out at the registration desk. I've even learned how to give massages to help the massage therapist," she added. Susan noticed the note of satisfaction and pride in her voice.

"My goodness. Aren't you a busy girl? I suppose you'll be wanting to become a photographer now too," Susan said, laughing.

The young girl smiled shyly and laughed with Susan.

"As a matter of fact, I would," Francesca replied.

"I've been learning photography in art class, and I've joined the photography club at my school in La Spezia."

"You live in La Spezia and work here in Monterosso?" Susan asked.

"Actually, I live in Manarola, go to school in La Spezia, and work here in Monterosso. It is the biggest village in Cinque Terre, so there is more work here. But I would really like to work closer to home," Francesca admitted.

Something about the young girl resonated with Susan. She seemed so independent and confident for such a young girl, much like herself when she was younger. She wondered if she was seeing a bit of herself in Francesca.

"Well, what a coincidence," Susan replied. "I have my portrait studio in La Spezia, and I run the small art gallery in Manarola. I've been thinking I need somebody to help me, both at the studio and the gallery. Are you interested?"

Francesca's brown eyes came alive with Susan's offer. "I can see you any day this week after school," she replied enthusiastically.

Susan reached into her purse and produced a business card.

"I'll be at the gallery in Manarola tomorrow afternoon. Would four o'clock be too early?" Susan asked.

"That will be perfect. Thank you so much!" Francesca answered. She reached out and pumped Susan's hand enthusiastically. "You will have to excuse me. I have to get back to work. See you tomorrow!"

SUSAN KEANER was a young girl in Bonner's Ferry, Idaho in 1950 when she first knew she was different. She couldn't put it into words, and it would be years before she would be able to do so. But she knew early in her life that she didn't fit well in the small Western-American town. Susan was always a tomboy and was the constant target of teasing from other girls. Not that Susan minded. She was happier cutting her hair short and playing sports with the boys, than playing with dolls or playing house, like most of the other girls her age.

By the time she was twelve, Susan began to wonder why she didn't giggle and have crushes on boys, like the other girls. To her, boys were just her friends. Instead, she started noticing the other girls who were developing breasts and figures. The other girls started calling her some different names that she didn't understand. One day, she was helping her mother, a devout Methodist, to hang laundry on the clothesline, when her curiosity got the best of her.

"Mom, what does *lezzie* mean?"

Susan remembered seeing her mother's jaw drop and her face turn crimson. She'd only recently had the birds and bees talk with her mother, but homosexuality wasn't something her mother was ready or willing to discuss. Her mother was caught off guard, blurting out the first thing that came to her mind.

"That's when women like other women. They're called lesbians. They're all sinners who are going to hell. It's dirty and I don't want to talk about it anymore. Is that clear?"

Crystal clear, Susan thought. At that moment, she realized she was going to have to look elsewhere for a supportive mother figure, and she was going to have to find her own answers. She felt confused, but had nowhere to turn for support.

By the time she was sixteen and in high school, Susan no longer felt confused. She understood her attraction to the other girls and women. She understood why she was different. She was beginning to accept her sexual orientation. But she felt devastatingly alone with her dark secret in the small, conservative town. She knew the discrimination she would experience if she revealed her secret and remained in town.

Early in her junior year in high school, Susan stayed behind after physical education class one day to help return softball equipment to the storage room. Miss Cruickshank, the new physical education teacher, came over to help Susan. Their eyes met. Susan saw understanding in the teacher's eyes.

"I think you have a secret," Miss Cruickshank said to Susan. "You feel different from the other girls, don't you?"

Susan was startled by the unexpected question, which was more a statement of fact. She swallowed hard before answering.

"How do you know?" Susan whispered.

"Don't worry, Susan. I'm not going to tell anybody. I've been keeping the same secret for a long time. I know how you feel."

Susan exhaled slowly. She felt like an enormous weight was slowly beginning to lift off her shoulders.

"How do you manage to keep it secret?" Susan asked, keeping her voice hushed.

"I keep my work life here in Idaho separate from my private life. Most of my like-minded friends live in Seattle, so I spend a lot of weekends there," Miss Cruikshank replied.

"Susan, you know you can come to talk with me anytime you need somebody to listen."

Susan smiled and nodded, and then resumed putting away the rest of the softball equipment.

Miss Cruikshank was true to her word, often staying after school to listen to Susan, and to give advice when Susan needed some. During her senior year, Susan remembered accompanying her teacher to Seattle on two occasions, on the premise of visiting the University of Washington campus and their sports programs. While there, the older woman introduced Susan to some of her gay friends. She felt accepted by Miss Cruickshank and her circle of friends. For the first time in her life, Susan started to get a sense of where she fit, and she began to feel that she wasn't alone.

During the latter part of her senior year, rumors started to circulate. The other girls started to notice how close Susan and Miss Cruickshank had become. It was all innuendo. They had never done anything inappropriate or sexual. But Susan knew the time was coming when she had to leave Bonner's Ferry behind.

Susan recalled working hard to save money during her senior year, and during the summer following high school graduation. When September came, she announced to her parents that she wanted to defer her acceptance to the University of Washington. She wanted to take the following year to see Europe, with the intention of returning to university the following year.

Susan set out to find herself. She worked her way through northern Europe during the fall, then moved further south during the winter. She managed to meet other gay people during her travels through France, the Netherlands, and Germany, feeling more and more comfortable with her orientation and her identity as the year progressed.

That's when Susan Keaner discovered the beauty and serenity of Italy and Cinque Terre. She knew instantly that this was where she wanted to live the rest of her life. She never returned home to attend the University of Washington.

SUSAN WATCHED Francesca carefully developing the black-and-white photographic print under the orange glow of the safelight. Her mind wandered back to earlier times when she was learning photography from the former owner of the portrait studio, a kindly old Italian gentleman named Giuseppe. Unlike Francesca, who was naturally drawn to photography, Susan remembered that she started working for Giuseppe because it was the only job she could find at the time. She recalled how understanding Giuseppe had been with her, while he patiently taught her the art of portraiture and demonstrated the skills of developing film and prints in the darkroom. She remembered how frustrated she was in the beginning, before photography started coming more naturally to her, and before she began to enjoy the work. In contrast to herself, Francesca was a natural at learning the finer nuances of exposure and composition.

It was Francesca's seventeenth birthday. Susan had grown fond of her young apprentice and wanted to do something special for her. The two had become close friends over the past year. With their mutual love of photography and their shared interest in art, the two had much in common. Francesca had accepted Susan's revelation about being lesbian without question. On the other hand, Francesca remained tight-lipped about her personal life.

After Francesca finished hanging the last photographic print to dry, the pair emerged from the dull orange glow of the darkroom into the bright daylight of Susan's studio.

"Do you have a moment, Francesca? I'd like to talk to you before you leave. Can you stay a few extra minutes?" she said, speaking English to the young apprentice.

"Certainly, Miss Keaner," Francesca answered. She spoke with the precise and businesslike English she was learning at school and from Susan.

"First of all, I'm pleased with your work, both here at the studio and at the gallery in Manarola," Susan began.

"Thank you, Miss Keaner," Francesca replied. Her speech was stiff and mechanical.

"And second, please stop calling me 'Miss Keaner'. It looks like we'll be spending a lot of time together, so can we please be less formal with each other? You can call me Sue, or Susan if you like."

Susan noticed Francesca struggling. She knew it was difficult for her to let her guard down and let people in. After a brief delay, the young woman looked at Susan with a look of resolve in her eye.

"I'll call you Susan. And you can call me Fran, if you like."

Susan smiled and reached out her right hand towards Fran, who smiled in return.

"Okay, Fran. It's a deal. I have a little something for you," she said, as she went behind the front counter and brought out a small gift. It was wrapped in blue paper with balloons and the words *Buon Compleanno* covering the gift on all sides. Susan had finished the gift with white ribbon, carefully fraying and curling the ends of the ribbon to make the gift more decorative and festive.

Fran's eyes opened wide in surprise. Susan saw them begin to turn red and become watery. The gift was totally unexpected. Susan didn't know it, but even Fran's *mamma* and sister often didn't get her a gift on her birthday.

"Go ahead. Open it," Susan said.

Fran patiently picked apart the knot in the ribbon, then carefully loosened the tape that held the wrapping paper together. She tried to save the colorful wrapping paper in her perfectionistic way. A plain cardboard box appeared as she peeled the paper carefully away. She jiggled the box. A heavy object shifted and changed the box's center of gravity each time the box was shaken. Fran carefully loosened the tape that held down the flaps on the top of the box.

As she flipped open the flaps, Fran's mouth opened and she held her breath. "Oh, Susan. You cannot do this. This is yours! Nobody has ever bought me a gift as nice as this. This is too much."

Fran reached into the box and brought out Susan's used Pentax K-1000 35 mm. camera, which she had loaned to Fran on a few occasions for her school art projects.

"Don't be silly," Susan replied. "I hardly use it anymore since I got the Hasselblad. You've been getting much more use from it than I ever will. I want you to have it, Fran. You're a gifted photographer."

Susan watched the tears trickle down Fran's face. Fran reached her arms out, and Susan felt them wrapping around her. It broke Susan's heart that Fran's family didn't treat her any better.

"Thank you, Susan! This is the best gift anybody has ever given to me. I do not know what to say. How can I ever repay you for this?"

"You don't have to say anything. It's a gift. Seeing the photos you take with this camera, and seeing you enjoy it, will be all the payment I ever need."

Fran's arms remained wrapped tightly around Susan for a few more seconds. Then, her formal, businesslike part took control again. "I have to go home now," Fran said.

Susan saw the joy slowly draining from Fran's eyes. She felt Fran's sadness and did her best to praise and reassure her, trying to boost her spirits. But despite her best efforts, she noticed that Fran often slipped into periods of depression.

"You're a strong, talented girl, Fran. Stay strong and stay true to yourself. If you do, you'll always be a success."

Fran didn't reply. She nodded her head in acknowledgment. Her eyes were watering again, but the strong, independent part of her held back the tears.

"I'll see you tomorrow. Thank you again," Fran said.

Without another word, Fran picked up her backpack, and then disappeared out the front door of the studio.

IT WAS about two months later when Susan noticed that Fran was moodier than usual. She had shown up late for work at the gallery again today. It was most uncharacteristic for Fran's responsible, businesslike nature. As they were closing up shop for the day, Susan noticed tears in Fran's eyes as she emerged from the toilette. She took Fran's hand, guided her into the workshop behind the gallery, and then sat her down.

"What's wrong, Fran. You're not yourself lately," Susan observed.

Fran looked down at her lap and couldn't make eye contact with Susan.

"Oh, Susan! I thought … I thought I might be pregnant!" she blurted. Susan put her hands on Fran's shoulder. There was a long pause as tears began to pour from Fran's eyes. She began sobbing inconsolably. Susan took her into her arms and began rocking back and forth.

Susan was caught by surprise. Fran had never mentioned anything about dating any boys. She only occasionally referred to a boy named Luca, saying he was just a friend.

"You thought you were pregnant? But you're not?" Susan asked.

"I was late, Susan. I was so afraid! *Mamma* would disown me if I ever got pregnant."

"I didn't know you were seeing anybody. Do you want to tell me about it?"

Fran gradually gained some control over her tears and stopped her sobbing. She released herself from Susan's arms. As she did, Susan noticed the girl's sadness changing slowly to anger.

"I wasn't dating anybody," Fran continued. "Luca and I have been friends for many years. We often walked home from school together. He has always wanted me to be his girlfriend. As much as I have always wanted to feel like somebody loves me, there is a part of me that will not trust boys. Do you understand?"

Susan nodded. "I think so. You haven't told me much about yourself, but I think some people haven't treated you very well. Am I right?"

Fran's eyes became glassy and distant. Her voice was speaking to Susan, but Susan realized that another part of her had reconnected to memories from her past.

"Luca walked me home along the Via Del Amore that night, like he always has. Only this time, he wanted me to kiss him. I said no, and he got angry with me. He said he knew I was lonely and that I really wanted him. He slapped me when I tried to walk away. He put his hand over my mouth and told me he would hurt me if I cried out. Then he … he … he made me do it, Susan."

Fran was sobbing uncontrollably again. Susan took Fran back into her arms, allowing her to let all of the emotions come pouring out.

"He made me do it. It was so dark. I was so scared!" The sobbing resumed. This time, Fran was on the verge of becoming hysterical. She began to hyperventilate, her breathing becoming shallow and rapid between her sobs of despair. Her sentences became short as she gulped for breaths after every few words.

"He was so heavy. I fought back. I tried to be strong, Susan, just like you always say I am! I screamed for help. But he was too strong! He was so angry. He started choking me, Susan! I couldn't breathe! I was so afraid!"

Fran's voice sounded more and more like she was a little girl. She continued to weep uncontrollably, curled up into a ball in Susan's arms. Susan held her and rocked back and forth, trying her best to console her.

"It's okay, Fran. You're safe here. Nobody's going to hurt you." She continued to rock Fran in her arms.

"But you said you're not pregnant, dear. You just got your period today, didn't you."

Fran nodded affirmatively as she continued to sob and gasp for breaths.

"And you're feeling so many different emotions that you can't even feel a sense of relief?" Susan asked.

Fran nodded again. She burst into another bout of heavy tears and wailing. She was inconsolable.

Susan patiently held Fran and let her weep until there were no more tears. Finally, Fran's eyes lifted and looked into Susan's. She seemed to be coming back from the dark memory and back into the present. Susan watched as Fran's strong, independent part struggled to regain control from the parts of her identity that had been feeling so helpless, terrified, and angry, just a few moments ago.

Fran finally wrestled her emotions under partial control. A look of quiet determination was trying to break through.

"It was my fault. I should never have let him hold my hand. I just want so much for somebody to love me, Susan! Is that so wrong?"

"I understand what you're feeling. But it wasn't your fault! You mustn't think that. It was Luca's fault. You deserve to be treated better than that! You know you always have me to talk to. You know I love you like a daughter. I believe in you, Fran!"

She kissed Fran gently on the forehead and held her head gently against her chest.

Fran finally pulled herself together and sat upright. The independent, businesslike part of her identity was finally back in control again.

"It will never happen again," she proclaimed. "I can be strong. I can manage on my own without getting married. I can manage, just like you have, Susan."

"Shhh, dear," Susan said gently. "Never say never. Someday you'll find a man who will treat you like you deserve. Just be patient. You'll find him someday."

CHAPTER 18

THE HOT, crowded train braked as it entered yet another of the dark tunnels along the Cinque Terre coast. As it emerged from the tunnel and slowed to a crawl, Philippe Morel saw the sign proclaiming the train's arrival at his destination, Manarola. He worked his way through the crowded railway car, trying to keep his burdensome suitcase from banging into the seats and other annoyed passengers. He finally reached the coach's exit, following the line of disembarking passengers down the steps. Once on the platform, he was swept along by a teeming mass of humanity.

There was no first class accommodation, nor any air conditioning, in the coaches on the local Cinque Terre train. Philippe was dripping with sweat from beneath the band of his wide-brimmed straw hat. He felt drops of perspiration running down his back. It was unseasonably hot for late September, and he was clearly overdressed for the weather. Rings of moisture wicked out from his underarms.

Philippe struggled to maneuver his heavy baggage through the throngs of tourists without banging the side of his own leg, trying to avoid the annoyed glances from other travellers who received unwelcome bangs on the side of their legs. He looked for an elevator or escalator, but was swept along by the mob until he found himself descending a set of stairs. The crowd pushed him through the tunnel, beneath the station platform, until he was confronted by another stairwell. He swore under his breath as he was slowly swept up the stairs, his luggage banging wildly into the stairs and the wave of humanity around him. Finally reaching the top of the stairs, he managed to extricate himself from the crowd and find a secluded area to set down his burden. His lungs were gasping for air, as he pulled a handkerchief from the pocket of his suit-jacket to mop the perspiration from his brow.

Philippe pulled the directions for his Bed and Breakfast from the inner pocket of his jacket. They seemed relatively uncomplicated.

Exit the tunnel from the train station, then follow the large red arrow at the end of the tunnel to the right. Follow the road uphill to the next landmarks - the town square bell tower, then watch for the sign for the restaurant known as Trattoria Billy.

Philippe looked up at the entrance to the tunnel. The crowds from the train had mostly preceded him, and had thinned to a trickle. He picked up his luggage and followed the stragglers into the tunnel, feeling some relief from the cool air as he trundled along the passage. The tunnel was lined with posters depicting Cinque Terre's five villages and the surrounding countryside.

As he exited the tunnel, he was assaulted again by another blast of hot air. His delight at seeing the large red arrow was short lived when he saw Manarola's main street, the *Via Renato Birolli*, climbing sharply upwards, then disappearing around a bend to the left. He saw his next landmark, the bell tower, but it was far up the steep hillside. By the time Philippe emerged from the tunnel, the handful of shuttle-buses and taxis had already filled up quickly and disappeared, leaving him with the option of waiting for them to return, or trekking up the hillside on foot.

Patience was not part of Philippe's character. He resigned himself to ascending the steep slope on foot. He began trudging up the street, leaning into the incline as he half-carried and half-dragged his heavy luggage beside him. As he reached the first bend in the winding road, he heard the sound of running water. Philippe was confused, since there was no obvious sign of a stream or a creek. After a few meters, he was able to see through openings beneath some of the town's buildings. It became apparent that the town's forefathers had built many of their buildings and the *Via Renato Birolli* over a creek that descended from the coastal hills.

By the time he made it up the hill to the bell tower, then found the *Via Rollandi* and the sign for *Trattoria Billy*, his legs felt like jelly, his shirt was soaked with perspiration, his lungs were wheezing, and his heart was pounding. Philippe was not in good physical shape for a man in his early twenties. He was careful not to overeat and avoided excessive alcohol and desserts, so he had not yet developed a belly, but his muscles were soft and weak. The sound of running water was louder now. To his left, he saw the small creek gurgling its way down the hill on the final part of its journey before it disappeared beneath Manarola, eventually emptying into the village's small marina.

After ascending a set of stone stairs and trekking another fifty meters along the narrow lane, he found the sign for *Trattoria Billy*. A sign for his Bed and Breakfast hung on a stone wall on the opposite side of the lane. An elderly woman in an apartment high above him, who appeared to have been awaiting his arrival, spotted his luggage and called out his name. She motioned him over to a long, narrow concrete staircase between two buildings. Philippe had to hold his bag high in front of him in order to navigate up the steep, constricted passage. As he finally reached a landing, about half way up the stairs, a door opened to his left and the old lady waved him into a small, but comfortable, apartment.

An hour later, refreshed by a shower, clean clothes, and the small bottle of sparkling water he found in the bar fridge, he felt ready to explore Manarola, to have some dinner, and perhaps locate the village's sole art gallery. This trip was for business, so he dressed in a cream-colored linen suit, with a salmon-colored shirt, and burgundy tie. He wore an expensive straw hat with a black band that went well with the casual, but stylish looking, linen suit. His mission to seek out unknown, but talented local artists in Cinque Terre, had been a waste of time thus far. The art he had seen in his stops in Monterosso, Vernazza, and tiny Corniglia, were inexpensive, low quality, and clearly priced for the budget-conscious tourist.

Philippe turned left, descending the stairs from his apartment, taking *Via Rollandi* until it began descending. He emerged at the small piazza, overlooking the train station and the Mediterranean. He noticed another set of stairs on the far side of the piazza, and began a steep descent that zigged and zagged between buildings and down the hillside, until he emerged on the Via di Corniglia, immediately opposite a restaurant. He could not have known that the restaurant was owned by the mother of young Francesca.

Philippe turned left and continued downhill towards the marina, passing two other restaurants and a number of small shops before arriving at a piazza that overlooked Manarola's tiny marina and harbor, sheltered by a natural rock breakwater. To his right, the street continued to wind its way around the cliffs toward Corniglia, the next village. To his left, another branch exited downwards and served as the village's boat launch.

Philippe realized that he had seen as much of the town as there was to see in this direction. He turned around and started making his way back up the hill. On his way, he made note of the three restaurants and looked at their menus of traditional Ligurian fare, comprised mostly of local seafood and pasta dishes. When he reached the stairs that climbed up to the small piazza over the railway tracks, he took the left-hand stairway. At the top of the stairs, he followed a walkway that curved around the outside of the piazza.

Philippe emerged at a large gazebo-like structure that housed yet another restaurant. He made a note of the name, *Ristorante Aristide*, studying its menu approvingly before moving on. As he descended the stairs on the far side of the piazza, Philippe recognized the exit of the tunnel from the train station. He chuckled to himself as he realized that the art gallery he was seeking, *Arte Dell'Aquila*, was immediately to the left of the tunnel exit. He had failed to notice it on his arrival, so focused had he been on following his directions to his lodgings.

The growling in his stomach and the smell of food in the air attracted Philippe's attention to his left, where he saw the same cafe he had first noticed when he exited from the tunnel earlier that afternoon. He realized he had come full-circle and stumbled upon the tunnel and the cafe from the opposite direction. He decided to have lunch before paying the gallery a visit. Philippe ordered a ham and cheese croissant and pulled a *Moretti* beer from the cooler, still feeling thirsty from his trek up the hillside to his apartment. He paid for the meal, and then carried it outside to a narrow patio. From there, he could watch people come and go from the tunnel, the gallery, and the piazza while he ate.

Philippe looked up after taking a bite from his sandwich. His eyes were drawn instantly to a striking young woman who hurried from the tunnel and into the gallery. She was wearing blue denim capris that hugged her lithe figure, and a yellow blouse that drew Philippe's attention to her tanned, olive-colored skin. Her hair was a deep brunette, so dark it was almost black, and was cut in a short pageboy style. Even from a distance of about fifteen meters, Philippe could see her dark brown eyes and friendly smile as she greeted people inside the gallery.

Philippe watched with fascination as he finished his lunch. It was obvious that the young woman worked in the gallery, and that she was congenial, knowledgeable, and helpful to the tourists who came into the gallery to browse. He wiped his lips with a napkin and left the patio, working his way through a crowd that had just disembarked from the train. As he entered the gallery, he was immediately greeted by the young woman's pleasant, melodic voice.

FRANCESCA CAPELLINI noticed the attractive young man, dressed in an expensive cream-colored suit, as he entered the gallery

"Ciao. May I help you?" she said in fluent English. Her tone was businesslike, yet friendly. She noted the charming smile that lit his face when she greeted him. She guessed that he was not a local, and probably not Italian.

"You certainly may, Signorina!" Philippe replied, in halting Italian. He removed his straw hat politely as he greeted Francesca, revealing a thick head of black hair that swept across his head, so that it fell partially over the left side of his forehead. The hair was held in place by significant quantities of hair-product that reflected highlights off its shiny surface. Francesca noticed that, although he attempted to speak Italian, he had a distinct French accent.

"I am looking for some local contemporary paintings, and your gallery was recommended to me," Philippe said. "From what I can see on display, I don't think that I am going to be disappointed." He gestured toward the art with a sweep of his hand.

"If you would prefer, we can speak either Italian or English," Francesca said.

"Thank you," Philippe answered in English. "I think my English is much better than my Italian."

"You like these?" Francesca said, referring back to the paintings Philippe had noticed." We are currently featuring these Impressionistic works by a local Cinque Terre artist, Sebastian Cavallo. They are a series of night views of the five villages and surrounding area. Because this is his first major showing, they are quite reasonably priced," she added.

"They're extremely good," Philippe observed. "Do you have more of his work?"

"Yes, we have more of his earlier work upstairs, if you would like to follow me," she said.

Philippe nodded and continued smiling at Francesca. She turned and led him up a tightly-coiled, spiral staircase in the corner of the gallery, which ascended to a narrow second level occupying the upper perimeter of all four sides of the room As she led the young man up the staircase, she noticed him gazing up intently at the sway of her hips. She knew that she was fit and that her arms, legs, and backside were firm and muscular. She had grown tired of having the eyes of Italian men follow her wherever she went. Yet, she was flattered that this polite young gentleman found her attractive.

As they reached the top of the stairs and the second level, Philippe reached into the inside pocket of his suit jacket and produced a small leather folder full of his business cards.

"I just realized that I haven't introduced myself yet," Philippe said, apologetically. "My name is Philippe Morel. I am an art agent and collector. I am searching for promising new artists to promote. Please have one of my business cards," he added, pulling one from the folder and handed it to Francesca.

"I am Francesca Capellini. I am pleased to meet you," she replied, reaching out to shake Philippe's hand.

"Are you the owner of the gallery?" Philippe inquired.

"No, Signora Keaner, an American lady, is the owner. She just stepped out for a while, but she should be back in half an hour if you would like to meet her," she added.

"I'm sure that it isn't necessary right now. I'm quite confident that you will be able to help me," he said, smiling.

Philippe listened intently to Francesca as she recited some background information about the artist, and pointed out the features of Cavallo's unique impressionistic style. Philippe reflected his appreciation with charming smiles and some occasional laughter.

Francesca was intrigued by the young man's charm. He was different from the tourists, who were usually only looking for souvenirs from their stay in Cinque Terre. He was knowledgeable and he seemed like a polar-opposite to the crude local boys who constantly leered at her. She knew they only wanted one thing from her. In contrast, this man was educated, refined, and charming. She found herself noticing a part of herself that she had never felt before - a part of her identity that longed for romance and to be loved. She was surprised at the pleasurable effect that the young Frenchman was having on that part of her.

Francesca finished her monologue and smiled back at Philippe, taking a chance on letting down her ever-present defensive wall of distrust. She allowed herself to relax, ever so slightly.

"So, what do you think, Signor Morel," she asked.

"I have to say that I am quite impressed by his work. I may be interested in speaking further with Signora Keaner and Signor Cavallo," he replied. He turned his body slightly, and as he did so, he caught sight of a series of black-and-white photographs on the wall behind him. They were a collection of both formal and candid portraits. As he looked more closely, he noticed the name *Capellini* signed in the bottom right corner.

"These are quite stunning. Is this a relative of yours?" he inquired, pointing to the signature.

Francesca blushed and her eyes looked downward, trying to avoid looking directly at Philippe's eyes as she answered.

"Actually, they are just some of my photos," she said, feeling partly embarrassed at the attention, but also feeling a faint sense of pride that somebody, other than Susan, was appreciating her art.

"Signora Keaner liked them, so she asked me if I wanted to display some in the gallery. They have only been there for a couple of days. I doubt if they will attract much attention," she said.

"That's ridiculous, my dear!" Philippe exclaimed. "You mustn't be so modest. It appears that you have a great deal of talent. So much, in fact, that I would like to discuss it further with you."

Philippe looked at his watch and sighed.

"I'm scheduled to take the train at ten tomorrow morning," he said. "But I would very much like to discuss your future as an artist. I don't quite know what to do. Tell me, what time do finish work tonight? Would you be available to join me for a late dinner?

Otherwise, I'm not sure when I may be able to meet with you next."

Francesca's fleeting sense of pride was quickly overcome by a sense of panic over the possibility of having dinner with this surprising contact with the world of art. She answered without thinking.

"Me? Dinner? I am not dressed to go out, Signor Morel," she stammered.

"Please," Philippe said. "You look lovely. The restaurants will be filled with tourists who are casually dressed. If anything, it is I who will appear overdressed for the occasion. I would be honored to have you join me, just as you are!"

Francesca was torn. On one hand, the distrustful side of her was panicking over the sudden intrusion of this young man into her personal space. On the other, her newly found romantic side was anxious that she would never see him again. She was lost for words and unable to speak.

"Where would you suggest we dine, Signorina Capellini?" Philippe continued. "I noticed three restaurants on the way to the marina. Do you know anything about them?"

Francesca felt another wave of panic at the thought of Philippe taking her to dine at *mamma's* restaurant. Her brain scrambled to find an alternative, finally finding a response.

"Those three are crowded and noisy," she lied. "For a more relaxing setting, I would suggest *Ristorante Aristide* in the piazza, or *Trattoria Billy*, up on the hillside. I know the owner of *Billy*," she volunteered. "He might be able to squeeze us in towards the end of the evening. I can phone him now if you like."

"Wherever you choose will be fine," Philippe said with a smile. "Actually, *Billy* will be convenient for me. I am staying just a stone's throw away. May I continue to browse through your gallery while I wait for you to call?"

"Of course, Signor Morel. Be my guest. If you have any questions, I would be pleased to answer them when I return," she said.

What is wrong with you, Francesca? Why are you so awkward and nervous? He must think you are acting like a child.

She took some slow breaths to calm herself as she waited for an answer from *Trattoria Billy*. Francesca's eyes met Philippe's, and she felt the warmth of his smile as he watched her from the other side of the room. There was something magnetic about the handsome young man and his smile, and she was helpless to resist. The love-starved, romantic part of her could not help being drawn towards him. Somewhere in the depths of her unconscious mind, the protective, distrustful part of her identity was trying to get her attention. But in that moment, Francesca's newly found romantic feelings were rising to the surface and would not be denied.

The ringing on the phone line stopped abruptly. With a loud click, Francesca's call was connected to *Trattoria Billy*.

"Ciao, this is Francesca Capellini. I was wondering if there was any chance that I might book a late dinner for two tonight. I am terribly sorry for the late notice … come at nine o'clock … we might have to wait for a few minutes … of course, I understand … "

PHILIPPE'S EYES were fixed on Francesca as she talked on the phone. She was exactly the kind of woman he was looking for! She spoke English fluently, a necessity in the world of business. But it was her looks that captivated him. As he gazed at the simple elegance of her slender face, deep brown eyes, perfect white teeth, her olive complexion, and her slim figure, a long forgotten feeling from his past started rising to the surface of his consciousness.

His mind drifted back to earlier times. He started remembering the feeling of power he had many years ago, when his plan to rid himself of Henri had started coming together. Then he remembered the satisfaction from how he had manipulated Isabelle into being first his model, then into being his lover.

Philippe was just beginning to remember how everything had ended so abruptly with Isabelle's death, when he realized that Francesca was no longer on the phone. She was now standing directly in front of him, speaking, and startling him back to reality.

"BILLY TOLD us to come around nine o'clock," she said. "We might have to wait a few minutes for a table, but he will be watching for us."

Francesca realized that Philippe's mind was someplace else, and her words had surprised him.

"I am sorry, Mr. Morel. I did not mean to startle you."

Philippe gathered himself quickly, smiling and making eye contact with Francesca.

"It is I who must apologize, Signorina. I'm afraid my mind was elsewhere. However, I was wondering if I can walk you to the restaurant this evening?" Philippe asked.

Francesca felt her heart and her breathing accelerate at the thought of Philippe coming to *mamma's* restaurant to pick her up.

"It is alright, Signor Morel. I am unsure whether I will have time to go home or not. It might be best if we meet at *Billy*."

"If you wish. I look forward to the pleasure of seeing you for dinner," he said. He took her hand in his, bowed forward, and placed his lips gently on her hand to kiss her adieu.

Francesca's heart fluttered and her face flushed as Philippe turned and retreated towards the gallery exit. He stopped and flashed one last warm smile in her direction, before stepping out the gallery door and onto the bustling street.

FRANCESCA and Philippe were seated in a prime location at *Trattoria Billy* - on the lower patio, with its spectacular view of Manarola and the surrounding terraced hillsides. The high-pressure weather system that was bringing the unseasonably hot days and cloudless blue skies to Cinque Terre during the day, created a clear black canvas for nature's masterpieces - the milky way and countless shimmering stars The pastel-colored buildings of Manarola were spread out below them against the rocky hillsides, illuminated by the warm orange-yellow incandescent glow of floodlights. On the opposite hillside, terraced gardens and vineyards were visible in light that reflected off the buildings of the village. The terraces stepped their way gradually up the hillside towards its peak, which was marked by a small religious shrine. Beyond Manarola, the lights of two other Cinque Terre villages, Corniglia and Monterosso, twinkled in the distance along the edge of a vast darkness that was the Mediterranean Sea.

Philippe was impressed with Francesca. She was obviously not an art expert, but she was knowledgeable enough and was extremely bright. She was exactly what he was looking for in an assistant for his business - somebody who was elegant, businesslike, and seductively beautiful. His mind detached briefly, scrambling to find a way to broach the subject with her, even though they had only just met.

The sound of Francesca's voice brought Philippe back from his reverie. He noticed that the young woman's initial veil of self-consciousness was lifting as she started to feel the effects of two glasses of wine. He also noticed that she avoided talking about her childhood or family, other than saying that her mother worked in one of the restaurants in Manarola. He nodded appreciatively as she told him of her love of art and photography while was in high school, and as she told of her chance meeting with Susan Keaner and her two jobs at the portrait studio and the art gallery.

"I have managed to save some money while I have been working for Susan during the last four years," she told Philippe. "I have just started a two-year course to learn massage therapy in Genoa, so I live in the city during the week. But I still come back to Manarola on weekends to work for Susan."

"I'm impressed!" Philippe exclaimed. "I can see that you're a dedicated worker, and you excel at everything you do. But I can't help but wonder, what does a talented young woman like yourself hope to do when you finish your schooling? Do you plan to stay in Cinque Terre?"

"Oh no!" she said emphatically. "Once I have my certification, I want to travel. I was thinking I might like to work on the cruise ships for a while as a massage therapist to save some more money. Then I would love to see America. Susan has told me so much about it!"

Philippe saw an opportunity presenting itself, and he seized it without hesitation.

"So you would like to travel and see the world, would you?" Philippe asked, working his charm and trying to appear empathic. "I understand completely. My parents gave me the opportunity to go outside of France for my university education. I'm grateful for that, but I'm afraid I was a disappointment to them. It seems it was decided at my birth that I would study business and follow the family tradition in the world of banking. Instead, I chose to follow my dream of becoming an artist."

"I am sorry to hear that they did not approve of your choice," Francesca said.

"In the end," Philippe continued, trying not to show his deep hatred for his parents, "we reached a peaceful compromise. My teachers were frustrated with my inability to be creative and original. It seems I can copy just about anybody else's work perfectly. Along the way, I have also learned almost anything there is to know about art. Yet, I am doomed to be frustrated as a creative artist. So, I persuaded my father to pay for me to attend business school. I am using my knowledge of art and business to become an artist's agent and an art dealer. Now I have the best of both worlds!" he said proudly.

"Now it is my turn to be impressed!" Francesca said, smiling shyly.

She's growing more confident, and she's opening up to me more as she drinks more wine.

Philippe realized that his smooth-talking style and his charm were quickly winning her trust.

"I'm so grateful for the opportunity to have studied in Florence, and to have travelled across your beautiful country to witness its spectacular art history. I would encourage you to take any opportunity to travel!" Philippe added.

A busboy appeared to clear their table. Their waiter followed closely behind, placing a selection of local Italian liqueurs on the table.

"Compliments of the house," he offered, bowing slightly as he did so. "Please feel free to sample as many as you like, Signorina. May I pour you one to start?"

Francesca's face flushed. It was obvious to Philippe that she rarely had more than one glass of wine.

She's probably never had the money to splurge on luxuries like liqueurs.

"Go on, my dear," Philippe coaxed. "This beautiful evening is still young. What would you like?"

Francesca wavered between the *Limoncello, Crema di Limon,* or the *Grappa.* Finally, she cast her inhibitions aside.

"I have never tried *Grappa* before," she admitted. "May I have just a taste, please?"

Their waiter poured a small sample into a liqueur glass. Francesca lifted the drink to her lips. Her face contorted as the harsh liquid burned its way over her tongue and down her palate. Both Philippe and the waiter, along with people at nearby tables, laughed at her sour face. Francesca gave her head a shake as the last of the liquid disappeared from her mouth. Her audience awaited her review.

"Not bad," she said unconvincingly. She managed to transform her wince into a wry smile. "But I will try some more, if I may," she added. Her response was greeted with applause from everybody around her.

The liqueurs were flowing at nearby tables as all the guests finished their meal. The volume of laughter in the restaurant rose proportionately as everybody on the patio enjoyed their drinks and the beautiful warm evening.

Francesca smiled at Philippe as they finished their glasses of Grappa. Philippe decided that the time was right for his gambit.

"I was just thinking, Francesca …," he began. Then he abruptly backtracked. "No, never mind, it was just a silly idea."

"Go on," Francesca said. "What were you going to say?"

"It was crazy," he replied. "I was just thinking that, with my knowledge of art and business, and with your talent as a photographer and a salesperson, we might make a good team in my Paris office. But, forgive me for even raising the idea," he added. "You are much too busy finishing your education."

Philippe saw the excitement flash in Francesca's eyes. He knew she wouldn't be able to resist taking his bait.

"I have another idea," Philippe added. "What if you moved to Paris and I helped you continue your studies there? You could finish your training, and also start learning about the art business at the same time. Would you like that?"

Francesca's eyes sparkled at the suggestion.

"Would you really do that for me?" she exclaimed. "I cannot believe this is happening."

Philippe realized that his charm had ignited a romantic spark in Francesca. And he knew that the independent side of her that longed for a better life outside Cinque Terre, would not be able to resist his offer.

"*Mais Oui*," Philippe answered, starting to slip some French vocabulary into his English, in his excitement. "I would be honored to help you, and to have you become a partner in my business, if you would consider joining me."

Francesca managed to overcome the effects of the alcohol. Philippe saw her put her responsible, businesslike face back on.

"Then I would be honored to accept your kind offer, Signor Morel," she replied. She reached across the table and shook Philippe's hand.

Philippe reached for the bottle of *Grappa* and poured them each one more glass of the strong liqueur. Then he raised his glass in the air in a salute.

"To our new partnership!"

THE FOLLOWING day, Fran's dry mouth and headache were all that remained of the alcohol's warm glow. She reflected on the warm feeling that had enveloped her body the night before. Although part of the warm feeling came from the unusual amount of alcohol she had consumed, she was also noticing a romantic and adventurous side of her that had made its unlikely, impulsive, and welcome debut on that beautiful September evening.

Later the same day, Fran introduced Philippe to Susan and told her the wonderful news. She noticed that Susan tried her best to be happy and supportive towards her new business adventure. She ignored the reservations Susan raised when they were alone together, after Philippe departed.

"This is so unexpected" Susan said. "Don't you think you should take some time to think about it? You've only just met this man. What do you really know about him?"

"But this may be my only chance to follow my dreams," Fran said. "We would complement each other perfectly. It almost seems too good to be true!"

Susan didn't say anything more. Fran wasn't in any mood for listening. It wouldn't have made any difference that Susan was thinking exactly the same thing - that Philippe, and everything he offered, seemed too good to be true. Nor was Fran interested in hearing about Susan's ultimate fear for her - that she might eventually pay a steep price for her impulsive, romantic decision.

WALLS

285

CHAPTER 19

FRAN'S EYES were wide-awake as she lay quietly in the king-sized bed, listening to the sound of Philippe's heavy breathing and snoring. She stared at the glowing red numbers on the alarm clock, unable to slow down the thoughts that were racing through her mind.

Her sleep had been fitful, interrupted by persistent nightmares. The first light of dawn was creeping into the room, and she was emotionally and physically exhausted. Her mind slipped into autopilot as she rose from the bed and wrapped herself in a simple white terry-cloth bathrobe. She tiptoed across the room to the sliding glass door at the far end of their elegant master suite. She clicked open the lock, slid the door open, slipped silently through the narrow opening, and slid the door closed in one smooth motion.

Once outside, Fran paused and breathed in the cool pre-dawn air before walking to the end of the swimming pool nearest the house. She dropped her robe and stood naked and motionless. She felt the chill of the March morning on her skin, taking a moment to enjoy the sensations of her nerve endings coming alive. She tried her best to relish the moment, trying to push the intrusive thoughts from her mind. Then, as she had done countless times before, she raised her arms in front of her and launched herself into the air. Her lithe, naked body sliced into the water, leaving only the slightest ripple behind her.

Fran's procedural memory took over. Her arms and legs began propelling her through the water without the need to think about what she was doing. As she moved smoothly through the refreshing liquid, her mind floated back in time, recalling the memories of her life with Philippe. She began to rewind that part of her life, unconsciously trying to pinpoint when things had started to go so wrong.

When she left Manarola, Fran felt like a princess whose dreams had all come true. She and Philippe had become lovers shortly after she joined him in Paris. Fran didn't know what to expect sexually. She was naturally frightened and tense, given that her only previous sexual encounters had been traumatic. Philippe was patient at first, yet also quite distant. It wasn't that Fran found sex with Philippe to be bad, but it didn't live up to the romantic expectations she had when she left Cinque Terre behind.

On the other hand, her business partnership with Philippe was an outstanding success. She vividly remembered their first official event together. Philippe had convinced his parents to allow him to show a promising new artist in their salon during one of Christian and Hélène's business dinners. Philippe had urged the artist to auction one of his paintings, with the proceeds going to Hélène's favorite charity.

The night was a spectacular success. They managed to introduce their new gallery and make social connections with many of his father's closest business associates and their wives. The guests were clearly enamored by the new artist's paintings, jumping at the chance to buy his paintings as investments, before he became better known. But most importantly, Philippe's enchanting new business associate, Francesca, was the talk of the party.

Fran recalled that they were subsequently invited to do the same type of private showings at dinners hosted by his parent's friends and associates. The shows became more lavish, until it was necessary to start hosting them in the larger salons of fashionable Paris hotels. They quickly outgrew their small gallery. Philippe made a deal to invest with one of his father's associates to purchase a small four-story building in which to house their new gallery, renting the remainder of the building. They found themselves in real estate and property management in addition to being in the art business.

As promised, Philippe paid for Francesca's massage therapy courses. But once she was finished, they were so busy with their business interests that she had no time to work in her new career. Fran remembered Philippe's dismissive remarks when she approached him about finding a way to pursue her massage profession.

"It is of no consequence, Francesca. Our business is making a thousand times more money than you will ever make doing manual labor on people's fat bodies."

As she swam, Fran made a mental note that it was probably the first time she felt hurt and rejected by Philippe. By that time, he was not only her business partner, but also her husband. As she felt more rejected by Philippe over time, she began to feel more worthless and started losing hope in her future.

As Fran's body slipped silently back and forth through the water, the eastern sky gradually became lighter. She heard early morning bird songs in the background, barely audible over the constant sound of water rippling in her ears.

Fran came to realize that their common interest in art, as well as their friendship, would never grow into anything more. As they became more successful, they also became more distant. Philippe lost interest in Francesca's photography. The only time she was able to find time for herself and her camera, was when Philippe was busy with real estate meetings, to which she was never invited.

The gala openings at their gallery, and the parties that accompanied them, became more opulent. The parties began attracting the elite of Paris society, along with the excessive alcohol, drugs, and sex that seemed to follow the celebrities like a black cloud. Fran remembered expressing her concerns about the parties to Philippe. She made a mental note that he was not only dismissive that evening, but it was the first time he became angry with her for broaching the subject.

Don't be such a prude, Francesca. These are our friends and associates. It is important that they have a good time at our parties, so they remember us, and our business! It wouldn't hurt you to relax and have some fun with our guests. Stop being so stuffy and professional all the time! Now don't bother me again about such trivia!

Fran realized that things went downhill rapidly after that, and she felt increasingly worthless. About a month later, Philippe invited a wealthy developer and his wife back to their luxurious apartment after a business dinner. Philippe and the other couple had been drinking, and Fran suspected that they might have taken some ecstasy. While touring the apartment, the man's wife was awed by the site of Philippe and Francesca's enormous sunken Jacuzzi. She immediately appealed to her husband and Philippe to fill the tub and "get naked". Without hesitation or discussion, Philippe agreed eagerly with his guests. With only his eyes, he ordered Fran to undress with him and to join them in the tub. By then, she didn't feel like she deserved to have her own opinion, so she stripped and joined them without hesitation. She felt dirty and ashamed.

Philippe had brought her another glass of wine in the Jacuzzi that night. She gradually felt more peaceful, relaxed, and less self-conscious for the rest of the evening. She recalled the other couple suggesting trading partners for sex. Her memories of the rest of the evening were sketchy. She barely remembered having sex, but she couldn't recall herself objecting. It occurred to her that Philippe had probably put some ecstasy in her wine that night.

The sun was getting close to rising over the horizon, and the sky above her was turning a lighter shade of blue. In the distance, Fran heard the peaceful Coachella valley starting to come alive. Her body continued to move instinctively back and forth through the pool, her mind unable to stop replaying her past.

After the other couple had left, Fran remembered having a dramatic argument with Philippe. She must have been coming down from the alcohol and the ecstasy, and was feeling more like herself. She refused to engage in any more swinging, with that couple or with any others. She felt dirty and disgusting for having given herself away.

It was the first time that Philippe ever struck her. As she remembered the beating, she became confused and her memories started becoming jumbled. A feeling of darkness and vague memories of a belt buckle searing into the flesh of a young child were trying to intrude into her consciousness. Suddenly, she was having difficulty remembering anything. Walls seemed to be going up in her mind, trying desperately to keep the darkness and memories out, and to keep her mind in the present. She tried to refocus her mind on the cool sensations of water flowing over every part of her body, on each stroke of her arms, and on every turn when she reached either end of the pool.

Fran succeeded, for the moment, in wrestling control over her thoughts and memories. She recognized that it was that night when she knew it was hopeless to argue with Philippe. She remembered thinking about going back to Cinque Terre, but realized that Philippe controlled all of their money. He bought her everything she ever needed, and more. She didn't have her own bank account, bank card, credit card, or more than 500 francs to her name at any time. By 1990, at the age of twenty-five, she had become totally dependent on Philippe, and he controlled virtually every aspect of her life. She couldn't leave him even if she wanted to do so.

Fran marveled at how young and naive she had been. Today, the independent, hard working part of her identity constantly struggled to keep her from feeling worthless, and to help her feel stronger. The romantic and hopeful parts of herself that had surfaced in Manarola on that warm September evening, had long since disappeared. They were gradually being replaced by those familiar old friends - distrust and hopelessness.

Fran recalled how exchanging sex partners, or having *ménage à trois*, became a way of making business deals for Philippe. Once the first ethical boundaries disappeared for him, there were no longer any ethical or moral limits for him. She remembered starting to feel like she was wandering between many different rooms in her mind, living each day like a zombie. In each dissociative room, there were distinctly different rules for how to act and for how to deal with life in that situation. She began feeling like she was many different people on the inside, even though each of those different parts of her identity seemed to be looking out through the same set of eyes.

Fran couldn't remember how Philippe had transitioned from swinging and trading sex partners for "vanilla" sex, to more extreme sexual acts involving bondage, submission, and sadomasochism. She made another mental note that he already seemed quite familiar and comfortable with those acts by the time he "asked" her to join him.

As if I had any choice in the matter.

The BDSM activities made her feel even more ashamed and dirty. She began feeling like she deserved to be dominated and humiliated. She became the ultimate submissive. She did what her master, Philippe, commanded. She started feeling like she had reached rock bottom in her life at that time.

About thirty minutes into her swim, Fran recalled the time when she finally learned how to exert some control over Philippe and her life. She learned how to take advantage of his greed, his need for more control and power, and his need to continue expanding his financial empire. She convinced him to set up offices in New York and Los Angeles. It was Fran who convinced him to build the opulent and reclusive estate in Palm Desert six years ago.

Philippe, since we are constantly coming to America for business, especially here in Los Angeles, would it not make sense for us to have a home here? You are always complaining about the winters in France. We could start expanding our art and real estate businesses in America, and also have a warm place to spend the winter.

Philippe was easily convinced. Then came Chateau Eden. While the Palm Desert Estate was under construction, Fran raised the idea of having a secluded, European-inspired nudist resort or spa somewhere near Palm Desert.

It would be a perfect place for some of our more open-minded business associates to relax. It would be a good real-estate investment. And managing it would give us something to do when we spend more time in Palm Desert during the winter.

Once Philippe agreed to the first part of her plan, the rest had been easy. They started the search for a suitable property and stumbled upon the run-down old 1950's-era motel in Palm Springs. Fran started reclaiming a small portion of her self-identity as they renovated the tired old buildings, and as she convinced Philippe to allow her to decorate and furnish each room with its own unique European theme.

Fran also allowed herself to think about the possibility of using her lost massage therapy skills at the resort. Just thinking about it had given her some faint hope of resurrecting yet another small portion of her lost identity. She was starting to find her spirit to fight back, if only in small ways.

The morning sun started spreading fingers of daylight across parts of the pool and deck. Fran's arms and legs were beginning to tire, and the physical sensation of fatigue was bringing her mind back into the present. The exercise of letting her mind retrace the events that brought her to this point in her life, and connecting all the dots in her mind, had been helpful. The independent, businesslike side of her realized that she hadn't been completely helpless in her life with Philippe, and the time she spent in Palm Springs and Palm Desert had made her existence more tolerable.

However, there was another part of Fran that was in deep denial, and was telling her that she really shouldn't complain.

After all, Philippe is still taking care of me, isn't he?

Deep in her subconscious, Fran became aware of another distant voice calling her by name, pulling her mind back more fully into the present. She coasted to a stop at the end of the pool and let her feet touch the bottom, her mind confused.

"Good morning. Beautiful morning for a swim, isn't it? Do you mind if I join you?"

She looked up, her mind still partially in a daze. The voice belonged to Dan Whitney, his naked body illuminated by the golden rays of the early morning sun.

294

PART THREE: THE TREE OF KNOWLEDGE

CHAPTER 20

DAN AWOKE to the sound of Michelle coming out of the bathroom, then rummaging through her suitcase for running clothes. Sunshine streamed through a space between the curtains at the eastern end of their room. It was clear and sunny again, as it had been for the last three days. Dan sat up in bed and rubbed his eyes.

"Morning, Chelly. Have a good sleep?"

"Yeah, I've been sleeping like a baby with that fresh desert air coming in the window for the past three nights. How about you?" she asked.

"Same here. It's so quiet up here at the top of the mountain. If you hadn't made any noise, I'd probably still be sleeping. Are you going for a run?"

"Yeah, I hope Fran or Philippe are up so they can let me out through that monster of a gate out there."

At the mention of Fran's name, Dan became aware of the distant sound of splashing water, drifting through the open window. He climbed out of bed and opened the curtains for a view of the pool.

Fran was already swimming lengths, her naked body gliding through the water. Seeing her, Dan was eager to get back into his regular swimming routine. Yesterday had been his first swim after ten days without exercise.

"I think I'll go and join Fran in the pool," Dan announced. "After we have breakfast, do you want to drive back to Palm Springs and look around in some shops? We didn't have a chance to do that while we were staying at the Chateau."

"Sure," Chelly answered. "I went for a long run yesterday, so I'll be taking it easy today. Then we can come back and look around Palm Desert, or just hang out by the pool this afternoon, okay?"

"Sounds good. Maybe tomorrow we can get up early and take a drive up to San Jacinto Park and hike around a bit?"

"Yeah, I'm okay with that. I'll see you when I get back."

Before Dan could answer, Chelly strode out of the guest suite. He realized that, once again, they hadn't even given each other a good morning kiss. He gave a dejected shrug, trying to ward off the resentment that was resurfacing.

He diverted his attention back towards the pool. He opened the sliding door and stepped onto the deck. His naked skin tingled as it came into contact with the brisk morning air. Yet, at the same time, he felt some warmth from the morning sun.

It's going to be another hot one today.

Dan walked over to the end of the pool where Fran had left her terry cloth robe folded on the deck. She coasted to a stop, where he was standing.

"Good morning, Fran. Beautiful morning for a swim, isn't it? Mind if I join you?"

Fran stared up at him, as if she was in a daze. She was breathing steadily from her exertion. After a delay, she seemed to recognize Dan, then started speaking to him in short sentences between taking deep breaths.

"Good morning, Dan … Yes, it is lovely … How are you this morning? … I trust you both slept well."

She hoisted herself up onto the edge of the pool and reached for her robe, using it to wipe the water from her face. Dan couldn't help but notice how her tanned body glistened and formed goose bumps as the morning chill and the sunrise both touched her wet skin simultaneously. Her hard nipples projected from her small, pear-shaped breasts and the hairs on her arms stood at attention, forming an ultra-fine fur over each limb.

"Yes, thank you," Dan answered. "That bed is so comfortable, we both had an awesome sleep."

He was trying to maintain eye contact to keep himself from staring at her naked body. But, from Fran's lack of eye contact, he realized she was feeling just as awkward as himself.

"I should go and help Philippe prepare breakfast," Fran replied. "Are you going to swim now?"

"Yes, but I don't think I'll be swimming for more than twenty or thirty minutes today."

"Please, do not feel you have to hurry," she said. "Breakfast should be ready when you are finished."

"Is anybody able to let Chelly out through the front gate this morning? She's headed that way to go for a run."

"Yes, Philippe is up there now. He will be able to let her out. Enjoy your swim."

They exchanged smiles, then Dan slipped into the pool, pushed off and started stroking through the cool, clear water.

PHILIPPE WAS cutting up strawberries and pineapple for breakfast as Chelly strode across the living area and into the kitchen. He looked up, noticing her red ponytail bounce up and down, and her running shoes squeaking on the tile floors as she walked.

Philippe's eyes devoured the sight of Chelly's compact, muscular frame, the voluptuous curves of her hips and breasts, and her red hair. She was totally aware of the effect that her skin-tight black running shorts and low-cut pink tank top, her muscular legs, her tight behind, and large bust were having on Philippe. And she loved it.

"Ah, bonjour Michelle!" Philippe exclaimed. "You look positively radiant today!"

"Why thank you, Philippe! You're too kind, but you must not have your glasses on yet. Otherwise you'd see that I just got out of bed and don't have any makeup! But thanks for the compliment anyway!"

He has a way of making me feel special every time I see him. And that French accent! It's so sexy and romantic!

"You are going running this morning?"

"Yes, but just a short one. I don't want to be running uphill when it's getting too hot out there. Maybe I'll take a day off and sleep in tomorrow," she added with a smile.

"But, of course, *ma chérie*. Then perhaps we can all stay up late, visiting in the spa, enjoying some wine, and getting to know each other better."

"That sounds like fun, I can't wait! Can you show me how to operate the main gate, just in case Dan and I want to go out when you or Fran aren't around?"

"Of course. But you don't have to worry. Either Francesca or myself will be here during the day to let you in or out. Just a moment," he said, while he rinsed and dried his hands.

Philippe led Chelly into the back hallway, through which they had first entered from the garage. She watched as he stopped at an intimidating-looking control panel on the wall beside the garage entrance.

Chelly could tell it wasn't your ordinary home security system. Philippe was careful to shield the control keys with his body, so she couldn't see the codes he entered.

He seems a bit paranoid about his security. But I guess I'd be paranoid too, if I had visitors in such an expensive home.

Chelly shrugged her shoulders and her thoughts disappeared when she heard three beeps, and Philippe opened the side entrance for her.

"Thank you! I'll be doing some stretching first, before I leave the estate. It will only take a few minutes."

"Of course, *ma chérie*. Just press the button on the intercom on your way out, and I'll close the gate. You can ring Francesca on the intercom when you return, since I will be gone to the Chateau by then. Do you and Dan like seafood? I was planning to make some for dinner tonight."

"Yes, we both love it, but please don't go to any trouble," she said.

"It's no trouble at all. I enjoy cooking for people, and I look forward to spending an evening relaxing with you and Dan. It will be nice to get to know each other better, don't you think?" he said, adding a friendly wink. "Enjoy your run."

Philippe disappeared back into the house. The massive wrought-iron gates started swinging slowly inwards, and remained open while Chelly completed her warm-up. She started into a slow jog down the driveway toward the open gate, paused to press the intercom button, and then jogged out through the only portal into or out of the estate.

Chelly looked over her shoulder as she turned onto the street, noticing the gates closing slowly behind her. She liked talking to herself as she ran. It helped her mind to relax completely. In those peaceful moments, her thoughts became a flow-of-consciousness, connecting all the different parts of her identity.

That security fence looks so odd ... It just makes me feel nervous ... The place looks more like a prison than an estate ... Oh well ... I guess they have their reasons ... My God that Philippe is sexy! ... I wonder what it would be like to be with him? ... It's getting hot out here already ...

Chelly pulled her water bottle from the belt around her waist, and took a gulp of water. Her flow-of-consciousness was distracted by the sumptuous estates she was passing as she jogged down the mountain towards Palm Desert. She didn't give the giant wall or Philippe another thought for the rest of her run.

"I DON'T know, Chelly. We went through just about every major gallery in Palm Springs and Palm Desert this afternoon. I'm on sensory overload right now."

"I know what you mean," Chelly said. "I loved all of the Native American art and the desert landscapes. But I just don't know if any of it's right for our place back home."

"You're right. I saw lots of pieces I liked too," Dan answered. "But I don't think that style is right for us either. I didn't see anything I liked better than Fran's portraits at the estate."

Chelly paused to think for a moment.

"Do you think she'd sell one of them to us? Chelly asked."

"I don't know, let's talk to her about it tonight. All she can do is say no … Looks like we're just about there," Dan said.

The mammoth wall of Philippe and Fran's estate loomed large against the late afternoon sunlight, as they made the final turn and reached the top of the mountain.

Dan's eyes were drawn to the imposing presence of the security wall and the ominous-looking razor wire.

I still don't get it. The whole thing still seems like overkill to me.

He guided the car to a stop beside the colossal iron gate, opened his window, and pressed the intercom button. Fran answered a few seconds later.

"Hello, who is it?" she inquired.

"It's Dan and Chelly. We're back."

"Just one moment," she replied.

There was a buzz from the intercom and the gate swung slowly inward. One of the garage doors also opened for them, allowing Dan to drive directly into the garage. He and Chelly met Fran in the hallway as they emerged from the garage.

"I am going out to pick up some groceries for Philippe," Fran announced. "Is there anything I can get for you while I am out? Perhaps there is something you like to snack on during the day?"

"No thanks," Chelly answered. "We mostly eat things like yogurt and fruit for snacks, and I noticed you already have lots of those."

Chelly and Dan watched from the kitchen window as Fran's blue Prius disappeared through the gate. They both had a banana and some grapes from a large bowl of fruit in the kitchen. The fruit seemed to be dwarfed by the enormous kitchen counters and cabinets.

"Well, it's time for me to get naked and get some sun!" Chelly remarked, as she finished her last grape. "Are you coming?"

"Absolutely," Dan said. "I can't wait to open up my book, feel the sun, and listen to that waterfall. I'll help you put sunblock on your back."

Once in the guest suite, it took no time at all to strip down. Seeing Chelly's ivory skin and the full, graceful curves of his wife's naked body had an immediate effect on Dan, as he approached her to put sunblock on her back.

Instead of squirting sunblock from the bottle, Dan put his hands on Michelle's waist and pulled himself close to her body. He moved his hands upwards over soft skin on her firm, flat stomach, until his hands reached the fullness of her breasts. His head bent down and he kissed her gently on the side of the neck. His growing penis rubbed against her backside.

Chelly's body went rigid, and she pulled away from Dan.

"Not now, lover boy!"

There was no playfulness in her voice. Instead, it was stern.

"I don't want a bunch of dried semen on me while I'm lying around naked! And I don't want to take another shower until just before dinner. Can't you keep that thing down until we have some privacy?"

Dan's frustration got the best of him and he couldn't restrain himself any longer.

"There isn't another person anywhere on the estate!" he shouted. "How much more privacy do you want?" He waved his arms in frustration.

"I thought we were getting away so we could spend some quality time together! What the hell's wrong with you these days, Chelly?"

"What's wrong with *me*?" she shouted back. "In case you don't remember, I'm still pissed off at you for having the audacity to speak for me when we were in the spa with Pam and Richard the other night! I still feel totally disrespected!"

"Come on!" Dan said. "How long are you going to hold onto that? I apologized and admitted I was wrong. What more do you want?"

"You're going to have to give me time, Dan. I guess I need to see if you're really going to change."

Chelly was defiant, her hands on her hips, her face red with anger. "So, are we going to put sunblock on each other's backs, or are we going to stand here and keep arguing for the rest of our holiday?" She thrust the bottle of sunblock back to Dan.

Unable to think of anything else to say, he reluctantly started rubbing the cream onto Chelly's back. An icy silence filled the room as his hands kneaded her skin until the white cream disappeared.

Chelly grabbed the sunblock and slathered some cream onto Dan's back in a matter of seconds. When she finished, she ended the awkward silence by wiping her hands on her towel, grabbing her book, throwing the sliding door open, and stomping to a lounge chair on the pool deck, where she spread the towel and hid her head in her book.

Dan followed, settling into a lounge chair about six feet from Chelly. He closed his eyes, trying to ease the tension in his body by focusing on the gentle splashing sounds of the pool's waterfall.

WHEN FRAN returned home with her groceries, she gazed out onto the pool deck from the giant windows of her luxurious living room. Dan and Chelly looked relaxed and peaceful, like the perfect couple having the perfect vacation. She was unaware of the festering tension between her two guests.

As for herself, Fran was anything but relaxed inside. She felt her fear intensifying. Her heart was pounding. She was losing control of her breathing and was feeling sick to her stomach. Philippe would be home soon. She was terrified that this perfect couple's perfect vacation was about to come to an end.

PHILIPPE ARRIVED home about thirty-minutes later. He was in an extraordinarily good mood as he took stock of the seafood and other ingredients Fran had purchased for the dinner he was preparing. He went to the living room and smiled as he saw his two guests lounging in the sun.

Turning away from the window, he shouted down the hallway towards their master suite. "Francesca, where are you!"

She emerged a few seconds later, looking timid and compliant. She was wearing a white bikini bottom and her sheer, peach-colored cover-up over her bare breasts.

"Yes, Philippe. What is it?"

Philippe's critical eye surveyed Fran's attire. He nodded his approval.

"Very nice. I'm sure my friend Dan will have a difficult time taking his eyes off you. Please take care of our guests while I prepare dinner. Offer them some wine or cocktails. You might also offer them a complimentary massage, due to the great inconvenience we have caused them!"

Philippe followed this last comment with a sarcastic laugh.

Fran went to the bar at the end of the dining room and removed an assortment of wine and cocktail glasses from the cabinet, setting them on top of the bar. When she was done, she went down the guest hallway and entered the smaller guest suite next to Dan and Michelle's. Her massage table was set up in that room, and she ensured that there were fresh sheets in place before leaving. She opened a glass door on the opposite side of the hallway, stepping onto the pool deck.

DAN SAW Fran coming towards them and gave her a wave.

"Is there anything we can do to help with dinner? I feel sort of strange sitting out here, while you and Philippe slave away in the kitchen."

"Please, it is no trouble at all. May I get either of you a cocktail or some wine? I will be bringing some cheese and crackers as well. We can have our own Chateau Eden wine and cheese party," she said, laughing nervously.

Chelly sat up in her lounge chair.

"Thanks. I'd love some white wine, if it's not too much trouble."

"I'll have the same," Dan added. "Can I help you with the wine and cheese?"

"That is kind of you. Philippe will have the cheese and crackers ready in the kitchen, if you would like to get them. I will get the wine."

Dan jumped up from his lounge chair, wrapping himself with his towel.

"Would either of you like a massage before dinner?" Fran asked. "It would be my way of showing how much we regret having inconvenienced you."

"You don't need to do that!" Dan exclaimed. "We'd be happy to pay you, like we would if we were at the Chateau."

"It is nothing, really. What about you, Chelly? I am sure your legs could use a good massage after running for the past two mornings"

"Are you sure? I don't want to take advantage of you," Chelly said.

"Not at all. I'll come and get you after you've had a chance to enjoy some wine and cheese."

Dan slipped his feet into his flip-flops, then went inside to the kitchen where Philippe had just finished preparing a tray with cheese, crackers, and vegetables.

"Hi, Philippe. You look busy. What's on the menu for dinner, or is that a surprise," he said with a laugh.

"No surprises," Philippe replied. "I'm preparing some traditional Italian dishes from Francesca's home, Cinque Terre, in the province of Liguria. I'm starting with seafood ravioli in a white wine and cheese sauce, then I thought we would enjoy a cold seafood salad. It doesn't sound like much, but I can assure you that both dishes are quite delicious and quite filling. I hope you and Michelle enjoy it!"

"I'm sure we will," Dan said.

He picked up the platter of snacks.

"Just let me know if there's anything more I can do to help you. I think Fran and Chelly will be busy with a massage, so I don't mind if you keep me busy."

"Merci. I will let you know if I need any help."

Dan carried the tray outside, set it on the patio table, and then raised the table's umbrella to shelter the food from the sun. Fran returned with a chilled bottle of white wine.

"I think you will enjoy this," she said. There was little emotion in her voice. "It is *Burasca* wine, from my home in Cinque Terre. I think you will find that it also goes nicely with dinner."

Fran poured them each a glass of wine, then disappeared into the house. Dan and Chelly each put some snacks on a plate, then took them back to their lounge chairs with their wine. The silence between them remained heavy as they both sat quietly, reading their respective books.

Dan felt relieved when he saw Fran returning to the deck.

"Okay, Chelly, I am ready if you are."

Dan couldn't help but notice the lack of enthusiasm in Fran's voice.

"I guess I'll see you two just before dinner," Dan said. "Enjoy yourself, Chelly!"

He didn't receive a reply, as Chelly followed Fran into the house. Dan was trying to keep things civil and light, but Chelly's mood seemed to get worse every time he spoke to her.

This is really going well! And I don't know what's got into Fran - something's bothering her too. She seems to be working too hard at everything this afternoon. And what am I going to do about Chelly? There doesn't seem to be anything I can say to make her happy. The only guy that seems to be happy around here is Philippe.

Dan was getting an unsettled feeling again - that feeling like something just wasn't right.

Maybe coming to the estate wasn't such a good idea after all. Or maybe it doesn't have anything to do with being at the estate. Maybe the problems between Chelly and I are worse than I thought.

At the moment, he had too many questions and no answers. It was no wonder he felt unsettled.

Dan tipped back his wine, taking a large gulp. He picked up his book again, hoping he could distract himself and push the questions out of his mind, at least until dinner.

PHILIPPE'S DINNER was exceptional. His culinary skills had indeed lived up to Fran's reviews. Both the seafood pasta and the seafood salad were distinctively Ligurian, and unlike any Italian meal Dan or Chelly had eaten before.

The conversation at dinner had been pleasant and much less stilted than it was before dinner. Chelly and Dan were both interested in Cinque Terre and what it was like for Fran to grow up there. Fran did her best to talk as much as possible about things that tourists would find interesting, while avoiding her personal life. Philippe did the same when talking about Paris.

I wonder why Philippe and Fran don't seem to want to talk about their childhoods. They always manage to turn it around so they're talking about us, Dan thought.

The *Burasca* wine was flowing freely. Everybody, including Dan, was becoming much more relaxed. Any reservations he had about Philippe's evasiveness seemed to disappear with the wine.

As the couples finished dinner, they were treated to a deep orange sunset over the San Jacinto Mountains and the Coachella Valley to the northwest. The lights of Palm Desert twinkled more brightly as the western sky gradually turned deeper shades of orange, then bronze.

"That was an absolutely terrific meal!" Dan exclaimed. "Wouldn't you agree, Chelly?"

After Saturday night's argument, he was being especially careful not to speak on her behalf again.

"I'm so impressed, Philippe!" Chelly squeaked. "I don't know about other women, but as far as I'm concerned, there's nothing hotter than a man who can cook! Isn't that right, Fran?"

"That is true," Fran answered. She fidgeted with her hands and her eyes looked downward. "I am fortunate to have a husband who is such a wonderful cook."

"Well, I think Philippe gets to sit and relax after all his hard work. I'll help with the clean up," Dan offered.

"You're too kind," Philippe said. "I'm sure Fran would appreciate your help in the kitchen. That will finally give me a chance to get to know your beautiful wife better. I fear that I have been so busy that I haven't been able to spend much time with my guests," he said.

"Okay, Fran," Dan said. "Let me give you a hand while our better halves get to know each other. I'll take the plates and cutlery."

Together, they carried a load of dishes into the kitchen. They returned to the table for a second load, and then disappeared inside the house to finish the cleanup.

PHILIPPE BEGAN making the best of his time alone with Michelle. As they talked, the eastern sky turned indigo and the full moon poked its head over the horizon. Much as it created the colorful sunset, the insidious smog that spread eastward through the valleys from Los Angeles, also tinted the rising orb a brownish shade of orange.

"Michelle, shall we open up the spa for when Dan and Francesca return?" Philippe asked.

"Sure, why not!" she exclaimed.

As he started folding up the spa cover, Philippe changed topics of conversation.

"Have you enjoyed the first week of your nudist experience so far? I hope you enjoyed the atmosphere at our humble Chateau. I must apologize once again for the sudden inconvenience and having to relocate you."

"Oh, you don't need to apologize again," Chelly replied. "We had a wonderful time this weekend with the other guests. And we had a relaxing day today. Your estate is so lovely and peaceful. I didn't think I would feel nearly as comfortable as I did with being nude around other people."

"Can you help me lift the cover and carry it over there?" Philippe asked.

Chelly picked up one end of the awkward cover, following Philippe to an area behind the spa, where they set it down.

"Richard and Pam were right," Chelly said. "It isn't really such a big deal, once you get used to it. And it felt so natural for me to be able to be naked by your pool today. It was just as relaxing as being at the Chateau."

"Then you won't mind if I go nude in the spa?" Philippe asked politely.

"Of course not! I assumed that you and Fran always relax in the nude. You don't mind if I join you too?"

"Please do!" Philippe replied, smiling.

He began disrobing, hanging his clothing over the back of a patio chair. Chelly was quick to join him as she removed her bikini and cover-up.

Philippe watched from behind as Chelly became naked. His eyes followed the round curves of her hips and firm buttocks. She turned towards him to hang her clothing on the same chair, pausing to tease him by giving him a healthy look at her large bosom, then turning away again. His eyes tracked the gentle swaying of her hips as she walked to the spa and climbed down into the bubbling water.

As he watched Chelly's ginger hair and the delicate freckles on her ivory-colored skin, Philippe's mind detached. He started reliving the images of a fourteen-year-old boy - the voluptuous curves of a red-haired, middle age woman he once loved. He remained distant and detached, even as he climbed into the spa with Chelly.

She reached out with her foot and nudged Philippe's foot with hers. He blinked and was momentarily disoriented, until the sight of Chelly's face and her real-life breasts brought him back to reality.

Philippe used the awkward moment of silence to gather his thoughts. Slowly regaining his composure, he took charge of the conversation again.

"You were speaking of the Holloways. They are an interesting couple, are they not?"

"They're so much fun," Chelly squeaked. "Richard's such a tease, and Pam has such a great sense of humor," she added.

"Ah, you found Richard to be a tease, did you? Some of the other guests have sometimes accused both Pam and Richard of being too sexually suggestive."

Philippe knew he had to put Michelle on the spot, and start putting his plan in motion before Dan returned. He knew Dan was going to be an obstacle, so he had little time to lay the foundations for his attack on the other man's defenses.

"Yes," Philippe continued. "It has been mentioned by some of the other guests that the Holloways have suggested … what do Americans call it? … Swaying? … No … Is it swinging? … You know … Exchanging each other's sexual partners? You know what I mean?"

"You're right. Swinging is the word you're looking for," Chelly said, blushing at her memory of the high sexual tension in the spa at Chateau Eden on Saturday night.

"I see from your blushing that I struck a sensitive nerve. I hope I did not embarrass you, *ma chérie*!" he said, although that was exactly what he intended.

"Did they ask you and Dan to trade partners?"

"Well, sort of," Chelly admitted. Her face and ears turned a darker shade of crimson. "They didn't actually ask us to swap. But there were lots of suggestions in the spa, and they invited us back to their room when the spa shut down."

"So you went back to their room and nothing happened?" Philippe pressed. He already knew what had happened, but he needed to coax Michelle to talk about her frustration with Dan.

"Dan declined their invitation," Chelly said, "so we don't know if they were going to ask us."

"So I assume that Dan was speaking for both of you," Philippe injected, knowing that he now had his finger on Michelle's button. He held his breath as he waited for her answer.

"No, he wasn't speaking for me," Chelly pouted. "He didn't even give me a chance to answer. We had a big argument about it afterwards. I told him how disrespected I felt because he didn't even have the courtesy to ask my opinion."

"You were only angry because he spoke for you?"

The deep red color returned to Michelle's face.

"Not exactly. I was sort of curious about what would happen," she admitted.

"So you would have said yes to switching partners?" Philippe asked, in mock surprise.

"Well, maybe … I really liked Richard. He was pretty hot." Chelly explained. "And I saw that Pam and Dan getting pretty cozy too. I was pissed-off when Dan declined."

Philippe knew the time was ripe to press Michelle's button.

"Ahhh … so you are looking for a little spice in your life. Something to put some spark back in your marriage?"

Philippe was going for her jugular.

She is becoming my marionette. And I am rehearsing her for her real performance, when Dan and Francesca return!

"I see," Philippe replied, feigning understanding. "I've heard there are many who choose that lifestyle. They claim there are many benefits."

"I know," Chelly answered. "But it's impossible trying to make Dan see that. He can be so frustrating sometimes. He's always quoting the 'Psychological Research' and his 'clinical experience' all the time. He can be so boring!"

Philippe watched as Chelly sat upright in the spa. She appeared to be growing more confident by the moment, sensing that she had an ally in Philippe. She reached for her glass of wine and took a long, relaxing sip.

"He won't try anything new unless *Psychology Today* endorses it," she added. "I still can't believe he got into skinny-dipping and nudism. It's so-not-him. I hope all psychologists aren't like that. If they are, they're more anally retentive than the rest of us! How ironic is that?" she said, laughing.

Philippe joined in the laughter, this time in genuine agreement with Chelly.

"Oh, here they come now. You won't tell him I told you about Saturday night, will you?" Chelly whispered.

"Don't worry. But I may try to engage him in some philosophical debate on the subject. It could be amusing, don't you think?"

Philippe winked and Chelly flashed a conspiratory smile in return.

"You're right. This could be fun. I'll play along with you," she added. She gave him a good-natured nudge on his arm, then leaned back into her seat on the opposite side of the spa, sipping on her wine.

Philippe felt smug as Dan and Fran stripped, ready to join himself and Chelly in the frothy water.

THE SKY was now almost black, except for an orange glow in the western sky from the lights of Los Angeles. From the spa, one could see small patches of lights stretching from east to west across the entire length of the valley. The lights from Palm Desert twinkled below them. In the foreground, solar garden-lights had come to life, bathing the yuccas and other natural desert vegetation of the carefully landscaped garden with their yellow glow. The lighting, both on the pool deck and beneath the surface of the spa, was muted, providing an intimate ambience for the bathers.

Before Fran could step down into the spa, Philippe glared at her, his eyes hard and penetrating. He gave her a distinct nod, sending a pre-arranged non-verbal signal between them.

"Francesca, before you join us, perhaps our guests would like to share a nice California Cabernet."

Dan, who had just seated himself in the spa beside Chelly, stood up again.

"Do you need any help, Fran?" he offered.

Fran looked to Philippe for help, panic showing in her eyes.

"No need, my friend," Philippe interjected. "You have done quite enough already tonight. Please stay and relax. You are our guests tonight!"

FRAN DISAPPEARED into the house. She headed towards the dining room and the bar, her legs trembling as she walked. An open bottle of Cabernet Sauvignon stood on the counter. She had removed the cork about thirty minutes earlier, allowing the wine to breathe.

Fran took a furtive look over her shoulder to make sure she was alone in the room, then opened a drawer in the bar, removing the small white envelope she had hidden earlier. She opened the package and poured the ecstasy powder into a crystal decanter that was standing beside the Cabernet. She carefully poured the wine into the decanter, as she had done so often for Philippe in the past, swirling it gently as she poured, until the powder dissolved completely.

The worthless part of Fran's identity was growing larger, as was a part that was feeling intense fear. Waves of guilt and nausea swept through her. She started to panic as she felt herself losing control of her body.

As the emotions increased in intensity, her walls came up and her mind dissociated back to Manarola. She imagined herself swimming in the Mediterranean, stroking steadily and breathing rhythmically, until she felt her heart rate and her breathing slowing. Only then did it feel safe to lower the mental barriers. Her mind gradually began to re-connect with her body, and she allowed herself to lower the walls and bring her focus back to the unpleasant task at hand.

Fran placed the wine decanter and four wine glasses on a portable cart, then wheeled it through the sliding door from the dining room to the pool deck, parking it beside the spa. She poured four glasses of wine, serving Chelly first, then Dan, and finally Philippe. She handed her own glass of wine to Philippe, who held it for her while Dan helped her down into the spa.

Philippe proposed a toast once Fran had settled into her seat.

"To our guests, and to making new friends!" he said, extending his glass.

"To new friends!" Dan and Chelly echoed. The foursome clinked their glasses together in the air.

AS DAN looked up at the raised wine glasses, his eyes strayed outward and he found himself gazing at the nocturnal beauty of the illuminated estate and the entire nightscape of the Coachella Valley below. He sat upright as something attracted his attention.

"Hey, Philippe, I just noticed something. I can't even see the security wall from down in the spa. It just disappeared!"

"You're very perceptive. It's one of the reasons I wanted this lot. The mountain drops off quickly at the back of the property. I knew I wanted a tall security wall, but I also wanted a view. So this was the perfect piece of land for me to have both."

"Well-planned," Dan said, nodding with approval. "I should have known that two sets of artistic eyes like yours and Fran's would have considered that!"

"Thank you. We are pleased with how things turned out," Fran replied.

"So, Dan. I have had a wonderful time getting acquainted with your beautiful wife," Philippe began.

"What about you? What kind of work do you do as a psychologist? It must be interesting!"

"It is, and challenging too," Dan said. "I work mostly with people who have experienced abuse or trauma - people who have Posttraumatic Stress Disorder."

"Fascinating," Philippe replied, dismissively.

"Do you ever find yourself dealing with more Freudian kinds of issues, such as people's dreams or sexual fantasies. After all, if Freud was right, we all have psychosexual fixations to some extent, do we not?"

Dan was taken aback by the abrupt change of subject.

"Occasionally," he answered. "Why do you ask?"

"Well, I was asking Michelle earlier about her experience with nudism this week. I asked her how she got along with the other guests, particularly Richard and Pam Holloway. She told me there was considerable ... shall we say ... erotic playfulness ... happening between yourselves and the Holloways. I was wondering if you believe that such playfulness represents a repressed drive for people to act out their sexual fantasies?"

Dan was caught off balance again, this time by the sudden change to the same subject that he had been arguing about with Chelly on Saturday morning.

"I suppose that may be true for some people," he replied carefully. "What's your point?"

"Well, I was also wondering if you think it's healthy for people to have sexual fantasies?" Philippe responded.

"Of course," Dan answered.

"So, you think it's healthy for people to act out those fantasies?"

"I suppose," Dan qualified. "But it depends on a lot of things, like whether they do it safely, or whether they're married," he added.

"Whether they're married?" Philippe asked.

"Certainly," Dan said. "I think it's healthy for most couples to encourage each other to play out their fantasies, but within the context of their relationship."

"I'm confused," Philippe said. He was enjoying every minute of parrying with Dan. "Does that mean each partner is only allowed to have fantasies they can fulfill with their partner, or are they also permitted to have other fantasies? May I give an example?" he added.

"I think I see the difference," Dan replied, "but please go ahead."

Philippe glanced across the spa at Michelle, who was seated between Dan and Fran, then gave her a warm smile accompanied by a small wink.

"Well, I believe research has shown that a common fantasy, for both men and women, is to have sex with somebody of a different color or ethnic background. Or even for heterosexuals to fantasize about having sex with a same sex partner. So hypothetically, let us assume your beautiful wife, Michelle, was having fantasies of having sex with an African-American man, like Richard Holloway, for example. And hypothetically, let us also assume that you were attracted to a beautiful black woman like Pam Holloway. Would it be acceptable for you to encourage each other to express your fantasies, and to exchange partners?"

Philippe sat back and Dan saw a satisfied smile spread across his face. He felt like the air had just been sucked out of his lungs.

Why would Philippe use Chelly and me as his hypothetical example? Did he know what happened in the spa on Saturday night?

Despite his shock at being confronted again with Saturday night's dilemma, Dan was surprised that wasn't feeling any hostility towards Philippe. Even though he knew he disagreed with Philippe on a cognitive level, he was starting to feel a confusing amount of empathy that he didn't understand.

From his peripheral vision, Dan saw Michelle smile openly at Philippe. He saw how much she was enjoying herself, and how a sense of intimacy was quickly developing between his wife and the Frenchman. Chelly's nipples were erect, and he knew she was starting to feel aroused.

"Do I ever like this wine," Chelly exclaimed. "I haven't felt this laid-back for such a long time!"

Dan looked at Fran, who was reclined in her seat, not saying a word. She appeared to be feeling much more relaxed as well. He had to concentrate to get his thoughts in order.

"Well … like I said before, Philippe. I think it depends on a lot of factors. My feeling is that both partners have to be emotionally secure and have great communication in their marriage before they even consider trading partners.

Dan looked directly at Chelly, raising his eyebrows so she knew he was talking about their marriage.

"If they do," he continued, "as long as they both know the physical and emotional risks, and as long as they both consent, then I have no problem with how mature adults express themselves sexually."

Dan turned his attention and the conversation back in Philippe's direction.

"However, my big issue is that I don't think there are many people who are emotionally secure enough to handle sharing their partners in such an intimate way. I've seen too many women in therapy who have been coerced into swapping because they're afraid of losing their husbands. I've also seen cases where it splits up marriages and families. Instead of making the marriages stronger, it ends up leaving two of the partners devastated and children confused."

"Francesca and I both agree that mature, consenting adults should be able to make their own decisions. Do we not, Francesca?" Philippe said, narrowing his eyes as he made eye contact with his wife.

"Of course," Fran said, with almost no emotion present in her voice. She averted Philippe's stare, took a sip of wine, and turned her attention to Michelle.

"What do you think, Chelly?"

"I think the decision to start swinging is similar to when Dan and I were deciding to come to Chateau Eden. Dan wanted to share his enjoyment of skinny-dipping and social nudity with me. I was really afraid to try it, but he didn't pressure me, did you Dan?"

"I hope not," he replied. "I let you talk to some other people, do your own research, then make up your own mind about it."

"Actually, I had a terrible nightmare about it the morning before we drove here," Chelly said, laughing. "But by Saturday, it felt like I'd been doing it for years! So I'd like to think that if I suggested swinging to Dan as a way of allowing us to broaden our sexuality, that we could talk about it just as openly."

"I have an important question for you, Dan," Philippe asked. "If we assume that all four people must be mature and emotionally secure, who gets to decide who is secure enough, and who is not? Surely we mustn't all have to be cleared by a psychologist or psychiatrist first?"

"That's just my point," Dan said. "I don't think we *can* ever be sure that all four people are secure enough. That's why I think it's risky. All four people have to trust that the other three are emotionally secure enough to handle swinging. It requires a huge amount of trust!"

"Ah, but isn't that what swinging is all about?" Philippe rebutted. "It's about building more trust in our relationships with our partners and other people! It's about being able to trust our partner, and to talk openly about each other's sexual and emotional experiences, is it not? All you talk about are the risks. But look at the possible rewards for your marriage!"

Dan couldn't fail to notice the cunning smile on Philippe's face as he finished making his argument. It made him feel increasingly uneasy. He was beginning to feel like the prey being herded into an ambush by predators. His response was tentative.

"I see your point … I guess its all about whether the potential rewards outweigh the risks."

"I have another hypothetical question for you," Philippe continued.

"If I told you that Francesca and I find you and Michelle sexually attractive, and that we would like to exchange partners and get to know each other on a much more intimate level, what would you say to such a proposition?"

Philippe flashed Chelly his most charming smile.

At that moment, Dan realized that his wife had fallen under the spell of the Frenchman's romantic accent, his charming personality, and his persuasive logic. Her romantic side had surfaced and had taken complete control of her.

As if on cue, Chelly stood up and crossed over to the other side of the spa, where she sat down beside Philippe. She leaned against him, put her head on his shoulder, and wrapped her arm and nearly empty wine glass around his neck.

Dan was dumbfounded by Philippe's question and Chelly's response. He now knew it was not just another hypothetical question. Too late, he realized that Philippe was playing him against Chelly, forcing him to choose between either staying true to his morals and professional judgment, or angering his wife.

I'm trapped!

Dan's old familiar self - the part that was always afraid of doing anything bad - was causing Dan to panic. It was struggling against two other parts: the loyal part of him that desperately wanted to please Chelly and save his marriage, and the part of him that feared she might leave him.

He looked to Fran on his left for help. As his eyes met hers, she looked down quickly to avoid eye contact. He was left totally on his own.

He met Philippe's expectant gaze, seeing the smug look of victory on his face.

Then Dan looked at Chelly. She wore the same satisfied look on her face as Philippe. He saw that she was waiting to hear what he had to say. She was daring him to say no like he did to Richard and Pam on Saturday night. It was clear to Dan that she was enjoying seeing him trapped in his predicament.

Dan sighed. He had no choice.

"Well ...," he began slowly. "Hypothetically, I would have to take into account all of the issues I just mentioned. I suppose, more than anything, I would want to make sure that both Chelly and Fran were willing to do it. If they were, then I suppose I would have no objections to the idea," he admitted.

"Most interesting, *mon ami*," Philippe replied.

He looked to his right at Fran, then turned his focus back to Dan.

"As you might have guessed by now from my conversation, Francesca and I have engaged in some exchanges of partners in the past. We have found the experiences to be most rewarding, have we not *ma chérie?*"

He fixed his eyes on her, waiting until she raised her head and looked him directly in the eyes.

Fran forced herself to smile back at Philippe and Chelly. Dan detected her submissive response. It only reinforced the uneasy feeling in his body.

"Philippe is right," Fran continued. "We have been able to get to know a number of lovely couples much more intimately." Her voice showed little enthusiasm as she spoke.

Fran finally met Dan's eyes. The walls in her mind were desperate to hide her fear from him. She slid to her right, so that she was now sitting closer to Dan than to Philippe. Her hand searched for Dan's under the water, taking it into hers.

"Dan, I want you to know that if Chelly is agreeable, I would like to share Philippe with her. And Chelly, if you are willing to share Dan with me, I would like very much to be with him."

Dan tried to make a connection with Fran's eyes, as they had done on Saturday. Today, however, he was unable to read anything. They were completely vacant at that moment. Her walls were fully activated. They were allowing the businesslike part of her identity to take complete control over her emotions. Unable to see anything in her eyes, Dan had no idea that her businesslike part had just resigned herself to doing exactly what Philippe expected her to do.

"DO YOU mind if I call you Michelle instead of Chelly?" Philippe inquired. "It is such a beautiful French name and such a shame not to use it."

He gazed directly into her eyes.

"If the four of us were to engage in such a social experiment, would you be willing to explore your sexuality more fully with me?" His eyes implored her to say yes.

Chelly had lowered any remaining barriers in her mind as the ecstasy and alcohol combination took control of her brain and body. Her long-frustrated romantic, sexual side was now in full control, overpowering any remnants of distrust or fear of intimacy that may ordinarily have been present. Feelings of relief and sexual arousal were rushing through her.

"Philippe, you have no idea how romantic and sexy I find you, and how much I want to explore with you!"

She drew herself closer to him, ran her fingers through the thick hair on his chest, and planted a passionate kiss on his lips. Philippe reciprocated with a sensuous touch of his lips.

As he did so, his right hand cupped one of her full breasts and his thumb stroked her nipple, sending a wave of sexual longing through her body that was so intense, it shocked her and left her breathless. Chelly had never taken ecstasy and was completely naive to how it was intensifying every sensation in her body.

Dan saw Philippe growing more confident by the moment. He watched in awe as Philippe skillfully aroused the romantic, sexual side of his wife's identity. There was no doubt in his mind that it was happening on both an emotional and physical level. But what Dan didn't know, was the full extent of the sense of power and control flooding through Philippe, and into his genitals, as he kissed Michelle.

The couple's lips separated and Philippe was the first to speak.

"So, Michelle. What do you hope to learn from such an experiment? How do you hope to broaden your sexuality and your relationship, as you said before?"

Chelly turned towards Dan. She was still clutching Philippe with her one arm around his neck.

"I don't want to knock you, Dan," she began. "You're an amazing guy and a loyal husband. You're a good listener most of the time, you're attentive, and you're tender. I know you only want to please me and show me that you love me. What more could a girl want, right?"

Chelly's eyes locked onto Dan's, letting him know she wasn't finished with him yet.

"But you're too tender. You're too afraid to hurt me or do something wrong. And it just gets … it gets boring! I'm sorry. I just want to be taken by someone with some fire inside him. I want to wonder what he's going to do to me next. I want somebody to take control of my body and use it to please himself! And I want to see how much pleasure that gives me!"

Chelly looked up at Philippe with tears starting to form in her eyes.

"I want so much for you to do that for me, Philippe," she pleaded.

Then she looked back towards Dan again.

"I'd like to see if you're any different when you're having sex with somebody else. I guess I'm just curious. Do you understand?"

"Not really," Dan admitted. "But I guess I need to try to understand what you need. I'll do this to see if it can help bring us closer."

"I am intrigued by your answer, Michelle," Philippe said.

"It sounds to me like you are tired of having Dan defer control of your lovemaking to you. You are tired of him being submissive and asking you to be the dominant partner. Would you agree? He inquired.

"That's it exactly! You understand! Thank you, Philippe!" She leaned over and planted another huge kiss, this time on Philippe's cheek.

"What you want is to let someone else be dominant. You want to trust him to do whatever he wishes with your body to give him pleasure. In return, you will submit to him and receive your own pleasure," Philippe concluded.

Chelly gave Philippe another kiss, this time a tender one on his lips, then settled back into his arms.

"Just talking about this with you is turning me on," she said. "I can't wait to be with you, my dear, romantic man. When can we start?"

"Immediately if you like. Since you and Dan are planning to leave on Friday, it would be a shame to waste any precious time, would it not?"

Chelly's eyes pleaded with Dan's. His shrug of resignation was all she needed to see.

CHELLY SNUGGLED closer to Philippe, clinging to his arm.

"Perhaps we should agree on a few courtesies and rules first," Philippe continued.

"I think we can all agree on using condoms for safe sex, even if Michelle and Francesca are both using the pill. If you like, Francesca and I can show you our recent test results indicating that we are free from STD's. What about yourselves?"

"We haven't been tested since we got married, have we Dan? I guess everybody will have to trust me if I tell you I haven't had sex with anybody but Dan since then. My guess is that Dan is too much of a goody-goody to have an affair. Am I right, Dan?"

Dan shook his head at Chelly for that comment. He usually hated it when she called him a goody-goody. Yet, oddly, he found himself unable to feel angry with her tonight. He didn't understand what it was, but something was making him feel laid-back. It just didn't seem to bother him tonight.

It must be the wine. I'm feeling so relaxed and agreeable right now!

"Chelly's right. You'll have to trust me too. I haven't had sex with anybody but her since we've been married."

"Would anybody else like some more of that wine?" Dan asked, changing the subject unexpectedly.

"Of course" Philippe replied. "Francesca, would you mind serving the rest of that bottle? And please remember to take out another two bottles for us to take to our rooms tonight."

"Now, let's finish discussing our rules," Philippe said. "Francesca will make sure we all have a good supply of condoms. Shall we leave it up to each couple to decide whether they choose to use dental dam for oral sex? And, shall we leave it up to each couple to discuss any limits to the activities any of us might object to? Does everybody approve?"

"I only have one other suggestion," Dan interjected. "I will only agree to this on the condition that the experiment ends immediately if any one of us objects and wants out. Does anybody have a problem with that?" he asked.

His question was greeted by complete silence.

"Then Dan and I agree!" Michelle squeaked. Her voice had climbed up into its higher register. "We all agree! I can't wait to spend tonight with my charming French lover."

Michelle showed her excitement by pulling Philippe closer and planting a series of short, sensuous kisses on his lips. Then she stood up and crossed back to the other side of the tub. She gave first Dan, then Fran, a tight embrace and a kiss on the cheek. As she planted the kiss on Fran's cheek, she whispered in the other woman's ear.

"Thank you for sharing. He's all yours, and he's a really gentle guy. You guys have a good time." She sat back down next to Philippe, snuggling up close.

Dan turned to face Fran. He forced a smile and gave his new partner an awkward hug. He felt confused inside as he looked into Fran's eyes. She was distant and tired. There was something in her look that troubled him. Something wasn't right, but she trying not to let it show.

I'm here on vacation to get closer to my wife. Yet, here I am giving Chelly to another man I hardly know, and spending the night with his wife. What the hell am I doing? What's coming over me? What in the world am I getting myself into?

CHAPTER 21

FRAN LED Dan by the hand into the second guest suite, both of them wrapped modestly in the large white towels they had used to dry themselves after climbing out of the spa. Fran switched on the lights and the room became illuminated in the soft, warm glow of recessed overhead lighting.

"Would you prefer candles, Dan?" she asked. There was still little emotion in her voice.

Dan still felt awkward and confused. Here he was, unexpectedly spending the night with this other, very attractive woman. He couldn't deny the sudden emotional link he had felt with Fran just two days earlier. He was feeling increasingly drawn to her since meeting her three days ago, but even more during the past few hours. He had to admit he felt increasingly comfortable being with Fran as they dined, worked together in the kitchen, and enjoyed conversation and the exceptional wine in the spa over the past few hours.

"Candles would be nice," Dan replied, as he looked around the guest suite.

There were two large wrought-iron candleholders on the bureau, each with a sizeable four-inch-diameter white candle. The candleholders blended perfectly with the room's decor, which was the same modern Mission style as the rest of the home. Even though it was smaller than the larger guest suite he was sharing with Chelly, it still had a large, solid pine bed. The room was simple, with matching bedside tables, each with a small reading lamp, on either side of the bed. Dan noticed a bowl that was well stocked with condoms, on one of the bedside tables.

A massage table, prepared with fresh linens, had been set up in the larger space on the left side of the bed. Dan found it a bit unusual that there were three large pine-framed mirrors in the room: one was hung over the bureau, another over the head of the bed, and a third on the wall beside the massage table. Finally, he noticed a tasteful assortment of prints and paintings in the Southwestern style that fit well with the spacious, yet warm, decor of the room.

"Would you like to light them while I get some more wine," Fran asked. "There's a CD player and some discs on the bureau, if you would like to load three or four of them into the player."

"Thanks," he said, taking a lighter from her, then lighting the two large candles. He looked through the stack of CD's, finding mostly New Age relaxation recordings for massage. He found a couple of Jesse Cook albums and a Zen relaxation recording of Asian music, and loaded them into the player. The calming sound of Jesse Cook's classical guitar washed gently through the room. Dan turned off the overhead lights then lay back on the bed, allowing himself to think about how he and Fran would be spending the night. He was starting to feel excited, and felt his penis beginning to stir.

Fran returned a few minutes later, carrying a tray with a new bottle of the Cabernet and two wine glasses. This time, she managed a weak smile at Dan as she entered the room.

Am I mistaken, or does Fran seem like she's starting to relax? She was so distant and distracted during dinner, but she seems to be growing less guarded as the night wears on. Maybe it's the wine. I know it's helping me relax and feel more comfortable.

Fran filled two glasses with wine, standing with her back to Dan to shield the small amount of additional ecstasy powder in each glass. She swirled each one slightly to help the crystals dissolve. Philippe insisted on a follow-up dose of the drug.

We need to make sure everybody enjoys themselves, he had said.

"Here, Dan," she said, as she smiled and passed his glass to him. "To new friends and experiences,"

They raised their glasses to each other.

"To new friends and experiences," Dan replied.

"So …" Dan began awkwardly, "how do we get started? You've done this before. What would you suggest?"

"You could just tell me the kinds of things you like to do," she answered softly. "I want this to be as pleasurable as possible for you."

"That's nice of you," Dan answered. "But what about you? This isn't all about pleasing me, is it? What would you like to do tonight?"

"To use Philippe's words, I feel more comfortable letting my partners be dominant during sex. I get pleasure from your pleasure," she explained.

Dan's mind floated back to the things Chelly said about him in the spa - how she wanted a man who took control during sex - someone who was more dominant.

I must be submissive in sex, just like both Chelly and Fran. It looks like somebody needs to take control here. I guess it might as well be me.

"I've got an idea," Dan said. "When was the last time anybody gave you a massage, Fran?"

"Who, me?" she asked. "I am afraid I cannot remember. I imagine it was when I was taking my massage course in Paris, and we had to learn on each other. That was many years ago. Do you know massage?"

"I don't know it well," Dan admitted. "Chelly and I took an evening course for a few weeks just after we were married. She enjoyed receiving much more than giving, so we didn't use it much. But I learned enough to give a relaxing massage. So, I think it's about time that somebody pampered you. Besides, we can talk and it will be a good icebreaker. Hop up on the table please!"

Fran reached out and removed the towel from Dan's waist, then dropped her own towel, leaving them both naked and vulnerable. Fran got herself settled on the table, then Dan covered her lower half with a sheet. He started rubbing some massage oil briskly in his hand to warm it.

"I am quite warm enough at the moment," Fran murmured, as she spoke downward through the hole in the headrest. "You do not need to cover me with a sheet."

Dan removed the sheet for her, exposing the entire backside of her body. He paused briefly to admire her muscular legs and butt, her slim waist, and her olive-colored skin. He started working on her back. Even to his untrained hands, he noticed immediately that the muscles in Fran's upper back and shoulders were tight and full of small knots.

"Things are pretty tight up there, Fran. Have you been under any stress lately?" he inquired. "You seemed preoccupied earlier today."

There was a long pause.

"No more than usual," she lied. "I imagine I should take better care of my own muscles," she added. She searched for a way to deflect the conversation away from her.

"Dan, do you love Chelly?" she asked out of the blue, quickly throwing the conversation back in Dan's direction.

The question caught Dan by surprise. He stopped massaging momentarily to consider his response, choosing his words carefully.

"Well, I try hard to love her and make her happy," he replied. "But she's good at throwing up barriers. I often feel like she's holding back her intimacy and sexuality from me. I know it's in there, because it comes out sometimes. But I don't know how to help her bring it out more. I guess I feel like it's hard work loving her."

He resumed massaging, and then threw the question back at Fran.

"How about you and Philippe?" he countered. "Do you love him?"

There was a noticeable pause before Fran's businesslike, professional voice replied.

"Philippe takes good care of me. What more can I ask?"

The talk about their spouses had just introduced a significant amount of tension and awkward silence into the room. Dan continued to knead the small nodules in Fran's back. She closed her eyes and concentrated on the warmth and surprising skill of Dan's hands on her body.

CHELLY SAT across Philippe's lap in the spa, sipping the last of her ecstasy-laced Cabernet. She was feeling the usual relaxing effects of alcohol, but even more pronounced than usual. She felt warm all over, her sense of touch was highly attuned, and the signals from all of her sensory receptors were amplified. She was also enjoying a heightened state of sexual anticipation and arousal. Philippe knew it was driving her crazy, and that he could have her any time. But that was the point - he intended to drive her crazy. He wanted to take advantage of her will to have him dominate her. He wanted to build her arousal at a painstakingly slow pace, until she had to beg him for a release like she had never experienced before.

Philippe was also sexually charged. While the wine and ecstasy were no doubt exacerbating his current state, his arousal had intensified over the course of the evening as he felt himself gaining more and more power and control over Michelle and Dan.

"*Ma chére*, Michelle," he said, tracing the curves of her voluminous breasts with the tips of his fingers. "Now that we are alone, do I understand that you are willing to trust me to take your sexuality to places it has never been before?"

"Oh yes, Philippe," she whispered. She began stroking the inside of his thigh, finding his well-endowed erect penis with the side of her hand. She turned her hand so her fingers could better feel it. She gasped slightly as her fingers worked their way towards the top his shaft, wondering when she was going to reach the tip of its impressive length. "I can't wait for you to have me," she sighed. "Any way you want to have me!" she added.

He reached down and gently took her hand, lifting it away from his genitals.

"All in good time, *ma chérie*," he answered, as he kissed her gently on her cheek. "If you want this from me, you must consider me to be your master, and you my slave. Are you willing to trust me enough to do this?" he said, looking sternly into her eyes.

"Yes, whatever you want me to do! I'm yours," she whimpered.

"Then I first need to know if there is any kind of activity that you absolutely wish to put off limits. Fellatio? Cunnilingus? Anal intercourse? Vibrators? Anything else? This is the time to speak up. Once you give me permission, you are giving me permission to pleasure you in any way I see fit!" he directed. "Do you understand?" he added solemnly.

"Yes, I understand," Chelly answered. She was more serious now. From somewhere deep inside her, fear was trying to work its way to the surface, making her hesitate before answering. "You may do anything with me. Except … except anal sex. Is that alright?" she questioned.

"Certainly, my dear," he replied. "And if you find that anything we do is simply too intense for you, and you wish to stop any activity, you will immediately shout the word *Red* to me. Do you understand?" he demanded.

"I do," she responded, this time in a more submissive tone. *Red.*

"One more rule," Philippe added. "From this moment on, when we are alone together, you will address me as *Master* or *Sir*! You will think of yourself as my slave. I will still call you Michelle or Madame, but you understand that you will consider yourself to be my slave," he repeated.

"Yes, Phil … Sir," she said. "I accept."

At that moment, Philippe saw Michelle become more distant, as though part of her mind was somewhere else. He suspected he knew what it was. All true Submissives have a part of themselves that feels defective, worthless, and undeserving of being loved, unless they are pleasing somebody else.

"Will there be any punishment if I disobey you, sir?"

Chelly's eyes went blank and she was momentarily confused. *Where did that just come from?* Just as quickly, her mind was brought back to reality by Philippe's voice in her ear.

"Perhaps later, Michelle," he answered. "But for tonight, it will be enough for you to become familiar with addressing me properly, and learning to trust me without question."

"Now, Michelle. As for tonight, you must tell me some of your most secret sexual fantasies. Nothing is sacred. I will try to find a way to fulfill one of those fantasies tonight, if I can. All you have to do is trust yourself to give your body to me completely," he explained.

Michelle thought about it for a moment, then squirmed in Philippe's lap and avoided making eye contact.

"I feel kind of silly," she giggled. Her face turned red with embarrassment. "I've always wanted to go to Venice, to a Carnival Ball. You know? Where they dress up in fancy robes and balls gowns, and wear those beautiful masks and hats?"

"Ah, yes. A very common fantasy," Philippe replied.

"But I fantasize of going alone, and having wild sex with a total stranger," she continued. "Like two strangers in the night, never knowing each other. Did you ever see Stanley Kubrick's *Eyes Wide Shut*?" she asked.

"Yes, of course - his adaptation of Schnitzler's *Dream Story* - a movie about a couple's sexual fantasies. How apropos!" he mused.

"Well, I was curious about it. So I watched it alone one time when Dan wasn't home, while I was lounging around in my pajamas. I felt so hot during that scene with the orgy, where everybody was nude except for their masks, I couldn't stand it. I reached underneath my pj's and made myself come while I was watching. Inside, there was a part of me that secretly wished I were one of the escorts at the orgy! Since then, I fantasize about going to a party just like that, hopefully in Venice. Is that too crazy?" she asked. Her ears were still red with embarrassment.

"Crazy?" Philippe scoffed. "Of course not, my dear. No fantasy is too crazy! Some are a bit more difficult to fulfill than others, but nothing is crazy."

Philippe lost himself for a moment as his eyes took in the beauty of Michelle's orange-red ponytail, her ivory-colored skin, the subtle freckles, and her wholesome breasts. An image of Isabelle, with her red hair and pure white skin, posing for a nude portrait, flashed into his mind momentarily. Michelle shifted in his lap. His mind snapped back into his present reality.

"I will see what I can arrange," he said thoughtfully. "I want you to go back to your room to shower. Do your hair and makeup like you would if you were going someplace formal, but don't put on any perfume or cologne. When you're finished, wear only a bathrobe and come to our master suite. There will be instructions waiting there for you. You are to read and follow them to the letter. If you fail to do so, you may be punished appropriately. Do you understand, Michelle?" he demanded.

"Yes Sir," she acknowledged.

"Then go now, and mind that you obey me!" he commanded.

Chelly did as she was told immediately. She gathered up her clothing in her arms and ran, still naked and dripping wet, back to their guest suite. As she ran, she was overcome with a mixture of excitement, sexual desire, joy, and anxious anticipation, at the prospect of finally being able to play out one of her fantasies.

CHAPTER 22

THE STATE-OF-THE ART video cameras and microphones, carefully concealed behind the two-way mirrors in the guest suite, were recording every action and word of the couple's intimate encounter.

Fran lay on her back in a tranquil state induced by the combination of wine, ecstasy, and massage. Dan had finished massaging her legs and back and was now massaging her thighs. He was feeling the effects of the ecstasy and was feeling an increasing sense of intimacy with Fran. As his hands moved closer to her genitals, he started to feel a stirring in his own. Fran opened her eyes and their eyes met.

"Dan, please massage me everywhere. I will not bite. Your touch is tender and beautiful, but you can be rougher with me if you like. Touch me anywhere you want, and do whatever you want to do with me. Do not be afraid that you are doing something wrong," she said.

"I don't think I'm afraid of being bad," he said. "You … you've just seemed fragile and vulnerable lately. I don't want to hurt you … emotionally," he explained.

"You worry too much. You are not hurting me. Please …" she begged again.

Dan's hands moved upward. He began massaging Fran's torso, lingering to massage her breasts and occasionally touching her nipples.

"I saw some scars on your butt when I was massaging your backside. How did that happen?" he asked.

There was a long silence. Fran carefully chose her words before answering.

"It was something I did once when I was young and I was bad. If you like, you can spank me when you make love to me. I like that," she said. She took Dan's hand and guided it to one of her nipples.

"Squeeze my nipples between your fingers, Dan. Be rough with them. It feels good. You are not hurting me."

Dan did as he was told, squeezing and twisting her nipples with increasing intensity.

"That feels better!" she urged. As Dan twirled and squeezed, her nipples became firm and erect in his fingers.

With a free hand, Fran took one of Dan's hands and placed it so it was cupping her pubic mound. She started moving his hand roughly up and down to make sure Dan knew what she wanted.

Once his hand felt her vaginal juices, Dan's arousal gained momentum, and he quickly became hard. He leaned down and began kissing the inside of one of her thighs. She spread her legs wider apart, to give him better access to her. She reached over for a condom from the bedside table, placing it at the ready beside her hip. She slid her body toward the end of the table, exposing herself more and giving Dan easier access for foreplay. Dan alternated his kisses and gentle strokes of his fingers, working gradually closer to her vaginal area.

"Not so gentle, Dan. Use your fingernails. Scratch my skin … yes, that's it," she directed.

Dan's fingernails scratched long, tantalizing trails up the inside of Fran's left leg, from her calf up to her groin. He repeated the ritual on her right leg, seeing his scratch marks on her thighs turning into red welts. He resumed kissing and letting his tongue wander through her thick, dark pubic hair. The fragrance of her juices was unusually strong, drawing Dan's tongue quickly towards its source. When he reached his goal, he was rewarded with nectar that was balanced like a fine wine: exquisitely sweet, but slightly salty, with a pungent and musky quality. She felt his tongue scoop it onto its tip.

The video cameras recorded every moment, as Dan reveled in Fran's taste and aroma. His tongue alternated between fluttering and probing between her inner labia, then circled round and round her swollen clitoris.

The tension was building inside Fran's vagina, and her body started letting go, oblivious to the cameras and microphones. She started rotating her pelvis and thrusting it towards Dan's tongue, more desperate to feel it working its way inside her. The sexual side of her identity had taken over. Its voice moaned as her longing intensified. She needed him inside her.

Fran sat up and reached for the condom. She ripped it open, then grasped Dan's arm, pulling him up to his feet, then towards her in one rapid motion. One hand found his erection and gripped it, causing Dan to moan in ecstasy. She unrolled the condom over his shaft, and then wasted no time guiding him towards her waiting body. She sat on the edge of the table and he stood between her legs. Her legs wrapped themselves around Dan's waist and her arms circled his neck, holding him tightly against her.

She felt him enter her, and then all movement ceased for a breathtaking moment. The video cameras kept rolling. Both Dan and Fran bathed in the exquisite sensations that were enveloping each other's sexual apparatus. His penis wasn't exceptionally long, but was thick. Her closed eyes, and the look of ecstasy on Fran's face clearly reflected the pleasant tightness, tension, and pressure she was feeling from his breadth, both on her clitoris and inside her vagina.

Their lips met, tentatively at first as they acquainted themselves with each other's touch, then followed by a long, passionate kiss as their tongues entered each other and began exploring eagerly. The kiss eventually wound itself down, ending with delicious, light touches of their lips. Then Dan's eyes locked onto Fran's. Their eyes became conduits into each other's completely vulnerable souls at that moment. Their breathing was now synchronized, as if they had become a single breathing entity.

IN THE MOMENTS of stillness that were recorded on video, the cameras could only capture the two lovers gazing into each other's eyes.

What they were unable to record was the confusion behind Fran's dark brown eyes. There was the long-dormant romantic part of her that was starved for sexual release. But more than that, it was also a part of her that desperately wanted to feel loved. It was a side of her that she tried to hide beneath her formal, businesslike exterior. There were also traces of the fear, sadness, and helplessness that Dan had seen when their eyes connected, so unexpectedly, two days earlier. She knew Dan was compelled to find out as much as possible about her.

Meanwhile, as Dan's soul made contact with Fran's through their eyes, she felt the depth of his empathy, his tenderness, and his ability to love. The level of intimacy was overwhelming for her. Even though it was everything she had ever longed to feel, her fearful and distrusting voices began shouting warnings to her, and the worthless part of her identity started screaming its messages of self-deprecation and guilt even more loudly. She began to feel panic building within, as the inner voices started erecting protective walls in her mind.

Fran's worthless, guilty side won the internal struggle this time. She quickly averted her eyes from Dan's, disconnecting the brief, yet powerful, exchange of emotional information that had just occurred between them. She pushed Dan away firmly and slid her pelvis back, breaking the coital connection between them. She turned her body over and thrust her buttocks into the air, exposing the underside of her genitals. The voice of Fran's worthless side shouted new instructions to Dan.

"Take me from behind, Dan. But first, spank me. Spank me as hard as you can. I want to feel it burn!"

Dan was stunned. A guilty voice inside him was shouting at him, telling him it was abusive and wrong. But his sexual desire and the loving part of his identity were burning to be back inside, making love to her. His guilty voice continued to protest, but it was no contest for the overwhelming urges of his long-frustrated sexual and loving parts. He smacked her repeatedly with his flattened palm, without thinking.

"Harder, Dan!" she shouted. "Everything you've got. I want to feel it all! All your frustration, Dan -make me feel it all. Harder!" she ordered.

Dan gave it everything he had. After five strikes, his hand was burning and had turned a fiery red. He felt pins and needles in it, and felt it going numb by the time she shouted for him to stop.

"Take me, Dan! Now," she shouted. As he moved his throbbing, swollen, and purple erection beneath her, she grabbed it and quickly slid its head into her opening, allowing Dan to push it home.

The cameras continued recording the thrusts and gyrations of the two lovers, capturing their lust and the physical act of coitus, yet completely unable to capture the depth of their mutual emotional transference.

THE MUSCLES inside Fran's vagina were now stretched tight and her clitoris felt a surge of tension and friction. Dan wasn't as deep as when he entered from the front, but the different angle of penetration was bringing the head of his penis against her G-spot. Even with the condom over his organ, she could feel his hard rim grinding over the densely concentrated zone of pleasure receptors. All of the sexual tension in her body seemed to be focusing simultaneously on her clitoris and G-spot, like sunlight being focused and intensified through two lenses of a pair of glasses. She felt the dual focus of her desire building like those two hot pinpoints of light, as she rammed her pelvis back and forth against Dan.

Dan picked up Fran's rhythm and started driving harder with each thrust, his own tension building as quickly as Fran's. It didn't take long for that pressure to reach the point-of-no-return for Dan. When he erupted into rhythmic contractions inside her, she heard his moans and felt all of his sexual tension and frustration exploding inside her.

Tears of mixed pleasure and pain flowed from her eyes as her vagina convulsed with its own rhythmic explosions, in perfect synchrony with Dan's orgasm. Her brain was overwhelmed and unable to differentiate between the blend of pain and sexual exhilaration she was experiencing. The magnitude of Fran's release was completely unexpected. Only rarely, on one or two occasions shortly after giving herself to Philippe, had she ever experienced orgasm as intense as what she had just felt.

Fran's pelvis collapsed as she knelt on the edge of the massage table and all of their contractions dissipated. Dan's body caved in on top of Fran's. Their lungs expelled long, exhausted breaths. Every muscle in their bodies sagged in relief. Dan wrapped his arms around Fran's abdomen and held her close to him. She reveled in the warm afterglow and the feeling of having him inside her.

After a few moments, when she felt him starting to shrink, Fran pulled her hips forward so that Dan slid gently from her. She turned and removed the condom from Dan, disposed of it, then took Dan's hand and moved towards the bed. She pulled back the covers and guided him between the sheets, climbing in after him. She moved close to him, putting her head on his chest, putting her arm across his stomach, and drawing one leg up on top of his. Their bodies rested, peacefully entwined together, not saying a word to each other in their exhausted state.

The video cameras continued recording the outer expressions of peace and exhaustion in the lover's eyes. However, beneath the outward appearance of peace and tranquility, both of their minds were racing. The multiple conflicting parts of their identities were confused and frightened by the speed and intensity of the emotional connection that was developing between Dan's loving and empathic parts, and the parts of Fran's identity that longed for both emotional and sexual intimacy.

Yet, despite their fears, neither Dan nor Fran had any physical or mental energy remaining for dealing with their respective mental struggles. Within a few moments, both had succumbed to exhaustion and were soundly asleep in each other's arms.

THE KNOCK finally came on the door. Anticipation and excitement streamed through Chelly's body. She had followed Philippe's written instructions to the letter. It repeated his warning that she would be punished if she didn't. The note also reminded her that she was not permitted to speak at all during tonight's fantasy. The lone exception was that she could say *Red* at any time if the activities became too intense for her. But it also stated clearly, in bold letters, that the experiment was over for good if she said *Red*.

When she had entered the master suite, she found a black thong undergarment, black high-heeled shoes, a bronze medallion choker on a black ribbon, and a stunning bronze-colored Venetian style *Columbina* mask, complete with long feather plumes, laid out neatly on the bed. A small bottle of Chanel No. 5 was placed carefully on top of the note and the neatly arranged costume items.

After putting the clothing items on, Chelly was surprised by how elegant her nude body looked in the perfectly fitting high heels, thong, choker, and mask. The plumes of feathers on the mask made her look like a lion with a black mane. She noted that the mask covered her eyes and nose, but left her mouth uncovered. Her exposed lips were plump and sensuous. She was pleased with the result. For the first time, she perceived her naked body as being truly sexy. She nodded her head in approval.

Chelly donned the ankle-length black cape with the long black sleeves and drank the glass of Cabernet that the note instructed her to drink. She felt the warm glow of the wine spreading through her body, intensifying the sense of wellbeing she was already feeling. The instructions were also clear that she was to wear no other fragrance except the Chanel when playing out her fantasies. She sat down on the side of the bed and waited impatiently for the knock on the door. Moments later, the silence was broken by three sharp raps on the door. Chelly reminded herself that she was not allowed to speak when she opened it.

When she swung the door open, she saw Philippe standing before her, attired in an ankle-length black cape, black leather boots, a traditional black *Tricorne* hat, and black leather mask. He looked as if he was straight from a Carnival ball in Venice! Like her mask, his disguise covered his eyes and nose, leaving his mouth uncovered. Philippe raised one arm, displaying a blindfold for Chelly, which the instructions told her to expect. Without a word, he walked around behind her and applied the blindfold, tying it tightly enough that she couldn't see, but not so tight as to damage the delicate plumes on her mask.

Philippe took her by the hand and silently led her down the hallway from the guest suite and then across the enormous living room of the mammoth home. He stopped and applied pressure on Chelly's hand, sending the non-verbal message for her to stop.

"Stairs down, Madame. Be careful." He took the first step and waited for Chelly to step down tentatively beside him. They repeated the process a dozen times, arriving on a surface that felt to Chelly like carpet on top of concrete. They began walking again. Despite the muffling effect of the carpet, she could hear their footsteps echoing slightly off the walls and ceiling of a concrete tunnel. Chelly had trouble estimating how far they walked, and she felt like they were descending further underground as they proceeded. After about a hundred or more paces, or about ninety seconds, she felt Philippe stop in front of her.

"Stairs up, Madame," he advised. As before, they took each step one at a time. However, this time she counted twenty steps as they ascended from the tunnel.

Where are we going? She thought to herself, as they emerged onto a carpeted landing. She heard Philippe turn a key in a lock, open a door in front of her, and then felt him take her hand and guide her through the doorway. Once through the entrance, he stopped again and she heard him close and lock the door behind her. She felt him loosen the blindfold at the back of her head. As it fell away from her eyes, Chelly's mouth dropped open in amazement. She was standing in a recreation of an enormous sixteenth-century European bedroom, with hardwood floors, and antique furniture. Authentic-looking area rugs from the period were placed on the floor around the bed and in front of casual chairs. There was a large open area of bare hardwood floor in front of them.

Chelly heard the gruff, subdued voice of Leonard Cohen singing poetically from speakers mounted in the corners of the room. Even though the music was from the twentieth century, Cohen's gravelly, dark voice and lyrics fit the mood and decor of the room perfectly. There were dark red curtains hanging down from the ceiling, which could be drawn into a ring around the canopy bed. The bed's canopy matched the curtains that hung from the ceiling. The room was illuminated only by the light from numerous candles.

From where she was standing, Chelly noted that she could see the metal rail from which the curtains were suspended, mostly hidden from view by the curtains. The ceiling looked like the rigging you would see in the backstage rafters of a theatre.

"Madame, please," Philippe said, as he guided her towards the middle of the floor by pushing her elbow gently forward. He took off his hat, and then bowed to her in a romantic gesture, causing Chelly's romantic side to go into a swoon.

My God. Is this for real? Just for my fantasy?

Philippe took her into his arms. They began waltzing to the strains of *Take This Waltz*. He was an expert dancer, and led her in sweeping circles around the bare dance floor, their black capes swirling around them as they went. When the song ended, Philippe once again removed his hat and bowed to her. He took her hand and led her to a spot just beyond the end of the bed, where there was a small area rug. He left Chelly standing in the middle of the rug, then went to a table beside the bed and lit some cones of incense, placing them in a ball-shaped incense burner suspended by three chains, which were attached to a ring-shaped handle.

Philippe brought the burner around the bed with him and stood in front of Chelly, small plumes of incense wafting from the burner. Her senses were already intensified by the ecstasy in the wine. The musky aroma of the incense added to the mysterious and erotic atmosphere in the room. She felt the blood starting to flow towards her genitals.

"Madame," Philippe began, in a solemn voice. "You are privileged to have been invited to this ball, and to an exclusive, private, and sacred sexual ritual. Remove your cape!" he commanded.

Chelly reached behind her as ordered. She pulled down the zipper in the back of the cape, creating an opening at the top of the robe large enough for it to slide off her shoulders and drop off her body. It landed in a heap around her high-heeled shoes. She stood before him almost naked, wearing only the thong, her shoes, the medallion choker, and her plumed mask.

Philippe kneeled on the rug in front of her. He bowed his head until his forehead touched the rug. He held his position for several seconds before returning to the kneeling position. He reached out and touched the inside of Chelly's legs, just above the ankles. Ever so slowly and one leg at a time, he began caressing her legs with only the tips of his fingers. She felt electricity start flowing up her legs and into her vagina.

Chelly felt him stop occasionally to kiss the inside of a leg lightly, sometimes letting her feel the slightest flick of his tongue. He alternated his touch from one leg to the other, rising at an agonizingly slow speed towards her genitals. His slow, deliberate pace was both breathtaking and agonizing as he moved higher. Any initial trepidation Chelly may have felt about what he was going to do to her, had changed to longing as she allowed herself to relax and enjoy the adventure. She felt herself becoming wet, smelling the musky odor of her sexual juices and the Chanel merging together. She felt Philippe's breathing quicken as the powerful aphrodisiac effect of the two scents further stimulated his brain's sexual response.

Then, just before his tongue reached her vagina, he stopped and stood in front of her. Chelly exhaled sharply, realizing that she had been holding her breath. Philippe cocked his head slightly and kissed her fleetingly on the lips. He started stroking the thick red hair that was falling freely down over her shoulders. His eyes became distant, and his fingers paused, as his mind seemed to go to another place or time.

Chelly watched the vacant look in his eyes, wondering where he had gone. She reached out and put her hand on his shoulder. Suddenly, Philippe's eyes refocused and his mind was back in the present with Chelly. His fingers continued downward across her shoulders and arms. He stopped occasionally to brush her skin softly with his lips, or to give her skin a soft flick with his tongue, as he had done on the inside of her legs. Slowly, his fingers traced concentric circles around one ample breast, then the other, slowly closing the circles until they brushed, teased, or gently squeezed her large nipples. Then his fingers and tongue continued their downward journey across her abdomen, over her waist and hips, then across her pubic region.

Chelly felt his fingers reach the creases between the inside of her thigh and her outer labia, lingering gently in those valleys, brushing her short ginger-red pubic hairs. He was driving her crazy with anticipation. Finally, she felt his fingers cross over the great divide, running along the inside of her outer lips, making contact with her moist inner labia, and tracing leisurely circles around the opening of her vagina. She felt the blood pounding in her swollen, hypersensitive clitoris. She felt it pushing its way out of its protective hood like a blossoming flower. With the help of the wine and ecstasy, it was fully primed. All of her sexual energy was being channeled and focused on that single point, causing the tension to start building in the walls of her vagina.

Philippe was on his knees again. She felt the tip of his tongue dart out, giving her clitoris an electric shock that surged through her entire body. She gasped and almost shouted, remembering at the last possible moment that any sound she uttered would lead to punishment.

Philippe made her wait. She saw him smile and sensed the surge of arousal that was sweeping through his body, as he took control of hers. Then his tongue darted again. She gasped again and held her breath. Once again he paused and waited. Then he extended an index finger and slid it along the length of her moist inner labia, before entering her slowly. He curled his finger towards himself and gently massaged the inner surface of her vagina until he found a slightly elevated and harder area, her G-spot. Again, his movements felt excruciatingly slow to Chelly as he methodically massaged his target.

Chelly felt her energy shifting and felt an entirely different, more powerful urge building within her vagina. Her legs were going weak. She felt his finger stop. It stood still on the center of the target, as if drawing energy from every part of her body towards it. She tensed and held her breath. Then, without any warning, he pressed the tip of his tongue against her clitoris. She felt the floodgates open and all her sexual energy flooded towards her duel sexual triggers. Then, just as suddenly, Philippe withdrew his tongue and his finger. She felt like all of the air had just been sucked from her lungs. Every part of her was longing for release.

Her body was reeling in disappointment, as if somebody had just pulled the plug on her sexual engine.

Philippe rose from his knees. Despite the mask he was wearing, Chelly could see his face beaming.

"Remove my cape," he commanded.

Chelly realized that it was fastened by buttons down the front of the cape. She worked as quickly as she could, but her fingers were shaking. She fumbled with the buttons and could not go fast enough. She wanted him inside her, right this instant. When she finally released the last button, she spread the sides of the cape wide and let it drop from his shoulders. He was naked except for his mask, black socks, and boots. She kneeled down, untied his boots and helped him remove them. She looked up at his erect penis. It was impressively long, but not as wide as Dan's. Philippe reached to his right and tugged on a rope that hung from the ceiling, beside the post of the canopy bed. It released a nylon sling that was suspended from the ceiling so that it was hanging beside Chelly.

Chelly raised herself up onto her knees and guided his engorged member slowly into her mouth with one hand, while her other hand massaged his hard, swollen balls. The silence was broken by Philippe's voice.

"You are too eager, Madame. Slow down. Savor every square centimeter of it. But be careful. If you make me come, I will have to punish you!"

After a few moments of stimulation, he placed his hands on both sides of her head, forcing her head and mouth away from his erection. He motioned towards the sling with his eyes.

"Sit," Philippe ordered. He helped her into the seat, and then he pulled on the rope, connected to a pulley system in the roof, raising Chelly and the seat to the perfect height in front of him. He reached over to the bed, where a small pile of condoms lay and picked one from the pile. After removing it from its wrapper, he placed it in Chelly's hands and nodded to her. "Madame, if you please!" he insisted.

Chelly eagerly unrolled the condom over the length of his erection. When she finished, he reached his arms around the back of the sling and swung it towards him, penetrating her waiting vagina. She couldn't help herself and emitted a long, gratifying sigh as he entered her. He looked past her mask and into her eyes.

"I may have to punish you for that, Madame," he said quietly. Then, Philippe began moving the swing back and forth slowly, causing Chelly to slide back and forth on his shaft. She wanted him to go faster, but he slowed down, causing the agonizing tension to build more slowly for her. He stopped the swinging motion, and then started rotating his hips, causing his organ to start moving in slow circles, stimulating larger areas inside her. She felt her tension building again. Then he stopped and withdrew from her. She couldn't hide the longing and disappointment in her eyes. She realized how much enjoyment he was getting from being in complete control of her body.

Philippe reached towards the bed again, wrapping his fingers around a large curved rubber vibrator with large ridges on the inner surface of the object's curved shaft and head. It was much wider than his cock and not as long. He saw Chelly's eyes go wide as she saw him moving it towards her eagerly waiting vagina.

As Philippe slid the vibrator into her moist insides, Chelly felt her cervix stretching wider, pulling on her swollen clitoris. She felt the object rubbing against her swollen pleasure center. Philippe flicked the switch to turn on the vibrations. Every sensation she had been feeling until now became amplified. She felt the pressure building inside her again. Then, Philippe expertly pushed down on the curved object, causing it to press forward against her G-spot. He started to move it slowly up and down, then around in circles. Chelly felt the energy rushing into both her clitoris and her G-spot, her arousal cascading like water from a bursting dam. Her breathing was coming faster. She knew she was building towards her climax. He took her hand and put it on the vibrator.

"Madame, you may bring yourself to climax," he said.

Chelly didn't hesitate. It took no time at all for her to feel the exact movements of the vibrator that were most intense. She took over control from Philippe, but with less patience. She worked the mechanical organ harder and faster, feeling her vaginal muscles starting to seize with tension. At that point, her nervous system handed over control of her sexual response to her body's fight-or-flight response. The need for release became increasingly urgent as she pumped the vibrator. Philippe sensed the imminent climax and reached towards the bed for a thick rubber strap.

Suddenly, Chelly's vaginal muscles went into rhythmic spasms of release. She let out a loud whimper that expressed her mixture of intense sexual ecstasy and relief. At that moment, Philippe drew back his arm and propelled it upward from beneath Chelly, slapping her backside without mercy and stimulating every pain receptor in her buttocks to start flooding her brain with emergency pain alarms. Chelly's central nervous system was overwhelmed and scrambled. It was unable to distinguish between her exquisite sexual ecstasy and the intense pain she was feeling from the strap. Every time Philippe sensed an orgasmic contraction, he slapped her backside again. Unable to distinguish between pleasure and pain, Chelly's brain only felt increased stimulation. Her orgasm intensified and the muscle contractions felt like convulsions. Her whimpers turned into screams of mixed joy and pain.

When it was over, Chelly's lungs heaved and her body was exhausted. Philippe stood in front of her. She looked at him in amazement and smiled. She now understood what she had been missing.

"Thank you … for punishing me … Sir," she managed to gasp between deep breaths.

PHILIPPE'S SEXUAL tension was still building. The immense power he was feeling from controlling Chelly's sexual response was exhilarating. He felt the blood pounding into his penis. He reached his arms behind Chelly and drew the swing towards him, then pulled the vibrator out of her vagina.

Chelly's eyes widened as she saw his erection coming towards her. He knew she was physically exhausted, but her sexual appetite had only just awakened. She took him into her, allowing him to penetrate deep inside. He felt her vaginal muscles tighten around his cock as he began thrusting. She wrapped her legs around his waist and eagerly helped him by pulling and pushing the sling back and forth with her legs. Her clenched vaginal muscles squeezed and pumped him mercilessly. He felt her tension building again, this time more rapidly.

Again, Chelly's fight-or-flight system took control of the heightening tension in her body, sending it into more spasms of ecstasy. Philippe felt the ultimate sense of control. As she came, and he heard her screams of joy, he finally let himself release. He felt her orgasm and his rhythmic contractions exploding in perfect synchrony inside her.

As Philippe continued to erupt inside Chelly, his eyes were fixated on her ginger-red hair and his eyes were distant. He was filled with a sense of fulfillment and completeness. From somewhere behind the walls in his mind, he heard an angry voice talking to the red-haired woman who held him inside her.

You came back to me, Isabelle. Now that we are together again, I will always take care of you. Nobody will harm you! But you must never leave me again! Never!

CHAPTER 23

THROUGH THE slits of his partially opened eyes, Dan noticed the morning sun streaming through the guest suite's blinds. His mouth was dry and his head was pounding uncharacteristically. Gradually, memories of the Cabernet and spending last night with Fran crept back into his consciousness. He reached across the bed for Fran and realized that he was alone. Dan brought his hands up to his face to rub his eyes and inhaled the musky fragrance of Fran's sexual juices, still clinging to his skin. The scent went straight to his brain, causing instantaneous arousal. He clambered out of bed, noticing that Fran had picked up his white towel and laid it neatly across the massage table. He wrapped it around his waist, making his erection less noticeable.

Dan exited the smaller guest suite, crossed the hallway, and opened the door to the larger adjacent suite he shared with Chelly. She was sleeping soundly in their bed. Dan felt torn. He debated whether or not to climb into bed and snuggle up to his wife in his current erect state. He felt like she was slipping away from him, and he needed to feel close to her.

He decided against it, feeling awkward after each other's unexpected sexual explorations with Philippe and Fran last night. He had no idea about how things had gone between her and Philippe. Instead, he moved the blinds slightly to one side and looked out at the pool. Fran's sleek body was moving effortlessly through the water, her ritual swim already in progress. He opened the sliding door quietly and slipped out onto the pool deck. He moved a chair into the warm morning sun, and sat while he watched Fran swim back and forth.

Dan's mind drifted back to the previous night's events. He felt uneasy as he recalled the intensity of the emotional and sexual connections they had shared. After about five minutes, Fran noticed Dan when she made a turn at the near end of the poor. She stopped herself and floated back toward the end of the pool, sending him a shy smile.

"Good morning," Dan said, unable to think of anything more eloquent at the moment. "How are you this morning? You slept well I hope?"

"Very well, thank you," she smiled. "And you?"

"I don't remember waking or moving at all," he exclaimed. "Thank you for a most memorable evening."

"It is I who should thank you. I realize how much I used to enjoy being massaged. Last night was especially sensual and beautiful. Are you going to join me? I have about fifteen minutes left before I must prepare some breakfast."

"Sure, I think I need to work off the wine from last night," he remarked. He slipped the towel off his waist, his erection having disappeared while he was sitting, and slipped over the side of the pool next to Fran.

"Whoa," he moaned. "That's chilly after sitting in the sun."

They stood awkwardly beside each other for a moment. Finally Dan leaned over and gave her a kiss on the cheek.

"I'll see you at breakfast," he whispered. Fran reciprocated his kiss, and then they pushed off together, stroking their way through the refreshing water.

CHELLY AWAKENED to the sound of Dan, closing the sliding door. She looked around the room, trying to get her bearings.

Where am I?

Her head was throbbing and she remembered consuming a lot of red wine.

Oh ... Philippe's and Fran's estate.

Then other details from the last night's remarkable series of events started falling into place in her mind, like Tetris pieces dropping into her consciousness. She smiled as she started to remember begging Philippe to go down on her again, and to repeat his dual stimulation on her clitoris and G-spot. She also remembered him taking charge again with the vibrator, masterfully bringing her to the edge of climax three or four times, before stopping periodically and letting her arousal come down, then creating more waves of sexual tension and frustration.

A broad smile spread across Chelly's face as she relived the memories. Philippe finally let her reach an agonizingly intense climax while he whipped her buttocks again with the rubber strap. The memory made her aware that both her backside and her vagina were pleasantly tender this morning.

Chelly smiled with satisfaction as she recalled taking him into her mouth a second time, skillfully making him hard again and bringing him into her vagina for a fourth mind-blowing orgasm. Her memory was foggy after that. She vaguely remembered collapsing on the massive canopy-bed with Philippe, but couldn't remember anything after that.

I must have been like a zombie! How the hell did he get me back here?

Laying half awake in her bed, Chelly was amazed at how understanding Philippe was of her need to feel wanted and dominated. It was harder still to believe how easy it had been for Philippe to persuade Dan to try swinging. She felt deeply satisfied and excited by how deftly the charismatic Frenchman could fulfill her secret fantasies.

She flipped the covers off and swung her legs over the side of the bed, then shuffled over to the blinds and peered out at the pool. She saw Dan and Fran swimming back and forth beside each other. She wondered what happened between them last night, feeling sure that it couldn't possibly measure up to what had transpired between herself and Philippe.

Chelly noticed the throbbing in her head again. She closed the blinds and headed toward the luxurious bathroom. *It's a good thing I went for some long runs over the past few days. I think it's time for a rest today.*

She found some Tylenol in her overnight bag and took it with her into the bathroom. The cold marble floors sent a shiver through her body, causing her nipples to stand at attention. She chased the Tylenol with a glass of water then turned on the shower. Chelly stood in front of the mirror and looked at herself while the shower warmed up. She conjured up images of herself from last night, in her black high-heeled shoes, black thong, necklace, and decorative mask. The sexy images in her mind caused the blood to start moving towards her vagina again. She looked away from the mirror to snap herself back to reality, and then stepped into the shower.

PHILIPPE FINISHED the long process of transferring the video files from last night's activities onto his computer. He started up the movie application on the new Intel Mac that he had customized solely for the purpose of video editing. He waited impatiently as the long video clips finished loading, so he could scan through them and select some highlights.

Philippe was glowing with satisfaction. The evening couldn't have gone better for him. He couldn't believe his good fortune in finding Michelle, who was so desperate for new sexual outlets, and for someone to be more dominant with her.

That fool, Whitney, fell into my trap perfectly. He's so afraid of losing his little redhead, he won't dare upset her! And I'm not stupid. He thinks I haven't noticed how much he is attracted to Francesca.

Philippe was impatient to look at last night's clips to see if the night's activities had ignited any small fires inside either his wife or Dan. The clips were finally loaded. He clicked first on the one of Francesca and Dan in the guest suite. The quality of the video, taken through the two-way mirror, was excellent. He dragged the computer's mouse impatiently through the clip, shaking his head at the pair's initial shyness and the lack of any significant action while Dan massaged the backside of Fran's body. He was scanning quickly when he finally saw Dan touching her breasts. He dragged the cursor backwards in the clip, then started moving it slowly, seeing the couple's sexual desire growing quickly into their initial tender connection. He shook his head sadly and frowned. He wasn't interested in watching vanilla sex. Then he noticed that Francesca was suddenly on her knees on the massage table, exposing her backside to Dan. Things changed quickly. He saw Dan start spanking his wife. The smile on his face returned.

Now that's more like it!

He watched the images of Dan's urgent thrusting and the synchronous pumping of Francesca's pelvis. Philippe felt himself getting hard, not from the sex he was watching, but from feeling like Geppetto, proudly admiring his human puppets. The feelings of power and control were intoxicating and addictive. And like any addiction, he needed more.

Philippe selected the portions of the clip he wanted to show. Then, he moved his mouse and clicked on the video of himself and Michelle, taken in the clandestine sixteenth-century set in the two-story shed next door. He selected a few portions of the clip - the parts when he was removing Michelle's blindfold and cape, when she was in the sling and he was driving her crazy with the vibrator, and finally the part showing him whipping her with the rubber strap, sending her into her ecstatic orgasm.

He hastily dragged his selections into two projects, and then clicked again to tell the Mac's state-of-the-art processor to transform the selected clips into two short movies. He was like a child waiting to open his gifts on Christmas morning. He would have it ready to watch within an hour, ready to show in the estate's luxurious home theatre. Philippe could barely wait until after breakfast to present Dan and Michelle with the results of last night's highly successful experiment. But even better, he knew they would not be able to resist taking another step deeper into his web tonight.

DAN AND CHELLY were sitting at the table on the pool deck, finishing their breakfast, reading the newspaper, and enjoying a cup of coffee. Neither had spoken much about last night, waiting for the other to break the ice. Philippe noticed them and walked cheerfully out onto the deck.

"Good morning, *mes amis*," he chirped, in his customary Frenglish. "How are my favorite guests feeling this lovely morning? I trust that everybody enjoyed last evening and slept well?"

As he spoke, he made a point of going to Chelly. He put his hand on her shoulder, then leaned over and placed his lips gently on hers. Chelly responded with a sensuous kiss, feeling no embarrassment, even with Dan watching.

"If you've finished your breakfast, I'd like to invite you to come with me into the theatre. I have some things I wish to show you, and then perhaps we can discuss our small social experiment from last evening. After all, our goal was to get to know each other more intimately, and to learn something about us in the process. It may be interesting to share our experiences with each other," he suggested.

Dan looked across the table at Chelly and nodded to her. Chelly jumped to her feet, eager to talk about her experience of sexual awakening. They picked up their cups of coffee and followed Philippe into the house, walking past the wall with Fran's photographs.

Dan couldn't help himself from stopping and looking at her portrait of the street-person again. In addition to the fear he initially saw in the woman's eyes, he felt something new this time. He felt like her eyes were pleading for help. Dan allowed himself to feel the sensation briefly, and then noticed he had fallen behind Chelly and Philippe. He hurried to catch up.

Philippe's home theatre was comfortably furnished with three rows of wide leather seats, attached together like regular theatre seats. Each seat had drink holders and a tray that could swing out in front of each viewer, much like being in an airplane seat. The seats reclined slightly to give a direct line of sight to the projection screen, which was elevated at the front of the room. Surround speakers were mounted on the walls. The projector was already on, and screen-saver images from a computer were wandering randomly across the screen.

"Dan, Michelle, please have a seat," he said, motioning for them to take seats in the front row. Fran followed them into the theatre and took a seat behind Dan in the second row.

"Because we have the luxury of having security cameras throughout our estate," Philippe began, "we are fortunate to have some video of our small social experiment last night. Rather than just talking about what we learned about each other last night, I thought it might be illuminating to watch our partners and ourselves first. Then, perhaps we can talk about what we've seen. I should first explain to you, Dan, that I asked Michelle to tell me some of her sexual fantasies. You will be watching my humble attempts to bring some of those fantasies to life for her."

Dan felt an uneasy feeling in his stomach as he realized he was going to be watching himself and Chelly in what amounted to a porn film. He looked quickly at his wife. Dan saw excitement in her eyes. He knew she was probably as curious to see what transpired between himself and Fran, as she was to watch herself and Philippe.

Philippe dimmed the lights and pointed a remote control toward the back of the room. Dan saw two icons on the screen, displaying two separate movies: *Philippe and Michelle* was the first of the two files, while *Dan and Francesca* was the second. Philippe moved the cursor over the first icon and double-clicked.

The video was captured from the far wall of the sixteenth-century room, through a two-way mirror opposite to the canopy bed. Dan saw two figures cloaked in long black capes in the scene, one with a man's *Tricorne* hat, and the other with an elaborate Venetian party mask. The quality of the video was much better than Dan expected from a security camera, and there was a high quality audio track as well. He felt increasingly nervous as he saw Chelly's cape fall to the floor and Philippe went down to his knees to begin worshipping her nearly naked body.

As he watched the short movie, Dan felt a confusing mix of emotions. On one hand, he was pleased and aroused to see Chelly letting her sexuality go and holding nothing back. He found himself getting hard as he watched, feeling envious that he wasn't the man in the scene. On the other hand, Dan felt disgust when Philippe reached for the rubber strap and began beating Chelly's backside. It felt abusive and foreign to him. He looked at Chelly with horror on his face as the movie clip ended and the sounds of her squeals of ecstasy abruptly ceased.

Chelly started laughing when she saw the expression on Dan's face.

"You should see the look on your face!" she howled. "You look like you were just watching Freddy Krueger!"

Philippe watched Dan and Michelle's different reactions with amusement.

"So, what is your reaction to seeing your wife living out a sexual fantasy with another man?" Philippe said to Dan.

"Wow," Dan said. He paused to reflect before continuing. "I don't know where to start. That was pretty unexpected." He turned toward Chelly, addressing her as he shared his feelings.

"My first reaction was feeling glad to see you let yourself go so completely during sex. I've always known you are a sexual person, and I've always wanted to see that side of you. On the other hand, I guess my ego feels a bit bruised that you can't seem to let yourself go like that when you're with me. I'm also confused.

You actually got off on being beaten? I'm having difficulty understanding that, Chelly. It just feels wrong to me. I don't think I could ever do that to you or anybody else."

"Well, Michelle, are you able to tell Dan what it was like for you, and what you learned about yourself?" Philippe said.

"Dan, I've been telling you for a long time that I need to have more excitement. But your idea of excitement is just trying different sexual positions, and talking about it a lot beforehand. Even if it's new, it's not exciting if I know what's coming. With Philippe as the stranger in my fantasy, I had no idea what he was going to do to me! It felt spontaneous and so exciting! I could feel the adrenaline rush the whole time! The strange thing is, when he was whipping my ass, it didn't really hurt. It just seemed to intensify every feeling in my body. I couldn't really tell what I was feeling. It was just indescribable ecstasy, Dan!" she said with a sigh.

"As a psychologist, Dr. Whitney, I assume you are familiar with the human *fight-or-flight response*, are you not?" Philippe asked.

"Of course," Dan answered. "Our body's fear response. It's hard-wired into all of us. It activates our body to save us whenever we think we're in danger."

"Quite correct." Philippe nodded. "Can you tell me if there is any relationship between our fear response and our body's sexual response?" he added.

"Yes," Dan answered. "Our fear response is controlled by our Sympathetic Nervous System. Our sexual response is more complicated, though. During sexual arousal, our response is controlled by the Parasympathetic System, the same pathway that's responsible for relaxation, among other things. But when we get close to orgasm, I believe our Sympathetic System, *the fight-or-flight system,* takes over."

"Correct again," Philippe confirmed. "So is it conceivable, that when we get closer to orgasm, and our Sympathetic system gets ready to take over, that we can create a much more intense orgasm by flooding the Sympathetic system with more stimulation? Much like you did when you spanked Fran, and like I did when I strapped Michelle?"

Dan thought about it for a moment, and then nodded his head in agreement.

"Logically, it seems like that could happen," he agreed.

"So, if our partners trust us to apply some painful stimulation, and if we keep that within their tolerance of pain, we may be able to give them a much more intense and pleasurable sexual experience. Would you agree?"

"Once again, it seems logical." Dan answered. "I'm not an expert in the area, so I couldn't say for sure."

"I have a question for you, Michelle," Philippe said. "If I had told you that I was going to use a rubber strap on you, and that I was going to strike you with such intensity, would you have agreed?"

"If I'd had time to think about it? Absolutely not!" she said. "I probably would have thought the same things as Dan," she admitted. "And I probably would have been afraid of feeling any pain."

"So," Philippe continued. "Are you glad you trusted me and gave me complete control of your body? Would you do it again," he added. "Especially if I told you that you have barely begun to explore the limits of your sexuality?"

"Oh, I'm so glad I trusted you! And I can't wait to keep exploring! Are we going to be able to do this again?" she asked, turning to look at Dan as she asked the question.

"Perhaps we should watch our other video before we ask Dan that question," Philippe said. "Let's continue."

He pointed the remote at the computer, clicking on the *Dan and Francesca* icon. Dan felt surreal as he watched himself and Fran together. He had difficulty associating the images on the screen with himself. On one hand, he felt guilty and dirty, like he was cheating on Chelly. It looked like porn to him and made him feel cheap, especially when he saw himself spanking Fran with such force. On the other hand, he was overcome by watching the intensity of Fran's sexual response, and he felt himself getting aroused. When he saw the moment that their eyes connected, he found himself reliving the emotions he had felt the night before. He felt the dual physical and emotional attractions that were drawing him closer to her, making him want to know everything about her. Dan looked over his shoulder, his eyes making brief contact with hers. Fran looked away quickly, just as she did last night, feeling uncomfortable with the intense emotional intimacy.

The video clip ended and Philippe brought the house lights up with his remote control.

"So what did everybody think?" he asked.

"Dan!" Chelly exclaimed. Her voice rose into her high, excited register. "I didn't think you had that in you. That was so hot, you two! How did you make yourself do that? You must have felt so guilty!"

"I don't really know," Dan admitted. He was blushing and wondering why he didn't notice any guilt last night. "I guess I was just caught up in the heat of the moment. Maybe it was the wine, or maybe I didn't want to disappoint Fran," he admitted.

"Michelle," Philippe inquired. "Would you agree that Dan seems to be naturally submissive during sex? Perhaps, like you, he prefers to give up control to somebody else, and to submit to their pleasure."

Chelly nodded her head vigorously.

"And what do you think," Philippe continued. "Do you think he could learn to have a more intense orgasm, and ultimately give his partners more pleasure, if he could learn to be more dominant with them?"

"Absolutely," she said. "I'm sure of it!"

"Well, then. It seems we all learned some interesting things with our little social experiment last night. Perhaps, after dinner, we can talk about continuing our experiment tonight. Perhaps some activities that will help us to build more trust with our new partners?" he hinted.

"Dan, what do you think," Chelly said.

"Like I said last night, Philippe, I have an open mind, as long as both Chelly and Fran are willing to continue." He looked at Chelly as he spoke, not daring to speak for his wife and deferring the question back to her.

"Excellent," Philippe exclaimed, as he rubbed his hands together. "I must stop by Chateau Eden today to see how our renovations are going and to discuss some things with Carmen. So I will be out for a few hours. Do you and Dan like Vietnamese food, Michelle?"

"We love it!" she squeaked. "Don't we, Dan. It's our favorite ethnic food."

"You bet," Dan agreed. "I've been craving some for the past few days."

"You're in luck, then," Philippe said. "I'll buy some groceries on the way home today. Michelle, would you like to join me in the kitchen this afternoon while I make some dumplings and some beef rolls? And Dan, would you mind helping by grilling some shrimp for us tonight?"

"I'd love to," Dan said. "How about you, Chelly?"

"Me too. We were thinking of going for a hike in the mountains before it gets too hot. When would you like us to be back, Philippe?"

"Three o'clock should give us enough time. Let's meet again then, shall we?"

As they agreed and started to leave the theatre, Dan couldn't help but notice how passive and quiet Fran had been during the gathering. Once again, she seemed passive and distant, while Philippe was in complete control of the proceedings. Dan still had an uneasy feeling that Philippe was manipulating him. He was also uncomfortable with the videos of their sexual activity, and

Philippe's nonchalant explanation that they were just a normal part of the estate's security measures. There was something about them that didn't feel right to Dan, but he couldn't explain what it was.

DAN AND CHELLY had been enjoying their hike on the trail in San Jacinto State Park for about half an hour. The temperature was in the eighties and they were getting thirsty. They stopped at a point that looked eastward over Palm Springs, and out towards Palm Desert.

Chelly took Dan's hand and smiled at him. "Thanks for taking a risk with me, Dan. I had the most amazing time last night. I learned so much about myself, and I loved seeing you take charge with Fran. I'd like you to learn to do that with me too. Did you feel jealous?"

"Surprisingly, I didn't," Dan answered. "Like I said before, I enjoyed seeing you let yourself go. I know you can be so hot and sexy. I just want you to learn to be that way more with me."

"So, are you still okay with me being with Philippe again tonight? And are you okay staying with Fran again?" she asked.

Dan knew he couldn't resist being with Fran.

"Sure, I really liked being with Fran," he admitted. "I just have a really uneasy feeling about Philippe. There's something about him that still doesn't feel right. Have you tried using your cell phone up at the estate yet?"

"No, why?"

"Well, I tried using mine this morning, but there was absolutely no signal. I asked Philippe, and he told me the neighborhood was still too new. He said AT&T has a tower, but the other carriers haven't caught up yet. It seems a bit strange. Most of the homes in the area are pretty expensive, and they look like they've been there for at least a couple of years. Doesn't it seem a bit odd to you?" he asked.

"No. Why would Philippe have any reason to lie to us?"

"I don't know. But he always seems to have the right answer all the time. He's a bit too smooth, don't you think?"

It was like Dan had tripped a switch in Chelly's mind. Her attitude changed instantly, from being sweet and conciliatory one moment, to being defensive the next.

"What is it about you, Dan? One minute I think you're loosening up a bit and starting to be more relaxed, the next you're being a paranoid, anal-retentive psychologist again! Can't you ever stop being so damned negative?"

"I'm sorry," he pleaded. "I don't think I'm being negative. I'm just trained not to take things at face value. In our research training, they taught us to always be looking for other possible explanations, even if a piece of research seems to be totally convincing."

"Well, this isn't research and I don't like it," Chelly snapped. "It feels negative, critical, and anal to me. I wish you'd stop being that way."

Chelly threw the water bottle back at Dan and stomped off down the trail on her own. Dan was upset with himself for saying anything to her about his concerns. Things had been going well between them today. He started getting the old feeling of rejection, as he felt Chelly pushing him away again, widening the gulf between them.

Dan kicked himself for forgetting to bring his phone with him this morning. He had intended to test Philippe's explanation by phoning his office in Detroit today, while they were outside the estate. Now it was going to be too late. He kept forgetting the three-hour time difference between Michigan and the coast. By the time they got back to the estate, it would be too late to call the office.

Chelly's probably right. I'm probably just being paranoid. I can try again tomorrow morning.

He replaced the water bottle in his backpack, and then started jogging down the trail, trying to catch up to Chelly.

"ACCORDING TO the hotel's manager, Morel and his wife are taking the week off and are staying at their estate in Palm Desert," Kelvin McKnight explained to his partner, Beverly Dixon. He had the phone pressed between his ear and shoulder, trying to type on his keyboard while he talked.

"I've set up an appointment this morning to talk with the manager, Carmen Hererra. I need to find out if Alvarez contacted her, or if she noticed anything unusual during that time," McKnight added.

"Couldn't you just do that over the phone? You just want to go back to see more bare boobs!" Dixon joked over the phone.

"It's a dirty job, Beverly, but somebody's got to do it!" McKnight replied, laughing.

"I'm over in Palm Desert sharing our info with their Investigation Bureau, and seeing if there is any way they can help us out. I'm with Detective Jameson now. She and I are just about to drive up to the Morel estate to make a social call," Dixon said.

"With any luck, maybe Mrs. Morel, Capulet, or whatever her name is, will be home and you can talk to her alone," McKnight suggested. "I wish we could talk to all these people when Morel isn't around. He seems to have all the right answers when he's doing all the talking."

"Yeah, I agree with you there. I'll be back in the office after I get back from Palm Desert," Dixon said. "We can compare notes when you get back from the Chateau. And don't get any ideas about interviewing all the female guests, Kelvin!" she joked.

"You're no fun at all, Detective Dixon," McKnight pouted. "I'll talk to you later."

MCKNIGHT PULLED on the heavy pine door as Carmen sounded the buzzer and the electronic door lock clicked open for him. He entered Chateau Eden's courtyard and noticed only one nude couple getting settled into lounge chairs on the pool deck. He looked at his watch, noting that it was probably just getting warm enough now for the bare-skinned sun worshippers to come out into the sun. It looked like the hotel was still relatively full of guests, since the parking lot had only one parking space left when he pulled in a minute ago. He turned left and walked across the east side of the courtyard, still shaded from the early morning sun.

He entered the cool lobby and waited for his eyes to adjust to the sudden change in brightness. As his eyes accommodated, he saw a short Hispanic woman in her early forties at work behind the reception desk. She had dark brown skin and black hair. She looked up at McKnight with dark brown eyes as he approached, flashing him a friendly smile.

"May I help you, sir?" she inquired.

McKnight noticed she was wearing a name badge with the name *Carmen Herrera*.

"I'm Detective McKnight, Palm Springs Police Department, Ms. Herrera," he said. He flipped his badge open for Carmen to inspect.

"As I mentioned earlier on the phone, my partner and I were here the other day to see Mister Morel about a missing persons investigation," he explained. "He was helpful, but we need to ask you some questions to confirm one or two things. Do you have a few minutes?"

"Of course, Detective. Go ahead."

"We're looking for this married couple from Columbia - Diego and Juanita Alvarez." He produced the same two photographs from his jacket pocket that he had shown to Philippe three days earlier.

"They landed at LAX on February 17, rented a car, and then vanished completely," he added. "LAPD has asked us to follow up on some information that they contacted your hotel by email."

"They contacted us?" Carmen asked.

"Yes. Mr. Morel remembered receiving an email from Mr. Alvarez, inquiring about room availability in mid-February. He turned him away because you were fully booked. Do you remember if Mr. Alvarez or his wife ever contacted you again to check for cancellations? Did they email or phone the hotel while you were working?" he inquired.

"I'm afraid I can't remember the emails from that far back. But I can check them again on the office computer, Detective. We archive all of our emails."

"Is there any other way they might have contacted you, besides phone or email? Could they have sent you a fax? Or could they try to contact you through a third-party reservation service?" McKnight pressed.

"I would have remembered if they had faxed us," Carmen replied. "And we're small and private, so we don't use any reservation services. Most of our clients either phone or email us, Detective. They rarely fax us anymore. But, I'll check the emails once more for you. Do you mind waiting a few minutes?" she asked.

"Do you mind if I come with you?" McKnight asked impulsively. He knew Carmen didn't have to share anything on the computer with him, but he was hoping to take advantage of her cooperative nature.

"Certainly, Detective," she said. "Please follow me."

Carmen took him into the office and offered him a chair beside her. He could see the monitor clearly as she scanned through the long list of emails. While she searched, his eyes took in everything else on the computer's desktop. He saw the usual icons for word-processing and spreadsheet programs, web browsers, and accounting software. He noticed a light blue icon with a large white "S", mixed in the midst of the other desktop shortcuts. It wasn't one he was familiar with.

"I'm afraid I don't see more than one email from Señor Alvarez, Detective. And I don't remember any phone calls from anybody by that name," she said apologetically.

"Thanks for checking again," McKnight replied. He leaned forward and pointed to the blue and white icon.

"Carmen, I've never seen this icon with the "S" on it before. Do you know which program it starts?"

Carmen shook her head from side to side.

"I am not sure, Detective. It's not one I've ever used."

"Would you mind double-clicking on it, just so I can see what it is?"

Carmen shrugged and double-clicked with her mouse on the desktop icon. A window opened, and McKnight suddenly found himself looking at an image of Carmen and himself, staring into the computer. He looked above the monitor and immediately saw the webcam that was sending their images to the screen. He also saw another open window beside the video image that looked like a contact list.

"Do any of the names or users on this list look familiar to you, Carmen?" McKnight inquired.

"Yes, Detective. I think one of them is for Señor Morel's Paris office."

McKnight was just starting to understand what he had stumbled upon. He saw from the Menu Bar that the program was called *Skype*. It looked to McKnight like it might be used for making videophone calls. He quickly filed the information in his head, and then got himself back to thinking about the other questions he wanted to ask Carmen.

"Thanks Carmen," he said casually. "That looks like an interesting toy, but I'd better get back to work!" he said, chuckling.

"Just one more thing before I go. Did you notice anything unusual here at the chateau between February 17 and now?" he asked.

Carmen became silent as she let her mind float back into her recent memory for a moment.

"Nothing unusual, Detective," she replied. "The only thing I can think of was when Señor Morel had the flu one day. I think that is the first time I can ever remember him not coming into the Chateau," she exclaimed.

McKnight lifted his eyes from his notepad, his mind snapping to yellow-alert.

"How do you know he had the flu," McKnight asked. "Did you talk to him?"

"No. Francesca … Señora Capellini … his wife … she came into work, but she told me that Señor Morel was ill with the flu and would not be here that day. He seemed a bit better the next day, but he did not seem to be himself for one or two days," she recalled.

"Can you remember what day that was?" McKnight asked.

Carmen went back into the hotel's reservation and guest-registration software, clicking the backward arrow on her keyboard several times until she found the data she wanted.

"He was away on Friday, February 24," she announced. "I made an entry because I had to cancel Señor Morel's meeting with the security service."

In his peripheral vision, McKnight noticed the main entrance gate open. To his surprise, Philippe Morel walked briskly into the darkened lobby, unaware of McKnight because his eyes were still adjusting from the bright sunlight outside. Philippe almost ran into the policeman before he noticed him. McKnight saw the look of surprise in Philippe's eyes, but noticed it was replaced quickly by the Frenchman's charming smile.

"Ah, Detective McKnight. May I help you again?" Philippe inquired.

"Good morning, Mr. Morel. I was just in the area, so I thought I'd follow up on your suggestion to ask Ms. Hererra if she had any contact with our missing persons."

Philippe's eyes narrowed and he looked directly into Carmen's eyes.

"And what did you tell the good detective, Carmen. Did you see the one exchange of emails on the office computer?"

"Yes, Señor Morel. And I told the Detective that he did not contact us again while I was here. I am sure of that."

Philippe felt relieved. *No harm done,* he thought to himself. He maintained his composure, being careful not to let the officer see any change in his emotions.

"Well, Detective. As you can see, the couple you are seeking was never here at Chateau Eden. I'm sorry we aren't able to help you any further."

"Not at all, Mr. Morel. Don't be sorry," McKnight replied. "I guess we'll just have to tell LAPD we have nothing for them. I'd like to thank you both for your cooperation."

"You're welcome Detective. As I said before, please call me if I can be of any more help. May I show you out?"

"No worries," McKnight said. "I can let myself out."

Philippe started to get an uneasy feeling as he watched McKnight exit through the main gate. Thoughts started racing through his mind.

Why did he come back alone? Where's his partner? What did he ask Carmen, and what did she tell him?

Suddenly it struck him and he began to feel a hollow feeling in his stomach. He pictured Francesca alone at home, being questioned by the female detective.

Merde! How could I be so stupid to leave her alone?

Outside Chateau Eden's gate, McKnight ran to his cruiser. He was on his cell phone the second he closed his car door and had the air conditioning running.

BEVERLY DIXON SAT IN the passenger seat of the dark-blue unmarked Crown Victoria, next to her Palm Desert Police host, Detective Julie Jameson. She regarded the woman with respect. Had she met Jameson's slim forty-five-year-old, five-foot frame on the street, she would never have guessed she was a hardened veteran police officer. She was much tougher than she looked. She had paid her dues and worked her way through the ranks of a number of police departments in the county, finally landing her current position as head of the Bureau of Investigation in the Palm Desert Police Department. Like Dixon, she was the loving mother of two children when she was off duty. But when she was at work, she was all business. Dixon gazed at the older woman's profile, and saw the determination and concentration in Jameson's firmly set jaw and facial muscles.

Jameson slowed the cruiser as they reached the top of the mountain, looking for the Morel estate. Long before they came to the wrought-iron entrance, the two detectives got a close look at the estate's imposing security wall.

"Whoa, would you look at that," Jameson remarked. "This guy is serious about his security. I wonder what he's trying to keep out?"

"Or keep in," Dixon suggested. "What doesn't he want people to see?"

"Good point," Jameson answered. "The razor wire on top is a nice touch, wouldn't you say?"

The cruiser finally reached the entrance gate. Dixon and Jameson couldn't see any activity. There were no cars in the driveway and the four garage doors were all closed. Dixon emitted a long, low whistle.

"Nice place," she commented. "Want to see if we can get a guided tour, Julie?"

"Okay. Let's see if anybody's home." She opened her door and walked over to the intercom on the wall beside the gate. She pressed the call button. There was no reply. Jameson waited about 10 seconds, noticing a security camera staring down at them from the top of the wall while she listened for a response. She gave the button a second push. This time, there was a crackle and the intercom came alive.

"Hello. Who is it?" asked a nervous-sounding female voice.

"Detective Jameson, Palm Desert Police. I'm here with Detective Dixon. Is this the Morel residence?"

"Yes. I am Mr. Morel's wife. How may I help you, Detective?" she inquired.

"We're involved in a missing-persons investigation, ma'am. We'd just like to ask you a few questions if you don't mind. It will only take a few minutes," she added.

Francesca felt panic. A visceral fear was growing deep inside her. She was trapped. Philippe would be furious if she talked to the police while he wasn't here. Yet, she knew he would also be upset if she refused to cooperate with them. She felt dizzy, and she was having difficulty keeping her mind focused on what was happening at that moment. She heard her own distant voice answering the police officers.

"Of course Detective. Please wait while I open the gate for you."

The giant twin gates began to swing slowly inward. Jameson returned to the cruiser, waiting patiently until they opened sufficiently to allow them to enter.

"Open sesame!" Dixon said. "Let's see if we can get our feet in the door and have a look around."

Jameson parked the cruiser in the driveway and the two officers made their way to the front door, where Dixon rang the bell.

"What a place," she said to Jameson with a sigh. "We're in the wrong business, Julie. I'll bet the rear of this place has a view of the entire valley. We haven't seen the half of it yet."

The two detectives heard the click of a deadbolt, then the front door opened. They were greeted by Francesca, who was attired only in a yellow bikini, cover-up, and flip-flops. Both women were immediately envious of her dark Mediterranean skin, unblemished complexion, and fit body. She was trying to smile, but Dixon saw that her eyes were wary and anxious.

"Detectives Jameson and Dixon," Jameson said. The two officers flashed their respective badges at Francesca.

"Please come in, officers," Francesca replied, in her stiff, businesslike voice. "I apologize for my casual appearance. I would have dressed more suitably if I had known you were coming. Would you follow me?"

Francesca led Jameson and Dixon down a hallway between the kitchen and dining room, then into the huge expanse of living area, where she offered them a seat.

"Do you have time for some tea or coffee?" she offered. "The coffee is already made and the tea will only take a few minutes."

"I'll have coffee please," Dixon replied quickly. She wanted a moment to talk with Jameson without Francesca hearing them. Jameson caught Dixon's glance immediately.

"I'll have coffee too," she added.

Francesca left for the kitchen, leaving the two police officers alone.

Jameson quickly scanned the expanses of open area in the home, noting that she didn't see anybody else inside, nor out on the pool deck.

"I don't see any sign of her husband," she whispered to Dixon. "Maybe we're going to get lucky and be able to talk with her alone."

The detectives left their seats and were examining Francesca's portraits when she returned. She was carrying a tray with a carafe of coffee, two cups and saucers, cream and sugar, and a small plate of fruit. They both noticed Francesca's hands shaking visibly as she poured coffee for her two unexpected guests.

"Thank you for allowing us into your home," Jameson began. "We're just helping out LAPD with a missing-person's report. Detective Dixon was able to talk to your husband the other day at your hotel, but we were told you were busy giving a massage at the time. Do you mind if we ask you some questions now?" she asked.

Francesca nodded silently for Jameson to proceed. Dixon handed copies of the Alvarez couple's photographs for her to view.

"Have you ever heard from or seen this couple?" Dixon asked. "They're Columbian nationals who disappeared after landing at LAX and renting a car on February 17."

Francesca's eyes darted quickly between the two detectives, the floor, the massive living room windows, and then back towards the officers. Both Dixon and Jameson noticed the tension in Francesca's jaws, the shaking of her hands, the perspiration on her brow, and the lack of eye contact. Dixon's coffee cup made a clinking sound on its saucer, pulling Fran's mind back abruptly into the present. Her eyes looked up quickly. She had a distant look in her eyes as she handed the photos back to Dixon.

"I'm sorry. I've never seen these people," Francesca said. It was her businesslike part, speaking in a dull, monotone voice.

Noticing that the photographs had struck a nerve, Jameson quickly changed topics. She called upon a part of herself that wasn't a cop, but shared a common love of interior design with Francesca. She realized that she needed to appear more human and less threatening, as quickly as possible, before the woman shut herself down, effectively ending the interview.

"Your home is beautiful, Ms. Capellini. I know we're supposed to be on police business, but would you mind giving us a quick tour before we go? We're just dying to see the rest of the house, aren't we Beverly?"

"Oh please, would you?" Dixon echoed. "We can only spare a few minutes before we have to get back downtown."

There was a long pause while Francesca thought over her options. Dixon could tell that the woman was emotionally torn and extremely wary.

"I would love to show you around," Francesca answered. She walked her visitors through the kitchen and dining room, and then pointed out the master suite at the end of that side of the home. She pointed out Philippe's office, the home theatre, and the small private art gallery. She walked part way down the corridor towards the guest suites, and then stopped.

"I would normally show you the guest suites," she apologized, "but we have friends staying with us now. I hope you understand if I don't show you through their rooms."

"Guests?" Dixon asked. "Do you entertain guests often?"

"Not often," Francesca replied. "When we do, they are either close friends or business associates of my husband. At the moment, we have some close friends visiting," she lied.

Once again, both Dixon and Jameson noted that Fran was avoiding making eye contact.

"May we go outside and look at the yard?" Jameson asked.

Francesca nodded and led them onto the pool deck through a sliding glass door.

"The grounds are beautiful. I'll bet they look stunning at night when the garden lights come on. You must be able to see the lights all over the valley," Jameson said.

"What's the other large building over there," Dixon asked. "It's still on your property, isn't it?"

"That is my husband's studio. As you already know, we are in the art business. My husband has some specialized workshops for restoring expensive art works. I'm afraid I can't show you around there for security reasons," she lied again.

Jameson continued to read the fear in Francesca's eyes. She nodded to Dixon, who got the message that it was time to go.

"Thank you for the tour. You must be proud of your home," she said, and then turned to Dixon.

"Well, Beverly. I think we'd better get back to the station before they think I've gone AWOL."

Francesca started to feel a trickle of relief as the two dangerous adversaries headed back into the house, then found their way towards the front entrance.

"Thank you once again, Ms. Capellini. If you happen to think of anything else that might be useful, please phone me at this number," Jameson said. She handed a business card to their reluctant host.

"Of course," Francesca answered. She was trying to appear cheery, but wasn't convincing. "Please have a nice day!" she said, as she ushered the officers out through the front door, then closed it behind them.

BEVERLY DIXON'S cell phone rang on the drive back down the mountain into Palm Desert.

"Dixon here," she announced.

"Beverly," McKnight shouted. "I think I may have stumbled onto something here. Morel didn't show up at the hotel on February twenty-fourth. His wife told their manager that he stayed home with the flu. So we have one day in Morel's life he can't account for, except for his wife's story."

"How did things go at the estate?" he continued. "Did you get to talk to anybody?"

"We managed to interview Morel's wife by herself. She's afraid of something, Kelvin. I think we struck a nerve when we showed her the photos."

"So, we have a guy who was off the map for a day, and his only alibi is his wife," Kelvin said.

"Yup. And a wife who is afraid of something, and might be too afraid of him to say anything," Dixon added.

"One other thing, Beverly," McKnight added. "I think I might have figured out how Morel could have contacted Alvarez, but I'm going to have to do some more research to see if I'm right."

"Good work," Dixon said. "You know, we might have been barking up the wrong tree looking for the Alvarez couple. Maybe we should have been looking at what Morel has been doing," she suggested.

"I agree," McKnight said. "I'll start getting warrants and running all of the usual checks to see what he was up to between the seventeenth and the twenty-fourth. We'll start with cell phone and credit cards, then expand the search to rental cars, airlines, Homeland Security, and so on. Anything else you can think of?" he asked.

"Not right now," Dixon answered. "I'll join you back at the office right away. It looks like we've got some work to do, Kelvin."

After she hung up, Beverly Dixon's mind started picking up speed. She felt that old familiar feeling as the adrenaline starting finding its way into her bloodstream. She loved the challenge of a good chase.

So, Monsieur Morel. What have you been up to lately? What dirty little secrets have you been hiding behind those big walls?

CHAPTER 24

DAN AND FRAN sat beside each other on lounge chairs in the bright March sunshine. Dan was reading Stephen King's *Insomnia* and chuckling to himself, realizing that the early parts of the book were having quite the opposite effect on him. He was distracted by the sight of Fran's bronze, naked body in the chair beside him. He noted that she seemed distant and preoccupied since he and Chelly returned from their hike.

Dan was still trying to make sense of how he and Chelly had landed in this surprising and bewildering situation. Question after question was circling endlessly through his mind, but no answers were forthcoming.

How did Chelly go from being terrified of being naked in front of strangers, to swapping husbands within a span of three days? How did I end up swapping my wife for this mysterious and beautiful woman beside me, when all of my professional instincts are telling me not to do it? Why am I so attracted to Fran, when I want so much to get closer to Chelly? What made me start spanking Fran, when every bone in my body finds it repulsive?

Dan's eyes drifted to the sight of Chelly, working and laughing side-by-side with Philippe in the kitchen, preparing dumplings and beef rolls in Lop-leaf for tonight's meal. He was troubled by the things that were attracting her to Philippe.

If she needed to be submissive sexually, and needed someone to dominate her, could he ever satisfy her needs?

Dan gave in to the distractions and put down his book. He needed to do a few lengths to cool down his body and clear his mind. He stood briefly on the edge of the pool, and then propelled himself over the water. The splash as he entered the water, shattered the serenity of the peaceful setting. He felt the cool liquid flowing past him and over every pore on his skin, seemingly washing away all of the tension he had been feeling only moments before. He kept his body beneath the surface, using powerful strokes to propel him as far as he could go underwater.

He made it to the far end of the pool, gulping a huge breath of air as he broke the surface. He floated on his back, looking up at the few wisps of clouds in the blue sky, when he heard a splash at the far end of the pool. Seconds later, Fran surfaced beside him, breathing deeply as she emerged from the cool depths of the pool. She wiped the water away from her face and swept her hair back out of her eyes, then looked at Dan.

"A penny for your thoughts," Dan said.

Fran looked away to avoid eye contact.

"I am fine. What about you, Dan? You are not saying much either," she observed.

"My mind won't slow down," Dan answered. "I think I'm confused about how all of this happened so quickly."

"Do you not want to be with me?" she asked.

"Yes … of course," Dan said. "I think you know how attracted I am to you. But, it's confusing. I'm trying to love Chelly, but I'm afraid I might not be able to give her what she needs. I don't think I can be the dominant partner she wants me to be."

"And what if that is true?" Fran asked. "What if that is your reality?"

"It scares me. I'm afraid of losing her," Dan replied.

"Do you and Chelly want to have children?" Fran asked.

"I'd like to have kids," Dan answered. "Chelly's just over forty now and her time is running out. Whenever we talk about it, she manages to find reasons to put it off. She won't come right out and say it, but I don't think she really wants to be a mother."

"What about you, Fran? Do you and Philippe want to have children?" Dan asked.

"No, we have decided not to have any. We both had experiences when we were young that should not happen to children. We do not want to bring children into a world where such things can happen. Philippe is quite firm about that. He has always insisted that I take the pill, so that does not happen," she answered.

"Fran, tell me about Manarola. Tell me about your mom and dad, and your family. What happened that made you not want to have children? "

"There is not so much to tell," she answered. "I do not remember much."

"Are your parents still alive?"

"Yes … uh … I don't know. *Mamma* is alive. I do not know about my *papa*. I have not seen him for many years."

"So, tell me about your mother. What's she like?"

"She owns a restaurant. She could not depend on *papa* because he was never home. He was a sailor and a drunk. The only time he ever came home was to beat her or make her pregnant. *Mamma* and Giulia, my sister, they were always busy in the restaurant. They did not have much time for me, but I managed to survive."

Dan looked into Fran's eyes as she told her story. He had heard similar stories of neglect far too often from his clients. He saw the depths of her loneliness and sadness, and felt her emotions touching and affecting him. Dan reached for Fran and took her into his arms, bringing her close to him. He felt the warmth from her body against his own, in stark contrast to the cool water surrounding them.

"I'm so sorry you had to live through that," he said softly. His hands stroked her back lovingly, then moved down and followed the smooth curves of her buttocks. He felt the scars that marred her otherwise silky skin. His eyes continued to gaze into hers.

"What could you possibly have done that was so bad for somebody to give you scars on your backside? Who was it, Fran?"

Dan saw her eyes becoming distant. He placed his hands on both sides of her face and brought it slowly towards his lips. He kissed her firmly, and then he raised his voice to her to bring her back into the moment.

"Who did it, Fran?" he said. He saw the walls coming down, making her more vulnerable, and allowing her to gather the strength to share one of her most painful secrets. Her eyes turned red, then tears began pooling until one spilled out of each eye and trickled gently down her face.

"My brother in law, Paolo," she whispered. "I was just twelve years old. I made sure it never happened again." Her businesslike voice tried to take over. Dan saw that she was trying to raise her walls to keep herself safe. But his eyes refused to leave Fran's. He was consumed with empathy for her. Her sadness, fear, and loneliness were reflected in his eyes. Fran wrapped her arms around Dan and pulled him tightly against her body. Their lips met in a kiss that was full of passion and longing. Dan felt a surge of blood in his loins, and he started growing along with their passion.

"Not here," he whispered, as his lips left hers. "Not now."

"We should wait until tonight," she whispered softly in return. She gave Dan one more kiss, and then let herself fall backwards into a smooth backstroke, gliding back in the direction of the house.

PHILIPPE LOOKED past Michelle as he stood at the island in the kitchen. His eyes gazed through the home's massive picture windows, and out towards the pool. He witnessed Dan and Fran in their passionate embrace, and followed Fran's movement as she swam away from Dan.

A pleased look gradually replaced the worry he'd been feeling since this morning's visits by the police. He felt a deep sense of satisfaction as he saw Dan and Fran falling for each other. The controlling, competitive side of him managed to push his troubles away for the moment. His confidence was returning. Apart from the persistence of the damned police, things were proceeding even better than he could ever have planned.

"MY COMPLIMENTS to the chefs!" Dan exclaimed, raising his glass to Philippe and Chelly. "I don't think we've ever had a green papaya salad this good, have we Chelly?"

"That's for sure," she agreed. "Philippe got the recipe from his favorite restaurant in Saigon. I just loved the dumplings, and the spicy beef in Lop-leaves was delicious."

"My thanks to Dan for grilling the shrimp to perfection for us tonight," Philippe responded, raising his glass to Dan.

Philippe wasted no time in changing the topic, now that his guest's appetites were sated. They were all relaxed and enjoying a fine Pinot Grigio, once again laced with ecstasy.

"So, *mes amis*," he began." Shall we talk some more about continuing our small social experiment tonight? Michelle has expressed a keen interest in some activities that will help to build her trust in me as her Dominant. She wants to learn to completely trust in my desire to give her the most intense sexual experience. Is that not right, *ma chérie?*"

"Oh yeah," Chelly squeaked. "The suspense is killing me! I can't wait to see and feel what you have planned for tonight!"

"And what about you, Dan?" Philippe asked. "Francesca is a natural Submissive, much like you. I'm sure she can suggest some activities that will increase your comfort and confidence with being a true Dominant."

Philippe's eyes met Fran's, sending a clear message from Dominant to Submissive.

"I have to admit," Dan continued, "I'm still a bit confused about how inflicting pain can help to increase pleasure. I think I understand how it can happen on a physiological level. But I have a tough time thinking that Dominance and Submission - or BDSM - whatever you call it - is healthy. I see far too many of my clients who learned to be passive in abusive or neglectful homes. I think they became naturally submissive because they lack the self-confidence and self-esteem to be assertive. They don't feel worthy enough to demand to be treated as an equal, whether it's during sex or in the rest of their relationship."

Dan glanced at Chelly, who was frowning in his direction.

"I have the same fears about people that feel the need to be Dominant," he continued. "I've seen people in my practice who need to manipulate, control, and abuse others as a way to hide their own insecurities. They do it because they are incredibly angry about the abuse or neglect they experienced when they were younger. So, while people in the BDSM community praise the transfer of power involved in BDSM, I'm afraid that some of them like it because they aren't comfortable with true intimacy and equality in their relationships."

Dan saw a look of anger flash briefly in Philippe's eyes, sensing that he had struck a nerve.

"So, are you saying that your lovely wife's need for a partner who is more dominant, and her need to be submissive, is because she is carrying around - how do you say this - much emotional baggage?"

"Well, no. I'm not saying that about Chelly at all," Dan replied, scrambling to defend his comments. "Chelly's an adult. She can make her own decisions."

"That's not what I heard, Dan!" Chelly snapped, glaring at her husband. "I heard it the same way Philippe did! I heard your implication that anybody who is into Dominance or Submission is unstable!"

"Let's assume that what you say has some truth to it," Philippe offered. "As I argued last night when we discussed the possibility of sharing our spouses, who is qualified to decide if people are psychologically stable enough to be in a BDSM relationship? Do they need approval from you? Or can we assume that we are all adults and are able to make our own adult choices?"

"You're right, of course," Dan admitted. "I agree that every one of us, including Chelly, has the right to make our own adult choices. I'm just arguing that those decisions can be heavily influenced by some people's emotional baggage. There are more emotional risks for those people, and they may not be fully aware of those risks."

"So, do you think all four of us are capable of making that adult decision for ourselves?" Chelly challenged.

Once again, Dan felt trapped and helpless. This was his chance to put an end to the experiment and walk away. He felt Fran's emotional vulnerability and knew there were risks for her. But he knew he was only going to make things worse with Chelly if he suggested that she, or anybody else at the table, had any emotional baggage. He was also certain that he would lose her if he backed out now.

The room was silent. Chelly, Fran, and Philippe were all staring expectantly at him. His heart was pounding and he felt like he couldn't swallow. He was feeling more nauseous and dizzy by the moment.

Well, Dan. It's time to man-up and make a decision. Chelly keeps saying I need to take more chances. So I guess if I'm going to keep her, I only have one choice.

"Of course, Chelly. I'm willing to experiment and accept the risks if everybody else is," Dan said. "Count me in. But the last thing I want to do is to see you or Fran get hurt."

"Excellent!" Philippe exclaimed, his face beaming. "Your concerns are noted. If you are so afraid of hurting Fran, might I suggest that she take the role of Dominant with you tonight? Then you can learn how pleasurable it can be to submit to her, and to trust completely that she is not going to harm you."

Dan paused to think about Philippe's suggestion, still feeling the conflict inside. The guilty side of him, which was so afraid of hurting Fran, was definitely tempted to let her take the role of Dominatrix tonight. He trusted that she wouldn't harm him. On the other hand, the side of him that loved Chelly and wanted to please her, knew that he needed to learn to be more dominant during sex, if he was ever going to keep her happy.

"I'll try being more dominant," he decided. He looked at Fran, who was sitting to his left. "But I'll need some coaching and some suggestions from you if you're willing to help."

Like everybody else at the table, Fran was feeling more relaxed as the wine and ecstasy began to exert their effects. Her walls were coming down and her romantic, loving side was finding its voice. She reached over and took Dan's hand in hers.

"I look forward to it, *mio caro*," she said. Her smile was warm and genuine. Dan felt a heightened sense of intimacy with her. He felt himself being drawn closer to her as he looked into her brown eyes and saw the vulnerability of her loving, romantic side.

CHELLY SAW the connection developing between Fran and her husband. But ironically, she wasn't feeling any jealousy. She remembered how she had often felt insecure in the past, when other women talked about Dan's handsome looks and fit body.

This must prove I'm getting over any of my insecurities. If anybody is insecure here, it's Dan!

"Very well then, *mes amis*," Philippe concluded. "After we clean up the dinner dishes, shall we meet at the spa? We can get naked, have some wine, and relax together for a while before we continue our explorations."

MICHELLE LAY blindfolded and spread-eagled on the giant four-poster bed in the Venetian room. Her breathing was ragged and her vagina was ready to go into convulsions with even the slightest stimulation.

Where is he? What is he doing now? Damn him! Why did he stop? Why won't he let me come?

Her mind was spinning. She had given herself to Philippe completely, from the moment he brought her through the concrete tunnel to his studio and up the stairs to the Venetian room. He had let her see where she was going tonight, but he blindfolded her after they entered the room. He removed her bathrobe, leaving her naked and vulnerable, wearing nothing but a hint of the Chanel No. 5 again. He led her over to an armoire in the far corner of the room that served as a storage locker for his BDSM toys. He made her touch a number of toys, including a collar, a giant feather, handcuffs, a spreader bar, the rubber strap, a suede flogger, a cane, and the same vibrator he had used last night.

Then he took her back to the foot of the bed, as he did the night before. He fastened leather cuffs around each wrist before suspending each arm above her head by ropes attached to the pulleys in the ceiling. She felt him shackle each ankle into the spreader bar so she couldn't walk or bring her legs together. As he did the previous night, he warned her of the consequences of talking, moaning, or screaming. He snapped a whip in the air beside her head, so close that she felt the air rush away from her, only inches from her cheek. She gasped in surprise.

It was exhilarating from the start. Philippe hadn't even touched her, apart from immobilizing her. Then, ever so slowly, he started teasing her. He began with a feather, touching her so softly she could barely feel it. Methodically, he worked his way from her head and neck, down her back, buttocks, and legs, and then slowly teased her inner legs, her breasts and stomach, and finally her genitals. When she was moist, she felt his finger slowly massage her, then enter her, leaving her wanting much more.

Then without warning, he withdrew his finger and everything was silent. The next thing she knew, she smelled the unmistakable fragrance of her own sexual juices in front of her nose. The musky smell sent a surge of blood to her vagina. Then, suddenly, she felt his finger between her lips. She touched it with her tongue and tasted herself on his finger. He kept teasing her until he finally pushed it into her mouth and allowed her to suck the remaining juices from it.

Then came more sensory deprivation. For how long? It seemed like minutes, but could have been only seconds. She felt the lubrication oozing from her vagina, cooling as it evaporated. Suddenly, out of nowhere, she felt something smooth massaging her labia and clit. She shivered at the unexpected stimulation, craving more, then felt her cervix stretch as first one, then another, heavy round silicon objects were squeezed into her. The objects came to rest at the base of her vagina, against her G-spot. She couldn't help herself. She began squeezing her vaginal muscles to get the balls moving around on her inner trigger, since she was unable to move her legs together. The effect was overwhelming. Philippe saw her writhing in ecstasy and warned her to remain still. Michelle felt the agonizing craving for more stimulation.

Philippe continued to torment her, using a suede flogger next. He alternated dragging the implement over her skin, then quickly flicking it, causing brief stings on her skin. His touch was exquisite, not hard enough to hurt, but sharp enough to make her nerve endings come alive. Michelle never knew where he was going to touch next, or whether it would be the soft sensation of the suede being dragged over her skin, or the sharp snap of the suede on her skin. The uncertainty and suspense was exhilarating. Each snap of the flogger took her breath away.

More tortuous sensory deprivation followed. Then, without warning, she felt him reach up and loosen the leather cuffs on her hands. When he was finished, he kneeled to release the shackles on her ankles, removing the spreader bar. She felt the increased pressure inside her womb from the balls as she brought her legs back together. The silence in the room was replaced with the soft sounds of the Blue Danube waltz, like the previous night.

Michelle felt Philippe take her by the hands, into a dance position, and felt his naked body press closely against her own. He began leading her around the dance floor and she immediately felt the weights in her vagina start undulating. The effect was breathtaking. She felt the tension building inside her. At the same time, she also felt Philippe growing larger, his penis rubbing randomly against her labia and clit as they danced. Her breathing became shorter and faster. Again, he cautioned her. She would be punished if she moaned, screamed, or let herself climax. She struggled to contain herself and her arousal.

Just when Michelle thought she wouldn't be able to hold it any longer, the music stopped and Philippe led her back towards the bed. Once again he fastened her wrists with the leather cuffs, then ordered her to climb onto the bed and to lay on her back. He fastened her arms to the bedposts at the head of the bed, then felt him putting leather cuffs on her ankles, spreading her legs wide apart and fastening them tightly to the bedposts at the foot of the bed. She was spread-eagled and completely vulnerable.

Michelle felt a pull on the objects in her vagina as Philippe tugged on a string, attached to the balls. Then he ordered her to clench with her vaginal muscles to resist his tugging. He eased off, and then pulled again, ordering her to clench each time. The sensation was delicious. She felt the tension continue to build inside her. Yet, every time she came close to orgasm and her breathing became short and ragged, he would stop tugging on the string. She craved release so badly she was almost in tears.

Once again, more sensory deprivation. Michelle smelled a candle burning. Suddenly, she felt a burning sensation on her sternum, between her breasts, that took her breath away. Just when it seemed like the burning was too intense, the wax cooled and she felt some relief, before feeling another sharp burning sensation from another drop of wax. The teasing continued on her breasts and continued downwards towards her genitals. Without explanation, she felt a different sharp sensation. This time it was ice. He alternated the two sensations, seemingly at random. She didn't know which one she would feel next, or where she would feel it. He was slowly driving her mad. Then it stopped and she felt nothing but more sensory deprivation. Finally, she felt another tug on the balls in her vagina. She expelled all of the air from her lungs at the unexpected stimulation inside her. It was all she could do to keep from screaming. Then the stimulation stopped again, just as suddenly.

Her breathing was ragged and her vagina was ready to go into convulsions with even the slightest stimulation.

Where is he? What is he doing now? Damn him! Why did he stop? My pussy is dying - why won't he let me come?

Michelle felt the tension on her ankles lessen as he loosened their restraints. "Lift your legs up into the air and back towards your head," Philippe ordered. Abruptly, she felt him yank on first one ankle, then the other. He pulled them back towards her shoulders and tied the ropes to the head of the bed. She felt the pressure of the balls on her G-spot almost immediately as her thighs pressed downward on her lower abdomen. The tension was almost unbearable. Then she felt increased pressure on her cervix and her swollen clit as first one, then the other ball, was pulled from inside her. The tension in her vagina eased somewhat. She responded by taking deep breaths to relax herself.

More deprivation and tension.

Oh, my God. My pussy feels like it's going to explode. What will he do if I come before he allows it? Oh, God ...

Then, Michelle heard a faint noise that sounded familiar. At first she couldn't place where she had heard it. Then it came to her. She gasped, just as she felt the stretching of her labia and more tension on her clit. It was the vibrator from last night. Philippe started working it expertly, first moving it in and out, then pressing on it and working around in circles to stimulate both her clit and her entire vagina. He was constantly changing the amount and location of stimulation. Her breathing quickened as she moved closer orgasm. Once again, the movement stopped and she felt the vibrator slide out of her, just before she reached her point-of-no-return. Michelle's sexual part was screaming for release, when she felt weight at the end of the bed, then felt Philippe kneeling in front of her exposed, vulnerable genitals. She heard the tearing of a condom pouch.

Please ... Please ... fuck my pussy ... I can't stand it anymore!

This time, Michelle wasn't disappointed. She felt Philippe sink deep inside her, the head of his penis pressing perfectly against her inner trigger as he pressed her legs back against her lower abdomen. She reveled in the exquisite fullness inside her.

Philippe deftly began thrusting, making sure to grind his rim over Michelle's G-spot with each push.

Finally!

Michelle almost screamed in frustration when, without warning, his thrusting stopped and he pulled out. Then, out of nowhere, she felt the sharp sting of the flogger on her exposed ass, fractions of a second before she heard the delayed snapping sound.

Michelle gasped in shock at first. Then she felt the sharp sting transform into even more sensual ecstasy.

Oh, yeah ... bring it on ...

Philippe plunged back into her. His thrusts resumed slowly, alternating with sharp snaps of the flogger on her sensitive bare skin. Red welts appeared against the ivory backdrop of her white skin. He picked up the pace, lashing with the flogger as he pumped harder and faster. Michelle felt like Philippe was her jockey, riding her furiously down the backstretch, using his flogger and his hard cock to urge her on towards the finish line.

"Come on, *ma chérie*," he urged as his thrusts became more urgent. "Let me hear you. Don't hold anything back!"

Like the previous night, Michelle lost her ability to distinguish between hot pain on her ass, and the surges of pleasure coming from her clit and her G-spot. They all blended together into an inferno of pleasure inside her vaginal walls.

"Philippe ... harder ... give me all of your cock ... faster ... whip me ... harder ... fuck my pussy ... whip me ... fuck me ...," she screamed.

Philippe's breathing became quicker and more ragged. Finally, he gave one huge thrust against her trigger. His entire body went rigid. Michelle's vagina exploded into a spasm of ecstasy at the same moment that his penis slammed into her G-spot the final time. She felt him throbbing inside her as their rhythmic orgasmic contractions continued in synchrony.

Philippe sighed a single word as his body froze and reached his release.

"Isabelle," he moaned softly, the breath rushing from his lungs.

After half a dozen more contractions, Philippe was spent. He collapsed forward, resting the full weight of his body on the exposed backside of Michelle's outstretched legs. Both of them gasped for breath.

Michelle barely heard the name that Philippe uttered. Her brain scrambled to try to make sense of what she thought she had heard. But in the midst of the incredible sensory overload coming from every nerve ending in her body, the sound of that single word was lost in the avalanche of her own overwhelming ecstasy.

As they lay together on the bed in the afterglow, their breathing gradually slowing and their muscles collapsing from exhaustion, Michelle's mind was in awe of the effect that this Frenchman, her new Dominant, was having on her.

What on earth can he ever do to surpass this!

But far away, beneath that conscious question, the sexual and romantic part of her identity was asking a different question.

Will Dan ever be able to satisfy me like this?

AS FRAN led Dan into the smaller guest suite, she nodded towards the assortment of sex toys she had laid out neatly on the bureau.

There was a large feather, a candle and matches, a riding crop, a long wooden cane, a large vibrator, and two long leather cords, each with a loop at one end and small weights on the other.

Another object looked like a pizza cutter with a long handle, except that the wheel was smaller and had pointed teeth protruding from it. There were four leather cuffs lying on the bed, each one with a rope leading to one of the four bedposts.

"What is this for?" Dan asked curiously, holding up the leather cords with the loops.

"It is a nipple clamp. You can slide this small metal fastener up and down the cord to make the loop looser or tighter around the nipple," she explained. "The weights give continuous tension and stimulation to the nipples," she added.

"Ouch!" Dan exclaimed. "And you enjoy that?"

"Yes, my nipples are sensitive. I enjoy having them stimulated"

"What about this?" Dan asked, picking up the strange looking pinwheel.

"It is a *Wartenberg* pinwheel," she explained. "Like scratching, it gives a most pleasant prickling sensation."

Fran handed the leather cuffs to Dan, and then climbed onto the bed, lying on her back and spreading her arms and legs so that each limb pointed to one of the bedposts.

"Put these on me and tie them to the bed," she said. "Make sure I cannot move at all. Then you can use the feather to tease me, if you like. Try everything on me - the riding crop - the pinwheel - be rough, and do anything you like - I do not mind, go ahead."

Dan picked up the riding crop.

"Stroke me with it, then try snapping it on my skin," she said.

Fran saw how uncomfortable Dan looked as he started applying sharp snaps of the riding crop on her skin, alternating the sharp sensations from the whipping action with long gentle strokes of the crop. She closed her eyes so she couldn't see what he was going to do next. She loved the unpredictable mixture of pleasure and pain. Her nipples stood up, firm and erect, and moisture started seeping from between her labia.

"Put the nipple clamps on me," she demanded.

His hand shaking, Dan opened one loop and laid it over a nipple. He slid the clamp so that the loop closed snugly around Fran's hard bud.

"Tighter - I cannot feel it," Fran urged.

Dan repeated the procedure with the other nipple, tightening the clamps until Fran sucked in a deep breath in response to the pain, and nodded her approval.

"Go ahead. Do whatever you want," she said. "Try the pinwheel - mix it with the crop - I don't want to know what you are doing next."

Fran opened her eyes. They became more intense, greedy for more stimulation as the intensity of his stimulations increased. Her breathing was quickening.

"Harder, Dan," she urged. "Make it hurt."

She saw Dan getting hard, despite the inner turmoil she knew he was feeling.

Instinctively, he reached out and started massaging her already moist labia with his fingers. Fran moaned softly as he slid his index and middle fingers into her. His fingers massaged the erogenous zone on the lower front of her vagina. He leaned down and blew softly on her clit as he massaged.

Fran's moaning grew louder. It was a purring sound, coming from deep in her throat.

Without warning, Dan stopped all stimulation. Fran's body relaxed, yet craved more stimulation. After an agonizing pause, she felt the light touch of Dan's tongue on her clit. His fingers kept up the internal massage on her G-spot. Fran felt the tension building inside the walls of her vagina.

After a few moments, he took his mouth away from her clit, slid his fingers out of her, then stood up and reached for the *Wartenberg* wheel. Fran realized she was no longer giving him instructions. He was responding to her pleasure, taking control, and becoming increasingly aroused himself. She turned her head to the side, seeing that his cock was now long and hard.

"How am I doing?" Dan asked.

"You are a fast learner. Go on, do whatever you want - do not be afraid to hurt me."

"Okay. But you'll tell me if I'm hurting you too much?" he asked.

"I trust you," Fran said.

Dan picked up the pace, randomly rolling the prickly wheel in different areas of Fran's body, teasing the inside of her thighs and her breasts unpredictably, then stimulating other areas of her skin. He tightened the nipple clamps again. Fran groaned loudly. She felt a surge of pain through each nipple. After a few seconds, the sensations changed into a hot pain, then eventually into a dull throbbing. Her eyes remained open, and the intensity pleasure in her eyes was growing into a fire that signaled Dan that she was greedy for more intense stimulation.

Dan increased the frequency and intensity of the whipping action from the riding crop, stopping occasionally to pull on the weights of the nipple clamps or to insert his fingers and massage inside her. The fire in her eyes was growing in intensity, but was gradually transforming into a look of anger.

"Harder Dan!" she screamed, as Dan did his best to administer whips from the riding crop. He slid his fingers into her again, her eyes narrowed, and she screamed again.

"Take them out. I do not deserve to feel pleasure. Use the cane, Dan. Whip me, hard!"

Dan stopped everything. Fran opened her eyes and connected with Dan's. He held the cane in his hand, but his eyes showed the conflict in his mind. He looked down at the all of the soft, vulnerable flesh on the front of her body. He reached down and began undoing the cuff on one of her ankles. She looked at Dan, her eyes narrowing.

"Lie down!" he commanded. "If you want the cane, we're going to do it my way." He walked around the bed, releasing the cuffs from the remaining ankle and her wrists.

"Off the bed! Walk to the massage table and bend over it!" he ordered. Fran did as he commanded, and Dan followed her, cane in hand.

"I'm going to do this six times, are you ready?" he asked.

"Ten!" she screamed. She looked back at him, her eyes flaming with anger. "I deserve ten. I deserve to be punished for what I've done!"

She looked back over her shoulder at Dan. Their eyes connected. She saw that he understood.

The punishment and Dominance had knocked down Fran's defenses - her walls were down completely. A part of her identity that loathed herself and felt unworthy - that usually remained safely hidden behind her protective barriers - was fully exposed and screaming to be punished.

The cane whipped through the air. Fran heard the whirring and rushing of atmosphere around the object as it flew towards her buttocks. She gasped at the sharp pain as the long object slashed at her flesh.

"You want me to hurt you like everybody else has hurt you?" Dan shouted. "You want me to punish you like Paolo did?"

"Yeeeessss …!" Fran cried. "Hit me again, Paolo! I deserve it!" she howled in anguish.

Dan could no longer stand it. He realized she was dissociating. Her mind was no longer in the room, but was floating back to her childhood in Manarola.

"Damn it!" he cursed under his breath. "I knew something like this would happen!" He reached down and pulled Fran up to a standing position and looked into her distant eyes.

Fran felt like she was looking through a long, dark tunnel. At the end of the tunnel, she saw a blurred image of a man's face - it was somebody she knew …

What do you really want, Fran?

In the distance, she heard the voice - soft, nurturing and compassionate, like a parent trying to console a child. It was urging her to come back towards the light.

What does that twelve-year-old girl really want, Fran? Does it really want to be punished? What do you want instead?

THE TENSION in Fran's body started to release. Her shoulders sagged and her body started curling up. She answered Dan, not with the voice of the businesslike, independent adult Fran, but with the voice of a twelve-year-old child.

"Hold me?" she said. Her reply was half-answering his question and half-pleading at the same time. A scared, lonely twelve-year-old voice deep inside her was begging to be held.

"Please do not hurt me. Just hold me. Just love me," she begged.

Fran shivered. Dan walked her over to the bed and helped her in, then climbed in himself and pulled the covers over them, holding her close to his body to keep her warm and safe.

The overwhelming feeling of empathy and the intense intimacy of their shared emotional bond, along with the warmth of Fran's naked body, caused a surge of arousal through Dan's body. Their hearts pounded as they lay in each other's arms. Their breathing gradually synchronized. Dan stroked Fran's hair and they stared into each other's eyes.

"There, you're safe now," Dan said. "Nobody's going to hurt you. I'll keep you safe," he repeated, as he continued to stroke her hair with one hand and her back with the other.

Fran's mind was gradually coming back into the present. She sensed that she was safe in Dan's arms and that the danger was over. Her protective walls were moving back into place. The self-loathing and the angry parts of her identity were successfully locked away for now. She felt the warmth of Dan's body. She needed to feel safe and needed to feel as close as she could possibly get to him. She felt his erection pressing against her thigh.

She needed to feel him inside her. She felt a longing and desperation deep within her and felt the blood surging into her sexual organs.

Fran worked her bottom leg between Dan's legs, and then raised her top leg so that it lay on top of his upper leg. She pushed her pelvis and their bodies moved closer. She felt for his erection and guided the head into herself, pushing her pelvis as close to him as she possibly could.

Fran felt Dan filling her inside, yet also surrounding her body on the outside with his arms and legs. She clung to him with their legs entwined in the scissor position, neither of them moving. Instead, they lay silently, listening to the beating of each other's hearts and the sounds of their breathing, savoring the stillness of their coital bond, and staring into each other's eyes.

"I don't have a condom," Dan whispered. "Aren't you worried about being safe?"

"I trust you," she sighed. "I believe that you and Chelly have only been with each other. I am okay."

Fran kissed Dan tenderly. His lips responded, repeating the soft kisses, basking in the tenderness and in their closeness. Fran felt Dan's erection shrinking inside her. She pulled her pelvis back and his penis slid out of her. She started slowly kissing Dan's neck and his chest. Her kisses moved ever so slowly and gradually southward. She rolled and pulled her one leg out from between Dan's legs so that she was now on top of him. She sat astride his lower legs, then took his semi-rigid organ in her hand and leaned forward. She took him slowly into her mouth and beginning to suck, tasting her own sweet, salty sex on him.

She felt Dan responding almost immediately. She continued the sucking movements until he was large enough for her to tighten her lips around his rim. She brought the edges of her teeth barely into contact with the velvet-like skin on that most sensitive part of his organ, taking delight in the taste and feel of him, and in the pleasure she knew she was giving.

Dan moaned as she repeated tightening her lips and pressing her teeth lightly. Without warning, she slid her lips down the length of his shaft, taking him deep. Dan groaned in ecstasy at the unexpected intensity and pressure of lips around him. She pressed her tongue firmly and moved it slowly up the shaft, pressing on the most sensitive areas on his shaft as she moved, finally working her way back up to his rim. She locked her lips and the edges of her teeth in place, eliciting another deep groan from him.

Fran reached down and placed her fingernails on the inside of one of Dan's legs, near the ankle. Slowly, she dragged her fingers up the inside of his leg towards his genitals, all the while keeping pressure with her lips and tongue on his exquisitely sensitive rim. His eyes grew bigger and his body began to stiffen. She sensed that he was getting close to the point-of-no-return, releasing her lips and setting him free.

Dan's breathing was short and irregular. He let out longer, relaxing breaths, trying to calm himself and decrease the sense of urgency. Fran slid up higher on Dan's body, taking him in her hand. She lowered herself on his swollen, purple cock, taking it all the way inside, feeling him fill and stretch her wet vagina. She felt the tension pulling on her clit. She clasped Dan's hands in hers, and then let herself lean backwards. She felt his rim pressing firmly on the front of her vaginal wall, against her G-spot. She began rotating her pelvis so that she could feel him grinding against her own internal trigger, grinding her clit between his pelvis and hers.

Fran moved harder and faster, needing to feel him moving inside her. She felt both herself and Dan tensing. They were both feeling their sense of urgency growing more intense. The grinding of her pelvis became more frantic, until she felt Dan's entire body tense, giving one final thrust deep inside her. She felt the bursts of hot semen exploding inside her with each successive contraction of his pelvic muscles. It was more than her body could stand. Her brain reached sensory overload and her vagina joined Dan, bursting into contraction, after exquisite contraction, of her own.

Fran felt tears starting to flow from her eyes. She had felt some good orgasms before, mostly from the rough stimulation of BDSM play. But, just like the previous night, she had never experienced this combination of intense intimate emotional connection and physical release before. She was overwhelmed and confused by her growing feelings for Dan.

Her body collapsed in exhaustion, her arms circling his neck and her head resting gently on his chest. She felt his arms around her back, holding her close to him, and felt him inside her. Their bodies were melded together in their post-coital bliss.

Dan heard her sobs and felt the tears falling onto his chest.

"That was beautiful, Fran. What's wrong?" he whispered.

"He is going to be so angry," she sobbed.

"Who is?" Dan asked, a puzzled look crossing his face. "Philippe?"

Fran felt the fear creeping back into her voice.

"You were supposed to hurt me. He will be so angry! He will punish us for this!" she sobbed.

PHILIPPE GAZED longingly at Michelle from the easy chair beside the bed. He had been staring at her for ten minutes, ever since he walked her from the Venetian Room back to the guest suite.

Certain that she was sleeping, he crept to the bureau where both Dan's and Michelle's Blackberries were connected to their chargers. He quickly unplugged both chargers and scooped up the equipment, stealthily exiting the room. His first stop was his office. He closed the door behind him and brought his computer to life. He worked quickly, copying the names and email addresses from their address books into a data file on his Mac.

From the office, he scurried across the open living area, and then descended the steps to the underground tunnel. Instead of continuing underground to the adjacent building and his studio, he pulled a ring of keys from his pocket and unlocked a door on his right, turning on the light as he entered the house's mechanical room.

He dropped his guest's electronics on a workbench, where he had already set up a powerful AC transformer, a universal DC power transformer and a universal cell phone adapter kit. Within minutes, he sent powerful surges of power through both the phones and chargers, overloading and destroying their delicate circuits and rendering them useless. Before leaving the room, he made sure to disconnect the main telephone line into the house.

Philippe crept, unobserved, back into the guest suite, replacing the Blackberries and chargers to their former positions. He seated himself in the easy chair again and smiled contentedly, gazing at her beautiful ginger red hair and ivory skin. He was both pleased and excited that she and Dan were now totally isolated and at his mercy.

If they refuse my demands, I will simply threaten to send videos of their sexual escapades to their friends, family, and coworkers.

Philippe's eyes suddenly become dark and distant. His mind now travelled back to his parent's estate. His eyes become the eyes of a fourteen-year-old boy. He sees the open bedroom door - the room appears empty. He glimpses a chair, lying on its side on the floor. Then the desk, looking strangely out of place. He cringes as he hears that horrific creaking sound. His eyes rise slowly upwards towards the grotesque, swollen, purple face, but this time he sees right through it. Instead, his delusional mind sees only her sweet smile and her beautiful red hair. An angry voice from deep inside him speaks to her.

You are back with me, Isabelle. Now you will never be able to leave me again!

CHAPTER 25

PHILIPPE ROSE at first light, and went straight to his office to review and upload the video clips from last night's sexual encounters onto his Mac. As he worked in the quiet of his office, the early-morning serenity was broken by the sound of Francesca's feet, rustling in the hallway. Even the softest footsteps on the immense living area's hardwood floors and area rugs, reflected off the wooden ceilings as crisp swishes and whispers. Philippe surprised her in the hallway, grabbing her arm as she walked towards their bedroom. He dragged her into his office and closed the door. His fingers squeezed and his nails bit into the flesh on her arm.

"Where are you going?" he demanded.

"I am going swimming. Let go, you are hurting me!" she cried.

"Shut up! I'll be hurting you more if you don't keep quiet," he muttered, trying not to raise his voice or make any commotion that would awaken their unsuspecting guests.

"Do you remember what you were supposed to be doing last night, *ma chérie?* You were to get that weakling, Whitney, to give you a good hard caning. I wanted to hear you screaming and moaning, shouting for him to do it harder! I needed you to make him look like a sadistic beast! And what do I see on the video clips? I see you going all soft and starry-eyed with each other. Who wants to watch that? I was counting on you to get me some quality, hardcore video to post on my web site. But instead, you miserable little whore, you failed me!"

Philippe lashed out with his right hand and slapped Fran across the left side of her head, knocking her off balance and into the bookcase. She pulled herself upright, her left hand shielding herself in anticipation of another blow.

"What do you have to say for yourself!" he hissed.

"I am sorry. Please … please … don't hit me again. He is so different from the others. He is not an animal, he is more complicated. He sees right through me, Philippe. Please stop this. Please stop before somebody else gets hurt! He cannot make himself be dominant."

"Is that so? Then I am counting on you, *ma chérie*, to do better. Tonight, you must be his Dominatrix. You will make him look like the weak submissive he really is. And you had better make it look good. I will get Michelle to persuade him to take some Viagra first, to make sure he stays hard for the camera. It will be up to you to slip some ketamine into his wine. Then Francesca, you will have your way with him. I think some nice rope bondage, a bit of cock and ball pain, and some flogging should make some excellent video. I also need you to put some GBH into his orange juice this morning so that he feels ill. We must keep them inside the walls today! They cannot phone anybody to tell them where they are staying. Do you understand? Do you think you can get it right tonight?"

Francesca nodded silently and Philippe released his grip on her arm.

"Now, get out of here and go for your damned swim, if you must," he muttered.

DAN'S MIND raced as he pulled himself through the cool water with powerful strokes. His second night with Fran had done little to resolve the conflicts in his mind. If anything, they had intensified. Dan's loving and loyal side was trying to get over his guilt. He wanted to feel okay about learning to take charge sexually with Fran. He wanted to believe that it was healthy, that it was what Chelly wanted from him, and that it would help to rebuild the trust and love inside their relationship.

But instead, the psychologist in Dan had seen the raw emotions inside Fran - her fear, loneliness, and sadness. His connection with Fran triggered overwhelming compassion and empathy that his own loving, loyal side was helpless to ignore. He couldn't shake the guilty voice inside him that scolded him for taking advantage of Fran's vulnerability, and for the intense, irresistible, emotional and physical connection they were forging. He also felt guilty for feeling like he should disagree more strongly with Chelly and Philippe. He couldn't get over the feeling that swinging and BDSM activities were an all-around bad idea. Every part of his identity had clearly seen the evidence in Fran's eyes and in her two different dissociative reactions last night - first her feelings of unworthiness and anger, and then her intense need to feel safe and loved.

The first golden rays of sunlight were just beginning to sparkle and dance on the ripples in the pool as Dan glided to a stop and climbed out. He figured that Fran must have finished her swim before he arrived, judging from the puddle of water at the end of the pool, and the track of wet footprints that trailed away towards the house, and then disappeared after a few steps. He felt the cooling effect of evaporation from his skin in the morning air, his body hair standing upright and goose bumps forming all over his body. As he dried himself with a large pool towel, and as his skin began to feel the warm rays of early morning sunshine, his body hair gradually laid down and the bumps on his skin slowly disappeared.

Dan opened the sliding door and entered their guest room. Chelly wasn't in bed, but he heard the sound of water coming from the shower. As he pulled some clean clothes from his suitcase, he remembered that he wanted to phone the hospital in Detroit today to check his messages. He disconnected his Blackberry from the charger and pressed the button to power up the device.

Nothing happened, so Dan pressed the button again. Still nothing. He plugged his phone back into the charger and noticed that there was nothing on the phone to show that it was charging. It was lifeless. He checked Chelly's phone. There were no signs of life on her Blackberry either.

That's strange. First, I don't get any signal around here. Now our phones don't seem to be working at all.

He stuffed his phone into a pocket in his shorts, meaning to talk with Philippe about it during breakfast. He left the guest suite and headed towards the kitchen. Fran was busy preparing breakfast as Dan strode into the kitchen.

"Good morning, Fran" he said. He placed his hands on her shoulders, tipped his head slightly, and gave her a warm kiss on her lips.

"How are you feeling this morning," he asked. "I hope you slept as well as I did last night. It feels beautiful falling asleep with you after we make love."

"It was beautiful for me too," Fran said. She averted making eye contact with him.

"Where's Philippe this morning?" Dan asked.

"He is in the theatre. He has some more video clips for us to watch after breakfast. He should be joining us in a few minutes. Can I cook you an omelet?" she asked.

"That would be great, thanks."

"What would you like in it?" Fran asked.

"Anything. I'll trust your judgment, since trust seems to be the big theme around here this week," he said, laughing.

"Freshly squeezed orange juice?" she asked.

"Sounds delicious. Do you need help with anything?" he asked, as she handed him a glass of juice.

"No, but thank you for asking. There is fruit, cheese, and pastries on the counter. Take what you like and I will bring your omelet and some coffee out to the pool when they are ready."

"Thanks, Fran. Don't be afraid to ask me for help if you need it."

Dan loaded a plate with some sliced banana, kiwis, pineapple, grapes, strawberries, and cheese, then carried the fruit and his glass of juice out to the patio table, which was now bathed in warm, early morning sunshine. He nibbled on pieces of fruit as he scanned this morning's newspaper. There was nothing of much significance going on in the USA today. He skimmed over the international news, noting reports on a civil war in Chad and some rioting by migrant construction workers in Dubai.

As Dan laid the paper back down on the table, a smaller headline grabbed his attention.

Police Stymied by Couple's Disappearance. He remembered Shelley and Pam talking about the disappearance of a South American couple, and the two detectives who had visited Chateau Eden over the weekend. He read on. The article quoted a Palm Springs detective as saying they were still working on some leads, but had nothing they could share with the press at this time.

A transient thought flashed through Dan's mind. He wondered if there was any connection between the disappearance and the police visit to Chateau Eden. The thought vanished as quickly as it had come. His mind was distracted by Fran's emergence from the house with his omelet and a carafe of coffee. Chelly followed close behind, carrying a plate with some fruit, cheese, a croissant, and a container of yogurt.

"Thanks. Morning, Chelly!" Dan said, smiling warmly at the two significant women in his life. "Are you going to join us this morning, Fran?" he inquired.

"I am sorry," Fran apologized. "I need to clean up in the kitchen, but after breakfast I will join you in the theatre to talk about last night."

"We'll see you in a few minutes," Chelly chirped. Fran gathered some dirty dishes and headed back towards the house.

"How are you feeling this morning," Dan asked, still feeling awkward about asking about his wife's sexual adventures with another man.

"Awesome!" Chelly exclaimed. She lowered her voice and continued. "Philippe has more tricks up his sleeve than a magician. I can't wait for you to see the things we did last night, Dan. And I can't wait to see what he has planned for tonight! How about you guys? Did you have a good time? How did it feel to be the Dominant?"

"Well … Not bad," Dan replied, shyly. "At least it started out feeling that way. I suppose Philippe has some video and you'll see how it went."

"By the way, Chelly. How do you feel about Philippe taping us every night? I'm feeling a bit uncomfortable about it. What if anybody ever saw us on those tapes?"

"Will you stop worrying?" Chelly huffed. "The security cameras are taking the video anyway. It's not like he's purposely making porn films! And besides, if there aren't any security breaches on the estate, he told me the tapes get overwritten within a couple of days, so it destroys any traces of us."

"That doesn't stop him from making copies," Dan countered. "How do you know he isn't doing that? I realize I don't know much about security video, but don't you think the quality of the video is a lot better than most of the security video you see on TV?"

"For Pete's sake, Dan. Stop being so paranoid! He's a wealthy man. He does everything first-class, including his security system. Why wouldn't he have a better security system than the local Seven Eleven store?" she said, unable to hide her exasperation.

"Okay, okay," Dan said. "I just don't want any of this to come back and bite us. What do you want to do today?" he asked. He decided to change topics to calm Chelly's mood.

"I don't know. Do you want to go for a hike to the Indian Canyon today?"

"Sure, sounds good to me. It looks like another nice day for hiking," he said.

Thinking about being outside the confines of the estate suddenly reminded Dan about their cell phones.

"Oh, one more thing. You'd better take a close look at your phone. When I took mine off the charger this morning, it was completely dead, and I didn't see any life on your phone's screen either. I'm going to ask Philippe to check the breaker for our room, to see if there's anything wrong."

As if on cue, the sliding glass door to the pool deck slid open. Philippe smiled as he joined them at the table.

"Bonjour, *mes amis!*" he exclaimed. "I trust you both had a good sleep and are enjoying your *petit déjeuner*. I have some clips from our little experiment for you to watch before we all get busy today. Perhaps you will both join us in the theatre. Will thirty minutes be enough time for you finish eating?"

"Of course. We're looking forward to seeing what we've both learned so far, aren't we?" Chelly said. She looked to Dan for confirmation.

"Thirty minutes should be lots of time," Dan said. "By the way, I was wondering if there's something wrong with the wall plugs in our room. Our phones didn't charge and they seem to be completely dead at the moment. Could I get you to check to see if the breaker was tripped?"

"Oh my," Philippe replied contritely. "Forgive me for not telling you. I heard on the news that a faulty transformer exploded in the neighborhood overnight. Apparently, it caused a large power surge to many homes. I heard them say that it shouldn't cause too much damage, but might be a problem for more delicate electronics like cell phones. I hope yours were not damaged."

"Me too. Thanks for telling us," Chelly replied. "Dan, maybe it's just the chargers, not our phones. We can pick up a new one when we go out later, and see if the phones will charge."

Dan nodded in agreement.

"That sounds like a good plan. Maybe they can even plug our phones into a charger in the store to see if they're working," he added hopefully. Suddenly, Dan's head felt light and he started feeling dizzy.

"Are you alright, Dan?" Chelly asked.

"That's weird. I just felt a little dizzy. Maybe I've been sitting out here in the sun too long. I think I'll go inside and freshen up a little. I'll see you guys in the theatre in about fifteen minutes, okay?"

He left Philippe and Michelle at the patio table and headed through the sliding door into the guest suite to use the bathroom. The dizziness had passed for the moment, but his stomach was also starting to feel upset.

Boy, maybe I'm just hung over again. I have to start cutting down on the wine I've been drinking every night this week.

Fifteen minutes later, still not feeling any better, Dan walked slowly down the hallway from the guest suite towards Philippe's theatre. He made sure he was close to a wall to keep from falling, since his dizziness appeared to be getting worse.

Back in the theatre, he sat beside Chelly in the front row.

"Are you feeling any better?" she asked.

"Not much," he replied. "If anything, I'm feeling more dizzy. My stomach is also starting to feel upset. I hope I'm not coming down with the flu."

Philippe and Fran entered the theatre together. Today, she took the seat beside Dan, rather than sitting behind him like she did the day before. Dan noticed that her brow was creased and she wore a look of concern on her face. Not knowing that Fran had put something in his juice, he had no reason to question why she was so concerned about him.

"Well, my friends," Philippe began. "As you can see on the screen, I have put together some more security clips from last night so we can all have a look at the results of our little social experiment. Overall, I think things went well. But I am sure the video will give us more ideas for things we can do this evening. Hopefully, we can continue to build trust in our partners and increase our sexual pleasure even more."

He dimmed the house lights and clicked the remote control, starting the first video clip of himself and Chelly. Dan heard Chelly's breathing becoming faster and shallower as they watched. Occasionally, she gave a sigh or held her breath, as she remembered the sensations that raced through her body the night before. Dan marveled at Chelly's beautiful full breasts and nipples, her muscular runner's thighs and butt, and the voluptuous curves of her hips on the screen. He was captivated by the sight of his wife's rapture at the hands of another man in the movie clips. He felt a flush of guilt as he noticed himself becoming aroused from watching the erotic spectacle.

He reached over to take Chelly's hand in his. She didn't respond. It was as though she was in a trance, her mind fully engaged in last night's events and unaware of Dan's presence beside her. The movie clip finished and Philippe raised the house lights enough for them to see each other's faces clearly.

"Well, now. We can all see that I was giving Michelle much more sensory stimulation last night. Some might say I was causing her more pain. My dear, perhaps you can explain to Dan how it felt for you."

"It was absolutely awesome, Dan!" she squealed. Her voice had risen into her high range, giving an indication of how excited she was at that moment.

"I wish there were words to describe the full intensity of what I was feeling! But I honestly can't think of any words to describe it. Not only did it not hurt, that flogger just multiplied the pleasure I felt from having Philippe inside me. And when he was building up my pleasure, then leaving me alone, I didn't know whether I was going to explode inside, or cry from frustration. Waiting for him to touch me was agony! But it made it even better when he started touching me again. You've got to believe me. It didn't hurt at all. I just wanted him to whip me harder and harder!"

Dan was having difficulty concentrating. On one hand he couldn't help being aroused by the video, but his dizziness and nausea were definitely getting worse.

"So what are your feelings about what you just saw, Dan?" Philippe asked.

"Well, like yesterday, I think I have mixed feelings," he responded. He turned to face Michelle. "I have to admit that it really turns me on to see you so excited. I love to see that side of you. If that's what it takes to really get you turned-on, I suppose I could get used to doing it, with some practice."

"Ah, practice," Philippe sighed, putting extra emphasis on the *S* sound as he hissed the word slowly.

"That brings us to the video of Dan and Francesca. Shall we watch?" he said. It was like Philippe was playing the role of a sports announcer setting up his next highlight. He turned up the audio volume so that everybody could clearly hear their words.

Dan watched himself starting to apply the cane to Fran. He had no idea that Chelly was feeling aroused as she watched, wishing that it were Philippe whipping the supple wooden instrument against her flesh.

Instead, Dan heard the change in his voice as he recognized, then began talking to, the child-like parts of Fran's identity in the video. Then he saw himself stop caning Fran abruptly, trying to soothe her. He was disappointed and frustrated with himself.

"Dan, that started off so hot!" she exclaimed in dismay. "I was getting so turned on when you were whipping her with that cane. Why on earth did you stop? She was begging you to keep hitting her! It made you look so weak!"

Dan felt himself becoming exasperated and defensive.

"Chelly, can't you see she was in emotional pain? She was dissociating and losing touch with the here and now! She was stuck in a lot of childhood pain and self-hatred. I had to bring her back into the room. That's what I have to do when I'm doing therapy with somebody and they start dissociating. I would have caused Fran more emotional harm if I'd kept caning her. Can't you see that? That's what I've been trying to tell you and Philippe. There's a great risk for harming Fran!"

"Here we go again, mister psychologist!" Chelly groaned, her voice getting louder and showing her growing frustration. "Just when you start letting yourself be a real person, you have to get uptight and start talking your crazy psychobabble. Why can't you just let yourself go for once and stop being so anally retentive? You're not at work and she's not one of your clients! We're swinging! We've given each other permission to fuck each other's partners! Don't you get it! I thought we decided yesterday that we were going to trust everybody here to decide for themselves whether to participate or not. Why don't we hear what Fran has to say?"

Chelly and Dan looked at Fran, who in turn looked at Philippe. His eyes were trained on Fran like lasers.

"I am okay, Dan," she said softly. She wouldn't allow her eyes to meet his. "I trust that you will not harm me. I will tell you if you are hurting me, or if I want to stop! I want to keep doing this with you."

Fran finally lifted her head and allowed her eyes to meet Dan's. He saw determination in them. He also felt like she was trying to send him a non-verbal message with that look.

You must trust me, Dan.

"Very well," Philippe interjected. "That appears to settle things again, Dan. Everybody else would like to continue our experiment. But I think we all need to confirm if you are still willing to continue. Are you going to be the one who disappoints everybody else, especially Michelle?"

Dan started feeling like he was being played again. But his dizziness and nausea were getting the better of him. All he wanted to do was go back to their room and go to bed. Deep inside, he was aware of his responsible voice, telling him to stand up for his convictions. But the loyal part of him and his physical discomfort

were too overwhelming. He didn't have the energy to stand up to
Chelly and possibly risk losing her, at least while he was feeling so
wretchedly ill.

"Okay everybody. Take it easy," Dan sighed. "I'll stay with it,
at least for tonight. That is, if I'm feeling well enough. Is our movie
screening just about over, Philippe? I'm really not feeling well. I
think I need to go lay down."

"Almost finished, my friend," Philippe announced. "Just one
more detail. Since you seem to be caught in a moral dilemma
about being Fran's dominant, I would like to suggest that you
switch roles with Fran tonight. Although she is a natural
Submissive, like you, everything is relative. It's likely that you
may be even more submissive than Fran. If so, you both might feel
more comfortable with her being your Dominatrix tonight. She has
had some experience playing that role in the past, haven't you *ma
chérie?* What does everybody think?"

"I think it's a great idea," Chelly echoed. "How do you feel
about it, Fran? I'd like to see what Dan is like when he has to give
up control to somebody else."

"I would be happy to switch roles with you tonight, Dan,"
Fran replied, continuing to plead with her eyes for Dan to agree.
He gazed into her eyes, seeing her fear. He was trapped again. He
nodded a silent affirmation.

"So, it's decided then," Philippe announced. "I hope you're
feeling better later today, Dan. I was going to prepare Salmon for
dinner."

"We both love it," Chelly said. "I'll eat it, even if Dan can't.
Would you like some company in the kitchen again?"

"*Absolutement, ma chérie!* I would be delighted to have your
help again. Perhaps I could also interest you in a tour of my studio
and I can show you some other fascinating toys that you might
enjoy tonight," he suggested.

"Oh, I'd love that!" she squealed, her voice once again
jumping an octave in pitch. "When can we go?"

"Well, I have some business I must take care of in town. But I shouldn't be more than an hour or two. Will I be able to find you by the pool?"

"I think so. I was planning on going hiking with Dan today. But it doesn't like he's in any shape to go anywhere, so I'll probably just be reading and getting some sun."

"While you and Philippe make your plans, I will help Dan back to your room," Fran announced. "He needs to get some rest, and hopefully he will be able to join us tonight."

"Come with me, Dan," she insisted, as she helped him to his feet. He teetered precariously. Fran put his arm around her shoulders and walked him slowly out of the theatre, then across the living area towards the guest suite.

She felt terrible for spiking Dan's juice and for making him feel so ill. She felt guilty and worthless for doing it, and for having to keep it from him. Fortunately, her businesslike voice helped rationalize her behavior and decrease her guilt. She knew he would feel better in about three hours when the effects of the drug wore off.

FRAN HELPED Dan navigate his way to the bed in the guest suite. He slumped onto the bed and curled up in a fetal position to help calm the nausea in his stomach. Fran sat on the edge of the bed, stroking his hair and forehead.

"I am so sorry you are not feeling well. I am sure you will feel better after you sleep. Please do not worry about being my submissive tonight. You are such a gentle man, I could never hurt you. You must trust me. Now, close your eyes and go to sleep, *il mio caro.*"

Fran leaned close and kissed Dan on his forehead, then rose from the bed and left the room, closing the door behind her. A shroud of fear descended on her - fear of what Philippe might do if she failed to dominate and control Dan enough to satisfy his craving for graphic new video. At the same time, Fran's romantic side was starting to feel increasingly stronger every time she was with Dan. But it was also increasingly afraid of the horrible feelings of emptiness and abandonment that were looming, when Dan and Chelly returned to Detroit in a couple of days.

On one hand, Fran knew instinctively that Dan was a man she should trust. Yet, another part of her, deep inside, believed she could not trust any man. That part believed it was inevitable that Dan would leave her alone - feeling trapped, afraid, and lonely in her life with Philippe.

Tears began to well in Fran's eyes as she thought of him leaving. A lone tear escaped and began its slow descent over her cheek. She allowed herself to feel it for a moment. Then her distant, businesslike part regained control. She brushed the single tear from her face and started walking towards her own bedroom, with determination in her step. She would wash the tears from her eyes, put on her makeup, and nobody would see the emotional turmoil she was hiding inside.

CHELLY WAS wearing the yellow bikini and cover-up, and the flip-flops she had worn to breakfast. She held Philippe's hand as he led her through the tunnel to the barn-like two-story building that stood about fifty yards from the house. It was the first time she'd seen the passage. She was either blindfolded or half-asleep when Philippe had previously taken her to or from the building.

Philippe smiled at her as he led her through the passage. He was entranced by her ginger-red hair. She was wearing it down today. She said it was because she wouldn't be running today, but Philippe sensed it was because she wanted to please him. She must have known he liked it that way, since he had ordered her to wear it down for both of their evenings together. He stopped in front of a locked door as they exited the tunnel and entered the basement level of his studio.

"Dominants describe the places where we act out our scenes with Submissives, either as playrooms or dungeons. You have already seen my romantic playroom upstairs, Chelly. You have done so well with the beginner's toys in that room. Behind the door in front of you, is a room that I call my dungeon. I have many more toys and many more ways of creating extreme sensation and pleasure. Would you like to have a look, *ma chérie?*"

Philippe felt Chelly shiver. She hesitated, and he sensed a mixture of trepidation, but also excitement, in her. He felt her pulse quickening. She was holding her breath.

"Let's do it," she sighed, exhaling as she spoke. "I can't wait!"

Philippe unlocked the door and swung it open, revealing a landscape that was almost the exact opposite of the romantic room on the floor above. The space looked and smelled much like the inside of a barn. The room's skeleton was constructed from heavy wooden beams, while the walls were covered with pine planks. Ropes and chains were suspended from the rafters, many of them running over pulleys, and with a variety of leather or steel cuffs or shackles on one end. Chelly saw a large table, about thirty inches high and long enough for a person to lay on, in the center of the room. Philippe saw her eyes grew wider as they moved to the left side of the room, when she saw a large wooden "X" for spread-eagling and immobilizing a submissive. Leather cuffs for the Submissive's wrists and ankles were located on each corner of X-shaped wooden frame. Philippe noticed her excitement as she took in the scene in front of her.

"Do you think you might like to try my cross sometime? I think you will find that we can do many exciting things with it. Come, *ma chérie*. Follow me," he said. He took Chelly's hand again and led her into the room, past a pair of compartments that looked much like stalls in a barn. There was straw on the floors of the stalls, metal rings at various locations and heights on the walls, and pulleys with ropes and chains attached to the beams overhead. Chelly noticed many lengths of rope of varying thicknesses coiled on wooden dowels on the walls all over the room. They passed a sling, similar to the one in the romantic room, as they proceeded further. At the back of the room, on the left side, they came to a large wooden closet with two large doors and a half-dozen drawers beneath. Philippe opened the doors wide and Chelly gasped.

"You approve of my collection of toys?" he asked rhetorically. The cabinet contained a collection of whips, canes, floggers, hoods, masks, blindfolds, and some long metal spreader bars. He opened the two tops drawers. The one on the left held a variety of different clamps and loops, while the one on the right had a number of dildos and vibrators of different shapes and sizes. Chelly's eyes spotted the pair of two round silicone balls with a cord attached. Beside it was a set of heavier, shiny metal balls.

"Are those what you put inside me?" she asked.

"Ah, you remember the balls do you? Yes, the silicone pair on the left were quite pleasurable for you, if I remember correctly!" he teased.

"What about these?" Chelly asked, as she reached for a loop with a metal weight attached.

"This is a nipple-clamp. If you take off your top, I can show you. Would you like to try it?" he asked, winking and flashing her a salacious smile.

"Sure, why not!" she giggled. She took off her cover-up and reached back to undo the top of her bikini, freeing her large white breasts and their large, reddish-brown nipples that were already starting to become firm.

"Now, close your eyes and enjoy," Philippe commanded. He rubbed his hands to warm them, then started to fondle one of her breasts, grazing and teasing her nipple a number of times, but not lingering. Next, she felt him gently twirling her nipple between his fingers, and then leaving it alone. The next thing Chelly felt was an object lying on top of her nipple. The object slowly closed as Philippe pulled on it slowly and the pressure on her nipples increased. Chelly was just about to say *ouch* when Philippe stopped applying tension. Once again, she had a difficult time telling the difference between pain and feeling aroused.

"What do you think, *ma chérie?*"

"It's delicious!" Chelly squeaked, her voice rising in excitement. "You can do this all you want!"

"Good. You will find that the best part is how good it feels when I take them off and the blood starts flowing again. But the secret is not to leave it on too long, or it can feel painful. If you have ever frozen your feet and toes while skiing or skating, you know how painful it can be if they warm up too quickly. Now, see how it feels," he said, as he released the clamp from her nipple.

Philippe noticed Chelly's face starting to flush. He knew the sensations in her nipple were intensifying as the circulation returned. And he knew from her face that she was getting aroused.

"I feel like putting myself at your command this minute, Philippe! You're turning me on so much already!"

She tried to plant a kiss on his lips, but Philippe resisted. Instead, he gave her a kiss on the cheek.

"Later, *ma chérie*. The longer I make you wait, the more beautiful it will feel. I want you to think about this feeling all day!" he teased, giving her a salacious grin.

"What about the other drawers?" Chelly asked demurely. "Any other little toys you want me to think about all day?"

Philippe opened the two lower drawers, displaying an assortment of different mouth-gags in one drawer and a number of shiny metal objects in the other.

"I don't like the looks of those," Chelly said, as she looked at the gags. "What about these?" she asked. She picked up one of the metal objects, which were smooth with a number of ribbed bulges.

"Those are anal plugs," Philippe explained. "We usually call them butt-plugs. They can provide an intense sensation by pressing against your vagina from the other side. It is especially pleasant if you pull it out while you are coming," he explained. He watched Chelly's eyes carefully for her reaction.

"Ooow," Chelly squealed. "I don't know if I could let anybody stick this up my butt. Are these all different sizes?" she asked.

"Yes, but you would want to start small and work your way up to larger sizes. Even people who find the idea disgusting can learn to enjoy them, if they start small and move up gradually in size," he added, hoping that she might show some interest.

"So, my dear. Now that you have seen everything, do you see anything else you might want to try tonight?"

"Well … umm … I think I might like to try some bondage - tying me up with rope. I really liked the spreader bar and the flogger you used before too. And I definitely want to try the nipple clamps tonight," she answered enthusiastically.

"I think I'd also like to try the cane," she continued. "That looked really hot when Dan was doing it to Fran. Does it hurt very much?"

"Everything is relative, *ma chérie*," he replied. "You have learned that already. I believe I can provide you with some interesting new sensations. Is there anything here that is definitely a hard limit for you?" he asked.

"Yes. No gags and nothing in my butt. I'm sorry, Philippe, but I have a thing about those two that I just can't get over. Is that alright?"

"Of course. I understand that they make you feel uneasy," he answered. He felt extremely pleased with himself. He knew Chelly wasn't going to be able to say no to trying out his dungeon. She was eager and so willing. She was making it so easy for him.

"Thanks for understanding. I'm still really looking forward to tonight. I think I'll be fantasizing all day!" she said excitedly, as she put the top of her bikini and her cover-up back on.

"Myself, as well," Philippe said, "Now, I must go to town for a while. Shall we go back to the house?"

Philippe locked the door to the dungeon behind him and escorted Chelly through the tunnel and back to the house. He knew her mind was racing with fantasies of what he might be doing to her, and how it was going to feel.

Philippe's mind also started drifting far away, to very different images of a different redheaded woman. Visions of toys he had not shown to Chelly were flashing in his mind, together with images of long red hair, alabaster skin with light brown freckles, large breasts, and graceful curves of her female hips. He could see her body writhing in a combination of ecstasy and pain.

Ah Isabelle, said an angry fourteen-year-old voice inside his head. *Now that I have you back, you will learn to feel the agony I felt when you left me alone.*

DAN'S EYES popped open. The room was getting brighter as the afternoon sun partially penetrated the blinds. He was momentarily disoriented, until he remembered Fran helping him to bed after breakfast. The clock beside the bed read two-thirty.

I must have slept for over five hours.

Something felt different. It took him a moment before it came to him.

I'm hungry. And I don't feel dizzy or sick any more.

Dan swung his legs over the side of the bed and sat for a few seconds, then decided to try standing up slowly.

No dizziness.

He walked over to the patio door and pushed the blinds aside. Chelly was lying in a lounge chair. She was alone on the pool deck, and it looked like she'd fallen asleep while she was reading. There was no sign of Fran or Philippe. He went into the bathroom and found the tube of sunblock, then stripped off his clothing and began slathering the creamy lotion over his body. When he was finished, he picked up his book and the sunblock, and then opened the sliding door to the pool deck. The concrete deck burned his feet, so he danced quickly to the shelves with the pool towels, then to the pool, where he dipped his feet in quickly to cool them off.

Chelly opened her eyes at the sound of Dan's feet swishing in the water.

"How are you feeling?" she asked.

"Strangely enough, I feel almost normal," he answered. "Apart from being really hungry right now. I hope that's a sign that I'm getting back to normal. I wonder what made me feels so sick, all of a sudden?"

"I don't know. Philippe wondered if you might have had too much wine last night. Maybe you'd better slow down a bit tonight. Besides, you don't want to be too drunk to be able to perform for your Dominatrix tonight, do you?" she said, giggling.

Dan found himself blushing. He still found it unnatural and awkward talking with Chelly about the sex he was sharing with Fran.

"I suppose not," he replied. "Can I get you to put some sunblock on my back, Chelly? I wouldn't want to be so burned I couldn't appreciate whatever Fran's going to be doing tonight. By the way, you're starting to look a bit pink. Do you want some more sunblock?"

"No, I'm going inside to shower. I think I see Philippe in the kitchen and I promised I'd help him. Sit down over here and pass me the sunblock."

Dan sat at the end of the lounge chair while Chelly covered his back with sunblock. Just as she finished, the sliding door onto the patio opened and Philippe strode into the bright sunlight, smiling as he saw Dan.

"Ah, *mon ami*. You are awake. How are you feeling?"

"Amazingly good, Philippe. Thanks for asking. Everybody seems to think I might have had too much wine last night! Maybe you're all right. I've had more wine in the past week than I usually have in six months, right Chelly?"

"Yeah, it's going to be tough going back to work and real life. I can't believe we're going home in two days!"

"Ah, *oui*. It will be sad to see you both go. So we must make the most of our time, *non*? You are ready to help me prepare the supper again tonight?"

"Do I have time for a shower first?" she asked, as she wrapped herself in a towel.

"Of course! I will come inside with you. I have a small surprise for you," Philippe said, his eyes teasing Chelly as he spoke.

"I'm happy to see you feeling better, Dan. Enjoy the last of the afternoon sun. I will see you at dinner."

"Okay, thanks Philippe. I'll see you both later."

He watched Philippe and Chelly walk back into the house.

I wonder what Philippe's little surprise is?

Dan stretched out on his lounge chair, savoring the warmth of the afternoon sun.

ONCE INSIDE the house, Philippe looked Chelly directly in the eyes, letting her know immediately that he was her Dominant.

"Into your bedroom," he ordered.

"Yes, Sir," she answered.

"Drop your towel, *ma chérie*."

Chelly dropped her towel and stood completely naked in front of Philippe.

"Close your eyes and do not peek. If you do, I will discipline you, do you understand?"

"Yes, Sir," she answered.

Chelly felt the excitement building in her body as she wondered what Philippe's surprise would be. Suddenly, she felt something soft and furry being dragged down her shoulder and between her breasts. The object continued to move around to her backside.

"Spread your legs!" Philippe commanded. Chelly responded immediately. She felt the object move down the center of her butt, and then Philippe's other hand dragged it between her legs and over her genitals. She felt herself starting to go weak in the knees. Then, out of nowhere, the object was over her eyes and she realized that Philippe was tying a blindfold over her eyes.

She felt his hands tracing circles around her breasts. The circles continued to get smaller until he was tracing the outlines of her areolae. She wondered whether he was going to put clips on her nipples, but nothing happened. The anticipation was making her moist. She felt Philippe's fingers tracing a path downward between her breasts, over her pubic hair, and in between her outer labia. She almost groaned out loud as two of his fingers penetrated her and began massaging the front of her vagina, causing the blood to start surging towards her inner trigger. Almost as quickly, his fingers were gone, leaving her wanting more.

A few seconds later, she smelled the familiar salty, musky aroma of her juices teasing her olfactory senses, and building her desire.

Then, for what seemed like eternity, Chelly felt and heard nothing and wondered if he was still there. Finally, she heard a slight rustle in front of her, and before she could catch her breath, she felt pressure on her labia and felt something stretching her cervix and sliding into her vagina.

The balls! Chelly squealed silently. After a moment, she felt another object rubbing back and forth between her labia and over her clitoris. The dual stimulation from the ball inside her vagina, pressing against her G-spot, and the friction over her clitoris was causing tension to build rapidly throughout her body. Her breathing became short and rapid, as she got closer to coming.

Philippe sensed she was almost there. Just as she was about to release and her body started to tense, she felt Philippe slide a second ball through her cervix and into her dripping-wet vagina. The sensation pushed her over the edge, causing her to erupt into convulsions of ecstasy.

As the intensity of her convulsions slowly receded, Philippe untied the blindfold. Chelly blinked. She saw him smiling lasciviously at her. His hand moved toward her genitals and he tugged on the string that dangled from her vagina. She gasped at the pressure on her trigger, still hypersensitive from her orgasm.

"So, I trust you liked my little surprise? If you want to avoid being disciplined severely, you will keep those balls inside you while you shower, while we are cooking, and during dinner. Now be a good Sub and go shower. I expect you in the kitchen in thirty minutes, or you can expect to be disciplined," he commanded.

Chelly's eyes went hazy as she began walking to the bathroom, the balls starting to move gently inside her. She smiled as she turned the faucet to run the water for her shower.

This is going to be a most enjoyable afternoon indeed.

She stepped into the shower under the hot water. As she shampooed her hair, Chelly's imagination ran wild with fantasies of what Philippe might do to her that evening. She also felt the balls moving around inside her. The romantic, sexual part of herself found her arousal, and her yearning for Philippe's touch, building again.

At the same time, the romantic, sexual side of her identity saw clearly, for the first time, that Dan just wasn't the right man for her. She was certain now that he couldn't satisfy her the way she needed to be satisfied. She felt a moment of conflict, as the voice of her loyal part tried to protest. But that voice was weak and distant, compared to the sexual longing that was intensifying inside and taking over her identity, sweeping all other inner voices aside.

Chelly reconnected with her fantasies. She imagined herself in total darkness, feeling only the softness of the fur lining on her blindfold. Her eyes were closed. In her mind, she was no longer in the shower. She saw herself in the barn-like setting of Philippe's dungeon. She imagined Philippe's vibrator running over her clitoris and lips, teasing her with brief penetrations. At the same time, her own fingers were greedily exploring her vagina and rubbing her clitoris. She felt her pleasure growing as the warm water from her shower and her fingers continued to caress her.

DAN LEANED back in his seat in the spa, feeling the warm waters massaging and relaxing his whole body. He was shocked at how quickly he was returning to normal. He had felt good enough to have one glass of an excellent California Pinot Noir with his dinner, laced, as usual, with some ecstasy powder to enhance everybody's mood for the evening, as they all relaxed naked in the spa. Tonight, Fran had also added Ketamine to their wine — Philippe wanted to make sure Dan and Chelly were compliant Subs tonight.

"Well, Philippe," Dan sighed. "You've outdone yourself again. That salmon was absolutely delicious!"

"It sure was!" Chelly agreed. "Are we ever in for a reality check when we get back to Detroit in a couple of days. Back to coming home from work and cooking for ourselves. We're really going to miss staying with you and Fran. It's been a pretty amazing experience, hasn't it Dan?"

Chelly was feeling flushed and excited from the wine and drugs, but was also feeling an almost unbearable tension building inside her from the silicone balls that were relentlessly massaging the inside of her vagina.

"I have to agree with that," Dan replied. It's not like anything we expected, that's for sure. Apart from feeling sick earlier today, I guess I have to be honest and admit that I'm enjoying the experience," he said. He smiled at Fran who was sitting next to him.

"We're pleased that you've enjoyed yourselves, aren't we Francesca?" Philippe asked. His eyes locked onto Fran's eyes, grabbing her attention away from Dan, and then giving her a look of dominance that commanded her to agree with him.

"Yes, we are both enjoying your company very much. But we must not be sentimental! We still have one more day and two evenings together. Shall we make the most of the time we have left?" she asked.

"I agree completely," Philippe echoed. He was smiling and clearly enjoying the week's events. "I propose a toast. To our experiment, and to expanding the limits of our sensual and emotional experiences. To testing our limits!" he toasted. Their four wine glasses clinked together in the air over the swirling water of the spa.

"To testing our limits!" they chimed.

"Speaking of limits, I think that is an excellent segue for us to discuss tonight's activities," Philippe interjected. "I gave Michelle a tour of another one of our playrooms this afternoon, and she appeared to be quite excited about trying it out tonight."

"I've even had a couple of samples to whet my appetite!" Chelly squeaked with a giggle. She blushed as she felt the round objects stimulating her from inside.

"Francesca, perhaps you and Dan would like to use the Venetian Room tonight. It will provide you with more flexibility for exerting your control as his Dominatrix."

"I look forward to it," she replied to Philippe, although her face did not show much excitement or anticipation. She was looking very much like a serious, stern Dominatrix.

"I have one more suggestion, my friends. Since we are all looking for ways to broaden our experience, I think we can all agree that it is in everybody's interest to prolong our sexual arousal as long as possible. But, sadly, there are some limits to how quickly, or for how long, we men can be erect. Isn't that right?" he asked, smiling and giving Dan a knowing wink as he spoke.

Dan smiled and blushed slightly as he nodded acknowledgment to Philippe.

"Yes, compared to the ladies, we do have our limitations," Philippe continued. "And we do not wish to disappoint the ladies do we, Dan?"

He stood and dried his hands on a towel, then reached behind him on the pool deck and retrieved a small plastic bottle from the pocket of his pants.

"In that case, Dan, I would like to suggest that we each take one of these tonight." He tipped over the bottle and poured two diamond-shaped blue tablets into his palm. "Just to make sure the ladies are not disappointed!" he said, chuckling.

"Oh, yeah!" Chelly squealed, as she saw the Viagra tablets in Philippe's hand. "That's awesome! I can't wait to see what it does for you guys! You have to try one, Dan! Are you going to take it?"

Dan started blushing again as he looked at the pills in Philippe's hand.

"Well, that part of sex has never really been a problem for me. But I have to admit; I've always wondered what it would be like to take one. Are there any side effects or reasons why I shouldn't?"

"Not unless you've got high blood pressure, heart disease, or problems with your liver or kidneys!" Chelly interrupted.

"In case you forgot, Dan, I'm an ER nurse. We have to know all of our drugs and their side effects. All the girls at work always laugh about Viagra and Cialis. We're still waiting for some poor guy to come into emergency with an erection that won't go away! How embarrassing would that be?"

The others joined Chelly in laughter.

"Since I don't have to go anywhere tonight, or go to work in the morning, I guess there's no danger of that," Dan said. "Okay, my curiosity has the best of me. I'll take one."

Dan took one of the pills from Philippe and chased it down quickly with a gulp of wine.

"Here's to a long and satisfying night!" he toasted, raising his glass into the air.

"No pun intended!" Chelly shouted, giggling lasciviously at Dan's unintentional double-entendre. Philippe and Fran joined with Chelly's laughter. Dan's face turned a deeper red as he realized his humorous slip-of-the-tongue.

When the laughter settled down, Philippe's face took on a more serious appearance.

"Very well then, all joking aside. As we discussed this morning, are we agreed that Michelle wants me to push her limits even further this evening? And Dan, are you in agreement with putting your trust in Fran as your Dominatrix tonight?"

"I'm definitely ready for more," Chelly replied. "What about you, Dan? You're not going to jam out on us and go mushy again, are you?" Chelly jeered.

"No, Chelly, I'm not going to jam out on anybody. I'm all-in tonight." Dan turned to Fran and smiled at her, trying to coax her into making eye contact.

"I'm at your service, my lady," he said sincerely to Fran. He took her hand, bowed, and gave her a submissive kiss on her hand.

Fran gave a weak smile in return, finally daring to make brief eye contact with Dan. In that brief moment, all Dan could see in her eyes again was fear.

CHAPTER 26

CHELLY SLUMPED forward against the ropes that were restraining her arms. She was still trying to catch her breath after the waves of orgasmic contractions finally ceased surging through her body. She was exhausted. Philippe brought a cup of water and put it to her lips, tipping it gently so she could drink. Her throat was parched from an hour of intense stimulation and heavy breathing. She gulped from the cup, water escaping from the sides of her mouth, as she greedily slurped more water than her mouth could handle. She finally emptied the cup.

The deep layer of fluffed straw on the floor had kept her knees from contacting the hard concrete below while Philippe was teasing her slowly and roughly towards ecstasy. But the straw also scratched the skin on her knees and lower legs, causing the nerve endings in those areas to come alive. The air in the dungeon was cool. Her nipples were standing firm and erect and she felt goose bumps all over her body. The rhythm of her heart and her breathing were gradually slowing in the afterglow of her climax.

She felt her fluids oozing slowly from inside her, and she smelled the musky odor of her sex. The silicone balls had done their job, priming her vagina and making it ready for Philippe's slow, but steady, assault on her senses.

Chelly felt the soft caress of the fur lining of her blindfold. The total darkness had kept her psychologically off balance - always anticipating, but never knowing what Philippe was going to do to her next. Kneeling on the straw-covered concrete floor in one of the wooden stalls in the stable-dungeon, her remaining senses were more keen, allowing her to bask in the delicious blend of odors surrounding her - recently cut pine, fresh straw, oiled leather, and jute ropes. The fragrant mixture felt primal and sensual. Subtly mingling with the smells from the stable, she detected traces of the Chanel No. 5 that Philippe insisted she wear.

Chelly heard more rustling in the straw behind her. Philippe had barely spoken to her while he administered the delicious smorgasbord of erotic sensations, continually frustrating her by denying her an orgasm, then finally bringing her to heights that left her begging for her release. He had not spoken a word to her since she finally climaxed. She waited in silence while she felt him loosen the ropes that had been immobilizing her arms behind her. She tried to anticipate what he could possibly do to surpass what she had already experienced. A surge of warmth and relief washed over her upper torso as her muscles relaxed and the blood began flowing normally through her shoulders and back again. He loosened, and then removed, the rope from her ankles. Then he loosened the ropes that had immobilized her knees and kept them spread apart.

"Stand!" he commanded.

Chelly attempted to stand, but her legs were wobbly. Philippe put his arm around her waist and helped her to her feet.

"You have done well, Michelle. But you will still be punished if you say anything other than acknowledging me, is that clear?"

"Yes, Master," she sighed.

"You have proven yourself to be worthy of the pleasures of *Kinbaku* - Japanese rope bondage. Are you ready now to stretch yourself even further, for the most intense sexual experience of your life, *ma chérie?*"

Chelly paused briefly and wondered if she should mention her safe word or the hard limits they had agreed to on their first night together. She decided against saying anything. She trusted Philippe. He had been true to his word so far. Every time she thought that Philippe's stimulation and her pain were going to be too intense to endure, it seemed to make their sex and her orgasm more intense and exciting. Philippe seemed to know exactly how much she could take, without pushing her too far. She was surprising herself with how much physical pain she could tolerate, and even enjoy.

"Yes, Master. I'm all yours, and I'm ready," she announced.

"Very well. Come with me."

Philippe led her out of the straw-filled stall onto the cool concrete floor, then they turned to her right and walked toward the back of the dungeon. She could tell from the way sounds were reaching her ears that they were now standing in the middle of the large open space at the back of the dungeon. But, because of her blindfold, she couldn't see the five thick, course, jute ropes hanging from a sturdy metal ring, which was itself suspended by a substantial single rope running up and over a large pulley. The other end of that rope was fastened to a large metal ring, anchored in the concrete floor.

"I'm going to re-bind you with the ropes, to make your pleasure more intense. Once again, you will do exactly as I say while I bind you. Do you understand?" he said.

"Yes, Master," she replied solemnly.

Philippe worked quickly and expertly. Chelly felt him place a round wooden pole against the small of her back, but in front of her arms. He raised her left forearm so it was pointing forward at a ninety-degree angle to her upper arm, and the wooden pole rested in the crook of her elbow. He quickly wound one of the bristly ropes two times around her forearm, just below the elbow. He also wound it around the wooden bar, effectively binding the pole tightly against the inside of her left elbow. He repeated the procedure with another rope on her right arm so that the bar pressed firmly into the crook of both arms, which pressed the bar forward and held it firmly in place against her lower back by the natural forward swing of her arms.

Next, Chelly felt Philippe start winding another of the five ropes around the top of her left thigh so that the rope was tucked into her groin, next to her genitals. She felt another wooden bar pushed against the small of her back, beneath the first bar, and she felt him winding the rope from her thigh loosely against the pole. He repeated the procedure on her right thigh so that it was now also bound to the lower pole.

Philippe placed a large, soft pillow on the concrete floor.

"I will help you sit," he announced. " Sit with your legs out in front of you like a large *V*."

"Yes, Master," she replied, doing exactly as he commanded.

When she was seated on the pillow, he grabbed her left leg and swung it outwards towards her left hip, surprising her and stretching her groin almost to its limit.

Once again, Philippe went quickly to work. He tightened the ropes that bound both thighs to the lower pole, so that her thighs were now firmly bound to it. He pulled her wrists upward so her forearms were parallel to the floor, and then attached ropes to each wrist. Finally, she felt Philippe wind two more ropes around her lower thighs, just above the knees.

Philippe stopped working on the ropes. She heard his footsteps moving away towards the back of the room behind her. Suddenly, she felt tension on all of the ropes and on the two poles that rested against her back. The ropes around her upper thighs began pressing into her flesh. She gasped as she felt her butt being raised slowly off the floor, her legs spread into a wide *V* in front of her, until both of her heels were barely touching the floor. She heard him tie off the rope behind her.

Philippe walked deliberately around in front of Chelly, wearing a lascivious smile as he surveyed his work.

"You will now learn to appreciate the thrill of being suspended by ropes!" he announced. "I have three more ropes to attach before you are ready to begin."

Philippe grabbed one of the two ropes that were still attached to Chelly's lower thighs. He pulled hard on the rope so that it pulled her left leg even further out to the left and into the air. It spread her leg so much that the muscles in her groin screamed in protest. He repeated the procedure with her right leg. When he was finished, Chelly's legs were spread-eagled into a wide *V* shape, with her genitals fully exposed and completely vulnerable. Both sides of her groin were strained to their limit. Her breathing became more rapid and she felt her heat starting to pound in her chest with anticipation.

Philippe started winding another rope in a figure-eight pattern around her breasts, and then circling her back until it came around and reconnected between her breasts. Chelly felt a slight tug on that rope. Philippe appeared to be attaching it to another rope. Suddenly, she felt the rope around her breasts tightening, and her body rose higher above the floor. She was now suspended from five ropes that were attached to the two bars beneath her back, to her lower arms, her wrists, her upper and lower thighs, and to her breasts. She heard him walk to the rear of the room again.

An involuntary grunt escaped from Chelly as she felt all of the ropes go tight, and her body started rising further off the floor. The course jute ropes bit into her arms, wrists, legs, and especially her breasts. Philippe continued to pull the rope over its pulley, raising Chelly higher into the air. Her vagina was about waist high when he stopped her ascent. She heard Philippe tying off the rope behind her. She felt herself swaying gently in the air and felt butterflies in her stomach. The rope that bound her breasts was being pulled tighter around the base of each breast, squeezing them and slowing their circulation.

Chelly tried to move her arms, but they were now totally immobilized at her sides by the ropes and wooden bars. She was completely helpless. Chelly started to feel some fear and panic spreading throughout her body from the strange sensations. But the fear was overpowered by her romantic, sexual voice, which was starting to anticipate another ecstatic orgasmic journey.

Philippe once again circled slowly in front of Chelly, surveying his handiwork. She felt his presence moving deliberately around behind her. Suddenly, out of nowhere, she felt his cool hands gently cupping her butt cheeks, stroking those large powerful muscles and gradually moving his hands around towards her inner thighs. His touch became lighter and he started tickling and teasing the insides of her thighs, gradually moving towards her labia, which were fully exposed and stretched wide apart. He began stroking her gently, teasing her labia and her clitoris. Tension started to build inside her, and she felt herself becoming moist again. Then, without warning, he stopped again. She felt nothing except the weight of her body, the heavy ropes pressing into her flesh, and the subtle swaying of her body in the air.

Philippe was moving away from her again, making a variety of small sounds from the direction of his selection of sex toys. She heard footsteps moving in her direction and felt him circling slowly behind her before stopping again. She detected a low humming sound coming from behind her, followed by a strange prickling sensation, like the hairs standing on the back of her neck.

Suddenly, Chelly felt a snap of electricity jolt through the skin on her neck, causing her voice to squeak involuntarily. Although unexpected and alarming, the shock was weak. Her mind was confused; not exactly sure whether the sensation was pleasant or unpleasant.

She felt the prickly sensation moving slowly across her shoulders for about ten-seconds, followed by another sharp snap of electricity. Philippe moved the violet wand slowly and skillfully around her back, moving slowly downward towards her buttocks. Chelly felt her tension mounting with each additional shock, and from the anticipation of never knowing where or when the device would give off another electrical impulse. He moved around to the front of her body. Slowly moving the stimulation up the insides of her thighs, but just missing her genitals.

The prickling disappeared for a few seconds, only to reappear over the front of her neck. The first shock struck on her sternum, then the electrical charge began to move over her breasts. Philippe applied electrical zaps to each breast and each nipple. Chelly found herself purring under her breath. The shocks weren't exactly painful - they were both annoying and stimulating at the same time. She wanted him to stop, but at the same time she needed him to continue. Her arousal continued to intensify. She was careful not to start moaning aloud and possibly risk additional punishment. The charges moved at an agonizingly slow pace, downwards towards her genitals. Philippe was gradually increasing the intensity of the discharge as Chelly learned to accommodate to the sensations. By the time the wand arrived at her labia, Chelly's brain was torn in conflict between wanting the electrical jolts to stop, and desiring more.

Chelly felt confusion in both her body and her brain. Her fight or flight response was feeling alarm and panic from the electrical stimulation and from being suspended in the air. But her sexual response was gradually winning the battle and taking control of her body and her mind. She exhaled as she felt Philippe's fingers slide into her, probing and exploring her moist vagina from his position in front of her. Sexual tension continued to intensify inside her. After a few moments of teasing and pleasure, he withdrew his fingers. She felt the frustration inside her body from the cessation of his stimulation. She sensed nothing at that moment, except the ropes pressing into her flesh and the nerve endings all over her body that had been excited by the violet wand.

After a moment of complete silence, Chelly sensed movement in the air in front of her face. She smelled the musky smell of her own sexual juices, and her olfactory nerves started sending signals that found their way to the pleasure center of her brain. She felt herself becoming more and more turned-on by the rising tide of multi-sensory stimulation that was building steadily inside her brain. The musky smell was getting stronger. Philippe was waving his fingers in front of her nose. Seemingly out of nowhere, the tips of his fingers gently touched and teased her lower lip. She opened her mouth and greedily licked some of the salty, musky liquid from his fingers.

But suddenly, without warning, she felt a hard, rubbery object being pushed roughly between her teeth and into her mouth, forcing her mouth open and stretching her masticatory muscles painfully wide. She felt Philippe tying the ends of something behind her head. Instinctively, she tried to spit the object out of her mouth, but it had forced her jaws so far apart, that they had collapsed tightly against the object, locking it in place.

What the fuck! Philippe, what the fuck are you doing?

Alarms were going off in her brain. She felt panic surging through her body. Her heart was racing and her breathing was rapid and labored. The panic caused every muscle in her body to go rigid. While her body urged her to breathe more quickly, the tension in her muscles made it impossible to do so. She felt like she was suffocating.

The walls were going up in Chelly's mind, trying to shut out the danger and the intense fear that was coursing through her body. In an attempt to block out her current nightmare, her mind tried to flee. But instead of escaping, her mind jumped over her defensive barriers before they slammed shut, linking to an even darker place in her past.

Chelly's mind flashed back in time. Through the darkness, she saw images of Derek. She felt him pinning her arms and legs with his body, restraining her and pinning her to the bed. She was helpless to move her arms and legs. She was completely powerless. Chelly's bound, naked, suspended body was on autopilot, trying to fight back against the stout jute ropes that were currently binding and suspending her in Philippe's dungeon. Yet, in her mind, she saw only the drug-crazed, maniacal look in Derek's eyes from many years ago. She only felt the weight of his body and the incredible strength and power that the drugs were conferring on him.

Out of the darkness, she was faintly aware of images of Derek's erect, angry penis coming towards her mouth. The image faded in and out of darkness as her walls struggled to keep it from her consciousness. Her mouth and throat were filled and she found herself gagging and choking. She felt like she was suffocating. She prayed that the darkness would take her away and put and end to her terror. She was suspended in time and space, feeling only her fear, her helplessness, and the suffocating presence in her mouth and throat.

Philippe sensed that Chelly was no longer with him. Anger began to build inside him from somewhere deep in his past.

"How dare you leave me!" he screamed.

Without warning, Philippe untied her blindfold and whipped it away from her eyes. The bright lights of the dungeon violated the safety of Chelly's darkness, rudely and abruptly jerking her back from her past and returning her to her present nightmare. She winced and closed her eyes against the sudden assault of bright light on her retinas. He grabbed her by her red hair and jerked her head roughly towards him so she had no choice but to look him in the face.

Philippe smiled sadistically. Genuine terror surged through her body like a red alert. She had never seen that maniacal look in Philippe's eyes before. The word *Red* popped into her mind.

My safe word! Give him the safe word!

Chelly frantically tried shouting the word *Red* at Philippe. The only sounds that emerged from behind the ball-gag were frantic, muted, mumbling sounds.

"What is this?" Philippe asked. "What are you trying to tell me? Surely you don't want to stop and leave me now, just when we're becoming so close again, and things are getting interesting?"

He reached out and loosened the loops of the nipple clamps on Chelly's nipples. Initially, she felt nothing, since the circulation had been cut off soon after Philippe tightened them. She felt the beginnings of sensation returning to them, as the blood slowly began to find its way back into the tissue. Her brain couldn't decipher whether she was feeling numbness, tingling, or the beginning of pain sensations.

Chelly's bright blue eyes stared blankly at Philippe. Her pupils were fully dilated. Philippe held up a small chain with two alligator-clips for Chelly to see. The tips of the clips were covered with protective rubber plugs, so they could be attached safely to nipples, labia, skin, or other body parts. She felt his fingers starting to stroke and tease the inside of her thighs again, moving ever so slowly towards her vagina, circling and teasing her clitoris. But her walls were already fixed in place. She felt violated, his touch suddenly disgusting. Her sexual, romantic side was locked safely away behind her walls. Her anger and her fear were firmly in control now.

Philippe felt Chelly's body grow tense and saw the anger and fear in her eyes. The sadistic smile left his face. While Chelly's walls were coming up to protect her, Philippe's walls were tumbling down. Long repressed memories and emotions from many years ago were surfacing and creeping around his crumbling defenses.

"So, you no longer want me. I'm no longer good enough for you! Is that it?" he shouted. His voice was becoming louder and more agitated. Instead of the voice of a man, it was becoming the voice of an immature adolescent.

"Are you planning on leaving me again? Think again, *ma chérie!* Do you really think you can escape from these ropes and from the hold I have over you? And my walls - do you really think you can ever get outside the walls of my beautiful estate?"

Chelly's eyes dilated even wider as reality sank in.

He's not even talking to me! He thinks I'm somebody else - somebody that left him once? I have to tell Dan. We have to find a way out of here!

Chelly struggled instinctively in a futile attempt to escape her restraints. Tears began filling her eyes. She started to realize the folly of her sexual, romantic side over the past few days. Overpowering feelings of guilt and sadness swept over her, mixing with the intense fear she was already experiencing. She realized she had forsaken the part of her identity that she had always valued the most - the part that was always loyal to her friends and family. But most of all, she was beginning to realize how badly she had betrayed Dan.

Why did I ever stop trusting him? She said to herself, sobbing.

Philippe grabbed Chelly's ponytail with one hand and snapped her head upright, so it was right in front of his face, to regain her attention.

"I'm not finished worshipping your beautiful body yet. That beautiful red hair and your white skin, just like fine china. I love caressing the curves of your hips, your thighs, and your wonderfully round derrière. Let's not forget those incredible breasts and nipples. You are a work of art, *ma chérie*. And I'm not yet finished capturing your beauty and your exquisite sexuality on film. The world will finally see the artist that I am! You will stay to let me finish the work that you selfishly interrupted many years ago!"

Feelings of dread ran through Chelly. She felt a sudden chill at the realization that Philippe was filming her for his own pornographic needs. She started imagining the faces on her family, friends, and co-workers when images of her sexual exploits made their way back to them over the Internet.

Chelly also felt something else running through her body. She felt a deep, intense burn that was focused in both of her nipples. She hadn't noticed the burning sensation until now, but it was becoming focused in her nipples like sunlight being focused through a lens. The burning was increasing in intensity and starting to spread outwards into her breasts. Her entire body was becoming more uncomfortable and she began squirming.

"Speaking of your nipples, *ma chérie*. Just how are they feeling now? Are they waking up yet? Have you ever frozen your toes in the winter, longing to put them up in front of a warm fire to warm them up? But instead of feeling comfort from the fire, you may have felt the agony as the blood returned and the nerve endings screamed at you in agony. Have you ever felt that, *ma chérie?* Well, you are going to feel it now as the blood returns to your nipples. You are going to feel exquisite pain like you have never felt before! I hope you will enjoy and remember it!"

Even while he spoke, Chelly's nipples started feeling like they were on fire. She felt the agonizing burn spreading more quickly, and she felt her breathing starting to quicken instinctively to help herself cope with the pain.

Philippe reached out and took her right nipple gently between his thumb and forefinger. The sinister smile returned to his face and he suddenly gave the nipple a hard squeeze.

Chelly's body went rigid and she screamed a muffled scream through the ball gag that Philippe had wedged into her mouth. Tears filled her eyes. She sobbed, imploring Philippe with her eyes to stop hurting her. But rather than feel any empathy or have any mercy on her, Philippe's eyes became more vacant, and his body became more agitated.

"You have no idea how much pain you caused me, do you?" he said. He was talking to Chelly, but his eyes were distant. Philippe's mental walls had disappeared. The memories and pain from his past were overflowing the mental barriers like a river bursting its banks, unable to contain a sudden spring thaw.

Philippe held up the alligator-clips in front Chelly's eyes and pulled the plastic protectors from the clips on both ends of the short chain, revealing the sharp metal teeth on the clips. Next, she felt his fingers probing her labia. Her lubrication had dried up and his fingers felt like rough sandpaper. Without warning, she felt a stabbing pain shoot through her genitals as he clamped one set of metal teeth to one of her labia. Chelly emitted another long, muffled scream through the ball-gag.

Seconds later, before she could catch her breath, a second bolt of shooting pain shot through her body as the second alligator-clip bit into her other labia. She struggled to breathe. Her genitals and her breasts felt like somebody was searing then with red-hot branding irons.

Philippe's eyes lit up as he watched Chelly writhe in pain. He walked quickly to the back of the dungeon, gathering a number of objects in his hands and carrying them back to the center of the room. He returned to the back of the dungeon, then slowly walked back to Chelly, this time unwinding an extension cord as he went.

Once again he gripped her by her ponytail and stared vacantly into her terrified eyes. With his other hand, he held up a DC transformer with a large black dial on the front to control voltage output. Dangling from the transformer were four wires, two black and two white, each with alligator-clips on each end.

"Sometimes there is a limit to the amount of stimulation your own body can produce, *ma chérie*. This small device can help you with that problem by adding to your stimulation. You see, I don't think you fully appreciate the depths of the pain you caused me those many years ago. Do you have any idea how much it hurt to see your body hanging from that rope? To see your beautiful face so distorted and grotesque? Unlike me, you did not stay to feel the anger and shame of my parents, did you? You do not know what it was like to have them reject me, and to feel the pain of being sent away to that horrible religious school? Do you have any idea what it felt like to be beaten and humiliated by those nuns?"

Philippe put down the transformer and picked up another object, waving it deliberately in front of Chelly's face, as he continued to grip her ponytail. The extra-large butt-plug was much wider and longer than the large vibrator he had used so effectively on her G-spot.

"Do you remember this, *ma chérie?* Since I haven't heard your safe word, I must assume that you are willing to feel some of my pain!" he hissed.

Chelly's body re-started her futile struggling - her eyes grew wider as the full extent of Philippe's intended tortures became apparent to her. She tried shouting her safe words, begging him to stop. But her muffled screams of protest fell on deaf ears, as Philippe was lost in the emotional pain of his past.

Chelly couldn't imagine any pain more severe than what she was feeling in her nipples since her nerve-endings screamed back to life, until Philippe began delivering electrical current to all four alligator-clips.

"You are mine again, Isabelle! Now you are feeling the pain I felt after you left me! Now we are together in our pain!"

Philippe's anger was now in total control of his mind. Yet, as he unleashed his anger on Chelly, an eerie calm descended over him. He was completely focused and absorbed on Chelly, and on the cathartic release he was experiencing as he administered his sadistic acts on her.

Philippe forced the giant butt plug into Chelly's rectum. Chelly's brain was struggling to keep her walls up now - trying desperately to keep out the nightmare of Philippe's torture. Instead, her brain escaped. Flashbacks of Derek flooded back into her mind. He was high again. She had tried to run, but he caught her and pinned her face down over the kitchen table, her skirt lifted high. He pushed her face violently into the table, and tore her panties away in his drug-fuelled rage.

Chelly couldn't take any more. Her brain was on overload. There was only one thing she could do to escape the flashbacks and the pain. Her brain shut down, allowing her to go numb. The images of Derek, and the scorching pain that was shooting through her entire body, faded away into a merciful, unconscious darkness.

CHAPTER 27

"ARE YOU sure you are feeling well enough to play again tonight, Dan?" Fran asked.

She and Dan remained by themselves in the spa, Chelly and Philippe having already departed for another night of exploring the blurred boundary between sexual pleasure and pain.

"I can't believe how much better I'm feeling now," he answered. "Don't worry about me, Fran. I'm just having a run of bad luck. First our cell phones seem to have got fried by a power surge, and then I get some kind of a weird bug. I hope nothing else happens."

"What about you?" Dan asked. "You looked afraid a few minutes ago. Are you still worried about Philippe? He's not abusing you, is he?"

Fran wouldn't let her eyes make contact with Dan's.

"I am fine," she lied. "I was only feeling emotional last night. It was nothing. He will just be disappointed if you and Chelly do not have the best possible impression of our lifestyle. That is all. Trust me, Dan. He takes good care of me."

Fran rested her hand reassuringly on Dan's thigh. The effect of her warm touch next to his genitals had an immediate effect on Dan.

"Okay. I won't ask again. Speaking of trust, I suppose we should be talking about what you want to do to me tonight, since it seems like my little blue pill is starting to work," he said, chuckling.

"What would you like?" she asked. "Do you have any fantasies that you would like to play out with me tonight?"

"Apart from trading partners and having sex with a beautiful woman like you?" Dan asked. "I can't think of a fantasy that would be better than this."

He smiled, lifting Fran's chin with one hand so he could see into her eyes. He tilted his head and gave her a tender kiss.

"Seriously," Fran countered. The businesslike, serious part of her was taking over, trying to stay emotionally detached. "You must have some other fantasies. What about being dominated by a Dominatrix dressed in black leather, or maybe by a female boss or a teacher?"

"Okay. How about the black leather? That sounds like it could be fun!" Dan answered, grinning.

"Is there anything you don't want me to do?" Fran asked. "Bondage, cock-and-ball torture, anal sex?"

"I don't really know much about it," Dan admitted. "Cock-and-ball torture doesn't sound like much fun. Same with anal sex. But I'll try just about anything else, as long as you take it slowly."

"Naturally," Fran replied. "We will use code words. If I am doing something that is too painful or intense, just say *Red*. If you are enjoying what I am doing, but it is too intense - if you want me to slow down or give you a break, just say *Yellow*."

Fran placed a hand on Dan's shoulder, giving him a reassuring smile.

She seems more relaxed and less businesslike. The wine must be helping her loosen up.

"Are you sure you feel comfortable doing this?" Dan asked.

"I do not want to hurt you or anybody else, Dan," she said softly. "I only want you to feel what Chelly is learning to feel from Philippe. I want to please you in a way you have never been pleased before. Will you trust me?"

"Of course," he replied. "I trust you. I'm all yours!"

The empathic part of Dan's identity knew the pain that Fran must have felt in the past. So he trusted that she would never want to cause anybody to feel pain.

DAN STOOD on the carpet in front of the canopy-bed. He was completely naked in front of Fran in the sixteenth-century European playroom, his arms behind his back. Fran was dressed in a black leather bustier that pushed her petite breasts into seductive mounds, but was cut so low that the edges of her areolae teased Dan's eyes. The garment was cut high on the sides, showing off her muscular thighs and slim hips. It was also crotchless. She wore black high-heeled shoes that were open at the toes. She wore no stockings, instead emphasizing the perfection of her smooth, olive-toned legs. Her outfit was accessorized perfectly by a black choker with a gold medallion suspended beneath it. Dan was already firmly erect as he took in the erotic spectacle before him.

An assortment of sex toys was placed neatly across the foot of the bed. Fran stepped forward and chose a leather collar. She walked in front of Dan and wrapped the collar around his neck. She adjusted it so it was snug, but not tight. Attached to the front of the collar was a metal ring for attaching a chain, if desired.

The businesslike part of Fran's identity, which was well suited to the role of dominatrix, took over as she spoke.

"As long as you are wearing this collar, you are mine. You will call me *Lady Francesca*, and you will only speak if I ask you to speak. If you do not obey, I will find some delightful way to punish you. Do you understand?"

"Yes, Lady Francesca," Dan said.

"Good," Fran said softly into Dan's ear, as she moved close to him. "I can see you are excited by my appearance. And I know you enjoy my touch, am I correct?"

"Yes, Lady Francesca."

She circled around him and selected one of the toys from the end of the bed. As she walked back around him, she ran her hands slowly and softly along his shoulders, over his neck, then downwards along both sides of his spine. She continued to move around him until she stood directly in front of him again.

"I am going to blindfold you now. It will add to the intimacy of your experience. It will heighten all of your other senses, and your arousal."

She placed a fur-lined black leather mask over Dan's eyes, then reached around behind his head and tied the it snuggly.

When she finished, Fran started running her hands through the hair on Dan's chest, slowly moving her hands downwards in erotic, teasing circles towards his genitals. She moved in closer, pressing her body tightly against Dan's, grinding her hips and rubbing herself against his erection. One hand moved lower and began scratching the inside of Dan's thigh, moving slowly upward, then slowly stroking his testicles. Dan felt himself swelling and feeling even more sensitive. Suddenly, Fran grabbed him firmly by his erection, causing him to moan. He let out a long, pleasurable breath of air.

"Oh, you like that? Does it drive you crazy not knowing where I am going to touch you next?"

Just as Dan was going to answer her, Fran reached up with her other hand and grabbed one of his nipples between two fingers, squeezing it hard. It took his breath away. She released her grip on his erection and pressed her body close again. With two fingers on her other hand, she pinched his other nipple tightly.

"Let us see how much you like this, Dan. I want to get some idea of how much pain you can withstand. Do not forget to code yellow or red if the pain is too intense for you. Focus on your breathing."

Fran continued to squeeze, twist, and pull on both nipples at the same time. A hot, searing pain was shooting through both sides of Dan's chest. He slowed his breathing, clenching his lips and teeth together, while he took deep, deliberate, grunting breaths through his nose. After breathing deeply five or six times, the pain began to subside into a dull, numbing pain. Dan was surprised that he was able to tolerate the continuous assault on the nerve endings in his nipples.

"You are doing well, Dan. You should be fine with everything I will be doing today," Fran whispered into his ear.

Without warning, Fran released her grip. She massaged his nipples and his chest lightly. Dan found the sensation of her light touch to be intensely pleasurable on the highly stimulated nerve endings. Fran's hand moved to Dan's penis, which had started to wilt while he was distracted by the searing pain in his nipples. Had it not been for the Viagra, he likely would have gone completely soft.

"Do not forget to focus on the pleasurable sensations in your cock," she said. She dropped to her knees and took his semi-rigid penis in one hand, guiding it into her mouth and closing her lips tightly around its rim and head. She touched the edge of her teeth against the sensitive tissue, causing Dan to moan. With the aid of the Viagra in his bloodstream, his erection recovered quickly. He felt her lips slide tightly down his shaft, taking him deeper. As she moved back up the shaft, she pressed her tongue firmly against the most sensitive areas of the hard shaft and moved slowly upwards. This time, Dan emitted a deep groan as her lips and tongue passed over the frenum and back over the rim. She let him slip out of her mouth and rose to her feet again.

Fran walked around Dan and took a step towards the bed again, this time choosing a long leather cord. She moved back around in front of Dan.

"I am going to tie up your balls to prevent them from being pushed back up inside you," she stated. She began winding the leather cord behind and under his scrotum, and then back over it. She pulled the cord so it was snug, tightly binding his testicles and putting gentle pressure on them. Dan felt a sensation of tightness in his scrotum once she was finished, but no discomfort.

His penis remained erect and swollen throughout the process. He found it highly pleasurable to feel the air swirling as Fran walked around him, and to feel the unexpected sensations when she stroked his shoulders, neck, and back, then his chest. The fragrance of her perfume, wafting occasionally into his airways, sent additional erotic messages to the sexual control-center in his brain. It felt exhilarating for Dan to entrust the care of his body to her hands, and to feel her hands and the leather moving expertly around on his sex parts. It was intensely intimate in a way he had never experienced before.

"Come with me!" Fran ordered. From the bed, she picked up four leather straps attached to lengths of chain. She attached a short length of chain to the ring on Dan's collar, and then tugged on it.

"Follow me," she ordered, tugging on the ring. Then, she pulled Dan to an X-shaped wooden cross on the other side of the room. Each wooden arm of the cross was equipped with metal rings for attaching chains.

"Turn around!" Fran commanded. With his blindfold in place, Dan tried to estimate half a turn of his body the best he could. One by one, Fran fastened leather cuffs to Dan's wrists and feet, pulling the straps snug. Each cuff had a short length of chain attached to it.

"Move backward slowly until you feel your back touching wood," Fran directed.

Dan shuffled backwards until he felt himself bump into the cold wooden structure.

"Lift up your left arm," Fran said. She attached the chain on Dan's wrist to the metal ring on the cross with a carabineer, and then repeated the process with his right arm.

"Spread your legs," she ordered.

Dan did as he was told, expecting to feel Fran attaching the chains on his ankle cuffs. Instead, he felt her presence in front of him as the air moved around him. A hint of perfume came to him. He felt her warm breath at his left ear. Out of nowhere, Fran grabbed his hard, throbbing cock with her hand again and squeezed. Dan groaned at the unexpected, exquisitely intense stimulation.

"Do you like being chained to my cross, Dan? I can do anything I want to you when you are chained to it. Do you like the way I am squeezing you now?"

"Yes, very much, Lady Francesca," Dan replied.

"I am pleased," Fran said. At the same moment, she grabbed and squeezed his right nipple with her left hand and squeezed his cock with her right.

Dan sucked in a huge breath of air as the pain tore unexpectedly through his chest and he felt the intense surge of pleasure from his penis. Both sets of impulses arrived at his brain at the same time, resulting in confusion. His senses were overwhelmed and he had difficulty determining whether he was feeling pain or pleasure at that moment.

Fran released her grip on his cock. Then he felt another surge of pain tearing through his left nipple. This time, his brain recognized the pain signal. Dan resumed taking deep breaths to cope with the intense pain sensations that were burning through his chest. He felt Fran breathing softly into his right ear as the pain in his nipples gradually transformed into a dull throbbing sensation. Dan was amazed at how erotic the combination of pain, combined with the closeness of Fran's breath, could feel.

Out of nowhere, Fran released both nipples. She continued to breathe in his ear as she tenderly massaged his nipples and chest again.

You're driving me crazy, Fran! What the hell are you going to do to me next? Pain? Pleasure?

Fran resumed fastening Dan's ankle cuffs to the wooden cross. As she worked, her loving, romantic part almost forced a brief smile. For a brief moment, she let herself enjoy the heightened intimacy from the complete trust and control that this unusual man had given to her. The businesslike Lady Francesca frowned and quickly regained control over her consciousness.

"I love very much that you are enjoying this," Fran said seductively. "Do you want to make love to me Dan? Do you want to be inside me?" She gently teased his testicles and penis as she spoke.

"Yes, Lady Francesca."

"Then you are going to have to earn the right to release inside me tonight. Make sure you do not come before I give you permission. If you do, I am afraid I will have to teach you a lesson. Do you understand?"

"Yes, Lady Francesca. I understand."

"Very well. I think it is time to give those nipples some more attention," she said. He heard her heels striking the hardwood floor as she walked back towards, the bed. After a brief pause, he heard the sound of her heels making their way back towards where he was chained to the wooden beams of the cross. He felt a cold sensation as Fran attempted to tighten a plastic loop, with weights attached, to his left nipple. Although they were firm and hard, his nipples were too small for her to attach the loop.

"That is not going to work. But, you are in luck. We just received a delightful new set of clover clamps with metal teeth that will provide even more intense stimulation!" she chuckled.

This time, Dan felt the sudden shock of cold metal touching his chest and nipple. Before he had a chance to recover from the surprise, the pain returned to his left nipple with a searing vengeance. Seconds later, he felt the same cold chill on the right side of his chest, followed immediately by a second searing pain on the right side. Dan felt like his entire chest was on fire. Out of nowhere, he felt a cold sensation on his lips.

"Hold this chain in your mouth," she ordered, giving it a small upward tug as she spoke. "Keep some tension on it and make sure you do not drop it!"

Dan felt another surge of pain as he pulled the chain tight, and the clamps stretched his hard nipples upward. The chain almost dropped from his mouth as he gasped from the pain.

"Do not let your head drop!" Fran shouted. "Keep it up. And do not forget about the pleasure in your cock!"

The pain continued to surge through Dan's chest, although the searing sensation was beginning to become more of a dull throbbing. Out of nowhere, he felt Fran's hand gently teasing the sweet spot on his shaft with her fingers, followed by a sudden squeeze from both her lips and her teeth on his increasingly sensitive rim. He found the throbbing pain sensations and the pleasurable sensations in his cock starting to merge into one excruciatingly intense ball of sensation. Fran released his penis and stood in front of him.

"I love the way you are trying so hard to please me, Dan," Fran whispered. She pressed her body tightly against his. Dan felt the increase in intensity of the intimate connection between them. At the same time, Fran tugged upward on the chain attached to the nipple-clamps, elevating the pain intensity in his chest. Dan moaned into her ear, then sucked in another deep breath. Moisture started to ooze from between Fran's legs. The businesslike Dominatrix was starting to lose control to the romantic, sexual Fran.

She moved away from Dan slightly, making random teasing strokes all over his body. Then Dan heard her heels clunking and clicking around in short, tiny movements on the hardwood floor next to him. He sensed that she was fiddling with something on a shelf beside him. After a brief pause, her shoes clicked and shuffled and he felt from the air currents that she was in front of him again.

He sensed her reaching between his legs. Out of nowhere, he felt a cold, wet sensation on the bottom of his right butt-cheek that caused him to shiver. The chilling cold was followed by a feeling as if Fran was pressing or massaging the area. Seconds later, he felt another wet chill on the right side of his scrotum, and more pressing and massaging. Fran repeated the process on the left side of his scrotum. Finally, Dan felt the strange wet sensation on the outside of the rim of his penis, followed by more pressure. There was another brief shuffling and clicking of Fran's heels, followed by other movement.

"Your head is down. Lift that chain!" Fran snapped from directly in front of him. Startled, Dan jerked his head upward, a surge of pain shooting through his nipples.

Dan thought he felt a warm vibration in his genital area. By the time he noticed it, the vibration seemed to have disappeared. A few seconds later, he definitely noticed the same sensation. Once again it disappeared. The third time, he felt a distinct, tingling sensation in his testicles, right butt-cheek, and the rim of his penis that was pleasant. Dan recognized the sensation as some type of electrical pulses. By the time he figured out that Fran must have attached four TENS electrodes to him, he felt the next set of electrical pulses. By now, the pulses created a distinct electrical buzz of increasing intensity. He felt like something was gently squeezing or massaging all of his genital area at once. The sensations were becoming increasingly pleasurable and he could feel himself swelling and getting harder.

The fifth set of impulses started with a noticeable buzzing, but increased rapidly until he felt like somebody was squeezing his balls. He wasn't sure the sensation was entirely pleasurable anymore, but the sequence of pulses stopped. Dan's breathing quickened and became shallower. Suddenly, he felt a strong buzz and felt a gut-wrenching pressure through his testicles and penis. The pulses continued to intensify. This burst was not only unpleasant, but also painful. Dan slowed his breathing, bracing himself for the next burst. When it came, he groaned and his head snapped back, causing more pain to scorch through his chest. At the same time, he felt the same sickening pressure in his balls that he could remember when he took a soccer ball to his balls. His body tried to fold together to protect himself, but the chains on his wrists held his torso upright. He began to feel helpless against the onslaught of pain.

As the sixth set of pulses gripped him, Dan groaned.

Yellow! He gasped, signaling Fran that she had exceeded his ability to cope with the sickening sensations creeping into his stomach from his genitals.

"I hear you, Dan," Fran said. "You have done well, but I see that it is too intense for you right now. I have moved the timer to the end of the cycle, and the pulses will be less intense now."

Dan was relieved by the decreasing intensity of the pulses. He was breathing slowly and deeply to calm himself. The contractions in his penis and testicles were returning to a pleasant tingling that made him feel his erection become harder and more swollen.

Fran pressed her body tightly against Dan again. He smelled the leather and felt it rubbing on him. He reveled in the intense intimacy of their closeness. The subtle fragrance of her perfume was mixing with the musky smell of her arousal. He felt her warm breath in his ear.

"You want me badly, Dan. Do you not?" she teased.

"Oh yes, Lady Francesca," he said.

"Do you think you have earned the right to be inside me, Dan?"

"Yes, Lady Francesca, I think so," he answered hesitantly.

"You are doing well. But it is early and there is so much more I can teach you! Now keep that chain in your mouth and lift your head while I turn you around!"

FRAN PRESSED her body against Dan's back, running her hands sensuously across his chest, his abdomen, and downwards towards him genitals. The seductive fragrances of her perfume and her sex, the closeness of her body, and the fact that he couldn't see what she was going to do next, were driving him crazy. Yet, at the same time, she tugged upwards on the chain of the clover clamps with one hand, torturing his nipples, while she squeezed the shaft of his penis lovingly with the other.

"Ahhhhh…" Dan moaned. His nervous system was overwhelmed by the contradicting extremes of pleasure and pain that were flooding his brain's sensory circuits. He both loved and loathed the exquisite mixture of sensations. He wanted her to stop, but he wanted her to keep going. Despite the pain, his brain did not want to blurt out his *Red* code to end the experience.

Time flew for Dan as Fran gave him a taste of every toy she had laid out for him. He was shocked at how much he had loved the exhilarating, heavy, whipping sensations of Fran's leather flogger. The skin on his back and buttocks was still warm and tingling all over. He was amazed at how disappointed he had felt when she didn't flog him any harder, and especially when she stopped. On the other hand, he remembered the sickening pain from the leather fronds of Fran's flogger striking his testicles, and the searing pain every time the clover clamps pulled and twisted his nipples.

Because he was blindfolded, Dan had lost track of time. It felt like Fran must have been dominating him for close to two hours. He was sweating profusely and losing fluids due to the non-stop stimulation of his sympathetic nervous system. His mouth and throat were parched from thirst.

Fran whispered into Dan's ear.

"You are trying so hard and making me so hot. I want you inside me. But not quite yet, my anxious lover!"

She released both the clover clamp chain and his erection at the same time, and then pulled her body away from Dan's. Without warning, she released the pressure on the clover clamps and removed them from Dan's nipples. They had become almost numb from the pain and Dan could barely feel them after the clamps were gone.

"Spread your legs," Fran ordered. She proceeded to attach a spreader bar equipped with leather cuffs to his ankles. When she was finished, she stood up and grabbed the metal ring on the collar around his neck.

"Follow me carefully," she commanded.

Dan shuffled his feet, feeling like a shackled prisoner as he followed Fran a few feet to his left. He heard the sound of Fran dragging something like a wooden table or bench into position in front of him, and then he heard a rustling sound near his feet.

"There is a cushion in front of you. Kneel down, and then feel for a bench in front of you. Keep your knees on the cushion and lay face down on the bench with your arms in front of you."

Because his legs were kept equidistant by the spreader bar, Dan struggled awkwardly to kneel without falling forward onto his face. Once his hands felt the bench in front of him, he was able to stabilize himself, and then lean forward onto the wooden surface. He heard Fran move walk to his right, to a position in front of him. She re-attached the leather cuffs to his wrists, and then attached the chains to a metal ring on the bench in front of him.

Dan lay silently on the bench, listening to Fran's shoes making short, clunking steps a few feet to his left. Once again, his breathing quickened with anticipation. His nipples throbbed. The blood was flowing again and his nerve endings were coming back to life after going numb from the clover clamps.

He didn't have to wait long. Suddenly there was a whipping sound in the air, first on his left, then on his right a few seconds later. After another pause, the sound was coming in the air immediately over his head. Then there was nothing but silence for at least ten or fifteen seconds.

Out of nowhere, he heard the whipping sound, followed by a sharp sensation on his right butt cheek. The air came rushing out of his lungs. He was caught completely off guard by the unexpected stinging in his flesh.

She's got a cane!

He felt excitement building inside him. After the heavy sensation of the flogger, and after using the cane on Fran last night, he realized that he had been secretly wondering what the cane would feel like on his skin. Now he would know.

This time, Fran brought the cane down on the left cheek. Dan felt a sharp stinging sensation on both sides of his butt that he didn't find unpleasant at all. Fran picked up the pace, alternating light snaps of the cane to each side of his behind, using fluid flicks of her wrist.

"Are you enjoying my cane, Dan?" she inquired.

"Very much, Lady Francesca!" Dan answered.

She gradually increased the frequency and intensity of the snaps to his butt cheeks until they were a rosy red. Dan felt a hot, stinging glow building in his behind and felt himself growing more excited. His breathing quickened and became synchronized with Fran's pace. His felt his erection throbbing. He was feeling far more pleasure than pain.

"Are you feeling any pain yet?" she asked.

"Not yet, Lady Francesca," he responded. "You can go harder if you like."

"My goodness. You are a bit of a pain-slut. I am impressed. Let me see what I can do for you! Do you remember your safe words?"

"Yes, Lady Francesca. *Yellow* if I enjoy it, but it's too intense. *Red* if it's too much."

"Very good," Fran answered. "Remember to focus on your breathing, Dan."

He felt the sharp snaps of the cane moving down onto his upper thighs. With smaller muscles and less padding over the thighs, every strike was sharper and produced a more intense burning in his flesh. Dan's breaths became more like grunts with each impact. He smiled to himself. What he was feeling at this moment contradicted everything he had ever known about pain. But he also realized he was becoming more and more aroused sexually as the hot glow spread throughout his muscles.

Fran worked like an artist, applying shorter strokes with the end of the cane to the inside of Dan's thighs as she saw him responding to her strokes. Dan felt the heat spreading upward towards his genitals and felt his sexual tension continuing to build as his enjoyment of the cane increased.

Fran's stokes became lighter and more rapid on Dan's thighs, then gradually tapered and stopped completely. Suddenly, Dan felt nothing but sensory deprivation. He was unable to sense any movement from Fran and couldn't tell where she was or what she was doing. The anticipation was causing his pulse and breathing to quicken, and he was aware of perspiring more.

Then, out of nowhere, Fran's cane landed with a sharp snap on the sole of Dan's bare left foot. His entire body jerked and Dan expelled his breath in a sudden grunt at the unexpected jolt of pain. He was stunned at how much more intense and painful the cane felt on his extremity, compared to his well-padded butt and thighs. Before he could recover, Fran dealt him another sharp stroke of the cane on his right foot. Dan's body gave another reflex jerk. In all, Fran landed four strokes on each of Dan's soles, each as painful as the first. By the fourth stroke, he felt a throbbing, numbing pain on the bottom of each foot.

Dan was breathing heavily, trying to manage the pain with slow relaxing breaths, when the strokes of the cane finally ceased. Fran said nothing, but Dan heard more rustling behind him. He waited as his breathing gradually relaxed, and his brain once again tried to sort out the confusing mixture of sensations: the pleasant, arousing glow of hot tingling sensations in his thighs and backside conflicted with the dull, throbbing pain he felt in his soles.

Dan's body shivered as he felt the cool, wet chill of gel on his testicles, shaft, and butt again. His heart started pumping faster and his breathing became shorter. With a sense of panic, he realized that Fran was putting the TENS electrodes back on his genitals for another round of electrical nerve stimulation.

"Let us see how you do with the TENS unit, Dan. You should start to feel some tingling in a few seconds," Fran advised.

Dan felt his body tense in anticipation. He slowed and deepened his breathing, preparing himself for more of the gut-wrenching squeezing sensation on his balls.

"Are you feeling it yet?" Fran asked.

"Yes, Lady Francesca," Dan replied. "It's just tingling right now."

Dan felt the intensity of the pulses increase gradually from a gentle, pleasant tingling to a more intense buzzing before the pulses reversed and subsided within each set of pulses. The second series of bursts was more intense, but the tingling and buzzing sensations felt pleasant to Dan. He was aware of his erection becoming harder again. The intensity of each series of pulses gradually increased. By the sixth burst, Dan found himself wanting to hold his breath as the electrical pulses caused a tight squeezing of his balls tightly. He felt the beginnings of that sick feeling in his stomach. But the intensity of the pulses did not get any stronger. He found himself tolerating and even enjoying the intermittent squeezing and letting go of his testicles.

"I am proud of you, Dan!" Fran said. "You are at the same intensity as you were the first time. How is it for you now?"

"Okay, Lady Francesca," he replied. "I can't believe it, but it's starting to feel enjoyable." He felt Fran's hand reaching underneath him, stroking the shaft of his penis.

"The timer will keep pulsing for another five minutes before it gradually turns itself off. Can you take that?" she asked.

"Yes, Lady Francesca. It's not a problem this time,

The combination of her gentle stroking on the trigger area of his shaft and the firm squeezing sensations in his balls made Dan feel like his penis was being stretched to its limit.

"Are you staying good and hard for me, Dan?" she teased. "Are you ready for me yet?"

"Oh, yes Lady Francesca," he sighed. "Very ready!"

Fran stopped stroking his erection and he heard the heels of her shoes taking slow, deliberate steps around behind him. He felt the air moving over his back again. Then he became aware of the gentle touch of the flogger's leather strands, moving ever so lightly and slowly across his shoulders, teasing the nerve endings in his skin again. She dragged it slowly down the middle of his back and over his butt crack. His nerve endings were craving something more.

Finally, as the TENS unit counted down the last three minutes of its cycle, Dan felt the heavy impact and the slap of the leather strands on the skin of his butt. Fran alternated strokes from one side to the other and gradually moved up his back. Dan felt himself cheering Fran on, as the flogger slapped him progressively harder with each strike. She picked up the pace, striking him harder and faster with every stroke, until he heard a small beep from the TENS unit. As the TENS pulses gradually weakened and disappeared, the intensity of the flogger's strokes slowed until the strands of leather were once again gently caressing the skin all over Dan's butt and back. He was conscious of a warm, tingling sensation all over, especially in his genitals.

Fran gently peeled the TENS electrodes from Dan's skin, then wiped away any remaining gel with a towel. She leaned over his back, her warm body pressing tightly against him, as she unclipped the chains anchoring his wrist cuffs to the wooden bench. Her fragrance and the closeness and warmth of her body were driving Dan wild with desire.

Fran took Dan's wrists in her hands.

"Back to a kneeling position," she commanded. His torso was stiff from remaining in one position on the bench for so long. Fran held Dan's wrists and guided him back onto his knees. He heard her drag the wooden bench back against a wall in front of him, her heels clicking and clunking against the hardwood as she did so. The sound of her told him she was walking back towards him. She slowly and deliberately circled him, pausing to run her hands through his hair, then across his chest to massage his nipples.

Unexpectedly, she squeezed, twisted, and pulled both of his nipples at the same time, causing him to wince in pain.

"We have been ignoring these for a while haven't we, Dan?" she teased. He controlled his breathing. This time, it was easier for him to manage the pain by slowing his breathing.

"Start kissing the inside of my thighs, Dan. Tickle me with your tongue. Go slowly, all the way up until you get to my pussy. Can you smell me, Dan?"

"Oh yes, Lady Francesca," he replied truthfully. The mixture of pheromones in her secretions, and the subtle fragrance of her perfume, was sending Dan's sexual center into a frenzy. As he alternated kisses, flicks of his tongue, and nibbles on her thighs, he heard Fran's breathing quicken.

Dan felt a finger on his lips. He both smelled and tasted the musky, salty moisture of her secretions on her finger.

"Suck on it," she ordered. Dan complied and savored the taste of her in his mouth.

"Higher now," she commanded. "I want your lips and tongue on my pussy."

As Dan learned forward and his mouth reached her crotch, the smell of leather mixed with the odor of her sexual fluids and her perfume. The mixture was sensational, luring Dan's mouth and tongue into the opening of the crotchless leather bustier. His lips and tongue found her outer labia. He spread them apart and dived in, savoring the rich, musky taste on his tongue and in his mouth. Fran's body writhed and he heard her starting to whimper as his tongue alternated between exploring inside her inner labia and teasing her clitoris.

Dan felt Fran's hands on his shoulders, and felt her body press close to his. Slowly, he felt her body slide down the front of his, her moist vagina moving downward towards his towering, swollen erection.

"Take me, Dan. You have earned the right to be inside me. Love me now," she moaned. Her labia met the head of his penis, and she slid effortlessly over his shaft, engulfing him in her warm, moist chamber of pleasure. She squeezed her vaginal muscles and moved up and down slowly, knowing it would be more than Dan could stand.

"Let go, Dan!" she pleaded. "Let me feel you explode inside me!"

It only took one more slow, tight, squeezing stroke on his shaft for Dan to feel the urgent ache rising quickly towards the head of his penis. His body tensed and he stilled for what seemed like an eternity, before he burst inside her.

"Ohh …" He moaned, as he felt himself release with one rhythmic burst after another inside her.

When the contractions ceased, Fran sat in Dan's lap, her legs wrapped around his waist, her arms wrapped around his neck, and his still-erect penis filling her. Her own desire was only just starting to build.

Fran leaned against Dan and he felt her hands move to the back of his head. She untied the leather ties of his blindfold and let it fall from his face. His eyes adjusted quickly in the dim lighting of the sixteenth-century theme playroom. The first thing he saw was the tears in Fran's eyes. He moved his face forward and touched his lips to hers.

As their lips parted, the businesslike Dominatrix returned, regaining emotional control and turning off her tears.

"If you think you are finished, you are quite mistaken," she said sternly to Dan. "You only have tonight and tomorrow night left to please me, so you had better make use of the Viagra and stay hard inside me. You have a long night ahead of you. If you fail to please me, I may have to try out my new *Wartenberg* pinwheel on your balls and cock. Is that clear?"

"Perfectly clear, Lady Francesca," he replied. A hint of a smile appeared on Dan's face as he thought about the prospect.

CHAPTER 28

DAN DESCENDED the stairs from the sixteenth-century playroom, wearing only his pool towel from the previous evening. He entered the tunnel connecting Philippe's studio with the house. His mind was spinning. He was struggling with his values and his ideas about both swinging and BDSM. His three nights with Fran, and especially tonight's mind-boggling mixture of pleasure and pain, were causing him to question many of his old sexual values, both personal and professional. He was struggling to maintain his identity, which he thought had been stable before he arrived in Palm Springs with Chelly.

Maybe Chelly's been the one who is right, and I've been wrong?

But, even worse than the struggle between old and new sexual values, Dan's feelings of conflict between his loyalty to Chelly and his growing sexual and emotional connection with Fran were making him feel extremely guilty this morning as he left her. He was starting to feel increasingly anxious and sad about having to leave her in less than two days.

As Dan neared the guest suite, preoccupied with his internal conflicts, he saw the first light of dawn, glowing softly in the eastern sky. Light was starting to creep through the massive glass windows that faced onto the illuminated pool deck and meticulously landscaped estate. He entered the guest suite and turned on a small table lamp, so he wouldn't trip over any of their luggage. He saw the shape of Chelly's body beneath the covers and felt a sudden need to be close to her. He lifted the covers, ready to crawl into bed beside her.

Dan froze as he caught his first glimpse of Chelly. Her lips were dried-out and chapped. The corner of her mouth was cracked and bloody. Her eyes were puffy, with heavy black rings beneath them. His eyes wandered lower to her large, ivory breasts. Her nipples were caked in dried blood. There was more dried blood on the inside of her thighs.

Waves of revulsion, anger, and sympathy flooded over Dan as the reality of Chelly's night of horror with Philippe began to sink in. He kneeled on the bed beside her and instinctively began stroking her hair tenderly.

"Oh, Chelly! What the hell did that bastard do to you?" he said. His eyes surveyed the extent of her wounds.

Chelly's body gave a start and her eyes opened wide as Dan touched her hair. He saw terror filling her eyes as she looked up at him. She didn't seem to recognize him, and he realized that she didn't know where she was at the moment. She was dissociating and reconnecting to the horrors she had endured during the night.

She coiled her body into fetal position and shrank away from Dan, her body trembling and her voice sobbing in fear. He put his hands gently on her face, holding it still so that he could maintain eye contact with her.

"It's okay, Chelly. It's me, Dan. You're safe now, babe. I've got you now. We're in our room and you're safe with me. Everything's going to be okay. C'mon, tell me who you see."

Chelly continued to whimper softly, but Dan saw her eyes relax as she started to recognize him. He felt the tension in her neck and shoulders releasing slightly as her mind began to come back slowly into the present time and place.

"Sorry … so … sorry … Dan," Chelly sobbed. "Should … should … have … listened … to you."

"Don't say that," Dan whispered, as he choked back his own tears. "Don't blame yourself, babe! You're safe now. That's all that matters." He drew Chelly into his body and held her close, rocking her gently and stroking her hair in an effort to calm her.

As he continued to rock Chelly, Dan's mind raced and a flood of emotions overwhelmed his ability to think rationally. He was overcome with feelings of empathy and a responsibility to take care of Chelly. But he was feeling a growing sense of danger - a fear that his initial instincts about Philippe were right. Dan started to realize that he had made a grave mistake by ignoring those instincts. It was becoming clear that he and Chelly were dealing with a sadistic sociopath. His mind jumped to thoughts of Fran and the fear he had seen so often in her eyes. It was all coming clear to him now. A new fear for Fran's safety was added to his overall sense of danger and fear. He tried to shift his mind into problem-solving mode, but he quickly bogged down. His thoughts were all over the place.

What should I do for Chelly? How am I going to confront that bastard, Philippe? Is Fran in danger, and how am I going to keep her safe? How are we going to get ourselves out of here?

Dan struggled to keep his focus. The flood of thoughts and emotions was overwhelming. His chest was tight and his breathing labored. His heart was pounding. He was feeling hot and claustrophobic.

Take it easy, Dan. You're going to have a panic attack unless you calm down!

He focused on rocking Chelly and stroking her hair. He slowed his breathing by taking slightly deeper breaths each time.

Okay, Dan. That's better. Let's just take one thing at a time.

He noticed Chelly's respiration stabilizing as his own breathing slowed. Her sobbing had stopped and she felt more relaxed in his arms.

"I'm going to lay you down now, Chelly. I'm just going to get a warm facecloth to clean you up a bit. Is that okay?"

Chelly tightened her grip on her husband. Her entire body tensed.

"Its okay, Chelly. You're safe now. I'll just be in the washroom. I'll only be a minute. You'll feel better once we get you cleaned up."

He laid his wife down gently on the bed, covered her with a sheet, then hurried into the washroom and started the hot water running. He grabbed a clean facecloth, soaked it under steaming hot water, and then hurried back to Chelly.

"Straighten out and lay on your back, babe," he whispered. "This might sting a little. Hang in there for me."

Dan winced and felt nauseous as he gently dripped water, dabbed, and cleaned away blood that had run from the torn tissues on her nipples and labia. Chelly winced at his initial touches, but laid still as she grew accustomed to Dan's soothing strokes with the warm cloth.

Dan went back into the washroom to rinse the bloody facecloth and soak it in more clean, hot water. He noticed Chelly's makeup bag on the counter and searched through it until he found a small container of lip balm. His revulsion and nausea turn into anger as he returned to the bed and continued to clean Chelly's wounds. He moistened the corners of her mouth and wiped the dried blood away, then coated her lips and the corners of her mouth with lip balm. As he worked quietly to clean her wounds, Dan focused on what he needed to say and what they had to do to get themselves away from their sociopathic host and immediate danger.

First you need to get us out of this mess. Then you have to do something to help Fran. But right now, just get Chelly someplace safe!

Dan felt his entire body trembling. Fear and tension were taking over. He continued to breathe slowly. He started rehearsing in his mind for the inevitable confrontation with Philippe, which he knew was only moments away.

DAN PULLED on a pair of shorts and a t-shirt. He took a couple of deep breaths before emerging from the guest suite in search of Philippe. He had only gone ten steps before his path intersected Fran, who had just completed her morning swim.

"Where's Philippe!" Dan demanded. "Is he in his office?"

Fran felt the anger in Dan's voice and saw it in his eyes. Her own eyes opened wide with fear. She realized that something terrible must have happened to Chelly, and Dan was going to challenge Philippe. She grabbed his arm impulsively.

"No, Dan!" she pleaded. "You must not make him angry. You do not know him! Please … I beg you …"

Her voice trailed away and she started sobbing. Her eyes became distant - they were still full of fear, but she seemed to be remembering something else from another time or place.

"I've had enough, Fran! The experiment is over. I'm taking Chelly and we're going home! Do you have any idea what he did to her last night?"

Don't take it out on Fran. She's starting to dissociate, and it's not her fault.

Dan gripped Fran's hands and wrenched them from his arm. He stomped off across the open living area towards Philippe's office. The door was slightly ajar. Dan burst into the room, startling the Frenchman, who was engrossed with the previous evening's video clips. Philippe's desk separated the two men.

"You sadistic bastard!" Dan screamed. "You aren't interested in anybody's pleasure except your own! What you did to Chelly last night was nothing but torture! What do you have to say for yourself, you narcissistic prick?"

Philippe turned slowly from his computer screen and rose from his chair. Dan thought he saw a flash of anger in the other man's eyes. His own body was trembling from a combination of anger and fear as he waited for Philippe to respond. But instead of becoming angry, Philippe's face turned into a sickly-sweet smile.

"You are over-reacting, *mon ami*," he said. "Please have a chair and we can discuss this like gentlemen."

"Gentlemen!" Dan shouted. "How can you call yourself a gentleman after what you did to my wife last night! You've been manipulating her since the day we arrived here. All you care about is using her to meet your sick, sadistic needs. All that talk about trust! You're disgusting! You took advantage of that poor woman's trust! Well, it's over, Philippe. We're leaving as soon as our bags are packed!"

Philippe's eyes went distant and vacant for a moment. The smile disappeared from his face. It was replaced by a look of intense anger that started setting off alarms in Dan's brain. Philippe took a moment to regain his composure, bringing himself back fully into the present before he answered.

"Nobody talks to me that way, you ignorant weakling! Now, sit down in that chair! I'll tell you what you're going to do, and you're going to do exactly as I say! You are in no position to demand anything from me! Would you like to know why?"

Suddenly, Fran burst into the office, startling both men. She moved quickly around the desk and tried to take her husband by the arm.

"No, Philippe!" she begged. "You must let them go! Please stop this game of yours. Somebody else will get hurt!"

Philippe reacted quickly, pushing Fran so viciously that her head slammed into a filing cabinet in the corner of the room.

"Get out of my way and stop interfering, you stupid bitch!" he shouted. "Nobody will get hurt if they just do what I ask! Why doesn't anybody understand?"

Dan jumped to his feet and started coming around the desk towards Philippe.

Philippe reacted quickly. He opened the top drawer of his desk. He whipped out a jet-black Smith and Wesson .38 caliber Governor, swinging his arm around so that the weapon was pointing at Dan's chest, halting him in his tracks.

"No, … no," Fran sobbed. She lay on the floor in complete despair, staring at the gun that pointed menacingly at Dan's chest. "Not again, Philippe."

Triggered by the sight of the gun, Dan saw the walls going up in Fran's mind. Her eyes were glassy and full of fear. He knew she was connecting to some dark memories, but had little idea it was because history was repeating itself in Philippe's office at that moment.

DIEGO ALVAREZ froze as Philippe pointed the taser at his heart. Philippe's face was red and twisted with rage.

"You fool. Who do you think you are! Nobody challenges me! Nobody leaves Philippe Morel until I say you can leave!"

"You think your threats frighten me?" Diego shouted in return. "I have friends in Columbia who will be most displeased at how you have treated my wife. If you harm even one more hair on us, you will experience a rain of shit that you could never imagine, my friend!"

"Be careful, Diego!" Juanita Alvarez begged. "He has a gun!"

"A gun!" Diego snorted in disgust. "He thinks he can frighten me with a stun-gun. I doubt that he even knows how to use it, Juanita."

Diego took a step towards Philippe, reaching for the taser as he spoke.

"Now give me that ridiculous toy, before you hurt somebody!" he said.

Philippe was enraged by Diego's lack of respect. The walls snapped up in Philippe's mind so that he was only partially present. The angry part of his identity had flown back in time to the small cottage in the woods behind his parents' estate. Instead of the face of Diego Alvarez, Philippe only saw the wrinkled, drunken face of Henri, the gardener, threatening him not to tell anybody about Philippe's secret visits to the cottage.

Nobody else loves you. Nobody would believe you. You know that nobody loves you except me. Who would love you if anything happens to me? Your parents?

Philippe saw a grotesque old man's face taking a step in his direction. A fearful, child-like part of his brain reacted in self-defense. His finger pulled the trigger of the taser, without even realizing what he was doing. A woman's scream startled him, jerking his mind back into the present.

Diego Alvarez lay on the floor of Philippe's office, every muscle in his body convulsing involuntarily from the two small projectile barbs that had delivered fifty thousand volts of electricity into his pectoral muscle. Juanita was at his side, wailing in Spanish. In a rage, she stood up and launched herself at Philippe, her fists at the ready. Philippe's fist collided with her face in mid-air. Juanita's head snapped back and the punch deflected her slight body into a filing cabinet. Her head struck the cabinet at an awkward angle, snapping her neck instantly. Her lifeless body collapsed into a heap on the floor.

Philippe couldn't shake the image of the old gardener's face from his mind. He was driven by rage. He grabbed Diego's feet and dragged him out of the office, into the hallway, and out across the spacious living area towards the exit to the pool deck.

Francesca heard the angry commotion over the sound of her shower in the adjacent master suite. She hurried to dry herself, and then rushed from the bedroom into the hallway. She caught a glimpse of Juanita's motionless body in Philippe's office, then heard the sound of something being dragged across the living area of the massive home. She caught sight of Philippe, dragging Diego's body, as he reached the sliding glass doorway to the pool deck.

"Philippe, what happened? What are you doing?" Francesca screamed. She grabbed his arm, trying to get him to stop. She was terrified by the vacant, angry look she saw in his eyes.

"Get out of my way!" Philippe screamed. "Are you against me too! Just look at what happens to people who threaten Philippe Morel!"

He pushed Francesca away viciously from him, then flung the sliding door open with such force that it bounced against its frame and started closing again on its track. Philippe caught it on the rebound, and then pushed it fully open again. He continued dragging his stunned victim onto the deck, until Diego's head lay beside the spa. Philippe picked Diego up by his shirt, holding the man's head out over the frothing waters of the spa, and holding his face directly over Diego's. Despite being paralyzed, the other man was conscious - but he was helpless and his eyes were filled with fear. Philippe shook Diego's head and upper torso mercilessly.

"What are you going to do?" Philippe screamed. "Are you going to walk away from me *now*? You'll see what happens to people who threaten me!"

Philippe rolled Diego over onto his stomach and grabbed him by his shirt. With the adrenaline flowing through his veins, he pulled his helpless victim forward until the man's upper body dropped over the edge of the spa and his face fell into the water. Philippe sat astride Diego's back, pushing the man's head under the surface. He continued to mutter obscenities in French, just as he had at Henri many years ago when the old man lay face down in the pond on his parents' estate.

Francesca was on Philippe's back, desperately trying to drag her crazed husband from the defenseless man, ripping Philippe's shirt in the process. Her attempts only served to enrage him further. He released his left hand from his victim and swung his fist around into Francesca's head, sending her sprawling onto the pool deck. Her body and her mind went numb as she hit the concrete.

The sun was rising in the eastern sky over Palm Desert. Philippe sat silently astride his victim for a full five minutes. The dissociative barriers in his mind slowly dropped away and the conscious part of his identity gradually came back into contact with reality. He gave a puzzled look at the drowned man beneath him, trying to make sense of what he saw.

Behind him, on the pool deck, Francesca stood up quietly and stripped off her clothing. She dived into the soothing waters of her pool, her mind fully believing that she was diving off the rocks and into the peaceful waters of the Mediterranean Sea.

FRANCESCA'S EYES opened to the sound of Dan's voice, his hands shaking her and patting both sides of her face to bring her back to consciousness.

"Fran, wake up. It's Dan, you're safe now. It's alright to come back, Fran. Come on back to me, girl."

Fran started to emerge from her dissociative fog. She vaguely recognized the features of Dan's face, then the outlines of Philippe's office. After a moment, she looked up and recognized Philippe. Then she saw the snub-nosed .38 caliber pistol in her husband's hand. The pieces of her present reality started dropping into place.

"Here, have some water." Dan said, holding a cup to her lips. The cool liquid was refreshing and helped to bring her back, more aware and alert.

"Help her into one of those chairs!" Philippe shouted, waving the gun towards the two chairs on the other side of his desk. Dan helped Fran to her feet and guided her to the nearest chair, then took the seat next to her.

"Alright, Dr. Whitney," Philippe said sarcastically. "Now I will tell *you* what you're going to do, and you're going to listen. Do I have your attention?"

Dan opened his mouth to reply, but the adrenaline had dried up his mouth and throat. Nothing emerged, apart from a hoarse whisper. He swallowed twice as he stared at the barrel of Philippe's pistol, trying to moisten his throat.

"I'm listening," Dan answered. "Let's all calm down and discuss this like adults, Philippe. There's no need for the gun."

"Silence!" Philippe roared, using the French form of the word. "You've done enough talking, Dr. Whitney. Now it's time for you to listen! If people would stop disagreeing with me, and would just listen, there would be no need for this gun. So, I repeat - are you ready to listen to what you and Michelle are going to do?"

"Just stay calm. I'm listening," Dan assured him.

"Bon! First, you and your beautiful wife are not leaving the estate until I am finished with you. If you cooperate tonight, you will be able to leave tomorrow, just as you planned. In case you think that you might want to leave early, I have locked away the keys for all of the vehicles. I have also changed the code for gate. Nobody can leave the estate unless I let them leave. Even Francesca, your new lover, will be unable to open the gate."

"So, what do you want from us," Dan asked, defeat registering in his voice.

"That's the spirit, *mon ami*," Philippe answered. "You and Michelle will simply continue our little social experiment for one more night. I am most pleased with Michelle's contribution to the experiment last night. But, I'm afraid I've been reviewing last night's film of you and Francesca. Despite your best efforts at being a Submissive last night, you were less than convincing. So, for tonight, we are going to try again. If your performance pleases me, you and Michelle are free to leave tomorrow. If not, you both stay until I am pleased. It is simple."

"People will start looking for us if we don't go back to work Monday morning," Dan challenged.

"Come now, Dr. Whitney. By your own admission, nobody in Detroit knows you are here. As far as they know, you checked out without warning or explanation on Sunday. If anybody asks, I will act surprised, and tell them that I assumed that you flew home early last weekend."

"And what if I don't care if you're pleased," Dan sniped in return.

The phony smile disappeared from Philippe's face and was replaced by an angry snarl. He waved the gun menacingly at Dan.

"For such an educated man, your stupidity amazes me," Philippe snapped. "Do you really believe that both of your mobile phones were destroyed by an accidental power surge? I destroyed them with my own high voltage power surge! And before I destroyed them, I made copies of every address and phone number in both of your phones. I now have them stored on my computer. With just a single click of a mouse, I can send videos of you and your wife, engaging in some of the most compromising sexual activities with strangers, to every friend, family member, and colleague you know. If you fail to please me, I will ruin both of your reputations! So, *mon ami*, I suspect that you will be highly motivated to please me! Am I correct?"

A chill ran through Dan's body as he realized the implications of Philippe's threat. He was trapped by Philippe's cunning manipulations, and he was completely helpless.

"I understand. What do you want me to do?" Dan said, sighing.

The smile returned to Philippe's face.

"I knew you would be accommodating. We will meet as usual to watch some film and to see what we can learn from last night. Shall we say nine o'clock again? Francesca will prepare a light breakfast for us, won't you *ma chérie?*"

Francesca nodded silently.

"Then we shall meet afterwards."

"I guess we don't have any choice, do we?" Dan said bitterly.

"Nonsense, *mon ami!*" Philippe said, chuckling sarcastically. "I am sure I can offer you some options for our little experiment that both you and Michelle will find most interesting and stimulating. Let me see what I can dream up for tonight!"

Philippe roared with sadistic laughter. Dan caught a brief glimpse of the man's eyes before he averted Dan's gaze. The cold look of anger, and the complete absence of remorse or empathy in Philippe's eyes, sent a chill of terror through Dan's body. In that instant, Dan learned what it was like to truly fear for his life.

"THERE IS plenty of room up here in the front, Isab … er … Michelle. Don't you want to be closer to me, *ma chèrie?* Come here, I insist!" Philippe said.

Dan observed that Philippe seemed hurt by Chelly's not wanting to be close to him. His eyes seemed distant and somewhat confused. He waved her towards the front row with his right hand, which still gripped the .38 caliber Smith and Wesson.

Dan took a seat between Chelly and Fran in the theatre's first row. He had his arm around Chelly, who was distraught and trying her best to avoid making any eye contact with Philippe.

"I thought we might do something a little different today, to add some variety into the last night of our small social experiment - to make it more … how shall I say … stimulating?" he added dryly.

"Instead of watching the security clips of ourselves from last night, I would like to show you some scenes from the Internet. I thought it might be interesting for you to watch the kinds of things that other trusting couples do in their BDSM play. Doesn't that sound exciting?" he asked.

"Don't you really mean that you want us to watch porn with you? Let's dispense with the crap, okay?" Dan challenged.

"Excuse me," Philippe answered, with a disappointed and distant look on his face. "I really do think you need to change your attitude. I saw how much you enjoyed Fran's introduction to the world of pain last night. If you would only open your mind, just imagine what things you could learn to enjoy."

Philippe's eyes suddenly seemed to regain their focus, and he returned his full attention to Dan.

"Dr. Whitney, you suggested earlier that I was keeping you and your lovely wife, against your will. You think you have no choice in the matter. Perhaps after we watch some videos from the Internet, you and Isabelle will see some things that you might like to try tonight. Let's watch, shall we?" he said. He dimmed the lights and brought his laptop's web browser onto the theatre's big screen.

Dan's head snapped to attention at Philippe's mistake. For an instant, he thought he didn't hear him correctly. Then he realized that Philippe was confusing Chelly with somebody else named Isabelle.

He's dissociating! No wonder he's so erratic today. Better not challenge him again - be agreeable and submissive. There's no telling what he might do with that gun if he loses complete touch with reality!

Philippe clicked the remote control in his left hand. The image of a pornography website appeared. The screen was filled with a large selection of images, mostly of women, in the process of experiencing various extreme BDSM activities. Philippe clicked on the member's login box and quickly typed in his password from memory.

Dan realized with alarm that this was a site that Philippe obviously visited often. Beside him, Chelly was becoming more agitated as the images of graphic sexual acts appeared on the screen. She began weeping. Her voice sounded more like an adolescent than a mature adult. Her body was shaking and she buried her head in Dan's chest to avoid watching. Chelly's brain was trying to keep the images out - to keep them behind its protective walls - trying to avoid both the graphic images on the screen and her traumatic memories from last night.

The videos showed a variety of extreme BDSM play, including forced oral and anal sex with huge dildos or extremely well endowed men. He moved on to other scenes showing the use of electrodes on a woman's labia and clitoris, huge electrified dildos in women's vaginas and rectums, and seeing objects as large as fists being shoved up the same female orifices. Dan was repulsed by the videos. Even though the women in the video clips invariably talked about the experiences with big smiles on their faces afterwards, the graphic images made Dan's stomach churn.

After ten minutes of being bombarded by the disturbing scenes, Philippe moved on to similar videos showing similar acts being performed on men. The video images became even more repugnant and frightening to Dan. He realized how much more painful and degrading most of the activities were, compared to the relatively mild pain he had received from Fran last night.

Finally, Philippe clicked the "stop" button on the current video, and then turned up the house lights with his remote control. Fran had remained motionless and completely silent throughout the entire screening. She put her hand on Dan's arm and moved closer to him.

"Well then," Philippe said. "As you can all see, there are a great many things we could all try. But we all have only one night left to sample them. So, I have a suggestion that should meet with Dr. Whitney's approval." His face wore a smug smile as he turned to his captive audience.

"Only one of you - either Michelle or you, Dr. Whitney - will have to participate tonight. Either Michelle will spend her last night learning to push her limits even further with me, or you will spend your last evening learning to push your pain limits further with Francesca - and also with me," he added, with a sadistic grin.

"Have you ever had any homosexual or bisexual fantasies, Dr. Whitney?" Philippe asked.

"No, I haven't," Dan answered. "I have no such fantasies or desire to try that type of scene either!"

"Never say never, *mon ami!* Just look at the fantasies your beautiful wife never thought she would play out. Look at how much more erotic your play with Francesca was last night. Had you ever fantasized about doing those things before?"

"Well … no," Dan admitted.

"Then don't be so quick to disagree with me again!" Philippe shouted, waving the gun menacingly in Dan's direction.

"One more thing, *mon ami* - and this is the best part. You and Michelle have a choice. I am letting you decide which one of you will be the lucky submissive, and which one of you will be able to watch and enjoy the proceedings!" Philippe gloated.

Dan realized that Philippe had them exactly where he wanted. He realized that Philippe didn't care which of them he was going to torture tonight. It was all about power and control. Forcing them to decide who would feel pain, and who would not, was feeding his addictive need for power and control.

Dan saw Philippe's eyes going distant again, unaware that Philippe was reliving his first triumph - a twelve year old boy standing over Henri's corpse, knowing that Henri would never abuse him again - and feeling that same power and arousal once again in this pivotal moment.

After a long pause, Philippe's absent gaze found its way back into the theatre, gradually turning into a grin.

"I do not need your answer now," he said sweetly. "I will just need to know by dinner time tonight. Take your time and discuss it all you want."

Philippe's tone suddenly became terse and businesslike. His hand shook the gun at Dan.

"But remember, Dr. Whitney," Philippe said. "If you or Michelle perform well and give me the quality video I desire, you will be on your way home tomorrow. If not, you will continue to be my guests! And people *will* start getting emails with some unflattering video attachments."

Philippe smiled and his mercurial mood once again became light and carefree.

"Speaking of dinner, would you all like to have beef tenderloin with a delightful wine sauce tonight? It is one of my delicacies, isn't it *ma chèrie?*" he said to Fran.

Nobody replied, but it was obvious to Dan that Philippe didn't care. He was lost in the euphoria of his sense of power and control. The question was purely rhetorical anyway.

CHAPTER 29

"I … I'M SO … sorry …," Chelly sobbed. Dan held her naked body close to him in the spa.

The soothing sensation of the turbulent waters were helping to soothe and calm Dan after his horrifying discovery of Chelly's wounds, and after his own frightening encounter with Philippe over the past hour. Dan's body was still trembling from the confrontation, and from the images of Philippe's .38 caliber revolver pointing at his own chest.

"It's … all … my … fault … I should … have … listened … to you." Chelly gasped. She managed to force the words from her chapped, dry lips between sobs.

"Shhhhh," Dan whispered. "It's nobody's fault. We all fell for it, babe - myself included. You were right too, Chelly. I *was* being anal-retentive and paranoid, just like you said. But I decided to take the chance on trying BDSM too. I could have said no, but I'm glad I did it. You were right - I actually started to enjoy it! And who knew Philippe was actually going to turn out to be a psychopath?"

"You … you …" Chelly sobbed.

"It wasn't anything more than a gut feeling. I need a lot more than that before I can diagnose somebody as a psychopath," Dan answered.

"It is not your fault," Fran added. She was sitting next to Chelly, stroking her ginger hair and trying in vain to comfort her inconsolable guest.

"He fooled you, Chelly. I should have warned both of you. I know him, but I said nothing. It is all my fault," Fran said.

"We only have to do this one final scene for Philippe, then we can go home," Dan said. "It's almost over, babe. All we have to do is give him the video he wants."

Dan was searching in his mind for a way out of their dilemma. But, no matter which direction his thoughts headed, they kept coming back to the only solution he could see for them.

"I'll do the scene with Philippe," he said. 'There's no way I could live with myself if I let him do that to you again. It's the only way, babe."

"No!" Fran interrupted. "It will never be enough. Can you not see? He never wants to let Chelly go. He thinks she is Isabelle, and that she has come back to him. He will never let her go, Dan. He will never let *you* go either. We have to stop him!"

Fran's eyes were red and watering. A single tear was making its way down her cheek. Her eyes were overflowing with sadness.

"Who the hell is Isabelle, anyway?" Dan demanded.

"She was his nanny when he was young," Fran replied. "That is all he will ever tell me. Something terrible happened and she had to leave him. But he cannot tell me."

"It must have been traumatic for him," Dan said. "As soon as he mentioned Isabelle, his mind took off someplace else. He was coming and going back and forth out of reality like a Ping-Pong ball this morning. He's extremely unstable right now, and he's scaring the shit out of me!"

"We have to stop him, Dan! Before he kills somebody else!" Fran implored.

Dan saw intense fear and helplessness replacing the sadness in her eyes. She was now weeping uncontrollably. He was stunned by Fran's words. As he stared into her eyes, he felt her fear seeping into his body. Chelly resumed her sobbing at the same time.

"What do you mean, Fran?" Dan asked. "He hasn't really killed anybody, has he?"

Suddenly, images of detectives Dixon and McKnight popped into Dan's head. The first pieces of the puzzle started dropping into place. His eyes opened wide and his mouth dropped open. He realized how grave their situation had become.

"Oh, shit!" he muttered. He reached around Chelly and grabbed Fran tightly by the arm, trying to look her in the eye. He shook Fran's arm to get her attention.

"Does this have anything to do with that couple that went missing around here?" Dan demanded.

But Fran was unresponsive. Dan knew her mind had gone someplace else, triggered by his mention of the missing couple. She sat, transfixed in her seat, weeping and shaking her head from side to side. Dan shook her arm, and then splashed water into her face. Her eyes appeared startled. She gazed at him, taking a few seconds to orient herself to where she was at this moment.

"Fran! Did Philippe do something to that other couple? Tell me, for God's sake!"

Fran continued to sob and to shake her head from side to side. Then, somehow, she managed to slowly string her words together.

"He … he … threatened … Philippe … just … just like … you did … Philippe … lost … lost … his mind … drowned him … we must … stop him … we must …!"

Dan continued shaking Fran's arm to keep her mind anchored to the present. Her eyes locked with Dan's. He saw the businesslike, resourceful part of Fran slowly emerging from the fog in her mind. She seemed to be rediscovering the strength in that part of her identity. Dan saw a renewed sense of resolve growing inside her as he gazed into her eyes.

"I cannot stay with him, Dan. You must help me. We must all try to escape from here. We are all in great danger!"

Dan was stunned. His mind was still struggling to comprehend the enormity of what Philippe had done.

"Philippe drowned him! What the hell happened?"

This time she stared directly into Dan's eyes with an intensity that his uncomprehending mind could no longer ignore.

"Diego challenged him, Dan. Just like you did this morning. Philippe just snapped. The look in his eyes … He was wild, out of control … It was awful!"

The businesslike Fran was back in charge now. Her eyes continued to maintain contact with Dan's, pleading with him to understand how dangerous it had been to challenge Philippe.

"He stunned Diego with a taser. He was furious. Then he just dragged him outside to the spa and held his head under water. He would not stop shouting at Diego. He kept shaking him and shouting at him while he held his head under. Diego was completely helpless!" Fran cried. She burst into tears and started weeping again.

Chelly, whose sobbing had subsided while Fran related the graphic details of Diego Alvarez's demise, reached out to touch Fran gently on the shoulder.

"I'm so sorry you had to watch that! It must have been horrible for you. But, it wasn't your fault. You know that, don't you?"

Fran nodded back unconvincingly.

"I know, Chelly. But I just cannot get that image out of my mind. It haunts me while I am awake. It comes back in my dreams. I keep replaying it over and over in my mind. I keep thinking there must have been something I could have done to save him!"

Fran looked into Dan's eyes, imploring him to hear the rest of her confession.

"He was awake and alive," Fran continued. "But he was paralyzed and helpless. He could not do anything to save himself, Dan! I tried to stop Philippe, but he punched me in the head. I was stunned and fell down!"

"What happened to his wife? Did Philippe drown her too?" Dan asked.

"No. Juanita tried to stop Philippe. He struck her in the head too. I think she must have broken her neck when she fell."

Dan was silent while he processed this latest information about Philippe.

"I still can't see any other way for Chelly and I to get out of this, Fran. We have to do this one last scene for Philippe."

Dan looked out over the back yard, towards the impenetrable barrier with its menacing razor-wire crown, surrounding the estate.

"We can't get over that wall without a ladder, some gloves, and some wire-cutters. If we try going over it without cutting the razor wire, it will slice us into little ribbons! If we just give him what he wants, maybe he'll let us go," he concluded.

"There might be one other way," Fran replied. "But it will only work if you are *not* the one doing the scene with Philippe!"

"What are you getting at? Why can't it be me?" Dan asked.

"You must break into Philippe's office while he is doing the scene with Chelly. He probably locked our car keys in his desk drawer. That is where he keeps my passport and identification so I cannot leave the country without him. He might even have the new gate code written down in that drawer, or on his computer. You *must* break in and search his office! So Chelly has to be the one to do the last scene."

"Absolutely not!" Dan shouted. "I'm not going to put Chelly through that again! Besides, how am I going to excuse myself from watching the scene, Fran? I can't just ask to leave so I can have a few minutes to go to his office to search for my car keys!"

"I have keys to the office," Fran said quietly.

"You're kidding me, right?" Dan asked, shocked at Fran's admission.

"No. I am sorry I did not tell you earlier, but I did not think it would come to this!"

Tears streamed down Fran's face. Dan saw the guilt in her eyes. He could only feel compassion, not anger, as he connected with her emotions.

"It's okay, Fran. Go on. How did you manage to get copies?" he asked.

"When Philippe was gone, the day after Diego died, I knew I had to find a way to leave him someday. He left his office unlocked with the office keys lying on his desk that day. So I went to town and made copies. If you can get inside, you might be able to get into the drawer, or find some car keys or the gate code!"

"Do you have the key to his desk drawer?" Dan asked.

"No, I took it into Palm Springs to a locksmith who had to order one for me. I could not take the one off the ring without Philippe noticing," Fran replied.

"Why didn't you just open the drawer, take your passport and run?" Chelly asked.

"I thought about that for a while," Fran admitted. "But I was too afraid. Philippe told me I had to act like everything was normal. I could not do anything that would attract attention to us. We killed two people, Chelly! Where could I run?"

"You didn't kill any body!" Dan insisted. "But, you're right. You can't run. You're going to have to come with us and report it to the police. Are you up to it? It's going to get ugly if he catches us!"

Dan saw the conflict in Fran's eyes. She was struggling with the same inner conflicts every abused woman feels. Fear versus her need for independence and freedom. Guilt versus self-preservation. Predictability versus an uncertain future - how would she survive?

After a moment, the sense of resolve returned to Fran's eyes. She swallowed hard.

"I'll do it," she decided. "I cannot live like this any more."

Chelly lifted her head from Dan's chest. She moved towards Fran, reached out, and held her in a tight embrace.

"We'll get ourselves out of this mess together, Fran," she whispered. Then she turned to Dan.

"She's right. I have to do the scene with Philippe. I managed to find a way to survive last night, so I guess I can do it again. Besides, everybody knows that women can take more pain than you guys, right Fran?" she added, a hint of a smile showing on her face.

"I agree," Fran answered. "Chelly and I have learned how to send our minds somewhere else when the pain gets to be too much. You have never had to learn that. Besides, we need you to find a way to break into Philippe's office."

Dan thought about it for a moment.

"Okay ladies. Suppose I agree with you. I think there's one thing you haven't considered. Philippe has been playing us like puppets all along, right?"

Chelly and Fran looked at each other and nodded in agreement.

"So why did he all of a sudden just let us choose who is going to be the Submissive tonight? Up until now, he's getting his thrill out of manipulating us! If we tell him it's going to be Chelly, I'll bet anything that he's going to make me do it anyway! I hate to be cliché you guys, but I think we have to use some reverse psychology on him. It's time *we* started manipulating *him*, don't you think?"

"So we tell him you're going to do it?" Chelly asked.

"Exactly. But you and Fran are going to have to be convincing. You're going to have to play along with whatever I say or do when we tell Philippe. You're both going to have to be Oscar-winning actresses if he's going to believe us! Do you both think you can do it?"

The two women in Dan's life looked at each other, smiles starting to appear on their faces. They nodded their agreement simultaneously.

"Okay, listen up ladies. This is what I think we should do!"

FRAN AND MICHELLE were trying to relax on the pool deck, their naked bodies feeling the warmth of the mid-morning sunshine. They watched in silence as Dan stroked smoothly back and forth in the pool. Chelly finally broke the silence.

"How did you know that I could send my mind someplace else?" Chelly asked.

"I saw it in your eyes this morning," Fran said. "Sometimes they were moving, alive, and showing emotions while we were talking. Then they would become distant and empty for a while. Who abused you, Chelly?" Fran asked.

"I think I mentioned my old boyfriend, Derek, while you were massaging me the other day. But I didn't know you well enough to tell you everything," Chelly admitted.

"You said you were in a bad relationship," Fran recalled.

"Yeah, that's for sure," Chelly replied. "It started off great. We met in the hospital during his last year in med school and I was in my last year of nursing school. His parents gave him a trip to Europe for a graduation present, and he asked me to go with him. I was so in love with him. And it felt so romantic being together in Paris, Rome, and Venice! He took me to every place I'd ever dreamed of!"

"So when did things start going bad?" Fran asked.

"Towards the end of the trip, Derek started getting moody. He seemed resentful and complained that we were only doing what I wanted to do. I didn't think I was being demanding, but he made me start second-guessing myself. So I asked him if there were things he wanted to do while we were there. He wanted to go to a health spa in Germany where everybody goes nude. I was mortified and didn't want to go. But he got so angry, I gave in and went with him."

"It must not have been so bad," Fran surmised. "Otherwise, I doubt that you would have come to Chateau Eden with Dan."

"Yes and no," Chelly answered. "I was surprised that I got over my sense of feeling embarrassed about my body quickly. But Derek was so abrupt and rude to me; I was far more embarrassed by the way he treated me, than I was about being seen naked by other people. Needless to say, the trip wasn't romantic in the end. There was a lot of tension between us."

"You did not break up with him?" Fran asked.

"No. I thought things would go back to being normal when we got back into our routines. We'd already made plans to move into an apartment together when we got back from Europe. He was starting a residency in anesthesiology in the hospital where I was working."

"You did not break up with him?" Fran asked.

"Of course not," Chelly confirmed. "I was stupid. I kept second-guessing myself and thinking that I must be doing something wrong. I tried dressing more seductively at night and on weekends, to see if I could get him to be more romantic again. I did everything he wanted to do. But instead of getting better, he just got angrier and more agitated. He started insulting me and calling me stupid! One night, I talked back to him. That's when the physical abuse started."

A tear ran down onto Chelly's cheek from beneath her sunglasses. Fran reached over and held Chelly's hand in hers.

"I was too embarrassed to go back home to my family." Chelly sniffled. "I kept blaming myself and feeling like such a failure! He started demanding sex and getting rough with me. I was afraid and just gave in to him. Then one day, he ordered me to have anal sex with him after he tore most of my clothing off. I made the mistake of saying no. He beat me pretty badly with his fists, but it didn't stop there. He took off his belt and started whipping me. I think that's the first time I managed to send my mind someplace else. After he whipped me, he pinned me on the bed and raped me orally. I was choking and thought I was going to suffocate!"

Chelly's face turned bright red, but she continued her sniffling and her cathartic sharing with Fran.

"It took me a long time to be able to go down on Dan after we got together," she admitted. "I thought Derek was finished with me that night. I locked myself in the bathroom and had a hot bath. I thought I heard the door slam and thought he'd left. When I came out of the bathroom, he was waiting for me again. He stripped off my robe and pinned me over the bed again. This time he used the belt on my ass. I was scared shitless and didn't dare fight back. He had the same look in his eyes that Philippe had last night. That empty, angry look was far worse than the physical abuse. It was absolutely terrifying!"

"That's when he fucked me in the ass!" Chelly sobbed. "I was emotionally overwhelmed. I felt humiliated, angry, terrified, lonely, and ashamed! I think it was the combination of the physical pain and all of the emotions that made it easy for me to send my mind someplace else. I just went numb. When my mind came back, I was confused, alone, and didn't remember much. There was a part of me that was ready to give up and resign myself to a life of abuse with him. But somewhere inside, I found another part of me - it knew I had to get out of there right away. So I packed a bag, went to my parent's place, and never looked back!"

Chelly's demeanor changed as she remembered leaving Derek. She put her shoulders back, sat up straight, and looked directly into Fran's eyes.

"I locked it all away behind some big wall in my mind and tried to forget it ever happened. I applied for the job in the ER and immersed myself in my work. I couldn't trust men and gave up on the idea of ever having a romantic relationship again. I think I buried that part of me behind the wall too!" she said, laughing.

"Then I met Dan. There was a softness and a gentleness in him that I felt I could trust. I let my walls down and tried to let the romantic part of me out."

Fran saw more tears trickling slowly from beneath Chelly's sunglasses again.

"So you have been cold and distant, and have not been able to let yourself love Dan fully," Fran concluded. She squeezed the other woman's hand, trying to let Chelly know that she shared the same feelings. Fran felt the bond growing between them.

"Yeah, I feel sorry for Dan. He's been so frustrated with me lately. I've been so defensive and I keep blaming him for being boring and unromantic. But, I guess I've been too stubborn to admit it," she said.

"But the romantic part of you still wants to be loved, doesn't it?" Fran said.

"Yeah," Chelly answered. "But I think part of me needed to prove that it was Dan's fault."

"So you started fantasizing about being loved by other men, especially when you came to the Chateau and were surrounded by naked men - like Richard Holloway," Fran added.

Chelly blushed. Fran understood how embarrassed and vulnerable she must have been feeling.

"Or Philippe," Chelly admitted. "I'm so sorry I started fantasizing about your husband!"

Fran squeezed Chelly's hand again.

"Do not blame yourself. Philippe sensed your infatuation the first time he looked into your eyes. He is a predator. He has been searching out hopeless romantics like you for years. How do you think we got together? He was scheming of ways to fulfill your fantasies from the minute you came to the Chateau. Do you really think that Philippe is doing repairs on your room at the Chateau?"

Fran saw the look of understanding flicker to life Chelly's eyes.

"So Philippe had to find an excuse to get us to stay with him at the estate! And you and Philippe have been swapping partners with other couples for a long time?" Chelly asked.

"Yes. And like you, I have accepted it and allowed him to play out his fantasies with many other couples. I am just as much to blame as Philippe. I should have left him many years ago, before he completely controlled me. Now, I have no bank accounts or money of my own, I have no friends to run to, and he keeps my passport locked away so that I cannot even go back home to Italy."

Chelly squeezed Fran's hand. Fran felt an overwhelming bond of empathy growing between them. Chelly got up from her lounge chair, then held her hands out towards her. Fran stood and the two women came together into a warm embrace, pressing their naked breasts and bodies closely together. Their shared empathy cemented a new bond between them.

"I hope you have learned what a lucky woman you really are!" Fran whispered into Chelly's ear. "Dan is a genuine and loving man. The more time I spend with him, the more I realize how lucky you are. When you leave here and go home, I hope you can let your walls down and set your romantic part free. You must learn to trust that Dan loves you. Go home and love him enough for both of us! Please promise you will do that for me!"

Both Fran and Chelly were sniffing. Tears of friendship were trickling down both of their faces.

"I promise. Please don't blame yourself for any of this. I'm so lucky to have met a survivor like you. I love you, girl!" Chelly whispered.

The two women pressed their bodies together again in a final embrace. Fran gave Chelly the traditional European kisses on each cheek, and the two new friends stood side by side on the pool deck. They watched together as Dan glided to a stop at the end of the pool.

"I should leave you two alone," Fran said. "I don't want Philippe to come home and think I have been plotting with the enemy!"

Fran turned her back to Chelly and Dan, and then walked towards the house. The smile on her face vanished. She felt her newly found sense of peace and acceptance fading, gradually being replaced by her familiar old feelings of helplessness, fear, and foreboding.

DETECTIVE Kelvin McKnight sat impatiently in front of his computer in Palm Springs Police Department headquarters. He was tempted to call Beverly to tell her about his progress, but he still needed one last critical piece of information to make a case against Philippe Morel. He stared at the contact list in front of him and marveled at the technology of the new program on the screen in front of him.

Who would have thought the day would come when we could make video telephone calls to anybody, anywhere in the world with a webcam, the click of a mouse, and a simple program called Skype!

So far, he had added three names to his own contact list. He had persuaded his colleague, Detective Fernandez in Bogota, to connect a webcam to his computer and to set up an account. He had done the same with a colleague in Paris. Right now, he was anxious, waiting to hear back from Fernandez to see if his theory was right. He was having difficulty focusing on his work while he waited. He had gone through the motions of taking a drive and interviewing a couple of witnesses about a recent case of domestic violence gone badly.

That poor guy was lucky his wife hadn't managed to cut off his balls and dick with that knife! I hope he learned his lesson about spending the night with strippers.

McKnight's computer screen remained silent. Beyond the monitor, he saw Detective Trey Sheppard walking towards him, waving a piece of paper.

"Hey, McKnight," Sheppard called. "You been expecting a fax from somebody in Columbia named Fernandez?"

Kelvin's body jumped and he almost fell backwards out of his chair. He leapt to his feet to meet Sheppard and tore the fax from his hands.

"Thanks, Trey!" he shouted. His eyes scanned the second page of the fax impatiently. He froze and held his breath as he read the message from Fernandez. The last piece of his puzzle had just fallen into place.

CHAPTER 30

PHILIPPE looked out from the kitchen, through the immense bank of windows, onto the expansive back yard and pool area. He saw Chelly and Dan sitting at the patio table, talking intensely over the sandwiches and glasses of wine that Fran had taken out for them.

"Come, Francesca. Let us find out if our guests have decided upon our entertainment for this evening!" he said with delight.

He strode confidently from the kitchen into the expansive living area, fondling the .38 in his right hand, with Fran walking obediently in front of him. As he crossed the open area, he glanced to his right at the four large portraits displayed on the back wall of the enormous room. The portrait of the street-person caught his eye. He felt uneasy, like the woman in the portrait was watching and judging him - her eyes following Philippe whichever direction he walked.

Why did you people have to go and take my picture? Why did you have to pry into my life? Why couldn't you have left me alone? Look at the mess your life is in - why couldn't you just mind your own business?

Philippe shivered as the woman's eyes seemed to bore into him. He turned his head away from the portraits, outward towards the pool deck where Dan and Chelly were sitting. He followed Francesca to the patio table.

"Bonjour, *mes amis!*" Philippe greeted. "Have my favorite guests been having an enjoyable morning? I hope Francesca has been taking good care of you."

"We're fine, considering that we really don't have much choice in the matter," Dan answered, his voice full of sarcasm.

"Ah, speaking of choices," Philippe gloated. His eyes narrowed and locked onto Dan's, like a wolf trying to establish his dominance. "Have you reached a decision yet about who will be my Sub tonight?"

Dan looked at Chelly, his eyes signaling that it was up to her to inform Philippe of their decision. She looked Philippe directly in the eyes.

"I want to push my limits even further with you tonight, Philippe. I know I can learn to enjoy the pain you give so lovingly to me," she answered.

Dan jumped to his feet and glared at Chelly.

"That's not what we decided this morning, Chelly! How dare you decide to do this on your own? After everything he did to you last night!"

"How dare you decide for me again," Chelly said. "Just because you found some blood and some bruises on me, it doesn't mean I didn't enjoy what I was doing last night!"

"Well, I won't stand for it," Dan replied. "You agreed this morning that I was going to be the Sub! It was already decided!"

Philippe gloated as he watched Fran jumped into the fray.

They can't even make up their minds. This is perfect!

"Chelly, you both told me that it was going to be Dan who would be the Sub tonight! You decided together!"

Fran walked around the table and stood between Dan and Chelly. She took Dan's hand to show her support for him.

Philippe kept grinning.

I love it when they argue - they are so vulnerable and controllable. And Francesca, supporting that idiot Whitney. If this were chess, they would make me look like a Grand Master!

"Well, well," Philippe interjected. "It appears that we don't have a consensus here."

Philippe walked up to Dan, so that he stood directly in front of him. His chest almost touched Dan's and their faces were only inches apart. The .38 pressed into Dan's ribs.

"You know, Dr. Whitney. There is nothing I would like better than to show you the true meaning of pain."

He waved the .38 menacingly in front of Dan's eyes with his right hand. At the same time he kneed Dan solidly in the groin, taking Dan by surprise.

"Ahhhhhh," Dan groaned. His knees buckled at the unexpected pain and he dropped to his knees in front of Philippe, on the verge of vomiting from the sickening sensation surging from his testicles to his stomach. Fran knelt beside him, holding him against her and running her hands through his hair.

"That is just an introduction to the type of pain I would like you to learn to appreciate. You think you can learn to enjoy what I have planned for you?"

Philippe reached down and yanked Fran's hands from Dan's hair. He gripped Dan by the hair, pulling his head up sharply. The result was an excruciating jolt of pain through Dan's neck and scalp.

"I am so tempted, because you have no idea what you are asking for!" Philippe shouted. He released Dan, stepped back, and turned his attention to Chelly.

"But since you and Michelle seem to be at an impasse, I will gladly make the decision for you. I am honored that you wish to push your limits further with me tonight, *ma chèrie*. I accept your offer," he said, running his hand through Chelly's long ginger hair as he spoke.

"And I do hope you enjoy watching the proceedings, Dr. Whitney. I am sure it will be something you will not soon forget!"

CHELLY WAS almost overcome by a wave of conflicting emotions, as she realized Dan's plan had worked.

Dan was right. Philippe wasn't ever going to let us decide. We out-guessed him, now we might have a chance!

But, at the same time, the reality of her decision to volunteer for more of Philippe's tortures started to sink in. Her mouth and throat were turning dry from fear. She reached deep inside for the strength to pull herself together. She needed to play out the last scene of her performance. She stepped forward, feigning self-confidence.

"Philippe, Sir. May I request that we do the scene this afternoon? Why wait for tonight? After we've finished, I'll help you make dinner and we can all celebrate the successful conclusion of our week together."

Philippe was caught somewhat off guard by her request. Chelly saw him crease his forehead. He seemed perplexed as he pondered her suggestion.

"Of course, Isab … Michelle. As you wish." He looked at his Rolex, noting that it was about twelve thirty.

"We will meet in the stable-dungeon at two o'clock!"

DAN AND CHELLY arrived, hand-in-hand, at the stable-dungeon promptly at two o'clock. Philippe was looking through the cabinets and laying out an array of sex toys and equipment on a large table at the back of the room. He was wearing a pair of black leather pants with matching vest and leather boots.

Chelly trembled at the familiar smells of straw and wood. Dan felt her body tense even before they arrived. He squeezed her hand a couple of times, trying to keep her present. He didn't want her to start dissociating too soon.

Philippe was busy tending to his sex toys. He lifted his eyes every few seconds to keep an eye on them. The .38 Governor lay on a shelf behind the table. Philippe made sure his body was between the others and the gun. Dan leaned towards Chelly and whispered in her ear.

"Hang in there as long as you can, babe. You've gotta give me enough time, okay?" Chelly nodded subtly to acknowledge, just as Philippe finished his preparations and turned to face them.

"Michelle. You will take off your clothes and put on your black robe!" Philippe ordered, letting Chelly know that she was now in her role as his Submissive.

"Yes Master," she replied.

"Dr. Whitney. You and Francesca will sit on that bench over by that stall to watch. Remove all of your clothing, both of you.

"Okay," Dan said. "But I should warn you, I seem to have a case of the runs today. I might have to run back to the house a few times to use the washroom. I'll try not to interrupt you."

Philippe flashed an annoyed look in Dan's direction. Then, just as quickly, it disappeared from his face. He was preoccupied with setting up the scene and couldn't be bothered by Dan's bowel problems.

"Alright. Just leave quietly if you need to," Philippe answered.

As Dan and Fran walked toward the bench with their backs turned to Philippe, Fran leaned closer to Dan and whispered.

"I put the key on top of the door frame to Philippe's office. All you have to do is reach up and feel for it."

Dan acknowledged with his eyes, just before they turned to face Philippe and Chelly. They took their places on the bench. Dan was horrified at the array of sex toys and equipment laid out on Philippe's table. Along with some of the more conventional toys such as vibrators, floggers, and a cane, there were much more alarming implements like a thick leather belt with a large buckle, enormous oversized dildos, and a cruel-looking array of electrical equipment. Dan felt a renewed sense of urgency about his mission.

You have to find something in that office to save us and get us out of here, Dan. You can't let that sadistic bastard hurt Chelly!

When everybody was in position, Philippe approached Chelly with a black, fur-lined blindfold.

"You will wear the blindfold to heighten all of your senses, *ma chèrie*."

He carefully tied the blindfold behind her head then went to the table, where he chose a black metal spreader bar with leather cuffs for both hands and feet.

"Spread your legs," Philippe commanded. He knelt on the floor and buckled the fur-lined, leather cuffs tightly to Chelly's ankles. When he was finished, he reached over to the table and picked up the vibrator that he had used to take Chelly to orgasm during their previous scenes together, along with a large pillow. Philippe dropped the pillow on the floor in front of Chelly, and then unfastened her black gown, letting it fall from her shoulders. She stood completely naked in the middle of the stable floor, her legs immobilized by the spreader bar.

Standing before them, with her long ginger-red hair flowing over her shoulders, the black blindfold over her eyes, and her legs held far apart by the spreader bar, Dan felt himself becoming overcome by her beauty and his love for her. Sitting behind Chelly and to her left, Dan had a perfect view of her short body, with her muscular buttocks and legs, and her smooth ivory skin. He had a side-view of her full, pear-shaped breast.

Dan had to give his head a quick shake to remind himself that this scene wasn't for pleasure today. This was no game and the stakes were high. It was now up to him to find a way for them to escape from Philippe's grasp with their lives.

Philippe placed the vibrator in Chelly's left hand.

"You will hold this behind your back with both hands unless I tell you otherwise, do you understand?"

"Yes Master," she replied.

"There is a pillow on the floor in front of you. Drop to your knees on the pillow, then lean forward so your forehead is touching the floor!"

"Yes Master." Chelly did as she was ordered. She dropped awkwardly to her knees, and then leaned forward so that her forehead was resting on the floor. Both hands were behind her back, holding the vibrator.

Philippe picked up a flogger from the table. He walked slowly and deliberately around Chelly, dragging the fronds of the flogger slowly over her right shoulder, then across her back, and down over her buttocks. He ran the fronds slowly up the inside of her right leg, under her crotch, then up through her butt crack.

Dan watched Chelly's breathing. It was even, but was becoming deeper with each breath. Unable to see what Philippe was going to do next, Dan knew that her fight or flight response must be kicking into high gear. Then he heard Chelly starting to moan with each stroke of the flogger. He was proud of her - she was playing her role like her life depended on it.

Philippe started flopping the fronds of the flogger rhythmically from side to side on Chelly's upper back, gradually picking up the pace. The flopping of the fronds gave way to heavier strokes, as Philippe's wrists developed a rhythm for snapping the flogger onto her back. Chelly's moaning increased in volume.

Dan decided to test Philippe with a trial run to the washroom. He slipped off the bench and walked quickly out the front door of the dungeon, into the connecting tunnel to the house. He jogged down the tunnel and then ascended the stairs from the tunnel into the house. He walked briskly through the living area, then down the hallway to the door of Philippe's study.

Dan tried the door handle. As expected, it was locked. He looked upward at the doorframe but couldn't see anything. He reached up and began running his hand along the top of the frame. All he felt was the wooden frame. His heart started racing and he began to sweat. Just as he was starting to feel some panic, his finger bumped into metal. He dragged it down off the frame. A sigh of relief escaped his lungs. It was the key Fran had planted for him.

It felt like he had been gone for an eternity. Dan felt his heart pounding and his naked body was sticky with nervous sweat. Not wanting Philippe to become suspicious, he quickly put the key back on the doorframe where he had found it. Satisfied that he could find the key next time, he jogged hastily back across the living area, down the stairs, through the tunnel and up to the dungeon door.

Take some slow breaths, Dan. Calm down and don't look nervous when you go back in there!

Dan opened the dungeon door and walked calmly back to his seat beside Fran. His eyes were drawn immediately to Chelly. Her buttocks, thighs, and back were a rosy red color from the flogger. Philippe was gently stroking her thighs and buttocks and was noticeably aroused at the sight of Chelly's colorful skin. His fingers found her vagina, searching for signs of arousal, but finding nothing yet.

Philippe drew his other arm back and brought his palm down with a resounding smack on Chelly's butt. Her body jumped and she expelled the air from her lungs at the unexpected change from feeling Philippe's probing fingers, to the sharp sting of his palm.

As his palm contacted Chelly's bare skin, he looked up in the direction where Dan and Fran sat. Dan saw a vacant, distant look in his eyes as he spoke angrily to Chelly.

"So you are not enjoying me yet? You are disappointing me. You know I am expecting much more from you today. What do you have to say for yourself?"

"I do not want to disappoint you, Master. Please be patient with me. I promise I will not fail you! If Master will use my favorite vibrator, he will see."

"That's more like it, Isabelle," Philippe exclaimed. "I'm happy to do as you wish. But remember, if you climax before I give my permission, you will be punished. Do you understand?"

"Yes, Master. Isabelle understands. I won't let myself come unless you let me," Chelly replied.

Dan was growing anxious. The success of their plan depended on Chelly being able to convince Philippe that she was highly aroused.

Come on, Chelly. Don't let everybody down. If he thinks you're Isabelle, then you'd better make it convincing! It's time to start putting on a show for him!

Philippe took the vibrator from Chelly's hands, which she'd been holding behind her back as instructed. He flipped the power switch and the phallus-shaped object came to life. He reached between her legs and began rubbing the object slowly over Chelly's clitoris. She started making soft moaning sounds as Philippe continued trying to arouse her.

Suddenly, Chelly felt a searing pain between her legs as Philippe forced the object into her dry vagina. She sucked in a deep breath.

Dan was horrified. It took all of his strength to keep himself from attacking Philippe. He felt Fran's hand on his arm.

Make this look good, Chelly. Let your mind go. You can do it. Work your magic, babe!

Dan could sense the walls going up in her mind -sending her mind someplace else so she could tolerate his abuse. She told Dan she was going to try to imagine that it was just like her first night with Philippe. She started moaning, just as she did that night.

The beginning of a smile appeared on Philippe's face as he started working the vibrator inside Chelly.

Both Dan and Fran gasped as they watched Philippe violate Chelly so cruelly. Fran looked into Dan's eyes and he nodded in return. He had to stop Philippe's sadistic rampage and spare Chelly as soon as possible. It was time for him to go. He leaned forward and put his hand over his stomach, feigning illness. He hurried out of the dungeon, bent over as if he was having severe stomach cramps.

The instant the door closed behind him, Dan sprinted through the tunnel, up the stairs, across the living area, and down the hallway towards Philippe's office. As he reached the locked door, he jumped, fished for the key, and had it in hand in one smooth motion. He inserted the key in the lock and turned it. Nothing happened. The key wouldn't turn. Impatiently, he twisted the key back and forth with no success.

Slow down and take it easy, Dan. Take a deep breath and relax. The key might not be a good copy. Just take your time!

After a couple of slow breaths, Dan resumed jiggling the key carefully while making gentle attempts to turn the key. It was close a couple of times, but it felt like there was just a fragment of metal that wasn't quite fitting into the lock properly. Dan continued to breathe slowly. Patiently, he jiggled, then turned, and then jiggled again. Without warning, the key slid smoothly into the mechanism and turned freely. The lock clicked. He turned the handle and the door swung open.

Dan breathed a short-lived sigh of relief, but he was aware that he had already wasted precious seconds struggling with the key. He had no idea now much time he had before Philippe noticed he was missing. He also knew Chelly was suffering, and he had to put an end to it!

The locked drawers, Dan! See if you can find the keys anywhere!

He moved quickly around to the other side of Philippe's desk. He tried the drawers with locks first. As expected, they did not budge. Next he tried a slim drawer in the middle of the desk with no lock on it. Inside was an assortment of everyday office supplies: pens, pencils, a ruler, whiteout, rubber bands, highlighters, and a box of staples. No keys. Dan's mind raced. He needed to find some kind of tool to break into the locked drawers. His eyes scanned back and forth over the desk and around the room. There was nothing that would help him.

Tools. Of course. The garage!

Dan remembered the small toolbox he had seen when they entered the house from the garage. He rushed around the desk, through the doorway, across the living area, past the kitchen, then down the back hallway towards the garage. He flung the door open, his eyes quickly scanning the top of the cabinet to the right of doorway.

"Yes!" he cheered, allowing himself one-second to celebrate his success. He grabbed the small toolbox and ran back to Philippe's office, taking a furtive look towards the hallway for any signs of commotion. The tunnel was quiet, but he knew time was running out.

Hurry up, Dan. He's going to notice you're gone soon. You'd better do something fast if you're going to save our asses!

Flipping open the toolbox, he found only the bare necessities for tools: pliers, a crescent wrench, a set of hex wrenches, an assortment of screwdrivers, some electrical tape, and a small hammer. The only useful objects he could see were a large flathead screwdriver and the hammer.

Dan grabbed the screwdriver and wedged it into the narrow opening above the lock on the larger of the two locked drawers. Using the screwdriver like a chisel, he began pounding it with the hammer. He felt the lock budge slightly. Two more hard blows with the hammer and the unsubstantial drawer lock finally gave way. Dan whipped the drawer open, disappointed to find only few hanging files.

Shit!

He turned his attention to the smaller of the drawers above the one he had just opened. Two powerful blows with the hammer and screwdriver and he was into the smaller drawer. This time, the contents were more interesting. Dan reached in and found Philippe's European Union passport, his birth certificate, and a number of frequent-flyer and loyalty cards. Fran's passport, birth certificate, and anything she could use for I.D. had also been locked in the drawer. He quickly sifted through a small pile of assorted papers and envelopes, but found no keys.

Damn!

He was starting to panic. Time was running out. He either had to find something, or get back to the dungeon to try to save Chelly.

He had no idea what he was going to do. Philippe still had the .38 on the table right beside him. Dan's eyes darted around the room. Behind the desk, partially concealed by an oak wall unit, he noticed a large floor safe.

We're fucked! He's locked the keys in his safe! We're never going to get out of here!

Dan's brain was starting to abandon Philippe's office as the source of a solution to his dilemma. He was sifting through possible scenarios for trying to get his hands on Philippe's gun. As he turned to leave the office, his eyes passed over the large silver tower of Philippe's Mac Pro. He stopped in his tracks.

The video files!

His eyes slowed down and he examined the area more carefully. Another set of shelves beside the tower held an array of hard disk drives capable of storing hundreds of hours of video and security images. Without further thinking, Dan sprang into action. He dragged the giant Mac out into the open, and then yanked all of the cables from the computer and each of the hard drives on the shelves. He knew he was going to have to make two trips to the pool.

Okay, Dan! If you don't get the chance for a second trip, do you disable the computer or the hard drives first?

Dan wasn't a computer whiz, but he knew enough about them to know that Philippe couldn't store the bulk of the large video files on his Mac. Most of the damaging evidence was on the external drives. But the summaries he showed in the theatre every morning were likely on the Mac. If he disabled the Mac, it would take at least a day or two for Philippe to get his system up and running again. The answer was obvious. He gripped the heavy tower, lifted it into his arms, and then headed towards the doorway as fast as his legs would carry him.

You can come back for the hard drives if you have time. Now hurry, man!

Dan ran awkwardly across the living area to the sliding door for the pool deck. The computer tower was too big to hold with one arm. He had to waste precious time putting it down while he flung the door open, and then hoisted the machine back into his arms. Still running, as he neared the edge of the pool, his arms heaved the heavy object into the air. The Mac hit the water with a giant splash, shattering the serenity of the backyard sanctuary.

He wheeled around as the computer sank quickly to the bottom, already running back to Philippe's office for the external drives.

PHILIPPE'S MIND was drifting and the defensive walls in his mind were trying to regroup. Something wasn't right. Isabelle was distant. She wasn't responding to his loving dominance. He was becoming frustrated and angry with her. Philippe became twelve years old again. She was the most beautiful thing he had ever seen in his life. It was his duty to record the beauty of her body and her sexuality in his art. It was important that he never allow her to leave him again. His eyes devoured the images of her flowing ginger-red hair, her milky white skin, and the fullness of her breasts, hanging gracefully from her body as she knelt in front of him. Her body jerked reflexly with each blow of the cane across the soles of her feet. Her whimpers were distant and unsatisfying. He was feeling the emotions of rejection and abandonment of the twelve-year-old Philippe. He knew she had abandoned him. But something was keeping him from remembering. She had done something terrible to him. He just couldn't remember what she had done.

Part of his consciousness occasionally floated back into the present, paying attention to the loving blows he was administering to his red-haired lover. His eyes wandered. He saw Francesca sitting on one end of the bench and he noticed the large vacant space next to her. Something wasn't right. He saw a look of fear in Francesca's eyes, and she looked away, avoiding further contact.

The uneasy feeling was growing into a sense of imminent danger. His mind snapped back to his present reality, analyzing the situation to determine the source of his danger. He blinked twice as he stared at Francesca. Then it struck him.

"Whitney!" he roared. "Where did he go?"

"He went to the toilet again. He already told you he had diarrhea," she pleaded. Her eyes couldn't meet Philippe's. Her eyes were giving her lie away.

"You're lying, you bitch!" he screamed, as he shook her by her shoulders. He slapped her savagely across her face. "Why are you doing this to me? Where is he?"

Francesca's walls snapped into place. Her mind drifted back in time to Manarola. She was swimming once again in the soothing waters of the Mediterranean, oblivious to the vicious slap and Philippe's anger. Philippe was panicking. He reached for the gun on the shelf beside him and rushed between the straw-filled stalls towards the exit. He burst through the door and into the tunnel, his short, heavy legs pumping as hard as they could carry him.

Fran trailed behind him in a daze. Chelly remained behind, her naked body kneeling with her forehead resting on the floor, her legs held apart by the black metal spreader bar. Her milky white skin glowed red on her back, buttocks, thighs, and the soles of her feet. Trickles of drying blood trailed down the insides of her thighs from her vagina.

Philippe ran up the stairs from the tunnel and into the expansive living area, his out-of-shape lungs already straining for more oxygen. He stopped in his tracks as he heard a loud splash. His head whipped around, his eyes scanning through the open sliding door and locking in on the image of Dan, standing naked by the side of the pool, with his back to Philippe.

Philippe raced to the pool in time to watch the last of the external hard drives sink to the bottom of the pool. A ring of waves radiated peacefully outward from the last point of impact. Images of Henri, the gardener, surged into his brain, accompanied by waves of anger. He turned his attention to the man who stood beside the pool, gazing over the water. As he did many years before, he started running, ready to unleash his anger at his unsuspecting victim.

CHAPTER 31

"WHITNEY! What the fuck do you think you are doing?" Philippe screamed. His face was red with rage, the muscles in his neck taut and his eyes bulging. He pointed the .38 menacingly at Dan as he advanced towards him. His arm, and the gun in his hand, was trembling from rage.

As he approached, Philippe saw the Mac and hard drives resting on the bottom of the pool. His mind flashed back into his past, locking onto the images of Henri, lying face-first in the pond, and the incredible anger he had felt towards his abuser. Then his mind jerked back to reality. The same intense rage was surging through him.

"You fucking prick!" he raged. "Do you think you can do this and not pay for it? Do you know what happens to people who do things to me? Nobody has ever defeated me. Nobody - not Henri, not my parents, not that cocky Alvarez - they've all lost. And so have you. What do you have to say for yourself, you low-life piece of shit?"

"It's all over, Philippe," Dan said. "The videos are gone. You can't blackmail us any more. Let us go now. I promise you, Chelly and I won't tell anybody about what happened here. I don't know what happened between you and the Alvarez couple, and I don't want to know. Give us our keys, we'll pack our bags, and everybody will be happy. Put down the gun, before somebody gets hurt and you make this worse."

"Over! You think this is over?" Philippe roared. He laughed uncontrollably, dropping his arm and the gun for brief instant. Dan took a step forward, but Philippe snapped to attention again.

"You imbecile! Do you think I'm stupid? Do you think I only have only one copy of my video files? Did you see the safe in my office? Did you not think that I would have backup drives somewhere? How stupid are you?"

Dan hung his head, his short-lived sense of relief replaced by a look of despair and helplessness. His knees trembled with fear.

"I should kill you right now!" Philippe screamed. He raised his right arm, pointing the .38 at Dan's heart.

"Stop! Before somebody else gets hurt," Fran shouted. She had appeared on the pool deck, and was moving towards her husband from behind.

Philippe slowly backed himself towards the west-wing of the house, so he could see both Dan and Fran at the same time. As he backed up, his heel hit the leg of one of the chairs that were arranged around the patio table. He lost his balance, almost falling over backwards. As he staggered, he accidentally squeezed the revolver's trigger. The crack of the exploding shell rang out. Dan heard the whistle of a bullet, just after he felt the rush of air go over his head.

Still in the process of taking a step forward when the shot rang out, Dan tried to take advantage of the opportunity to get the gun. But Philippe regained his balance quickly. Dan froze. He had no chance to catch Philippe off balance.

"Get back!" Philippe ordered. "If you try that again, I won't miss next time! If you doubt me, just do it again and see what happens."

Philippe shifted his attention to Fran.

"And you! Are you conspiring against me too, you ungrateful bitch? After I took you in and made a lady out of you? Everything you have is because of me. You used me, and now you dare to betray me? You are no better than that bitch that called herself my mother. Go, stand beside your new boyfriend. Do you think I do not see the look in your eyes when you are together?"

Philippe waved the gun at Francesca, motioning for her to stand beside Dan. She moved carefully as Philippe followed her movement with the weapon. Dan took Fran's hand and they stood side-by-side, naked and vulnerable. She felt his body trembling and squeezed his hand to help calm him. Philippe moved the revolver from Fran and re-focused on Dan's chest. He moved slowly back towards the pool again, keeping himself between the couple and the house.

"Why should I let you live, Whitney? You come into my home as my guest, and you dare to take my wife away from me? Then you have the audacity to challenge me and make me look like an idiot! Tell me why I should not bury both of you together!"

Philippe's eyes went glassy again at the mention of burying Fran and Dan. Images of Diego Alvarez, lying face down and motionless in the spa flashed through his consciousness, making it difficult for him to see the couple in front of him. For just a moment, it was dark and there was a distant sound of a shovel scraping in gravel, and images of two lifeless bodies lying in a shallow desert grave. Philippe was confused.

WITHOUT WARNING, Chelly's white-skinned body appeared in the doorway. She was naked, but had the three-foot-long spreader bar gripped tightly in her hands. She stepped cautiously onto the deck, her slow, barefoot steps completely silent.

Both Fran and Dan saw Chelly at the same moment. Neither one of them flinched or gave her away. They didn't have to move their eyes away from Philippe, since she appeared directly behind him. Seeing her with the spreader bar, Dan felt a renewed sense of hope.

We might have a chance if she can hit him hard enough with that thing. I need to stall him so she can get close enough to strike.

Dan noticed the distant look in Philippe's eyes, realizing that he was dissociating again. For a second, he thought about rushing the Frenchman.

It's too dangerous. What if I startle him and bring him back into the present too quickly? What he sees Chelly?

"What do you want us to do, Philippe?" he said, using his soothing therapist's voice. "Let's go back to the dungeon and finish the scene. Fran and I can join you and Isabelle if you want. We'll help you. Just tell us what you want us to do. We'll do anything you want, won't we Fran?"

The fog in Philippe's eyes cleared. He was coming back into the present.

"You really have no idea what you're asking for, do you Whitney?" Philippe said. "What Francesca did to you last night was mere child's play. Do you know how swollen and painful a man's balls can become? Do you have any idea how much pain you are capable of inflicting on Francesca or Isabelle? Do you think you are man enough to do either?"

Chelly was closing the distance. She was half way to Philippe and was raising the spreader bar in the air, readying herself to strike a blow. Dan's mind scrambled to find something else to distract Philippe for another couple of seconds. He appealed to Philippe's narcissistic need for control.

"I think I'm up to anything you can hand out, Philippe. I accept …"

Chelly was so intent on watching Philippe, she didn't notice the legs of one of the patio chairs sticking out in front of her. She caught it, ever so slightly, with her small toe. The sudden scraping sound startled Philippe.

The scene started moving in slow motion for Dan. He saw the look of shock in Philippe's eyes, and saw him starting to turn towards his assailant. Chelly's arms were bringing the spreader bar down on a collision course with Philippe's head.

Fran froze and screamed a single word at the nightmare unfolding in front of her.

"No ... "

The moment he saw Philippe's attention leave him, Dan lunged. He managed to grab Philippe's right arm just below the elbow, trying to lift it so that the gun would point harmlessly upward. A shot went off, followed by two more in quick succession, and then the weight of Dan's body brought the two men crashing down onto the pool deck. In the distance, Dan heard Fran scream again.

He was on top of Philippe, who was face down on the deck. He grabbed the larger man's arm and slammed it twice against the pool deck, managing to dislodge the gun and send it flying from Philippe's grasp with the second slam. Philippe was growling like a wild animal, trying to raise himself on his hands and knees. The gun was three-feet in front of him. It lay balanced on the edge of the pool, on the verge of falling into the water.

Dan scrambled over Philippe's back and lunged for the revolver at the same time as Philippe rose to his hands and knees. The momentum of Philippe's rising body lifted Dan into the air. He sailed over the .38, his fingers just grazing it enough to knock it over the edge and into the water. Dan's momentum carried him over the edge, and he splashed into the pool. He surfaced and opened his mouth enough to fill his lungs with air, just before Philippe landed on top of him.

Dan felt himself being pushed below the surface, staring up at Philippe's raging face and hatred-filled eyes. Philippe was trying to get his hands around Dan's throat. Dan struggled to keep the Frenchman's hands away from his throat, at the same time trying to get his body out from beneath his larger adversary.

Dan's lungs were starting to burn. He saw small bubbles of gas escaping from his mouth, floating upward. He felt his limbs becoming weaker as he continued to struggle with Philippe. He started to feel panic. His lungs were starting to demand oxygen, commanding his mouth to open. His limbs started flailing aimlessly. Then he felt Philippe's hands squeezing on his throat. In that moment, he realized he was going to die. His limbs went limp. He stopped fighting. His mouth was ready to concede to his body's demand for air. A strange sense of acceptance and peace came over him.

Suddenly, there was a large splash and a dark shadow appeared above him. Philippe's hands released their grip and Dan was suddenly free. Alarms began firing in his brain. His limbs began flailing again, desperately clawing and kicking their way upward towards the blue sky. His head broke the surface just as his mouth gaped open. His lungs gave a huge, wheezing gasp, desperate for life-saving oxygen. He bobbed on the surface, dazed and unsure what was happening. His heavy arms clawed their way toward the side of the pool. He clung to the edge, sucking in more gasps of air, trying to orient himself.

Then he saw Fran on top of Philippe, struggling to keep herself on top of the large man's body. He had the weight advantage, but Fran had something Philippe didn't have. Her lungs were full of air, and she was used to holding her breath under water. Philippe started to panic. He would have outlasted Dan, having enough time to surface for more air after Dan had filled his lungs with water. All he needed was five more seconds to finish off Dan, when Fran jumped into the pool on top of him.

As Dan watched in shock, Philippe's eyes bulged with fear. Then his mouth opened and a large ball of gas escaped, at the same time the water surged into his lungs. His eyes went wide, and then gradually turned lifeless. Fran continued holding him underwater until she needed to refill her lungs. She took a large breath of air, and then began shouting frantically at Dan.

"Dan … Chelly … hurt … called 911 … help coming …"

It took a moment for Dan to realize what Fran was saying. Chelly was hurt.

Oh, my God. She's been shot!

He sucked in another big breath and tried to hoist himself up onto the pool deck, but his arms felt like rubber. He swam to a ladder about ten feet away, and then managed to drag himself up onto the deck. He looked back towards the house. He went numb.

Chelly was lying in a pool of blood about fifteen feet away. She was covered with a blood-soaked towel. Dan's legs came alive as his adrenalin kicked in. He was at her side in seconds, lifting the towel to assess her injuries. She had a large wound in her upper chest and was still losing blood.

Fran must have been trying to stop the bleeding with pool towels.

He checked for a pulse, panicking when he couldn't find one. He was having difficulty concentrating. Sirens and commotion were coming from the other side of the estate. Then he found it. It was weak, but she still had a pulse. He pushed the towel back over the wound, desperate to stop the flow of blood.

"Oh God, Chelly. Please hang in there, babe. You can do it, I know you can," he whispered to his wife.

There was a large crash, then the sound of twisting metal from the far side of the house, as a fire truck crashed the estate's main gate. The sound of urgent shouting followed, as police and emergency personnel poured into the estate.

Dan continued stroking Chelly's ginger hair with one hand, and applying pressure with the other.

"Hold on, babe," he pleaded. "They're almost here. Help is on the way. Just hold on a bit longer!"

Then Fran was at his side, breathing heavily and dripping wet. She placed one hand on top of Dan's, both of them applying pressure on Chelly's wound. She and Dan clasped one of Chelly's hands with their remaining free hands, so that all three of Philippe's victims were joined in the moment.

Chelly's eyes blinked, then opened. They were hazy and she was barely conscious. She seemed to recognize Dan.

"Dan ...," she gasped.

"Shhh babe," Dan said. "Don't talk. Save your energy. They're almost here."

"Dan …," she repeated. She turned her head slowly and looked at Fran, then turned slowly back towards Dan.

"She's … good … for … you … Dan."

There was a long pause as Chelly tried to take another gasp of air.

"Take … good … care …"

Chelly's eyes closed and her head slumped.

"No Chelly! Don't do this! Don't leave me!" Dan screamed. He saw the first of the EMS crew rushing through the open sliding door onto the pool deck.

"Over here! Please help her. Don't let her die!" he shouted. "Oh, God. Please don't let her die!"

The EMS personnel hurried towards Dan and Fran, who were huddled over Chelly, and were oblivious to being completely naked.

A female paramedic pushed Fran aside while her male partner came around the other side and pushed Dan away. They felt for a pulse and found nothing.

"Get back, you two!" the woman shouted. "Give us some room!"

She and her partner had the defibrillator operational within seconds. Fran and Dan watched in horror as they gave Chelly the first jolt of electricity. The male paramedic kept searching for a pulse. A second shock caused Chelly's body to jump again.

"I've got a pulse!" the man shouted. Within seconds they had Chelly hooked up to an intravenous drip and had an oxygen mask over her face.

The paramedics were shouting numbers into their radios and responding to commands from hospital ER doctors. Dan felt terrified and helpless, but felt some comfort knowing that Chelly's life was now in the hands of peers.

Police were pouring out of the house and onto the pool deck now. Detective Julie Jameson was the first on the scene.

"What have we got here, guys?" she said.

"Female victim. Gunshot wound to the chest. She's lost a lot of blood and she's in shock. We already had to jump-start her! Looks like it coulda hit her aorta. Gonna be touch-and-go!"

"Thanks," she replied.

"Hey, Julie!" shouted one of the other uniformed cops. "We got a floater in the pool! Looks like a gun down there too!"

"Don't touch anything! The crime lab guys should be here in a few minutes," Jameson replied.

An officer brought two large towels over to Jameson. Julie examined the attractive, naked woman, confirming that it was Francesca Capellini. She didn't know who the good-looking naked guy was yet, but she was willing to bet he was the victim's partner. She handed towels to Dan and Fran.

"Here, cover up you two. I'll be back to talk to you in a couple of minutes."

"Are you kidding me? That's my wife!" Dan bellowed. "She just about died on me! I have to go in the ambulance with her!"

"Nobody's going anywhere until I've had a chance to talk with both of you!" Jameson snapped. "Now stand back and give those guys some room!" she ordered.

Julie Jameson found a quiet spot on the pool deck and flipped open her cell phone. She punched in a number and waited for the call to connect.

"Beverly? Julie. You better get your ass over to the Morel estate right away. There's been a shooting. We've got two gunshot victims - a middle aged, red haired female in critical condition and another male victim and a gun at the bottom of the pool. Wanna bet it's Morel? We also found the Capellini woman and another unidentified male, both wearing nothing but their birthday suits, huddled over the female vic when we arrived … Yeah, that's right

… Not a stitch … Yeah, no kidding, eh? Doesn't look like I'm going anywhere for a while. Talk to you when you get here."

DETECTIVE Kelvin McKnight leaned back in his chair, stretching leisurely. He was basking in the glow of his discovery that Philippe Morel had been in contact with Diego Alvarez via Skype. More of the pieces were starting to fall into place. He had just received a call from Homeland Security. They had photos of Morel crossing into Mexico on February twenty-fourth, the day he allegedly had the flu. The photos showed him driving the Alvarez rental car into Mexico, but showed him re-entering the States as a pedestrian.

McKnight's cell phone started ringing and vibrating simultaneously on his desk, startling him out of his short-lived state of satisfaction.

"Damn," he muttered. "Can't a guy get a minute of peace around here?"

"McKnight," he shouted into the phone.

"Kelvin, it's Beverly. Meet me down at the car, pronto. Jameson just called me from Palm Desert. She just responded to a 911 call at the Morel estate. There's an unidentified woman with a critical gunshot wound and a floater in the pool. Jameson's betting the floater is Morel! Let's go!"

"Shit," McKnight cursed, as the phone went dead in his hand. He grabbed his suit jacket and headed for the door. "That bastard better not have died on me, just when I had him nailed!"

Dixon had the squad car waiting as McKnight ran into the parking lot. He flung the passenger door open and jumped in as Beverly hit the gas, their momentum causing the door to slam shut behind McKnight.

"Let's hope the guy in the pool isn't Morel," Kelvin said. "I just confirmed that he's been contacting Alvarez on the Internet with a video-telephone program called Skype. I just got the confirmation from Fernandez in Bogotá a couple'a minutes before you called. And Homeland Security just came through with photos of Morel driving the Alvarez rental car into Mexico on the twenty-fourth - the day he allegedly missed work with the flu. I just *knew* that guy was lyin' to us, Beverly. He's clever. He's up-to-date on all the latest tech stuff. I guess he was hopin' we weren't."

"Awesome work, Kelvin. Let's hope it wasn't all wasted," Beverly said, driving as fast as she could without her siren and lights. They were out of their jurisdiction now and were only visiting the crime scene courtesy of Julie Jameson.

"You got anything more than you told me on the phone?" McKnight asked.

"Not much," Beverly answered. "Only that they found a big shed with rooms full of kinky sex stuff and video equipment. Morel's wife, some other guy, and the female shooting vic were all stark naked beside the pool when they arrived.

McKnight's face lit up.

"That's more like it," he exclaimed. "It's been far too dull around here lately. This sounds like it's gonna be a juicy one!"

"That's what Julie said," Beverly confirmed. "I guess we'll find out how juicy in a few minutes. Buckle up Kelvin!"

She punched the gas and spurred the squad car forward, eager to find out what Morel had been hiding on the other side of his estate's massive walls.

BEVERLY DIXON and Kelvin McKnight were escorted through the house, and out onto the pool deck, by a young female African-American police officer. Her black hair was pulled up neatly into a bun at the crown of her head. A name badge pinned on her uniform had the name *Washington* on it.

"Detective Jameson's over there talking to the shooting vic's husband," she said, pointing to the patio table that was shaded by a large yellow-and-white-striped umbrella.

"Thanks, Washington," Dixon acknowledged, as she and Kelvin stepped into the bright afternoon sunshine on the pool deck.

They surveyed the scene, which was alive with crime scene detectives, painstakingly processing the crime scene. Philippe Morel's body, clothed in black leather pants and vest, recently pulled from the bottom of the pool, lay lifeless on the deck beside the pool while a CSI detective scoured his body for evidence. Another detective was dusting the black spreader bar on the pool deck for fingerprints.

Beverly noticed Francesca sitting sideways on a lounge chair, her hands folded in her lap, her head bowed, and her body rocking slowly back and forth. She appeared to be off in her own little world.

Julie Jameson was engaged in a heated conversation with a man, whom Beverly suspected was the shooting vic's husband. Jameson acknowledged Beverly and Kelvin's arrival with a nod. After another animated exchange with the man, Julie excused herself to greet her Palm Springs colleagues.

"Hi Beverly, thanks for coming. I thought you'd want to be in on this."

"Thanks, Julie" Dixon replied. "Have you met my partner, Kelvin McKnight?"

"I have now. Good to meet you, McKnight."

"So you were right. It was Morel in the pool. Hey, what else is on the bottom of the pool? Is that a computer?" Beverly asked.

"Looks like it, and some external hard drives too," Kelvin replied. "They must have been having some kind of a party for that stuff to end up at the bottom of a pool!"

"I'm just starting to get some of the details from the vic's husband. His name is Dan Whitney. He's a psychologist from Detroit. His wife, the shooting vic, is Michelle Whitney. Morel's wife, Capellini, is in shock and isn't coherent right now," Julie added.

"What have you got so far?" Beverly asked.

"If you believe what Whitney says, he and his wife were being kept at the estate against their will. It sounds like they were into some kinky S&M, or whatever they're calling it these days, with Morel and Capellini. He claims Morel was making porn tapes and using them to blackmail him and is wife," Julie said.

"Against their will? How does anybody get 'held against their will' to play kinky sex games at a fancy estate like this?" Kelvin asked.

"Sounds like they were guests at Morel's nudist resort last weekend. Whitney claims Morel told him they had to do some emergency repairs on their room, then offered them a chance to stay here at the estate for free to make up for the inconvenience."

"How convenient," Beverly injected. "So who shot Whitney's wife and how did Morel end up at the bottom of the pool?"

"Well, according to Whitney, he broke into Morel's office to try to find a way out of their mess. All he could come up with was to throw the computer and hard drives into the pool. He was hoping he'd destroy all of the incriminating porn. I guess Morel got suspicious and caught him in the act - went berserk, according to Whitney - and was threatening to shoot him when his wife appeared. I guess she tried to sneak up and take Morel out with the spreader bar."

"The what?" Beverly asked.

"Don't ask," Julie replied, raising her eyebrows. "Let's just say that it's a suitably-named sex aid."

"Okay," Beverly grinned. "So what happened next?"

"Apparently, Morel heard Ms. Whitney at the last second and turned the gun on her. Whitney tried to jump him, but it looks like he was too late and the gun fired. He and Morel struggled and ended up in the pool. Whitney claims Morel pretty much had him on the ropes under water, but Capellini jumped in to save him."

Beverly glanced at Francesca, who was still sitting on the lounge chair, rocking catatonically.

"Whitney said he didn't see what happened between Morel and Capellini because he was half-drowned and trying to recover at the side of the pool," Jameson continued. "When he managed to get out of the water, he found his wife bleeding-out beside the pool. Capellini managed to make the 911 call before she jumped in to help Whitney. And that's what I've got so far," Jameson concluded.

"Any word yet on Whitney's wife?" Beverly asked?

"Nothing yet. The guy's pretty agitated and pissed at me for not letting him go in the ambulance with her. I feel bad for him. This was a pretty terrifying ordeal for him. But I've got a crime scene to manage here!"

"Yeah, you did the right thing. But, I guess we'd be pissed too if it was one of our spouses who got shot."

"By the way, Julie," Dixon continued. "Kelvin just linked Morel to the Alvarez couple's disappearance. I guess it's too late to catch Morel, but hopefully his wife can shed some light on what might have happened to them. Anything we can do to be useful here?"

"Sure," Jameson answered. "Wanna try questioning Capellini while I get back to Whitney?"

"Okay. I'll see if she's in any shape …"

They were interrupted by the ringing of Jameson's cell phone.

"Hang on a minute, Beverly … Jameson here … yeah … uh-huh … uh-huh … no way? … shit! … okay, thanks for letting me know."

"Change of plans you two. My guys just called from Eisenhower emergency. The paramedics had to jump-start Michelle Whitney in the ambulance again. She never made it to Emergency!"

TEN MINUTES after Julie Jameson informed Dan Whitney of his wife's death, he was still overwhelmed and numb with shock. His brain shut down and he wasn't able to process anything more about the afternoon's events. She gave him a break from any further questioning.

Jameson felt bad for Whitney. This was the toughest part of being a cop - seeing the aftermath of crime and having to deal with the survivors, without letting it get in the way of doing her job. Her gut instinct was to believe his story. Years of experience told her that nobody could fake a shutdown like she was witnessing at this moment. But she kept telling herself she had to rule out every other possibility. It was her job.

Jameson looked up at Beverly and Kelvin. Capellini, who was sitting with Beverly and Kelvin, had finally stopped rocking in her lounge chair. Tears trickled down the woman's face. She was gradually coming out of her trance, and her eyes searched until they found Whitney.

Francesca stood up. As she did, the towel fell from her naked body, emphasizing her state of raw emotional vulnerability to Jameson. Julie watched as Capellini re-wrapped the towel, and then trudged to where Whitney was sitting at the patio table, wearily dropping to her knees in front of him. She put her head in his lap and resumed weeping. Whitney, still in a state of shock, was no longer shedding any tears. The couple had no words to describe the overwhelming mixture of emotions they must have been feeling.

Jameson left Whitney and Capellini together and rejoined Dixon and McKnight.

"I'm gonna have to take them downtown for questioning," she said. "Let's give them a while together before we go. Do you think you two could help them find some clothes and get them dressed? The press circus is already starting, so we'd better make them presentable for when we hustle them out of here."

"No problem," Beverly said. "We can take care of it, can't we Kelvin?"

Kelvin nodded to Jameson in silent agreement.

"Thanks, guys. I haven't checked out the rest of the scene yet. I'll be taking a look around if you need me," she added.

Jameson paced slowly around the pool deck, taking in all of the details of the carnage. Morel's body was just being put in a body bag. From Whitney's description of the man, and from what

McKnight had found out about him, it was becoming clear that the man was a sociopath. She shook her head sadly from side to side.

How does a person get that way? What happened in his life to turn him into such a sadistic creep!

She continued her survey of the crime scene. A large pool of dried blood remained where Michelle Whitney had been shot. The two survivors, Dan Whitney and Capellini, were huddled together in the shade under the patio table umbrella.

Jameson refocused her mind on making mental notes, trying to recreate the scene in her mind as related to her by Whitney. So far, everything she saw fit with his story. She went back into the open living area of the house. To her right, a media area was being set up at the back of the large room, in front of four large black-and-white portrait photographs. She turned left, descended some stairs, and then followed the tunnel to the adjacent building, where Officer Washington was standing guard outside the stable dungeon.

"CSI is still processing, Detective," Washington said.

"Thanks, Washington. I'll be careful not to touch anything."

Julie Jameson opened the heavy steel door and was immediately engulfed in a sea of different scents - straw, freshly cut pine, and leather. She walked carefully to the back of the room. She saw a table with an array of different sex aids. She noticed a large, bloody dildo on the table. Her body gave an involuntary shudder.

Jameson surveyed the assorted canes, floggers, and whips. Her eyes were drawn to an ominous-looking whip with knots in the leather strands. From there, her eyes travelled to an electrical transformer. A number of wires were plugged into the device. She followed the wires to their source.

Julie Jameson was a seasoned detective. She had seen her share of hard-to-stomach scenes. But the large copper alligator clips attached to the transformer were testing her limits. She started imagining the types of sadistic acts that might be associated with electricity and the sharp, jagged teeth of the vicious looking metal clamps. She was starting to feel like she'd had enough for one visit to the stable. She whirled on the balls of her feet and walked quickly from the dungeon, with graphic visual images etched in her mind of what she imagined had been happening in the secrecy of Morel's estate.

Jameson ascended the stairs back to the luxury home's living area. She looked through the patio door, noticing that Whitney and Capellini were no longer present.

Dixon and McKnight must be getting them ready to transport downtown.

To her left, Jameson noticed a striking blonde woman setting up a remote broadcast for CBS Local-2. She was Jenifer Daniels, one of the local news anchors, setting up in front of one of the four giant black-and-white portraits. Jameson's eyes couldn't resist looking past Daniels, and being drawn into the portrait behind her. She couldn't have known that the portrait had the same effect on Dan and Michelle Whitney when they had first seen it.

The woman in the photo was a street-person being photographed while she was panhandling. She was unkempt, her clothes were old and dirty, and her blonde hair was stringy and knotted. Jameson was drawn to the woman's eyes. She was staring straight into the camera.

Jameson noticed immediately that something didn't fit. The woman was alert and intelligent. She was highly aware that she was being photographed and appeared extremely wary. She seemed out of place on the street.

You want to be there, don't you? You're hiding from somebody!

Jameson gave her head a shake. She pulled herself away from the magnetic grip of the street-person's image and brought herself back to reality. Beverly Dixon was waving at her from the doorway of the guest suite, signaling that Dan and Fran were ready for the ride downtown.

Okay folks. It's show time.

Jameson knew that life would never be the same again for Dan Whitney and Francesca Capellini, once they emerged from the safety of the guest suite.

"OKAY, Doctor Whitney. Than you for your cooperation, you're free to go for now. Please don't leave the valley over the next few days without letting me know. Is that clear?" Julie Jameson said.

Her eyes narrowed and her forehead wrinkled. Dan knew that she meant business.

"Yes, Detective," he said. "I'll let you know when I have to go back to Detroit."

Dan left Jameson's office and found himself a chair in the waiting area of the Palm Desert police station. He had no idea what he was waiting for. The hands on the analog clock on the wall said it was after ten o'clock at night. He had completely lost track of time. During the final struggle with Philippe, time had become suspended for Dan. What was probably no more than two minutes in real time, had seemed like an hour to him.

Then, strangely, time started speeding up once the police and EMS personnel arrived. Events seemed to be flying past him. He felt like he was in a time warp, watching things from a distance like an outside observer, feeling completely detached from reality. He had trouble focusing and keeping track of everything that was happening.

He assumed that Fran was still being questioned, probably about the fate of the Alvarez couple.

Free to go? Where am I going to go? What do I do now?

Dan felt cut-adrift and completely lost. He couldn't push the images of Chelly, gasping for breath and struggling to get her final message to him, out of his mind. The part of him that had always been afraid of doing something wrong was ashamed that he had allowed all of this to happen. He felt so horribly guilty. Guilty for getting Chelly into this mess in the first place. Guilty for putting her at risk in their escape plan. But worst of all, he felt so guilty that he never had a chance to say goodbye to her.

If only I'd realized I wasn't ever going to see her again.

The thought never crossed his mind. It was incomprehensible.

Dan was distracted by movement in his peripheral vision. A tall African-American man in jeans and a USC sweatshirt was walking down the hallway towards him. It took a moment, but Dan recognized him as Detective Kelvin McKnight, out of uniform.

"Hey man," McKnight said. "Julie gave me a call and told me she was finished with you for tonight. She thought you might need somebody to be with you. How ya' doin', man."

"I'm not sure, Detective. To tell you the truth, things seem pretty surreal to me right now."

"Stop with the 'detective' thing, man. Call me Kelvin. I'm off duty."

"Thanks, Kelvin. My head's spinning right now. Too many things to think about, I guess."

Dan went silent. His eyes were red and filling with tears. He took a moment to gather himself, trying to sort out his scattered thoughts. He managed to re-focus on his most immediate needs.

"I … I really need to see Chelly, Kelvin. Is she still at the hospital?"

"Yeah, I think they're keeping her downstairs, bro. They have to determine the cause of death, you know?"

Silence followed the question as Dan gradually started acknowledging the reality of what had happened.

"I guess I'm also going to need to start making some arrangements. I'm going to need to find a hotel too. Can I get you to help me find one? I really appreciate it," Dan said.

"No problem 'bro," Kelvin answered. "Wherever you want to go. I'm off tomorrow an' I got all night. Let's get you outta here!"

Dan walked out the front door of the Palm Desert Police station, Kelvin McKnight at his side, into the cool March night. His immediate priority was to get some control back over his thought processes, and to do what he needed to do for Chelly. Beyond that, he had no idea what he was going to do.

CHAPTER 32

THE COURTROOM in nearby Indio was overflowing for Fran's Monday-morning bail hearing. The deaths of Philippe Morel and Michelle Whitney had made both the national and international news. The incident had all of the necessary ingredients to capture the public's attention - Philippe's celebrity status in the world of art, swinging, kinky sex, multiple deaths, and murder. Riverside County Criminal Court was set to convene, waiting only for Judge Ernest Hartley to enter and bring the Court to order. Fran sat next to her lawyer, Joanna Sullivan, at the Defense table. Sullivan's reputation for successfully defending battered and abused women was attracting even more interest to Fran's case.

Fran watched Dan, who was sitting in the first row of the gallery with Shelley Paul, Tim Jennings, and Carmen Herrera. Carmen's husband and daughter were taking her place at Chateau Eden so she could give moral support. Shelley and Tim had both taken the day off to support her. Fran had no other close family or friends for support. She and Philippe had only been part-time residents of the valley, and Philippe had been careful to keep her socially isolated. She felt a mixture of conflicting feelings. On one hand, she felt embarrassed and ashamed that her few friends had to see her in this situation. She was having difficulty making eye contact with them. But on the other hand, she was grateful for their support.

It was the first time she had seen Dan since they had been taken into custody in Palm Desert on Friday afternoon. His eyes were red and teary. She knew he had likely spent a difficult weekend dealing with Chelly's family. What she didn't know was that Dan received an even worse reaction from his three older brothers, who were unanimous in not hiding their disgust and disappointment with Dan and the recent events.

With Chelly gone, Fran saw in Dan's eyes how lost and lonely he was feeling. As their eyes met, she felt the same emotional connection that had taken them both by surprise only about ten days earlier. She felt an overwhelming urge to hold, and to be held, by Dan at that moment. She was jolted back to reality by the Bailiff's announcement.

"All rise!" bellowed the uniformed court officer. "Riverside County Criminal Court is now in session. The Honorable Ernest Hartley presiding!"

Fran and Joanna Sullivan looked at the table to her right. The County's prosecutor was a tall Hispanic man, about thirty years of age, with jet-black hair and a black goatee. Kevin Vasquez was dressed in a poorly fitting grey suit. Sullivan had never met the young man in court before, but told Fran of his reputation. He was young, intelligent, and driven to succeed. He had not yet lost a case in his first two years since his admission to the bar and joining the DA's office. Joanna had told Fran not to underestimate their adversary in this case.

As Judge Hartley took his seat at the Bench and everybody in the courtroom took their seats, Sullivan leaned to her right and spoke under her breath to Fran.

"Just leave everything to me, Francesca. This shouldn't take long today."

Judge Hartley nodded to the Bailiff, indicating that he was ready to proceed.

"The people of California versus Francesca Capellini," the Bailiff announced.

"This is a preliminary bail hearing," Hartley said. "The State has brought charges of Capital Murder against Francesca Capellini in the deaths of Philippe Morel, Diego Alvarez, and Juanita Alvarez. Mr. Vasquez, you're first."

"Thank you, Your Honor," the young prosecutor began. "Ms. Capellini is accused, not only in the drowning of her husband, Mr. Morel, but also as an accomplice in Mr. Morel's murders of Diego and Juanita Alvarez. The State feels Ms. Capellini has shown herself to be a dangerous offender, capable of killing repeatedly. She is also a citizen of the European Community and is at risk for fleeing the country. The state asks that bail be denied for Ms. Capellini."

"Ms. Sullivan?" Judge Hartley said, looking over his glasses towards the Defense table.

"Your Honor. The State knows well that my client was a victim of Mr. Morel's emotional and physical abuse. Mr. Vasquez is also aware that Ms. Capellini has cooperated fully with the police in helping to locate the bodies of Mr. and Ms. Alvarez. He knows that she was an unwilling bystander in their murders. The Defense is asking that the defendant be freed on bail, and that bail be set at ten thousand dollars."

Vasquez was on his feet before Sullivan had finished her last sentence.

"Your Honor," he insisted. "The Defense's request for bail in the amount of ten thousand dollars is a mockery of the gravity of the multiple murder charges facing the defendant. It also fails to take into account her extensive assets. The State maintains that she should remain in custody until her arraignment."

"Very well, counselors. Mr. Vasquez, I am inclined to agree that a ten thousand dollar bail does not fit with the serious nature of the charges and the circumstances in this case."

"Ms. Sullivan. Your client is to be released on two hundred and fifty thousand dollars bail. She will surrender her passport and may not leave Riverside County. Ms. Capellini will appear for arraignment in this courtroom on Friday, April 28 at nine a.m."

DAN AND FRAN melted into each other's arms after the court was adjourned, feeling an immense sense of relief at seeing each other again. It was the embrace of two people who had just shared an experience that nobody else could possibly understand. Tears of relief flowed from the two of them as they clung to each other.

"I'm so glad to see you," Dan whispered in Fran's ear. "How are you holding up?"

"I am okay, Dan. How are *you* doing?"

"I've been better, that's for sure. Just taking it one day at a time," he answered.

They squeezed each other one more time, before Dan broke the embrace. He turned to Joanna Sullivan.

"Glad to finally meet you, Ms. Sullivan. I'm Dan Whitney. Thank you so much for taking Fran's case." He offered his hand to the imposing, prematurely grey barrister.

"Please call me Joanna, Mr. Whitney. I'm pleased to meet you too. I'm sure the past three days have been extremely difficult for you. My condolences on your loss," she said.

"Thank you," Dan replied. He felt himself getting choked up again at the mention of Chelly's death.

Dan and Fran each embraced Shelley, Tim, and Carmen in turn, before introducing their friends to Joanna.

"It's nice to meet you all," Joanna said. "Francesca is lucky to have such supportive friends. Now if you'll excuse me, I think I'll sneak out and try to avoid the media gauntlet. I'll be in touch in the next few days, Francesca," she added.

Francesca embraced Joanna, giving her the traditional European kisses to each cheek, and then Joanna waded into the crowd and slowly disappeared.

"It's going to be quite a circus in front of the court house," Shelley said. "Where do we want to go for some peace and quiet?"

"We could all go back to Chateau Eden. The walls should give us some peace and quiet," Fran suggested.

"I'd like that," Dan replied, taking Fran by the hand. "There's nothing I'd like better than to hang out with all of you at the Chateau."

But Dan was having a tough time keeping his mind focused on Chateau Eden. Instead, it was jumping ahead to tomorrow. He was dreading the flight back to Detroit. The prospect of having to start settling Chelly's estate, as well as facing the scrutiny of their families, friends, and coworkers, was going to be the most difficult thing he had done in his life.

DAN AND FRAN stood hand-in-hand beside the empty baggage carousel at Palm Springs airport. It had been two weeks since Dan left for Detroit. Although they had talked almost every day by phone, they were both craving the intimacy of being together again.

Dan was exhausted. His late flight from Detroit to Los Angeles didn't arrive until after ten o'clock. By the time the shuttle from LAX arrived in Palm Springs, it was after two in the morning, Detroit time.

"I know this sounds strange because of what happened at the estate, but it's good to be back," Dan said. "I've missed talking with you in person and seeing into those beautiful eyes."

"Me too," Fran answered. "We only spent a few days together, but I have missed you too. How long will you be able to stay?"

Dan saw that Fran was agitated and fragile. He knew the symptoms of PTSD well, and he sensed she was struggling emotionally on her own.

"I'm in no rush to go back to Detroit soon," Dan answered. "That was the worst two weeks of my life - having to go back to that empty house - thinking about and missing Chelly every day. Then there was the funeral - everybody made me feel so guilty - as if I didn't feel guilty enough on my own already! Finally, there was having to take care of her estate. I just felt overwhelmed."

Dan swallowed hard, trying to fight back the tears as he remembered that past two weeks.

"So I took a three-month leave of absence from work. I need some time to deal with everything that's happened. I had a couple of pretty intense sessions with my own EMDR trainer back home, but I need to hook up with somebody else out here. I guess I didn't realize how much my old issues got stirred up by everything that happened."

"How about you, Fran. Did you manage to call any of the names I gave you for EMDR therapy?" asked Dan.

"I phoned the lady in Rancho Mirage," Fran answered. "She sounded nice, so I am going to meet with her tomorrow. I asked her if she was also willing to see you. She is okay with it, as long as we both agree. You can meet her tomorrow if you want to come with me."

"Sure," Dan said. "I'd like that."

The carousal gave a loud bang, then came clunking to life in front of them.

"Are you still having the flashbacks and nightmares?" Dan asked.

Fran nodded slowly.

"And you?" she asked.

Dan's eyes started watering. The mere mention of the intrusive images and dreams of Chelly, lying in the pool of her own blood, were enough to bring him to tears.

Fran tightened her grip on Dan's hand and her body drew closer to him.

"You never said on the phone where you were going to stay," Fran said. Her voice was timid and emotionless. "You are welcome to stay with me at the Chateau, unless there are too many bad memories for you."

"I was hoping you'd say that," Dan said. "You know we need to talk about everything that's happened between us, don't you?"

Dan knew they were both afraid to have *the talk*. He was afraid to come back to Palm Springs, because of the terrible memory of Chelly's death. He was also afraid that Fran wouldn't want him to come back. But he also knew that Fran was probably terrified that he *would* come back. He was afraid too. After the difficulties each of them had encountered in their marriages to Philippe and Chelly, he knew that he and Fran were both afraid of the intense feelings of intimacy that had developed between them so quickly.

"I decided to do the CNN interview with Anderson Cooper," Dan said, breaking the awkward silence between them. "Chelly was right. I need to take more risks and learn to step out of my comfort zone. I may as well start right now."

Dan spotted his luggage coming towards him on the carousel.

"There it is," he said, as he moved toward to his bag. "I told him that I couldn't talk about our situation because of the impending court case. But he told me he's wanted to do a segment on PTSD for a long time. When he saw what happened to us, he thought I'd be the perfect person to have on the show to talk about PTSD and trauma. I'll have to phone Joanna Sullivan first, though, just to clear it with her … oh, there's my bag!" Dan said.

He hoisted the large suitcase off the moving carousel and extended the handle. Fran led him out of the terminal to the parking lot where her Prius was parked. Dan loaded the bag into the back of the car, and then sat in the passenger seat while Fran drove the short distance to Chateau Eden.

Fran finally broke the silence.

"What happened to Chelly was not your fault, Dan," she said. Dan sighed.

"I try to think that way," he said, pointing to his head as he spoke. "I know Chelly was unhappy and wanted to try something more exciting. And I know Philippe was a psychopath who manipulated all of us to get what he wanted."

"But down here, Fran," he said, pointing to his heart, "there's part of me that says I should have trusted my instincts and should have said no to Chelly and Philippe. And that part still thinks I'm guilty as hell!"

"It was all my fault," Fran said. "I knew what Philippe was doing. I helped him do it. I could have given you my key earlier and let you use the phone in Philippe's office. But I was too afraid of him, so I did nothing. I let it happen, but I could have stopped it!"

Dan saw tears flowing from Fran's eyes, and heard her sobbing. She pulled the car to the side of the road and parked. Dan leaned over in the darkness and took her into his arms. He realized she was feeling just as much guilt as he was, maybe even more. Tears of empathy welled up in his eyes.

"What's going to happen to us, Fran?" he sniffled. "Except for Shelley, Tim, and Carmen, most of the country thinks we're a pair of sexual deviants, at best. You know what people are going to start thinking if we stay together. They're going to start believing the Enquirer's conspiracy theory. Everybody's going to look at us like we plotted to murder Philippe and Chelly!"

"What do *you* think, Dan? Do you think we have anything in common besides what happened to us?"

"I ask myself the same thing," Dan said. "Believe me. I'm so attracted to you! I felt it from the first minute we met. I keep asking myself if it's just a physical attraction - if it's just the kinky sex."

"And what answer do you get?" Fran said, looking into his eyes.

Dan saw the fear in her eyes as she waited for his answer. "I feel like there's something a lot deeper," he answered. "I've never felt anything like what I felt with you right from the start. I'm willing to see where it takes us, if you are, Fran."

"Do you remember what Chelly said to you before they took her away?" Fran asked.

Dan was stunned by the question. The few short minutes he spent with Chelly before the paramedics came were still just a blur to him.

"I don't know if I remember," Dan answered. "When the images come, they're so vivid and clear, it's just overwhelming. But her words … what we said to each other … they're just a jumble of sounds. I can't be sure what anybody said."

Tears appeared in Fran's eyes.

"I think I remember," she said. "'Take care of her, Dan'. Do you think she knew she wasn't going to make it?"

Dan's eyes were glassy and distant. There was a long pause while his brain tried to make some sense out of Fran's question.

"I'm trying to remember, Fran. But there's something getting in the way, like that part of my brain is trying to shut it out, or put up a big wall or something. It kinda' sounds familiar. But it doesn't seem real."

Dan was getting more frustrated, the harder he tried to remember.

"You understand what I'm feeling, don't you?" Dan said. "That's what happens when you dissociate, isn't it?"

Fran nodded and squeezed Dan's hand.

"It's one thing to see this happen to people when I'm doing therapy with them," Dan said. "But I can't believe it's happening to me!"

Fran kissed Dan on the lips, then pulled herself away and brushed the remaining tears from her eyes.

"It has been a long day for you," she said. "I should get you home to bed."

They drove the last ten blocks in silence. They had started talking about the big elephant in the room - about whether there was anything meaningful between them. Now that it was out in the open, Dan felt an enormous sense of relief.

They arrived at Chateau Eden. Fran used her key to open the massive pine door. She took Dan to the Italian theme room - where she had been staying since the bail hearing. It was the same room where Dan and Chelly had stayed. There was no sign of construction anywhere in the room.

They quietly undressed each other and slid under the sheets, pressing their bodies close together. For the first time in more than two weeks, both Dan and Fran finally felt the warmth and safety of each other's arms. They were both asleep soon after they kissed each other goodnight.

THURSDAY MORNING, April 27, the morning before Fran's arraignment, found Dan in a deep REM sleep. The recurring dream had chosen this particular morning to intrude into his sleep. He was back in Calgary, in high school. He and his sixteen-year-old girlfriend, Anika, were about to consummate their friendship sexually for the first time.

Dan's shaking hands explored every soft curve of her freshly exposed breasts. He marveled at the silky smoothness and the milky glow of her skin in the dim light of his bedroom. The pair pressed their naked bodies tightly together, feeling their genitals in contact for the first time. Their lips melted together into a long, passionate kiss, their hands eagerly stoking each other's backs and necks, and then running their fingers through each other's hair. Anika pulled his body down onto the bed. She climbed on top and straddled him. Dan felt her fingers taking his penis and guiding it towards her, gently pushing until he felt her labia move apart. He felt himself sliding inside the warm heaven of her vagina.

Anika was hungry for release, gyrating her pelvis back and forth and from side to side, searching wildly for any movement and sensation that would satisfy her craving. Dan clutched at her youthful, white breasts. Her eager, tight vagina gripped Dan and kneaded his throbbing penis mercilessly. Before long, the two virgin lovers erupted simultaneously into their first coital orgasms. Dan marveled at the ecstasy of his own rhythmic explosions, against the background of contractions that were radiating outwards from Anika's vagina, and engulfing her entire body.

Anika leaned forward and rested her breasts against his chest and her head on his shoulder.

"I love you, Dan," she sighed.

"I love ..."

Suddenly, the rude beeping of an alarm clock interrupted the afterglow and serenity of the dream.

Dan's eye's popped open. He looked around the room, disoriented. He wasn't back in Calgary. Gradually, he noticed the modern European-styling and furnishings in the room, and the pastel shades in the Italian watercolor landscapes decorating the walls. Realizing that he was in Chateau Eden, he reached to his right, feeling for Fran's body. The other side of the bed was empty. Dan felt his heartbeat quicken and his chest become tight. Then he remembered that Fran had risen early to meet the movers and a real estate agent at the Palm Desert estate this morning.

Dan sighed, and then took some slow breaths to calm himself. He reached out and switched the alarm to the radio setting, the mellow harmonies of *Hotel California* filling the room.

That song again? How often do they play it, anyway?

Dan let the words and Don Henley's voice penetrate his consciousness for a while, and then sat up abruptly. The meaning of the lyrics was finally starting to make sense. His thoughts drifted to Chelly, and how she had become so seduced by Philippe that she was helpless to say no to him. He realized that by the time they were behind the walls of the Palm Desert estate, Chelly's romantic side was addicted to Philippe's charm. By then, it was too late for them to checkout of the estate. Tears filled his eyes as he listened, then remembered Chelly's brave attempt to save them. He let the lyrics sink in for a few more lines, then wiped the tears from his eyes. He forced himself to shift his thoughts back to Fran and the present.

Now that the crime scene was finally released by the police, Fran was wasting no time disposing of Philippe's belongings, including the estate. Dan became aware that his penis was erect and straining beneath the sheets. Then he remembered his dream.

Where the hell did that come from? Why was I dreaming of Anika? Why now?

His current inner conflicts had nothing to do with her, or so he thought. He knew he was still feeling guilty over how quickly his emotional connection with Fran was growing, and how he was starting to forget the frustration in his marriage with Chelly. He knew it was going to take time and more therapy to help him get over his guilt, not to mention the nightmarish images of Chelly dying in his arms.

Dan was surprised that his nocturnal fantasy hadn't turned into a wet dream. He threw back the covers and swung his legs over the side of the bed, then shuffled into the bathroom. His morning erection waved from side to side with each step along the way. He reached into the shower and turned on the water, waiting for it to warm up.

Why would I be thinking of Anika at a time like this? I should be more worried about Fran? Her arraignment is tomorrow morning. Joanna says the case should be a 'slam-dunk'. Her case for self-defense from an abusive spouse is pretty much airtight. She figures the DA has no case and all of the charges will be dropped.

Dan stepped into the shower, his cold skin erupting into goose bumps as the hot water droplets confused his skin's chilled nerve receptors.

It's not like I need the sexual release. Sex with Fran has been amazing! We made love again just last night. I have to admit I'm enjoying the kinky bondage and flogging. And I'm loving the intimacy of massages and vanilla sex too. So why Anika? Why now? And why did the dream end differently this time?

Dan's mind continued working on his dilemma as he shampooed his hair. His preoccupation with his thoughts was helping the morning erection disappear. He started thinking about Fran. He knew she'd get over their recent horror, but it would take time.

She's a survivor. It's a good sign that she's been able to go back to the estate so soon. It will help her to move on.

Dan knew her personality-type well from his work as a psychologist. She had a natural resourcefulness and resiliency that, somehow, always helped her to survive her traumas. She only needed some more therapy to help her get back in touch with that inner strength. People like Fran, when they tap into their resourcefulness, manage to function in this world. Those who fail to find it, struggle constantly. Dan admired her resiliency. He also knew he was falling more in love with her with each passing day.

He turned off the water, pulled the shower curtain aside, stepped out of the shower, and grabbed a towel to dry himself. He was still obsessing about the dream while he dressed.

Things are going so well with Fran. Why would Anika pop into my mind? And why was my dream different this time?

After putting on a pair of shorts, a t-shirt, and a pair of sandals, he picked up his MacBook, exited the room, and made the short trip across the patio to Chateau Eden's lobby and kitchen.

"Morning, Carmen," Dan said. "How is everything going today?"

"*Buenos dias*, Señor Whitney. Everything is good. Señora Francesca is over at the estate this morning?"

"That's right. She should be back by noon because she has a couple of massages scheduled for this afternoon. I'm going to take care of the spa and pool after I have some coffee and something to eat. Anything else I can do to help?"

"No Señor. Everything is good."

In the kitchen, Dan ground some coffee beans and brewed himself a fresh coffee. He found a small yogurt and a bagel to eat, then turned on the kitchen's TiVo and small TV. He pulled a stool up to the counter and searched for the recording of his CNN interview with Anderson Cooper. He'd started watching the recording last night, but turned it off in favor of a night of massages and lovemaking with Fran.

He found the interview and clicked the remote to resume playback.

... Dr. Whitney, a lot of viewers would like to know why two different people could experience the same traumatic event, but one of them will get PTSD and the other won't.

That's a good question, Anderson. It depends on a few things. The most important factor is how many other traumas a person has already experienced in their lifetime. The second is whether or not that person is able to find a way of processing, or thinking about the event, so that it makes better sense to them. And the third is whether the person's mind tends to dissociate a lot.

Okay then, Dr. Whitney, here's an example from my life. I spent a lot of time in Rwanda during their civil war. After a while I noticed I was becoming numb to many of the things I was seeing. I didn't like what was happening to me, so I decided to leave. I don't think I was suffering from PTSD. Or maybe I was ... You tell me! How do you explain my reaction to what I was seeing every day?

That's a great example. Although I don't know much about your past, I suspect that you haven't had too many horrible things happen to you in your life. And if you did, you were fortunate enough to be able to either learn how to block things out, or to find ways to make sense of what was happening. But it sounds like your mind learned how to dissociate, or block things out, while you were in Rwanda. I don't think any normal person would be able to make sense of those types of atrocities. So blocking things out - making yourself numb - was a way for your mind to avoid dealing with what you saw ...

Dan finished his food then sipped on his coffee while he finished watching the rest of the recording. Overall, he was satisfied with how he had done. Cooper's easy-going personality helped to calm his nerves, so he felt confident and relaxed while answering the veteran reporter's questions. The taping had gone so well that CNN offered him part-time work as a guest commentator when they needed an expert on psychological issues.

Dan had been wrestling with the offer before watching the taped interview. Now that he had seen the whole interview, he felt a renewed sense of self-confidence in himself and his expertise.

Before last month, I don't think I had the self-confidence to do that interview. But I'm glad I did it. Chelly would have wanted me to take a chance on stepping outside of my comfort zone. She was right. I was a bit of a chicken-shit. As much as I hate to admit it, I'm glad she pressured me into trying swinging and BDSM - despite everything that happened. She showed me that there are no guarantees in life. If I really want to start living my life, I'm going to have to start taking some chances. I'll talk it over with Fran. But I'm leaning towards saying yes to CNN. And I think I want to stay out west and take a chance on starting my own practice!

Dan was feeling invigorated by his self-talk and his new sense of resolve. He had been enjoying the casual lifestyle of living with Fran and helping out at Chateau Eden for the past three weeks. Most importantly, he was starting to feel a sense of optimism about his future. He was looking forward to getting his life back into some kind of normal and moving on.

... Plink ...

Dan's MacBook came to life, signaling an incoming email message.

I wonder whom that's from?

He hadn't received many emails since Chelly's death and he was starting to feel like an outcast.

When he saw the sender's name, Dan's hopes for getting back to a normal life seemed to vaporize in a matter of seconds. Instead, he began to feel a shadow being cast over both the present and his future. He held his breath as he double-clicked to open the message:

From: Anika Kristiansen
March 30, 2006
9:27 AM
Subject: HELP!!!!
Hello Dan,
I know it's been many years since we last talked.
I got your email address from your brother in Dallas. I hope you don't mind.
I was saddened to hear about your recent tragedy and I am sorry to have to bother you now, but I don't know whom else to turn to.
My husband and our son Jonah have disappeared! I'm so afraid Soren has kidnapped him! It's been two days and there's no sign of them! I'm going crazy and don't know who to turn to for support!
Please help me, Dan! I need to hear your voice. You are the best friend I've ever had.
Your friend,
Anika.

DAN WAS enveloped in smoke as he stood in front of the barbeque on the patio behind Chateau Eden's office and kitchen. He was grilling chicken to go with the pasta and salad that Fran and Shelley were preparing inside. He and Tim were engaged in man-talk over a couple of cold, dark craft ails.

"It's great of you and Shelley to take time off to be at the arraignment hearing, Tim. I really appreciate it. I know Fran doesn't say much, but I know it means a lot to her," Dan said.

"It's the least we can do," Tim replied. "We haven't come down to the Chateau for a weekend since Fran's bail hearing. It's nice to take an extra day so we can spend a long weekend with you guys. So how did Fran react when you told her about getting the message from Anika?"

"A lot better than I expected," Dan answered. "She was a bit shocked at first. But we had another long conversation about where the two of us are going. She made an excellent point. She's concerned that we both need to find out who we are as individuals, without Philippe and Chelly in our lives. She doesn't want to see us both fall into the trap of redefining our identities only by our relationship with each other. She's pretty sharp, Tim. She should have been the psychologist."

The two men laughed and tipped back their beer mugs. Dan opened the lid to turn the chicken pieces, coughing on the thick smoke coming from the meat's drippings and the smoking hickory-chips at the back of the grill. He closed the lid and took another mouthful of ale, enjoying the initial bite of hops on his tongue, followed by the delightful aftertaste that lingered after each swallow.

"Yeah, I agree," Tim said. "Fran's learned a lot about life from all of her life experiences."

"She's right about our relationship, too," Dan said. "We both have to think about what we want to do in the future, whether we stay together or not. I'm encouraging her to think about opening a photography business. She's so talented. With her connections in the world of art, and with the celebrities she knows, I'm sure she could do well. Of course, she still has the option of keeping Philippe's art agency going if she wants."

Tim nodded in agreement as the two men each took another mouthful of ale.

"She's encouraging me to follow my dream of having my own practice, somewhere out west if that's what I want," Dan added. "She says that if we're meant to be a couple, we'll find out over time. She doesn't want me to feel like she prevented me from seeing Anika. She doesn't want me to resent her, and to always wonder what it would have been like to see Anika again."

Tim's eyes narrowed and his face became serious. "Do you think there's still anything there for Anika?" he asked.

"I didn't think so," Dan answered. "But, there must be something unresolved in my mind if I keep having those dreams about her. Besides, she was there for me once when I really needed her. I owe her."

"So when are you leaving? She lives in British Columbia, right?" Tim asked.

"Yeah. Victoria, on Vancouver Island. I'm going to leave tomorrow afternoon, right after the arraignment hearing. I'll fly into Seattle and rent a car so I can take the ferry from Port Angeles. I'm not sure there's much I can do except provide some moral support, so I'll probably only stay for a couple of days. Hopefully, the police will have found her husband and son by then."

Dan lifted the lid again and checked the chicken pieces.

"I think these babies are pretty well done. Let's get them off the grill and see what the ladies are up to."

SHELLEY WATCHED Tim and Dan from the kitchen window as Dan placed the chicken pieces on the grill. The two men were talking, laughing, and drinking beer while Dan kept an eye on their dinner.

"Dan and Tim really get along well together, don't they?" Shelley said to Fran.

"Yes. They have a lot in common. They are both so dedicated to their work and they love helping people," Fran replied.

"It doesn't hurt that they both enjoy a good brew too!" Shelley said, laughing. "That reminds me. That gin and tonic you're drinking really looks good. I think I'll try one of those next, while we're finishing dinner."

Shelley searched the counter while Fran checked on the linguini. She found the six-pack of tonic left over from Fran's drink, but couldn't find the bottle of gin.

"Where did you hide the gin, Fran?"

"In the small cupboard above the refrigerator," she answered.

Shelley pulled a stool over to the fridge to reach the cupboard, continuing the conversation as she rooted around, finally finding the gin behind some other bottles.

"Dan's a good man," Shelley said. "Are you worried you might lose him if he connects with his old girlfriend? She's going to be vulnerable, just like him, if her marriage has gone down the drain."

"Same thing for Dan and me," Fran added. "We are both too vulnerable right now. We need to find more in common than just surviving the ordeal with Philippe."

A puzzled look came over Shelley's face as she climbed down from the stool. The look was slowly replaced by a small smile.

"You didn't have any gin with that tonic, did you Fran?"

Fran's eyes avoided Shelley, and her face blushed enough that she couldn't hide it from Shelley's scrutiny.

"You're pregnant, aren't you girl?" Shelley said.

Fran's blush turned a deeper shade of red, giving her away without even answering.

"Is it Dan's?" Shelley asked.

"Yes. I am sure of that," Fran said.

"Does he know yet?" Shelley pressed, the whites of her brown eyes getting larger with each question.

Fran shook her head.

"So the father of your unborn child is going away to see his long-lost girlfriend? My God, girl. Your emotions must be all over the map right now!"

Fran's eyes were turning red and starting to water. The independent, businesslike part of her identity, which had been trying so hard to be rational, unemotional, and supportive of Dan since he told her about the email from Anika, was losing the battle with that old familiar part of herself that felt abandoned so easily. Her defensive walls were crumbling, and they were no longer able to keep the painful old emotions away.

Shelley saw the tears forming in Fran's red eyes. She extended her arms and Fran melted into her friend's warm, empathic embrace. She realized how the independent, businesslike Fran had been putting on a brave face after hearing about Dan's email from Anika. Fran's tears, and all of the emotions that she had stuffed behind her walls since her period failed to materialize three weeks ago, came flooding out in one giant, cathartic wave.

"It's okay, girl," Shelley whispered into Fran's ear. "No matter what happens, I'm here for you. You're not alone."

EPILOGUE

THE HOTEL room was dark, except for the glow of the man's chest and face, appearing like a ghostly apparition in the luminescence of his laptop's screen.

He replayed the video of the newscast again. He had been obsessed by it since he first saw the news of Morel's death on television five weeks ago. The blonde CBS news reporter was reporting two deaths at a secluded Palm Desert estate. He looked past the reporter, staring instead at the wall behind her. He froze the video and zoomed in on a huge black-and-white portrait. The background photo was slightly out of focus and grainy, but he locked onto the eyes of the street-woman in the photograph. Even slightly out of focus, he was certain that the face in the portrait belonged to her.

"So, there you are, Angela," he whispered under his breath. "You thought you could run from me forever? Well, perhaps you can run, but you can't hide!"

The creases in his forehead, the flared nostrils, and the cold glare of his eyes gave away the intensity of his anger.

Who took that portrait, and where did they find you?

He reached for his burner cell phone, pressed the *Dial* button, and waited for the woman at the other end to answer.

"Mulholland," a curt voice answered. "What do you want?"

"Good evening, my dear," the man replied with condescending sweetness. "You sound upset. You really should be getting some help with managing your stress. It's bad for your health, you know."

"Thanks for the health advice. Now what do you want," she repeated.

"Is everything arranged for tomorrow? I don't want anything to go wrong."

"Vasquez will do the best he can," she replied. "We won't be pressing charges against Capellini in her husband's death. She's got the best lawyer in the state for battered-spouse cases. We wouldn't have a chance if they argue self-defense. We have a better chance at implicating her in the deaths of the Alvarez couple."

"That's not good enough, Kelly. I need more than 'a better chance'! I need those charges to stick. Do you understand?"

"You know it's not that easy. Vasquez says they also have a good chance at arguing battered-spouse to get her off those charges. He doesn't like our chances."

"Well, you tell him he'd better get working on improving your chances. I need him to make a case that will stand with a grand jury. It's up to you to make sure he does his job. It's all on you, Madame District Attorney. I don't deal well with people who fail me. Just do your job, and I can help make those gambling debts of yours go away. You wouldn't want your little problem to go public, would you now?"

There was only silence on his phone.

"Don't let me down, Kelly!" he shouted in a loud whisper. "Make sure she gets charged in the Alvarez murders, and make sure her bail is revoked! If that doesn't happen, you can be sure some eager little news reporter is going to get a hot tip to start looking into your finances! Is that clear?"

"Yes, sir," Mulholland answered. "Don't worry. I'll make sure it happens."

"A couple more things, Kelly. I need you to get some more information for me. Watch the CBS video from the estate on the day of Morel's death. There's a large black-and-white portrait of a woman hanging on the wall behind the reporter. I need you to get Capellini to tell you where she took that portrait."

"You know I can't do that. It has nothing to do with this case! There's no way her lawyer would let her answer that question." Mulholland replied.

"Then find a way!" he hissed. "Get the Palm Desert cops involved. Tell them you got a hot tip that the woman in the picture is the subject of a missing person case in Florida. You need more information to confirm. It's all true, counselor. She is a missing person. I just need to be the one who finds her."

"I'll do what I can," Mulholland repeated. "You said you need a couple of things. What else do you want?"

"I need as much personal information as you can get for that psychologist, Whitney, and his wife. You know the drill - birth dates, Social Security numbers, driver's licenses, and credit cards. Anything you can get. You should have collected most of that when you brought him in for questioning and made the identification on his wife's body."

"Okay. I think I can get that. Is that everything?" she asked. Her voice was weary and resigned to complying with his demands.

"That's my girl, Kelly. When you get the info on Whitney and his wife, use your burner phone and call me. I'll give you instructions for making a drop."

"Yes, sir," Mulholland answered.

"Remember, Kelly. I'll be watching tomorrow. Don't disappoint me!"

He pressed the *Hang-Up* button on the cell phone, and then re-focused on the image of the enigmatic blonde street-woman in the portrait. Anger was still etched into his face.

"I *will* find you, Angela!" he muttered. "And you *will* regret the day you crossed me!"

THE END

ACKNOWLEDGMENTS

To my loving wife and best friend, Peggy, for your love and infinite patience with my exploration into the world of writing, and to my daughter Lashia, for your support, constructive criticism, and for daring to be the first-reader of the first draft of this, my first novel.

To Susan Fish at Storywell, for getting me in touch with Hugh Cook, who provided his valuable feedback on parts of the first draft. And of course, to Hugh, for his very helpful constructive criticism.

Thanks to the entire team at Telemachus Press for guiding me through the daunting process of publishing the first edition of **WALLS** in 2013.

Finally, to all my friends, family, coworkers, and the other writers I've met through the social media, who have been so supportive and encouraging throughout the writing process.

David Alex Jones

December 2022

OTHER BOOKS BY DAVID ALEX JONES

THE NIGHT CLASS
An Alternative Tale of Reconciliation

***

Originally written as Alex Jones:

FACES:
The Survivor Trilogy, Book Two

ANGELA'S EYES:
The Survivor Trilogy, Prequel

SPIRITS:
The Survivor Trilogy, Book Three

Find out where to purchase David Alex Jones' books
by visiting his website:
http://www.davidalexjones.com

ABOUT THE AUTHOR

David Alex Jones is a retired Clinical Psychologist who lives in Ontario, Canada. In his writing, he combines his understanding of human identity and personality, his passion for helping victims of trauma, abuse, and Post-traumatic Stress Disorder, and his love of reading fiction, to create a unique brand of psychological suspense and political commentary. His writing is rich with complex characters and controversial social issues, resulting in an abundance of internal and interpersonal conflict, dysfunction, and tension. Dave also enjoys spending time with his grandchildren, travelling with his wife, photography, and home brewing craft beer.

CONNECT WITH THE AUTHOR

Independent authors, like David Alex Jones, provide readers with quality books at low prices. We can do this because we don't pass along the costs of traditional publishing houses to our readers. In doing so, we take on the responsibility for marketing our own books. Thus, we depend on our readers to visit our social media sites and our web sites to make us more visible on search engines like Google. Every "Follow,", "Like", and "Click" on our sites helps raise awareness of our writing and spreads the word!

Dave thanks you in advance for taking the time to follow him on Facebook, Instagram, and Twitter, and for visiting his website to stay current on events and news about his books. Be the first to find out about upcoming offers and projects, and discover his new blog: *The Null Hypothesis*. Here's how you can connect with him on social media:

Facebook: https://www.facebook.com/DavidAlexJonesWriter

Instagram: https://www.instagram.com/d_alexjonesauth/

Twitter: https://twitter.com/Alex_J_Writer

Web Site: http://www.davidalexjones.com

Email: dave@davidalexjones.com

FACES (EXCERPT)

The Survivor Trilogy, Book Two

by David Alex Jones

(Originally as Alex Jones)

A NONDESCRIPT grey mini-van made its way down Blanshard Street towards downtown. It was ten-thirty a.m. on a sunny late April day in Victoria, the picturesque capital of British Columbia. The blond-haired man behind the wheel drove cautiously, making sure to avoid doing anything that would attract attention to the vehicle.

"Are we almost there, Daddy?" asked the five-year-old boy in the back seat. A brand-new Blue Jays baseball cap covered his freshly shaved hair and cast a shadow over his face.

"Yeah, almost there," the driver mumbled. He turned to the woman seated beside him in the passenger seat. "Can you keep him quiet? All we need is for him to open his mouth and wreck everything. Do your job, Beth!"

The van made a right turn onto Bellville Street. The harbour and the Empress Hotel came into view.

"Look, Jonah," the woman said. "There's the harbour. We're almost at the ferry. Do you remember how important it is to remember our story? We don't want the bad people to catch us, do we?"

Jonah's mouth turned down at the corners, a confused look covering his face.

"Why are the bad people chasing us? Why isn't Mommy coming?" he asked.

"Shhhh!" Beth whispered. "Remember, we're pretending that I'm your mommy right now. If the man at the ferry asks you what your name is, what do you say?"

"John … John Dailey Junior," Jonah said by memory.

"And what's your dad's name?"

"His name's John Dailey too. And your name is Elizabeth Dailey. You're my mom," Jonah said.

"Excellent," the woman said. "You're going to do a good job of fooling the bad people."

"But why isn't Mommy coming with us?" Jonah repeated.

"I've already told you!" the driver shouted. "The devil has sent some very bad people who don't like Daddy's church. They don't like us spreading God's word, so they're spreading lies about Daddy and our church. If Mommy comes with us, they'll be sure to find us all. So Mommy is going to stay at home for a while. In a few days, she's going to try to run away from the bad people so she can be with us in Seattle. Now, smile and pretend that we're a happy family. We're going to visit Grandma and Grandpa, okay?"

"Okay," Jonah pouted.

Soren Kristiansen slowed the van as they approached the ferry terminal.

"You've got the passports ready?" he grunted to Beth.

"Yes, don't worry. I've got everything. Just relax."

"Don't you worry about me," Soren snorted. "Just make sure you and John Junior don't screw things up!"

Soren made another right turn onto a short road that carried them down a ramp to the Black Ball Ferry Terminal. He pulled up to the ticket booth and rolled down his window. A cheery middle-aged woman greeted him.

"How many passengers?" she asked.

"Two adults and one child," Soren answered.

"Do you have acceptable photo ID for entry into the U.S.?" the woman asked.

"Yes, we all have passports." He turned to Beth. "Do you have those passports, honey?"

Beth smiled and handed the passports to Soren.

"You'll need to show those at U.S. Immigration Pre-Clearance, just ahead. That'll be seventy-five dollars."

Soren handed the passports back to Beth and reached for his wallet, counting out a number of bills and handing them to the ticket agent.

"Thanks, sir. Have a pleasant trip."

"Thank you, ma'am. You have a nice day too," he said, flashing his warmest smile at the agent. He turned his head and looked at Jonah in the back seat.

"Okay, Jonah. This is it. All you have to do is remember that you're John Dailey Junior, and Beth here is your mom. That's easy, right?"

"Yes, Daddy."

Soren focused ahead at the security cameras, mounted on posts as the ramp descended towards U.S. Immigration. He donned his dark glasses and ball cap, making sure not to show his newly cut, very short blond hair.

"Okay then, everybody. Put on your best smiles!" he said.

Soren let his foot off the brake, allowing the van to creep along down the ramp behind a line of other vehicles, making its way towards Customs pre-clearance.

THE M.V. COHO slowed as it neared its mooring at the ferry terminal in Port Angeles, Washington. Clearing immigration pre-clearance in Victoria had gone without a hitch. The trio's crossing of the Strait of Juan de Fuca had been smooth. The almost fifty-year-old car ferry swayed gently from side to side with the small swells that rolled from west to east through the passage.

Deep inside his body, Soren felt energized by anticipation, like an athlete preparing for an important game. He was psyched. He looked at Beth and Jonah, who both looked tense. There was only one other thing that could possibly go wrong. But Anika was still at work, and she wouldn't be picking Jonah up from kindergarten for another two hours. She wouldn't even know yet that her son was gone. Soren donned his dark glasses and removed his cap, making sure his new look was captured on security video surveillance.

"Smile and relax, you two," he said. "Just make believe you're visiting Grandma and Grandpa, Jonah. Show the officer how excited you are to be in the United States. And Beth, just pretend we're really visiting your parents. Everybody ready?"

Beth and Jonah nodded in silent acknowledgment. The van was now at the head of the Immigration line. Finally, the light turned green. Soren lowered his window, allowing the vehicle to roll up to the Immigration booth. A short female agent in full body-armour, gun on her hip, greeted them with a frown on her face.

"Citizenship?" the agent demanded, craning her neck to look through Soren's open window at Beth and Jonah. Soren took the passports from Beth and handed them to the agent.

"Canadian," he answered.

"Reason for your visit?" the agent asked. She was all business, not cracking even the faintest smile.

"We're visiting my wife's parents in Seattle," Soren answered casually.

The Immigration agent scanned each of their newly acquired, forged passports, one at a time. Soren wasn't anxious. He knew the forgeries were almost perfect and the chances of detection were slim. He smiled and waited patiently. The agent was taking her sweet time. Finally, she looked through Soren's window and looked directly at Beth; then looked at the photograph on her passport.

"Your full name, ma'am?"

"Elizabeth Dailey," Beth answered.

"Your parents' address in Seattle?"

"666 West Raye Street," Beth said.

The agent looked closely at Beth's passport one last time.

"You're a Canadian citizen now?"

"Yes. I was born in Seattle, but I got my Canadian Citizenship after I married my husband. My maiden name is Andersson."

The agent leaned into Soren's window again, this time looking at Jonah.

"And what's your name, young man?" she asked.

"John Dailey Junior," he announced with pride. "But Mommy and Daddy call me John Junior."

"Do they, now," the agent said, finally cracking a faint smile at the young boy's response. She turned her attention to Soren, first looking at his shaved head, then his passport photo, which had a full head of blond hair.

"Can you remove your sunglasses, please?"

She glanced back and forth between the passport photo and Soren's exposed face.

"Anybody ever mistake you for the golfer?" she asked.

"All the time," Soren answered, laughing. "It gets tedious after a while, but what can ya do?"

This time the agent's face broke into a smile. She handed the passports back to Soren.

"I'll bet it does. Have a nice visit, folks."

"Thanks," Soren answered. "We will. Have a good day yourself."

The agent handed the passports back to Soren, who immediately donned his sunglasses. As they drove away, he raised the van's window, smiling to himself. He just cleared his first major hurdle.

He hadn't planned on running quite so soon, but Soren sensed it wouldn't be long before the authorities started looking into the church's finances. He also sensed that Anika was ready to leave him, and he couldn't let a custody battle get in the way of having Jonah. It wouldn't be the first time that trusting his intuition had saved him.

But now, it was only a matter of hours before Anika and the police would be after him. It was time to disappear.

ANIKA KRISTIANSEN rushed from her medical office. She was late for picking up Jonah from kindergarten. Her car beeped back at her as she pressed her remote to unlock it. She flung the door open, dropped into her seat, and slammed the door behind her. She grabbed her phone from her purse and tossed the bag into the passenger seat. Flipping open the phone, she dialed the kindergarten's number.

"Hello? … This is Dr. Kristiansen … I'm terribly sorry, something came up and I had to deal with it … I'm on my way now, but I'll be about ten minutes late picking up Jonah," she said hurriedly.

The female voice on the other end hesitated before answering.

"Anika?" the woman answered, confusion in her voice. "Is that you?"

"Yes, is that you, Janice? Why? Is something wrong?"

"I thought you knew. Soren picked up Jonah at ten o'clock this morning. He told me about your parents' accident. He said he was meeting you at home so you could leave for Calgary as soon as possible. I hope they weren't hurt badly!"

Anika shivered. A chill surged through her body. A feeling of dread began to descend over her. Something was terribly amiss.

"I haven't heard any details yet, Janice. I probably missed Soren's call. Things were crazy at the office. I'll call you to let you know if Jonah's going to miss some days. Thanks," she said, as she pressed the hang-up button on her phone. She dialed Soren's mobile number. It rang repeatedly and then went to voicemail.

Hello. This is Pastor Kristiansen. I'm not able to answer the phone right now. Please leave me a message and I'll call you back as soon as possible. Have a blessed day.

Anika's heart was racing. Her thoughts started racing.

I know things haven't been good between us lately, but surely he wouldn't take Jonah? Where would he go? Where would he take him? Maybe he's at home!

Anika dialed their home number, praying that Soren would answer. With each ring, she felt her heart pounding harder. When the call went through to voicemail, she hung up and tossed her phone in the passenger seat. She fastened her seatbelt, turned the key in the ignition, and slammed the vehicle into reverse. As she backed out of her parking spot, she sensed a blur in her peripheral vision and slammed on her brakes. The other car screeched to a halt, blaring its horn at Anika. The man behind the wheel flipped her the bird, then drove on.

Anika took a couple of deep breaths, let her foot off the brake slowly, and then backed the rest of the way out of her parking spot. She jammed the vehicle into *Drive* and her SUV flew out of the parking lot, tires squealing as she turned right onto Blanshard. She headed for the highway back toward Brentwood Bay.

Rush hour traffic was heavy on the highway. It seemed to take forever to reach the Brentwood Bay turn-off. Anika's mind raced and her hands were locked onto the steering wheel as she sped along Mt. Newton Cross Road. Two more turns, and she came to their cul de sac. Anika swung into the driveway, slammed on the brakes, threw the transmission into *Park*, and flung the driver's door open, all in one motion. Her hands shook and she fumbled impatiently with her keys, trying desperately to open the front door to her home. Finally, her key seated in the lock and she turned the deadbolt. She threw the heavy door open.

"Jonah! Soren! Anybody home?" she screamed.

Anika was greeted by an ominous calm. Except for the steady ticking of the grandfather clock in the hallway, the house was silent. Anika's heart pounded. Her chest was tight and she struggled to catch her breath.

"Jonah," she whimpered. The clock ticked relentlessly and Anika's heart sank. Reality started to set in. She ran upstairs and then down the hallway to her bedroom. Her jaw dropped when she threw open the door. Soren's closet door was agape. His bureau drawers were hanging open. He'd clearly gathered up some clothes and left in a hurry. Anika ran to Jonah's room and was greeted by the same sight.

With a growing sense of dread, Anika marched down the hallway, down the staircase to the main floor, then downstairs to the basement. The basement light was already on. Her eyes were drawn to a glaring gap on their storage shelves where two suitcases had been stored. Her mind was now spinning out of control. She began to feel violated—worse than if somebody had put a knife to her throat and threatened her life—she felt angry and betrayed. Then the floodgates opened and she became overwhelmed by a flood of emotions—anger, betrayal, fear, helplessness, sadness, loneliness and guilt. But most of all, it was anger that raged inside her.

Anika felt like there was an anvil on her chest, preventing her lungs from sucking in any air. She dropped to her knees on the concrete floor, gasping for breath. Tears filled her eyes.

She sobbed inconsolably while she struggled to breathe. Time seemed to stand still. She had no idea how long she spent on her knees. Gradually, she felt the pressure easing off of her chest. Her knees throbbed. She managed to hoist herself to her feet and slowly ascended the stairs, first to the main floor, then to the upper floor. She wandered into Jonah's bedroom and sat on his bed, reaching for his favourite stuffed animal; a tattered and worn panda that Anika's parents had given him for his first birthday. She pulled it close to her body, and then curled up on the bed. Her sobbing didn't stop until she had cried herself to sleep.

ANGELA'S EYES (EXCERPT)

The Survivor Trilogy, Prequel

by David Alex Jones

(Originally as Alex Jones)

I REMEMBER that day, almost one year ago, like it was yesterday. My eyes were wide open and alert to my surroundings, as they had been every day since I stole 4.7 million dollars from Soren Kristiansen and went on the run, vanishing from the lives of everybody I knew and loved. From that day on, my eyes have kept a constant vigil. I've been paranoid of every person I see, unable to trust a soul and waiting for the day when Soren eventually finds me.

The setting sun was sinking behind the towering landscape of downtown Los Angeles, the daytime heat giving way to long, late afternoon shadows. I sat on the grass in the San Julian Park, leaning up against a cinderblock wall, trying to blend into the shadows. This had become my usual afternoon and evening routine - hiding in plain sight in this small green oasis amidst the most unfortunate of humanity. As usual, the park was crowded with people; leaning up against trees, lying on the grass, or sitting cross-legged on the ground. In the park and out on the street, throngs of other street-people staked their claim to a small square of sidewalk or grass to set up temporary sleeping quarters for the coming night. They unpacked portable tents or cardboard boxes from the shopping carts that contained the sum total of their possessions.

The small mass of humanity in East Los Angeles was winding down another day of subsistence survival in the unseen underbelly of America.

Many of the park's residents knew each other well, jabbering casually with each other. I knew many of them by sight, as they knew me. But I rarely allowed myself anything more than raising my eyebrows in acknowledgement, or a curt greeting to any of them. I wasn't willing to risk conversation or the possibility of revealing anything about myself to anybody.

I liked San Julian park. It was a place where I could sit in the shade when it was warm, or find some sunshine when it was cool. I could keep my back to the cinderblock wall or the trunk of a tree, where I could keep a wary eye on every person who passed or entered the park. I blended in well, wearing the same pair of torn jeans, threadbare t-shirt, hoodie, and well-worn boots that I wore each time I visited the park. My shoulder-length blonde hair was purposely tousled and unkempt, and there wasn't a trace of makeup on my face. On that spring day, I wasn't wearing the grey hoodie I'd been wearing through the cooler winter months, but I was glad I still had it with me, using it to cushion my behind from the hard ground.

I first noticed the woman with the camera while she worked her way down the opposite side of the street. I'd never seen her in the area before, so she roused my attention immediately. She had an old-school SLR with a large telephoto lens attached, and she appeared to be taking candid photographs of people from a distance. The hairs on the back of my neck tingled. I riveted my eyes on her as she moved slowly towards the park.

The residents of skid row were used to seeing photojournalists who sometimes ventured here to document their existence. But this woman was different. She spent more time composing and taking each shot, manually focusing and setting the shutter speed and aperture for each exposure. She was completely engrossed, but relaxed at the same time. She was doing this for art and her own relaxation.

She was tall and thin, with an olive complexion and short dark hair. As I studied her carefully, she looked down at the SLR and checked its settings. Apparently satisfied, she raised her head and started surveying the area for potential targets. She noticed San Julian Park and started moving in my direction. I reached beneath me for my hoodie, wondering if I would be less noticeable if I pulled the hood over my head.

I decided against doing anything to attract attention, averting my eyes and hoping she wouldn't see me. It was time to leave the park. I stole a quick glance in my peripheral vision, hoping to see that her camera was focused on other residents of the park.

It was too late. I felt fear take control over my body. Instead of getting up and running, I froze. She had already spotted me and our eyes met. Automatically, she raised the camera and focused the large lens on me. Before I could look away, I saw the the camera's shutter opening and closing, capturing on film the fear and distrust on my face and in my eyes. It was all over in a couple of seconds. She lowered the camera away from her face and our eyes met. She could tell that I was different from the other residents of the park - she knew I didn't belong here. If I stayed where I was any longer, I knew she was going to come closer to start asking questions.

It was time to go. I reached for the used plastic grocery bag full of personal belongings beside me, and rose quickly to my feet. I pulled the hoodie over my head and lowered my eyes, walking briskly past the mystery woman and onto the asphalt pathway that led to the park's only exit at the corner of the green space. I turned right and quickly crossed St. Julian Street. Once across the street, I hunched down and slid behind a large blue dome-tent - somebody's lodging for the night. Shielding myself from the woman's view, I moved quickly along East 5th Street, leaving the park and the woman behind.

Now, hiding from the world in my makeshift bed in the darkness of a Las Vegas floodway, I recall the ominous feeling I had about those photos. Somehow, I knew they were going to come back to haunt me. I didn't know when or how, but I knew the day would come. I couldn't risk having anybody seeing them. As far as the rest of the world was concerned, I was dead. I walked away from everything - my two kids and my parents - and I ran away from my job. As far as anybody was concerned, I had simply vanished from the face of the earth.

My premonition came true three weeks ago. Suddenly seeing my face in the background of a TV news report took me by surprise, but it wasn't a total shock. I recognized the look of fear and distrust in my eyes in the candid portrait. The same feeling of fear swept through my body as I realized the implications of what I saw. With one quick glimpse of myself on TV, my entire world had turned upside down.

Since that day, my mind has been spinning - continually replaying the events from eighteen months earlier. Could I have done anything differently? How did I, Angela Baranyi, an innocent, religious, hard-working single mother of two, ever manage to get involved in Soren Kristiansen's web of dishonesty, deceit, and crime? How did I become a criminal myself? No matter how many times I analyze the events in my mind, I haven't come up with any good answers to those questions. But the events keep replaying in my memory, like a nightmare that never ends …

* * *

www.ingramcontent.com/pod-product-compliance
Lightning Source LLC
Chambersburg PA
CBHW070729120726
47910CB00001B/35